Carl Scholz is an American architect and amateur historian with an international background. He was born and raised in Chile, to where his grandparents had emigrated from Germany in the 1880s. His professional practice was based in California. He travelled widely and is fluent in English, Spanish and German. Currently he is working on another novel and a collection of short stories. Carl lives in the San Francisco Bay Area.

To Eric, for many conversations seeking enlightenment in nuances of the written word and the vexations of computers.

Carl Scholz

The Twin Behind the Curtain

Austin Macauley Publishers™
London • Cambridge • New York • Sharjah

Copyright © Carl Scholz 2023

The right of Carl Scholz to be identified as author of this work has been asserted by the author in accordance with sections 77 and 78 of the Copyright, Designs and Patents Act 1988.

All rights reserved. No part of this publication may be reproduced, stored in a retrieval system, or transmitted in any form or by any means, electronic, mechanical, photocopying, recording, or otherwise, without the prior permission of the publishers.

Any person who commits any unauthorised act in relation to this publication may be liable to criminal prosecution and civil claims for damages.

This is a work of fiction. Names, characters, businesses, places, events, locales, and incidents are either the products of the author's imagination or used in a fictitious manner. Any resemblance to actual persons, living or dead, or actual events is purely coincidental.

A CIP catalogue record for this title is available from the British Library.

ISBN 9781035812820 (Paperback)
ISBN 9781035812837 (Hardback)
ISBN 9781035812851 (ePub e-book)
ISBN 9781035812844 (Audiobook)

www.austinmacauley.com

First Published 2023
Austin Macauley Publishers Ltd®
1 Canada Square
Canary Wharf
London
E14 5AA

Table of Contents

Prologue	9
1. Appleton, Wisconsin	12
2. Budapest, Hungary	22
3. Bratislava, Czechoslovakia	41
4. Vienna, Austria	52
5. Washington, D.C.	61
6. Long Beach, California	73
7. Prague, Czechoslovakia	84
8. Wolkenstein, East Germany	100
9. Karl Marx Stadt, East Germany	105
10. East Berlin, East Germany	114
11. Leipzig, East Germany	126
12. Dresden, East Germany	147
13. Warsaw, Poland	173
14. Long Beach, California	206
15. Appleton, Wisconsin	223

Prologue

In our recent history, we have a period known as the Cold War, roughly the time from 1949 to 1991 according to most historians. Mankind was still reeling from World War II, mourning the deaths of millions, the survivors slowly rebuilding lives and bombed out cities.

The early post-war years brought great changes, from wartime economies to peaceful endeavours, from uniforms and military service to civilian dress and jobs, building instead of destroying. It was a period of hope, perhaps wishful thinking, that the future was going to be safer, more peaceful, more prosperous. It was a time to start families, build houses and plant fruit trees and flowers; a time to believe that children would grow up to start families of their own, not to become cannon fodder.

Not all was well in paradise. We tried to ignore the dark clouds in the horizon for a short while, then national survival started to preoccupy us again. The end of the war not only brought us the change from war to peace, but also the geopolitical shift of military and political power. The United States and the Soviet Union emerged as the new superpowers, replacing Britain, Germany, France, and Japan.

The United States allied with Western Europe, the British Commonwealth and Japan; the Soviets allied with Eastern Europe and Communist China.

Both sides actively pursued alliances with other countries, especially in the Third World. What made this era different from many other post-war reconfigurations was a strong ideological component, the rivalry between a capitalistic free market economy and a government-owned Marxist Communist economic system. The ideological rivalry was reminiscent of old, long religious wars, some continuing to this day.

The arms race between the two camps escalated, particularly after the Soviets managed to acquire, through espionage, the atomic bomb. The fear of nuclear annihilation and mutual destruction—the end of mankind—fuelled military preparedness and the need of finding out the other side's intentions, through espionage, advanced technology, analysis of data, detection systems. We were afraid of a nuclear Pearl Harbor.

There were several conflicts that changed the Cold War into a hot one, where miscalculations could threaten irreparable harm to the world. The Korean War from 1950 to 1953, the Vietnam War from 1955 to 1975, and the Soviet invasion of Afghanistan in 1979 were the principal shooting wars.

There were additional dangerous events and close calls throughout the Cold War period: the Berlin blockade and airlift in 1948, and the uprisings in East Germany in 1953, in Hungary in 1956, and in Czechoslovakia in 1968, all three stopped with brute force by Soviet tanks. In 1961, we had the Bay of Pigs failed invasion in Cuba, and in 1962 we looked at nuclear confrontation during the Cuban Missile Crisis. American presidents Kennedy in 1963 and Reagan in 1987 gave famous speeches at the Berlin wall. There were skirmishes in Third World countries around the globe.

We built tall towers with air-raid warning sirens and constructed air-raid shelters, big ones in subway stations and cellars of large buildings, a few small ones in back yards. We instructed school children to dive under their desks when they saw a super bright flash of light in the distance, to protect them from flying glass and other shock-wave debris. The ensuing radioactive fallout was not discussed.

We built early warning systems and Air Force bases in extraordinarily difficult, remote, and inhospitable locations, at huge cost, to be closer to enemy targets.

Behind the ups and downs of public events, the shift from aircraft to guided missiles, the replacement of world leaders, the race for space, behind everything that was in the open, continued the clandestine war of the secret services, the world of spies, saboteurs, disinformation specialists, informers, sleeper agents and moles, code breakers, traitors and patriots. Huge sums and resources were invested by all players in search of information, for the big prizes as well as little bits that might contain the missing letter in some minor puzzle.

Very few of these stories become public; most will never be known except to those involved, and some will be told only after many years. The following novel is based on one of those stories.

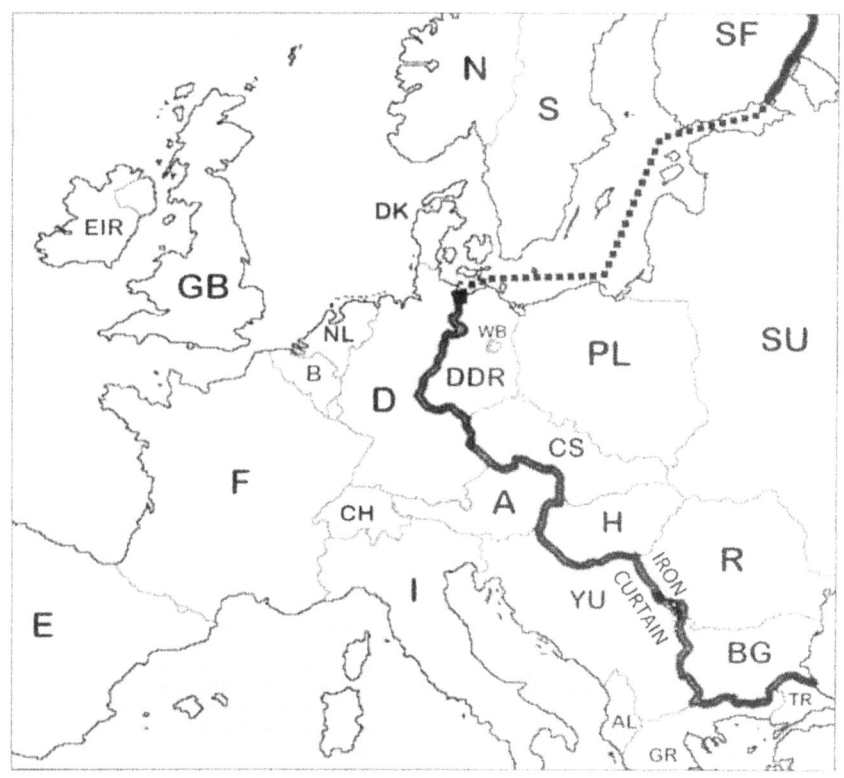

MAIN PART OF EUROPE DURING THE COLD WAR – BORDERS OF 1968

A	AUSTRIA	GR	GREECE
AL	ALBANIA*	H	HUNGARY
B	BELGIUM	I	ITALY
BG	BULGARIA	N	NORWAY
CH	SWITZERLAND	NL	NETHERLANDS
CS	CZECHOSLOVAKIA	PL	POLAND
D	WEST GERMANY	R	ROMANIA
DDR	EAST GERMANY	S	SWEDEN
DK	DENMARK	SF	FINLAND
E	SPAIN	SU	SOVIET UNION
EIR	IRELAND	TR	TURKEY
F	FRANCE	WB	WEST BERLIN*
GB	GREAT BRITAIN	YU	YUGOSLAVIA*

*The Iron Curtain separated the West from the communist countries in the Soviet sphere of control, except for 1. West Berlin, an island inside East Germany, 2. Yugoslavia, communist but not Soviet controlled, steering its own path between East and West, and 3. Albania, a fanatic xenophobic communist country at the time allied with Communist China.

1. Appleton, Wisconsin

The flight from Washington National to Chicago Midway had been routine, uneventful, boring, yet Alan felt a gradual increase in excitement and anticipation. He had to wait about an hour for the connecting flight to Appleton, Wisconsin. He watched television news dominated by the Soviet-led invasion of Czechoslovakia, crushing the so called 'Prague Spring', the brief period of liberalisation in the communist country. The violent use of tanks was a replay of what he had experienced years before in Budapest, when the Hungarian uprising had been crushed.

The TV news commentator took a break from the events in Prague, noting that 1968 was becoming a year of shocking events, recapitulating that North Korea captured the USS Pueblo, North Vietnam launched the TET offensive, Martin Luther King and Robert F. Kennedy were assassinated a few months apart. The year had also brought two big technological events, the introduction of the Boeing 747 jumbo jet, and the astounding voyage of Apollo 8, the first manned spacecraft to orbit the moon.

Now Alan was going to visit people with whom he had escaped from Hungary crawling through a minefield many years ago, unsure about what reception he would have. He was restless sitting in the airport waiting area, got up and walked around, then sat down, got up again. He was thrilled by his new assignment and could not help grinning frequently.

This behaviour was observed by a woman waiting in the same area. She decided to move to another row of seats, to watch him from safety. He was tall, well dressed, with grey hair turning white, a slightly wrinkled sun-tanned face, moving with the gait of a very fit young man. As he paced around, she moved again. He noticed her moves and her unease, becoming painfully aware that he had lost his touch. For much of his career, his life had depended on his ability to remain totally inconspicuous while crossing borders, legally and illegally, into and out of countries behind the Iron Curtain. This little incident in the Midway airport waiting area was a wake-up call for his survival instinct, asleep for many years.

He controlled his restlessness during the short flight to Appleton, where he was pleased by the small county airport welcoming travellers to Wisconsin, extolling local cheeses and the Green Bay Packers. The terminal was operated by a friendly staff that appeared to share jobs for ticketing, car rentals and the coffee shop. They did not have the Plymouth he had reserved and upgraded him to a De Soto at no extra cost.

After settling in at a nearby motel, he telephoned the number he had been given. A woman answered, and he asked to speak with Mr Yravszolok. There was a long silence, then she said he had a wrong number.

"Please, madam, in that case, may I then speak with Mr Ferenc Kolozsvary? I am an old acquaintance of his. I'm just passing through Appleton, and I thought I'd call to say hello."

There was another long silence, then she said, "She, he is retired."

"So am I. I just want to say hello. Could you please ask him to the phone, or would it be more convenient if I stop by your house? My name is Alan Mackenzie. He will remem …"

She interrupted, "I know who you are. Wait." He heard a garbled argument, possibly in another room, probably in Hungarian.

Kolozsvary came to the phone. "Better you come to my house for coffee."

"Could you give me your address?"

"You don't have my address? Why do I find that hard to believe? But okay, let's play it your way. We live on South Lee Street, let me tell you how to get here. Do you have a pencil?"

It was a large, unassuming, well-kept house in a nice neighbourhood, with light grey horizontal wood siding and a dark grey roof. The main portion of the house had two stories, with a one-story wing on the left side featuring a garage and a small entrance porch. The garage door was open, displaying a Studebaker sedan and a Rambler station wagon.

The garden was well-groomed, with freshly mowed lawns on both sides of the driveway, flowering bushes, a swing hanging from one of the tall trees in a cluster to the right. A colourful ball rested in a flower bed, and a yellow balloon was incongruously wedged in one of the bushes. Tall trees in the rear projected over the roof.

Alan studied the house and tried to form an impression of the occupants, as was his custom when approaching a new meeting place. He understood that precautions warranted in some war-torn hell did not make sense in a peaceful Wisconsin small city, but old habits die hard. His impression was that the people were a well-to-do, but not rich, solid middle-class family, proud of their house, friendly and good neighbours.

Kolozsvary opened the door. He had not changed much, a short, broad-shouldered muscular man, with an intelligent, round face, bright dark eyes, and a ferocious nineteenth century officer's moustache. His hair was still black, but with a few white streaks in the sideburns.

"Well, Big Mac, what brings you to Appleton?"

"Hello, Ferenc, long time, over twelve years."

"I'm American now, no longer Ferenc, now my name is Frank."

He invited Alan into the house and called his wife Maria, a pretty, vivacious woman with brown eyes and dark brown hair. She had not changed much, except she had gained some weight and seemed slightly plump compared with the skinny girl he remembered. She offered coffee or tea and brought some cookies. She was polite but radiated hostility towards the visitor. The living room featured paintings of Hungarian themes, framed children's school pictures, and large framed photographs of the Pope and cardinal Mindszenty.

"You told Maria that you just happened to be passing through Appleton and wanted to say hello. Nobody just passes through Appleton. People come here for business with the paper companies, or to visit family, or Lawrence University, or shopping. So, we have said hello, now let's talk about the purpose of your visit."

Maria added, "Frank has been retired for a couple of years. He is no longer involved with your company or your line of business."

Alan replied, "Mrs Kolozsvary, as I told you on the phone, I am also retired. I am no longer involved with our past employers. I just wanted to …"

She interrupted with "You don't need to address me as Mrs Kolozsvary, call me Maria. We are American citizens now, less formal."

She rose to leave, but Alan said, "Thank you, Maria. Please stay and hear what I wanted to discuss with Ferenc, I mean Frank."

She seemed surprised at being invited to stay, but her hostility did not disappear, and she continued with, "You were responsible for the deaths of sixteen Hungarians. We do not want to have anything to do with you. It was your operation, and they are all dead. We now have carved out a new life here in Wisconsin, we have a second chance at living a normal life, we do not want to jeopardise that. I do not want to hear what you want to tell us!"

Frank said, "Maria, let's just listen to what he has to say. There is no harm in listening. He came a long distance to see us, okay, to see me, and we can grant him the courtesy of listening."

She replied angrily, "Frank, you want to listen to he, him, but you are not listening to what I have to say. We have three children, two girls and a boy, have you forgotten? Our oldest girl, he wants to study to become a nurse to help people."

Alan interjected, "He, you mean your boy?"

"No, he, I mean she, our oldest girl."

She spoke with an almost accent-free Midwestern American English, but had the problem with the 'he', 'she', and 'it' pronouns that often affected native speakers of Hungarian and other languages that make no gender distinction. Frank did not seem to have this grammar problem; however, he spoke with a strong Hungarian accent. Alan found it interesting that people learning a new language as adults under shared circumstances had such different speech outcomes.

"Look," Alan said, "I just came to ask for some advice. I do not want to disrupt your life or ask you to do anything. Maria, you mentioned a second chance. Second chances are what brought me here. If you do not want to listen, that is fine, I will leave you alone. I do, however, resent you accusation that I was responsible for the killing of the Hungarians. Yes, it happened on my watch, and they were my team, but they died because someone betrayed them to the East German Stasi, who boarded the bus with a list of names and proceeded to arrest them. Our group tried to run away and were shot, executed. They were my friends too. They also were spies and saboteurs being infiltrated into East Germany through a …"

Frank interrupted, "We prefer to call them freedom fighters."

"All right, then, the freedom fighters were clandestine professionals who knew the risks and were betrayed and caught. It was bad all around. Not only were lives lost, but also years of hard work to engage and train this group went down the tubes, together with several careers. My cover was also blown, I was recalled and never had a chance to pay back the Stasi murderers. I still managed to get a few of your so-called freedom fighters out, including you two, and about the only thing I want to hear from you is 'Thank you for helping us escape and resettle us in the United States,'" and, starting to get angry, "I want to know whether you want to listen to me or not."

"Please, we are all ears," said Frank. Maria pouted.

Alan proceeded, "I am assuming your loyalty oaths are still valid and respected, and that you still understand the need for discretion. I sense you, especially Maria, still know fear. Fear is good for survival. Are we in agreement?" Both nodded.

Alan continued, "Perhaps you can help me to locate a bus operator that currently provides tours through the East Bloc countries, preferably out of Austria or Czechoslovakia."

"Why not go to a travel agency?" Maria demanded.

"Because I have a special requirement that most travel agencies cannot fulfil."

"I knew it, with you there always is a special requirement that may or may not kill some Hungarians," she exclaimed heatedly.

Frank raised his voice, "Enough, Maria, stop it, let the man speak! What is the special requirement?"

Alan continued, "I need a bus company that can arrange a tour that can be in a specific location at a specific time, perhaps with only a few weeks of advance notice."

Frank pondered this for a moment and asked, "What happens at the specific location?"

"Nothing. The bus stops for the night at some hotel, then leaves the next morning and continues for the reminder of the tour."

"Aw, Mac, if you want my advice you need to explain a little more. What do you mean by nothing?"

"Truly nothing. As far as the tour operator is concerned, nothing."

"Does a passenger have a heart attack at this special location, or is there an accident, or does a woman have a baby?" Maria asked, adding, "We all know what happens in bus trips organised by Big Mac. The stormtroopers arrive and arrest and execute the …"

Frank interrupted, now quite angry. "Be quiet, Maria, that's enough!"

"Don't you talk to me that way! In the United States of America, husbands cannot …"

"Shut up!" This was followed by some brusque few words in Hungarian, which kept her silent and unhappy.

Alan continued, "As I said, as far as the tour is concerned, nothing happens. Perhaps one of the passengers is quietly replaced by his or her twin, perhaps not, but this has no bearing on the tour."

"What about passports and other papers that our dear socialist republics require?"

"Twins can interchangeably share a passport."

"Perhaps in some places. In what country is this special stop?"

"The German Democratic Republic, your beloved GDR, or the DDR, if you prefer the German abbreviation."

"Shit, that complicates things. I can imagine a switch in Poland or Czechoslovakia or Austria, but not in Stasi land. As you well know, they mark passports and papers with some secret mark that gets checked upon exiting, to prevent switching."

"The same passport would be used. Only the twin, the person, would be substituted if it happens."

Frank had a sip of his coffee and munched on cookies. Maria was about to say something, hesitated, looked at her husband, who lifted a cautionary finger.

Alan let some time pass, then insisted, "Do you know a suitable bus company I could contact? That is all I need from you. If you can give me a name and where to find them, I'll be out of here."

Frank said, "Yes, I know an outfit that fits the bill, but they will not talk to you. They have stayed in business, and alive, by dealing only with people they personally know. I would have to introduce you in person and explain more than what you are willing to tell. They are Hungarians with Austrian partners and operate out of Vienna. However, I cannot afford the trip and I have no desire to go there to help you with whatever strange scheme you are involved in. Tell me one thing, why do you come to me for such information? You have enough company resources and contacts to find what you are looking for by telephoning from your desk. What can I offer?"

It was Alan's turn to sip coffee and eat cookies while deciding on his explanation. He really had no choice but to tell more than he originally intended.

"Look, Frank and Maria, I was retired, living comfortably, as you are. My wife died three years ago, I have two grown children, a boy and a girl, and four grandchildren. In old age, one often reminisces about past successes and failures, sometimes dreaming that old dream of mankind, getting a second chance to do something, or finish some unfinished business. One of my big regrets, better say disappointments, was that I did not have the opportunity to get back at the Stasi for the murders of our Hungarian network that Maria so fervently blames me for. My cover was blown, I was damaged goods, recalled to Washington in the nick of time."

"For a few years, I had a desk job organising and evaluating operations, then I retired and got used to civilian life, often nostalgic about my years in the field. I lost touch with my employers. As you know, when you are out, you do not even get a Christmas card, and they certainly cannot share any information with you. Your pension checks do not offer a clue about your former line of work."

"Then, specifically because I had been completely out of touch with the secret agencies and had no contact, social or otherwise, with my former colleagues, an opportunity presented itself to participate in a small confidential operation that would help the United States and inflict some real pain to the DDR hierarchy."

Frank said, "And you need a collaborating tour bus. Are you trying to infiltrate someone into the DDR or trying to get someone out?"

"Yes, something like that."

"That does not answer the question. But, well, in our business you rarely get a straight answer. Let us assume then. If we are infiltrating, there are simpler ways to get someone into the country, and if we are trying to rescue someone, why not kidnap them?"

Alan considered the extent of his explanation, offered, "The reason is that regular channels and agencies have been infiltrated and cannot be told. The prize is the identity of several moles. The whole thing must be done by people not connected, or no longer connected, to any government agency. I am sure there are many details you would like to know, but that is all I can tell you. I also pray that you both take the need for secrecy very seriously and remember that 'independent contractors' are not protected by the nice, law-abiding disciplinary procedures that governments—by that I mean our law-abiding Western governments—must follow. Independents are exposed to a different justice, rather hard and swift. That is why I have to be thorough." Both nodded.

"Are you flying solo? How did you become involved?" Frank asked.

Alan replied, "No, I am not freelancing. I have a sponsor, actually a college classmate and former boss, later station chief, who contacted me."

Frank thought for a while, then asked, "Are referring to your law school? Perhaps the same school attended by our distinguished president and our equally distinguished secretary of state?"

"As a matter of fact, yes, the same school, but these two gentlemen were a couple of years ahead of me and moved in different circles."

"I see," said Frank, grinning. "This coincidence is truly coincidental, right?"

"Yes, it is truly coincidental. Can we return to our bus line?"

"As I told you, I know an outfit, but they will not talk to a stranger, and I cannot go to Vienna to introduce you."

Alan replied "I can pay for your travel expenses. Introduce me to your … friends and you can fly back."

Maria started to sob and yelled that she would not let her husband go to Europe alone to become enmeshed in dangerous dirty work again.

Alan inquired, "Have you travelled abroad since you escaped Hungary?"

Frank replied, "We went to Canada and to Europe."

"Where in Europe, and when?"

"About five years ago, when we became citizens and could get American passports. We went to Austria, spent a week in Vienna, then went to Italy, to see Rome and the Vatican, and stopped in London for a few days on the way back."

"Are your passports still valid?"

"Yes, still good for several years."

"So, you went to Europe and enjoyed a vacation. Why, Maria, is it now a problem for Frank to spend a few days in Vienna?"

"Because we are no longer involved in your activities. We went to Europe as a family, as tourists, not to become involved. We visited places that were important to us, not to some political mission. We visited churches and museums," she argued, adding, "I have a good idea: Why don't you go away and leave us alone?"

Alan shot back, "I have a much better idea. How about taking the whole family to Vienna, both of you and the three children? I will pay in advance for the trip, hotels, reasonable spending money, for two weeks. You yourself would book airlines and accommodation to suit. You can go sightseeing or do whatever you want. All you must do, Frank, is introduce me to your bus service, which I assume would not take more than an hour. The rest of the time is yours."

Maria was startled by the offer, then asked, "Is this one of your tricks? Trying to lure us into another lethal bus trip by promising first class air fare and fancy hotels? Now you are into jeopardising children?"

Alan replied, getting quite angry, "I did not offer first class air fare nor five-star hotels. That would not be wise, calls too much attention. I will pay for travel and accommodations of the same level you would book if you were paying for your family. It must look normal. I suggest you two talk it over. If you decide to help me, and our country, and the memory of the Stasi victims from your old country, I will deliver all the travel funds to you immediately, so you can travel within two weeks or so. And, Maria, if you decide not to go, I do not give a shit. I am tired of your attitude. Here is a card from the motel where I am staying. If I do not hear from you by 2 p.m. tomorrow, I will fly back, and you will not see me again. Thank you for your hospitality."

He left abruptly without shaking hands and slammed the door on his way out. That evening he had dinner in a pub, then watched TV for a while in his room and retired early.

Next day, annoying Alan by waiting until exactly 2 p.m., Kolozsvary phoned. "We will go to Vienna, but we have a problem. You need to apologise to Maria; she feels you insulted her."

"Frank, we don't have a problem. You have a problem, you married it. Either you fix it now or I will withdraw my offer. This is becoming a security issue. We do not need all the noise and drama. I will phone you in half an hour. If everyone is then happy, I will drive to your house and give you a cashier's check, but only after I talk to Maria, and she convinces me that she is 100% in agreement with the trip and will obey all my security precautions and instructions. She is not new to our world and knows this is serious and that sloppy behaviour is dangerous, deadly dangerous. There will be no apologies, changes in plans, vague dates, complaints, or conditions. Your family can have a nice vacation in Austria or stay here, in which case I will find someone else to locate a reliable bus line. I guess you have about half an hour to discuss it with your wife and decide. Do you understand?"

After receiving telephoned assurances that everyone was in general agreement, Alan drove to the Lee Street house, where he was greeted by an angry Maria.

"Whenever there is trouble brewing somewhere, you seem to appear," she said, belligerently. "We had not seen you for a long time. Now there is a repeat slaughter going on in Czechoslovakia, and you show up. You pretend that your current interest is in buses and East Germany. I guess we are supposed to think that your periodic appearances in times of trouble are just coincidental."

Alan rebutted, "All I know about Czechoslovakia is what I hear in the news. That is not why I am here. Let us get back to the purpose of my visit. I need some names and addresses that Frank perhaps knows or can find. I need to know what I can do to get his help. I also need to know if I am wasting my time and yours."

2. Budapest, Hungary

Alan was concerned that Maria's hysterical moments could attract attention to his mission, but he needed Frank's unique kind of investigative talent to find the right people for the job.

The primary issue with Maria was her deep fear that her family, her children, were going to be pulled into dangerous undercover work behind the Iron Curtain, and she was determined to prevent it, by whatever obnoxious means she could think of. Alan was equally determined to try to reassure her, by whatever means, that her family was not at risk. She would not let her husband travel to Vienna alone, and she was afraid to go with the family. Alan wondered if there was some hidden skeleton in the family closet that needed to be exposed and neutralised.

Alan suggested, "Perhaps we can resolve our mutual anxieties. The way we resolved ambiguities, hunches, and bad vibes in my line of business was to review the whole story, often more than once, and see what falls out. When we debriefed defectors, we reviewed their stories many times, often over several weeks and with different people, and we would eventually find the discrepancies or a problem that was nagging in the background. I want to have a brief version of that kind of debriefing with you."

"What, now we are defectors needing a hostile debrief?" demanded Frank.

"No. You were defectors once, sort of. Now I just want to make sure that some unresolved issue or careless word does not put someone at risk. I know parts of your story. I want to hear it all. Who are you, Maria?"

After a long pause, Alan continued, "Please remember that I have witnessed many odysseys behind the curtain in the years that I was stationed in Vienna. I must evaluate whether I can trust you not to mess things up. If I decide your participation is too risky, I will leave you alone, no hard feelings, no further contact. I do hope, however, that I will be able to trust you to help me with the needed introductions." He looked at the couple. "Can we have a serious talk? All I want is your entire life story from your happy days in Hungary until you escaped, very unhappy. Okay?"

Frank asked sarcastically, "That's all you want?"

"I am really, really tired of this whole discussion," sobbed Maria. "Perhaps if I tell you what we went through you will have a better understanding and leave us alone."

Frank started to object, then kept quiet. Maria sobbed, sighed, asked her husband whether to share her private story. He nodded encouragement.

"You know that I know the details of your escape, probably better than you do," Alan said, and added solicitously, softly, "It would help all around if you could share the beginning parts of that period."

Resigned, Maria and Frank took turns with their narrative, each reminiscing about the segments they knew best, either from their own experience or learned from witnesses and participants.

The story of Maria and Frank was intertwined with the turbulent events of the Communist regime in Hungary. The lightning rod of the opposition was Jozsef Cardinal Mindszenty, head of the Roman Catholic Church in Hungary. He personified uncompromising opposition to fascism and communism in Hungary. He was imprisoned by a succession of governments.

After World War II, he opposed the Communist persecution in his country. He was imprisoned again, tortured, and after a show trial featuring a visibly mistreated man reading a coerced confession, he was given a life sentence that fuelled international condemnation of the regime. He spent eight years in prison, then was freed in the Hungarian uprising of 1956. During this brief revolution, all kinds of political prisoners were freed, and many hidden opponents of the Communists came out of the shadows.

In November of 1956, the Soviet Union invaded Hungary to restore the Communist regime. Retaliation against opponents was swift and brutal. Cardinal Mindszenty managed to obtain political asylum in the United States embassy, where, unable to leave the grounds, he lived for the next fifteen years while the Vatican and the United Nations engaged in frustrating negotiations to free him. Due to international public pressure, after all these years he was finally allowed to leave the country. He died in Vienna.

Maria's parents had been killed during World War II. She was raised by an aunt, and gradually more and more by the Communist state, having a rather happy childhood and adolescence, with friends and a busy social life in the many well-organised socialist youth organisations.

While studying at the university to become a teacher, she was raped by a professor, an episode that turned very violent as she vigorously tried to defend herself, biting, scratching, screaming at the top of her lungs. She was overpowered and beaten up. She reported the assault to authorities. He denied it, charged her with attempting to seduce him in exchange for good grades. He was supported and provided with alibis by faculty colleagues, and Maria was expelled from the university.

Hurt and furious, she escalated her complaint to the highest court of the land, who referred the case back to the academic authorities.

Having lost her college room-and-board scholarship, she got a job as a waitress in a poor neighbourhood. There she met and cautiously befriended a few other damaged people.

She wrote a long letter about her case to the leading newspaper, which was never published nor acknowledged. About a week later she was savagely beaten by a gang, and left in a gutter with two broken ribs, a broken arm, and severe cuts and bruises. Police stumbled on her during the night and took her to a hospital, where she was examined, stitched, and bandaged. They X-rayed her but deferred the broken bone setting for the morning. She had been kicked in the chest, abdomen, and legs. Her legs and feet were so swollen and bruised that she could not walk.

The police did a routine check on her and found she had a record of antisocialist behaviour and had made false accusations against a professor, causing her expulsion from the university, and leaving her subject to arrest if involved in any further dissent or disorderly conduct. The very short police report was attached to her chart. She was left on a gurney in a corridor, without any pain medication, to wait for the orthopaedic morning shift. As a 'political', she was of low priority.

In the early morning hours when the corridor was quiet, she managed to get up and crawl away, taking her chart, X-ray, and police report with her. She stole a pair of crutches from a sleeping patient but could only use one with her good arm. She dropped one crutch, got out unobserved through a fire stair, and managed to hobble to a church eight blocks away. Using her last strength, she banged on the residence door with the crutch, then fainted from pain and exhaustion.

The young priest who had to get up at five a.m. to do early morning chores thought he heard something outside and went to look, at first finding nothing, then noticing a woman's body in the shadow of the building. She was breathing in an irregular, stuttering way. He was about to call an ambulance when he saw the corner of a folder peeking out from under the body. Curious, he examined the papers and the police report, which listed her name as Maria Illenyi, then went to awaken the senior priest for guidance. They decided to take her inside before early sidewalk traffic started.

The Roman Catholic Church in Hungary was under enormous pressure from the Communist regime in those days. The martyrdom of Cardinal Mindszenty was on people's minds. Priests were barely tolerated, and officiated in their duties with extreme caution, afraid of using a wrong word in a sermon or helping anyone with anything that the state may disapprove of.

The two priests knew they were risking serious trouble by not calling the police immediately. The young woman was dressed only in a thin hospital gown without underwear, a very awkward situation. They found some sheets to cover up the girl in a more modest attire, and tried to revive her with communion wine, but she did not respond. As they laid her on a couch the younger priest recognised her, and told the older, "Father, I know this young woman. She works in a pub I sometimes visit to mingle with our flock and to have a beer."

The older priest gave him a stern look. The younger confessed, "On occasion I have more than one beer, Father, depending on what is being discussed with the parishioners." The older chose not to comment.

They would have to inform the housekeeper who came later in the morning to care for the household and church, and likely also to report priestly activities to the police. They discussed options, decided to inquire at the pub if they had any ideas. The younger knew, and the older suspected, that the pub was a clearinghouse for all kinds of information, not necessarily approved by the state or the church.

The younger priest got on his bicycle and pedalled to the pub, which still was closed. He banged on the door until an angry voice told him to go to hell, it's six in the morning. He kept banging on the door until the manager, who lived on the second floor, opened his window and yelled, "I told you to go to hell. O my God, Father, I'm sorry, I didn't expect you. Isn't it a bit early for a beer? I'll open the side door for you."

After he let the priest in, he wanted to know why this early morning visit. The priest told him about the woman.

"I found her this morning just outside the church residence, unconscious. She has been savagely beaten, with broken bones and some other scary injuries. It appears that she escaped from the hospital. I think she works here, but her face is so swollen and bruised that I am not sure. Her chart gives her name as Maria. The chart has a police report attached. Would you have any suggestion what a good Christian should do?"

The bartender looked scared, and said, after some hesitation, "Father, perhaps I know this woman. We have a Maria Illenyi working here, who disappeared last afternoon and didn't come to sleep. She has a small room in the back. Perhaps she was trying to get here, to her room, but only managed to get as far as the church."

The priest said, "Yes, Illenyi is the name on her chart and the police report," adding, "It seems that God has taken an interest in her. I hope the dear Lord will guide us on what to do next."

The bartender thought for a while, offered, "Would you like a beer?"

The priest asked if instead he could a have plum brandy, the most potent Hungarian drink he knew, and added that he had left in a rush without any money, could he pay later.

"It's on the house. You can have anything you want, Father. And I'll join you."

He poured them both double. After some thought, he asked the priest, "Tell me, Father, if you hear something in confession, you cannot tell anyone, ever, not even the Pope or the party. Is that correct?"

"Yes, the priest's lips are sealed forever."

"What about under torture?"

"Then it is in God's hands."

The bartender reflected, then abruptly requested, "Father, I'd like to give confession."

The priest hesitated. A bar was hardly a substitute for a proper confessional in a church, but under the circumstances he could not think of a reason to refuse. Sitting down on a couple of empty boxes, they were hidden behind the bar counter and pretended it was a confessional.

"Father," the barman said, "I think this girl has to disappear, and we need to help her, now, and fast, before the streets get busy. From what you tell me, she needs a doctor, also now, and fast, but not in a Budapest hospital. The beating was a last warning. I have seen that before. She is lucky to be alive, but she never will be safe around here."

"In our little neighbourhood pub, we hear many stories. Occasionally we can help someone, discreetly, quietly. Some of our patrons are well connected to a variety of services and sources of assistance. Sometimes we can connect a need with the right resource. Sometimes, only sometimes, not always. We can help someone escape from a … a difficult situation."

"Maria had told me some of her troubles and the expulsion from the university when she applied for the job. She was a good worker and I thought she would quietly disappear into anonymity, but then she stirred up some big hornets' nests. I think she was stupid, but naïve innocents often do stupid things that can't be undone. You cannot bring her here; the cops will come looking. I have to report her missing and be able to swear that I have not seen her."

He lit a cigarette and gulped the rest of his brandy. "I expect a bread delivery about 7:30. Your church just decided to buy fifty loaves to donate to your poorest parishioners as a gesture of Christian goodwill. I will pay for it, brief him, and send him your way. You can receive the bread and help load the girl into the van, really fast. He will take her to a safe doctor; we have the right connections. Make sure no one sees her. You go now, quickly." Confession ended with absolution and a sentence of one Hail Mary, deferrable to another day.

Back at the parish house the father superior was told about the bread deal but could not be briefed in further detail without breaking the sanctity of the confessional, which he understood. His assignment was to keep the housekeeper distracted in the church and away from the service door until the bread delivery was completed.

The van arrived shortly before eight. The young man was very decisive in his manner. He greeted the priest with, "Wake up, let's get her into the van, now, fast, before the bread is unloaded. No time to pray, stop that, you can pray later. Move!" They got her into the van, the driver unceremoniously dumped her on the floor, dragged her towards the front and piled loaves of bread all over her. The priest was shocked at the harsh handling and the lack of courtesy of the driver. As they were unloading the bread the driver said, "I hope the woman doesn't regain consciousness and start yelling at the wrong time. You better pray for that, just in case."

They unloaded the bread in great haste, piling the loaves on the floor on a clean white paper the driver provided. He slammed the rear doors shut and drove away, in a cloud of blue exhaust smoke, just as the housekeeper arrived on her bicycle.

"Good morning, Father. Was that van delivering something to our church?"

She was told about their decision to donate a loaf of bread to each poor parishioner, as a gesture of Christian goodwill. She was terribly upset about not being included in the decision and kept harping about it for the entire day, until they gave her two loaves.

The young priest had learned something about the pub's underground activities and became appreciative of the young driver's brusque haste. He wondered where the girl had been taken to. It had been an exciting adventure. He hoped God would grant him another opportunity to help someone in similar circumstances.

In the hospital, the night shift assumed the day shift had taken care of the young woman. The morning shift assumed the night shift had treated and discharged someone. There were no patients in the waiting room or resting on gurneys, these held on to their own paperwork until called. There was no chart or paperwork in the pending basket or the new arrivals file. The file was not closed; it had never been opened.

Alan Mackenzie listened carefully to Maria's story, paying particular attention to the source of the recollection, partly her own experience, partly what other participants or Frank had told her. Maria resumed sobbing.

She added, "The bastards not only raped and beat me, but they took away my country, my party, my university, my life. I was happy, a good student. I loved Hungary, my lovely country, and I still do, but not the bastards who now run it."

"I loved the Communist party, was grateful for all the good things they provided for our youth. I loved the camaraderie, I loved to sing patriotic songs, participate in sports with my group, go to dances and picnics and movies and ballets and concerts. I felt respected and protected. The bastards stole everything from me, my youth, my hopes, my dreams."

"In Wisconsin, we found our second chance. Frank started selling insurance and did well. Over the years he learned everyone's name between Appleton and Green Bay and started his own insurance agency. He is blessed by a prodigious memory. He knows everybody and can find anything. When he retired, we were looking forward to happy times. Then you showed up."

Alan commiserated and commented that Frank's prodigious memory and ability to find anything was the reason he was so badly needed, and only to make an introduction to the bus people in Vienna. In exchange, Maria and her family would enjoy two weeks in Europe with all expenses paid. Alan also reiterated that he fully understood her fears of involving her family in the clandestine world, and that her fears were completely valid and appropriate considering the events in her past, and that all that was needed was an introduction.

"Thank you for sharing your terrible experience. It is always hard to talk about those events. However, please continue with the bread truck. I know the rest of your story in broad strokes, but you need to fill in the details. We were talking about your ride in the bread truck."

Frank took a turn with the narrative, "As you know, I was driving a taxi in those days. The ideal job for someone with my assignments. I could go all over, work any hours I pleased, do favours, deliver goods, often I would hear interesting things from my passengers. I did some discreet errands for party hacks, and they protected me in turn. I was a convenient guy to know. They of course had no idea of my real loyalties. You will be amazed to learn about some of our escapades."

"Frank, the bread truck," Alan interrupted. "What happened with the bread truck?"

"Our friend the bartender phoned me to pick up an unconscious female at a corner near the bakery and take her to a farm we did business with. I met the bread truck, and we transferred her to the cab, and I went for a ride in the countryside."

"Was your trip uneventful?" Alan wanted to know.

"I was stopped once by a cop. He wanted to look in the trunk, where I only had a spare tire. He asked about my passenger, and I told him she was passed-out drunk, sleeping it off. He wanted to know why she was wrapped in a sheet. I told him that she had vomited all over her clothes, and that I hoped she would not vomit in my cab. He just shook his head, disgusted, and we parted company."

"Then what happened?"

"I drove to a farm, about twenty kilometres north of Budapest. The farm had been confiscated by the regime, but the original farmers were allowed to stay and run the place. In exchange, they provided fresh fruit, vegetables, homemade pickles and preserves to local officials, also contributed good cake to officials' birthday celebrations."

"They were helpful to our group in many ways. They provided shelter for persecuted people, food, and old clothing to the needy. I kept them informed about city events and possible dangers, and supplied them with cigarettes, candy, spices, fabrics for dressmaking, radio tubes, gasoline syphoned from my cab, booze and newspapers, and many special requests for hard-to-get items."

Maria added, "I remember the cab ride. I did not know where we were going. I was really scared when the cab driver was talking to the policeman, and I pretended that I was still unconscious. After the policemen left, I asked you, the driver, you, where I was, and you said I was in a cab and going to a safe place. I told you I had no money for a cab, and you said not to worry, it was a free ride. I could not remember what happened at the church. I had a vague recollection of the smell of fresh bread."

She started to cry. Frank came over, knelt by her, and held her hands, and asked, with a hint of anger, "Do we need to continue with this interrogation? You know the rest of the story."

"Maria and Frank, it's decision time," Alan admonished. "Are you in or out? If you are in, please continue and do not argue with my line of inquiry."

Both looked upset, Maria teary-eyed, Frank angry. Alan got up and started to put on his overcoat. First Maria, then Frank, asked him to sit down.

"Okay. Stay calm. We are doing all this for everyone's safety. I must know if anything is lurking in your background that may come and bite us at some inconvenient time. I am not expecting sainthood, I am just seeking clarity in your background."

"So now you are a psychiatrist?" asked Frank, with hostility.

Alan looked at his overcoat but made no further move. "No, I am not a psychiatrist or psychologist or priest. As you both well know, I survived a long career in a dangerous business because I am a careful observer of people and a reasonably skilled judge of character."

Maria offered coffee or tea or something else, acknowledging that the meeting was continuing. Frank seemed less enthusiastic. Alan observed with interest that a slight shift was taking place, Maria becoming more conciliatory and Frank more hostile.

"Tell me more about the farm. Tell me where you found medical care, and how you got there from the farm."

Frank responded, "There was an elderly doctor at the farm, name of Goldberg. He was fired for criticising an incompetent hospital administrator appointed by the party. He fought it, lost his medical license, was sentenced to do menial farm work. He cleaned out manure from pig sties and chicken coops and spread it to fertilise vegetables. His scientific knowledge soon showed good results in the quality and quantity of vegetables."

"He also discreetly provided medical advice and treated farm injuries. His experience resembled Maria's, and they immediately got along. He studied her chart and x-rays, and set her broken arm and taped her ribs after I delivered the necessary plaster, bandages, antibiotics and pain medicines, which I got from a hospital worker who owed me some big favours."

Maria continued the narrative. "The women in the farm cleaned me up and they she gave me some old clothing, much too big for me, as he, she all was quite hefty, but it kept me warm and felt wonderful. There was plenty to eat, people were kind to me, and I started to have some happy days again. I helped her, them with whatever the farm work I could do with one arm, later when the cast came off, I could do more."

She smiled at her husband; there was evident love between the two, and blushing slightly, she confessed, "I kept seeing our favourite cab driver almost every week. He always found me to say hello. Him, he was so dashing, he looked like pictures of hussars from the imperial era, with his military bearing, big moustache, ready smile. One day he brought me a gift, a real elegant city dress, my size, it fit perfectly. He saidhe had a good deal from a dressmaker he, she owed him some favours."

"Did you ever return to Budapest?" Alan wanted to know. "Did you travel anywhere away from the farm? Did you go to a nearby village? Did you have visitors?"

"No, not to Budapest, but we did go a few times to the village, to get supplies, deliver vegetables and fruit. I had no visitors, but Frank often brought visitors in his taxi. Sometimes they stayed for a few days, sometimes they returned with him." Alan asked many questions about the visitors; they were answered by Frank. There were other questions about life on the farm, what transportation was used to visit the village, was there rural mail delivery, were there troublesome visits from party officials.

"We had one official visitor who arrived unannounced and worried the farm people," Maria said. "I did not meet him."

"She, he talked with the elder and went for a walk around the premises, seemed to be interested in the two tractors and farm equipment. He asked many questions and wrote things on a clipboard. He had a nice car with a driver. Later the elder told us that we may be losing one of the two tractors, that our operations did not warrant so much valuable equipment. However, nothing seemed to change while I was there."

"She recovered amazingly well," said Frank. "Clean air, good food, decent treatment by kind, simple, Christian farm people. After the cast came off and she started to make or mend clothing that was of her size, she looked wonderful."

"We shared college tales. I had studied engineering in the same university. After graduating, I tried but could not get an engineering job. The university employment office said I had been lackadaisical in socialist and Marxist studies and would not recommend me. The available positions went to the more politically proactive graduates."

"I resigned myself to waiting for another opportunity, perhaps in some provincial town. For the meantime, I became a cab driver and freelance entrepreneur."

"I spent time with Maria whenever I visited the farm. She had started to laugh, her cheeks were pink, she combed her hair stylishly, she had become a totally different person from the sad wreck I had retrieved from the bread truck. I was in love."

"Me too," confessed Maria, blushing again. "We both knew it but did not talk about it. In those unsettled times, we were afraid to admit anything or commit to anything, although Frank did things that might have been normal in other parts of the world, but unusual in our country."

"What country do you mean?" Alan asked.

"Don't be such an ass," Frank responded for Maria, his temper flaring up. "You know full well that then our country was Hungary, and that in our hearts and in our souls it still is. We get tears in our eyes listening to some old Hungarian music. We don't get tears in our eyes listening to American music, which is new to us. However, make no mistake, our country now is the United

States of America. We love and respect and support our new country, and there should be no question of loyalty in your mind."

"Do you really think that by listening to our reminiscences you will detect what is in our hearts? Not Maria, but I can lie better than you. Our old occupations were supported by lies and make-believe and knowing secrets. I was among the best, you remember it well, and that is why you are here. So, cut out those stupid juvenile inquiries, and treat us as reasonably intelligent adults. Jesus, man, you have lost your skills. Now I am starting to question your suitability for clandestine work, or anything associated with it, or whatever it is that you are scheming."

"Sorry."

"Sorry doesn't cut it," Frank went on. "Sorry is not an excuse for your indecision. I think it is time to decide whether you—not us, but you—are in or out."

"For what it is worth," Maria said, conciliatory, "I love our flag, our American flag, I feel emotion, patriotic pride, whatever you call it, when I see it fluttering in the breeze, in schools and government buildings, on ships, on our embassies, on our houses, and, yes, also on some kid's tee shirt, or some hippie's pants. I used to be shocked, I found it disrespectful. In Hungary, you would have been arrested."

"Over time, I realised that some of these disrespectful flag displays actually represented a much deeper respect, the respect for the knowledge of free people that their country was stable enough to tolerate dissent, lack of respect, stupidity and insolent, filthy bad manners."

"Bravo!" said Frank. "That was a speech worthy of a left-wing hippie student defending flag burning on campus, all supported by the communists, of course."

Maria argued, "If the communists are free to incite campus trouble and disrespect our flag, how come that them have no political power, that she, they have not a communist political party? Nobody cares about communist socialist dogma here. He, we all are too busy with little league, our cars and appliances, we can go to church or to the beach by our choice, criticise government or salute flag or not."

Alan was amused by the continuing shift in attitudes between Maria and Frank, Maria becoming more supportive, Frank the doubtful one. It also became evident that both wanted to participate and did not want him to leave.

"Do you want to continue rehashing our escape? You know the story, so what is the point?" Frank asked, belligerently.

"Yes, please. Go back to the farm and your romance."

Alan continued to ask questions about farm life, visitors, and interaction with the regime. He had some reminiscences of his own. During that time, he had been stationed in Vienna and from there coordinated a large group of agents in Hungary and Czechoslovakia.

He had been sent to Hungary to study, very discreetly, the possibilities of extracting Cardinal Mindszenty from prison and taking him safely out of the country. It was a farfetched idea that may never be implemented, nevertheless it had to be planned and analysed, as well as the political fallout of such a mission.

He had entered Hungary legally, under his own name, as a representative of an American import firm seeking to establish a relationship with Hungarian industry to manufacture and export light bulbs to the United States. Negotiations were going well, and the idea was turning into a real business opportunity. It was the autumn of 1956.

In mid-October of 1956, there was talk of some unrest among students in Budapest. On October 23, a nationwide uprising started.

It spread like wildfire. The Hungarian army joined the revolution. A new government announced that Hungary would leave the Warsaw pact and ally Hungary with the West. Cardinal Mindszenty was released from prison to loud cheers across the country. The long nightmare had ended.

Maria recollected, "We all were glued to the radio. All farm work stopped, we just fed animals and milked cows. There was a joyous party that went on for days. Suddenly we had a future that would bring back the past, a past where people could live and work in peace and freedom, feel safe and be happy."

She looked at her husband, hesitated, who give her a big smile and nodded, encouraging her. Blushing again, she continued, "One afternoon Frank's familiar taxi arrived. Frank was dressed in his good suit and she, he had a bunch of flowers. In front of the assembled farm group, he knelt and asked me to marry him, and I joyfully accepted, and the farmers clapped and cheered and congratulated us."

"We decided that the priest who had saved me would marry us as soon as things calmed down in Budapest. Perhaps, we could have a party in the neighbourhood pub where I had worked, invite all farm hands. It was an incredible time in my life. It also was a time of collective euphoria across Hungary, and the most beautiful autumn we had ever seen."

"Our hero, our martyr Cardinal was free. He supported the revolution and prayed with us and for us and for our faith and our country. The Cardinal's books emerged from hiding places and reappeared on bookshelves. We were drunk without drinking, although we had drinks when offered. We laughed and hugged."

In Moscow, Khrushchev became increasingly alarmed at the breakaway of Hungary, particularly at the astonishing speed of events, and the threat of a domino-like collapse of the Eastern European bloc.

The Soviets decided to chance a confrontation with the West by starting an invasion of Hungary on November 4, 1956.

Hungary had allied with Germany during World War II and fought vigorously against the Soviets. When the Soviet army returned to Hungary in 1956 to quell the uprising, the Hungarian army tried to fight back. There were feelings of unfinished business from the war for both sides and the hostility was intense. However, the Hungarians were soon overwhelmed by the massive Soviet forces and the entire country ended back under Communist control.

Retaliation against the revolution's participants was swift and brutal. Many opponents of Communism that were in hiding had come out in the open to celebrate the revolution. Many had been involved in minor illegal activities under accommodations with the police or party members. All these people, as well as the policemen and party officials who had collaborated with them, were now on lists and systematically tracked down, arrested, or killed. About 3,000 persons were killed, over 12,000 were arrested. Heavy sentences were imposed, between 400 and 500 were executed.

Cardinal Mindszenty managed to obtain political asylum in the United States embassy in Budapest. It is estimated that over 200,000 managed to escape to another country before the borders were closed tight, fenced, patrolled with dogs, protected with minefields. The Communist regime provided information to friendly fraternal socialist countries, who managed to intercept some of the enemies of the people.

The East Germans captured a group of Hungarians traveling by bus on a workers' exchange program. They were charged with espionage and sabotage, shot to death, allegedly while trying to escape.

Their infiltration into the DDR had been organised by American businessman Alan Mackenzie, who also was accused, among others, of assisting in the escape of Cardinal Mindszenty to the American embassy, and of running espionage networks in Hungary. His picture was on every police bulletin, with orders to capture him alive if possible, but kill him if he resisted arrest.

Ferenc Kolozsvary remained out of trouble for nearly a month, then was accused of assisting the American in his espionage and also engaging in black market activities. Soon his picture was displayed next to Mackenzie's.

Alan remembered those days well, as did Frank and Maria, who had to fight back tears again, lamenting, "It seemed to me that whenever I found peace, safety, perhaps even happiness, the devil or his agents would destroy it all. When we heard the news about the Soviet invasion, we again were glued to the radio, listening to contradictory reports, gradually realising that the revolution had failed, and terrified when we recognised that we were going back, not to the Communist regime we had before, but to one much more brutally oppressive, straight out of Stalin's playbook." She looked at Frank, asked him to continue. He nodded and proceeded.

"For several weeks, I was free to move around and thought I had managed to avoid any charges. I telephoned Maria a few times, until the line was cut. Then you called a taxi, Alan, to meet and discuss your escape. You were bad news, my friend. Every cop was looking for you. Being around you was dangerous. It was obvious that the first thing to do was getting you out of Budapest. I suggested the farm if there was a way of getting you there."

"Let's be precise," interrupted Alan. "We agreed that it would be in your taxi, and that you would inform people at the farm in advance to avoid any surprises or misunderstandings."

"Why don't you tell, if you want to be so precise?"

"Why don't you stop arguing. Please go on."

Maria said, "Let me tell it for a bit. She, he, I mean Frank arrived one evening in a big rush, asking us to hide this American he had been working with, who was the object of a police manhunt. There was great fear that this would put everyone at risk. Frank said we were at risk already for our previous participation in various trespasses, including me finding shelter there. They asked what the charges against the American were, and you, Frank, said that among other charges, the American was accused of helping our dear Cardinal

Mindszenty to find shelter in the American embassy. The elder said that if the American helped in the cardinal's escape, we are honour bound to help him."

"Now, Frank, tell us how we reached the farm," suggested Alan. "And, on another subject, when do your children get home from school? Do you need to pick them up?"

"No," answered Maria, "They ride bikes. Our youngest will be here any moment, the other two in about an hour. Back to you, Frank."

"That was a pretty scary trip. That day I found out that I also was wanted by the cops. We decided to get out of the city with Alan as a passenger, hiding in plain sight, so to speak. We would go through smaller country roads, where rural police are not as savvy as the urban ones. Alan would pretend to be a Russian, inspecting rural police to determine if they were properly collaborating with our Soviet liberators. We discussed our ploy. We would pretend that he was a foul-tempered high-ranking official who had little patience with underlings, it being best for all concerned to get him on his way as soon as possible. We drove past the city limits, were stopped once by a young cop, who listened to my explanation, took one look at you, Alan, you appearing dangerous in your fake Russian fur cap and angry expression, saluted and let us go."

"About ten kilometres into the countryside, at a wye in the road, we were stopped by another policeman. This one was older and more thorough. He asked to open the trunk, then requested documents. He checked my papers slowly and asked a few questions. Then he requested the passenger's documents. You waved a binder with a Soviet flag on the cover and yelled at him in Russian, then wrote down his badge number and looked at your watch. I asked for the cop's name, rank, and unit. He seemed undecided and scared, but complied, then he asked for my documents again and wrote down my license and registration numbers and the car license plate numbers. He saluted and waved us through. You said to take the wrong road in the wye, away from the farm."

"We drove for a short distance, pulled over in a wooded curve, out of sight. We looked back through the vegetation, just in time to see the police car make a U-turn and head back towards the city at a high rate of speed. It was obvious that he had his doubts and radioed his dispatcher, now was racing to report. They would show him pictures of Alan Mackenzie and Ferenc Kolozsvary, then start a massive manhunt. We knew that our time was extremely limited. We turned back to the wye and on towards the farm. That's it."

"Not so fast. I want to hear the end of the story."

Maria chose to continue. "We were having dinner when you drove into the farmyard. You introduced Alan Mackenzie to us. We were sorry to meet you, Alan. Hiding you meant trouble and high risk for us. Then you, Frank, said that Alan would not be staying, that he had to flee, and we were relieved that this danger had passed."

"Then you, dear Frank, broke my heart saying that your cover had been blown and that you had to flee as well, immediately. I feared I had lost you forever. Again, a happy time in my life had been ripped away from me. Dreams of marriage evaporated. I was overwhelmed by sorrow."

"You said that the police would show up at any time and arrest everybody if any wanted or suspected individuals were found here. Those who must leave immediately were of course Alan and Frank, and also Laszlo, the assistant manager, and his wife Danica, and Geza, the widower manager and elder of the farm, the three who were primarily responsible for sheltering criminal elements and under investigation on suspicion of hoarding tractors."

"Then you added that it also was prudent to take the two lesser criminals, Dr Goldberg, who had been reported for practicing medicine illegally and hoarding medicines, and Maria, who had been expelled from the university for slandering a distinguished professor, and thereafter, continuing to engage in anti-socialist behaviour. And then you looked at me smiling and said that you had to keep me close to you, to prevent me from causing more troubles."

"I was choking because so much glad that I was going to be together with you. Then I was briefly angry with you for putting me through the emotional roller coaster of going away without me and then taking me with you. Then I was ashamed for being angry, then I was happy again, then afraid that someone was going to take it all away again …"

She started to sob. Frank looked at Alan with angry determination, ready to fight if Alan said anything pushy. However, Alan surprised them by saying in a soft voice, "Maria, thank you for confiding your private thoughts during that emotional event. You and Frank have lived through some extraordinary adventures, shared many dangers and great joys, consequently living a richer life than most people. I think you can deeply appreciate your good luck because you can measure it against some not so lucky times."

The narrative paused while the three drank coffee, munched on cookies, smoked, briefly discussed the paintings of Hungarian scenes on the walls, compared winters of Budapest with northern Wisconsin, the latter declared to be colder.

Alan asked, "Do you feel like continuing your story? We are still at the farm, a long distance from Bratislava."

Frank warned, "Don't push. Perhaps, this is as far as the story goes."

Maria said, "Please, I am okay. It just had been a long time since we last talked about those events in sequence and in detail, although we remember them from time to time. It was an emotional time, and the emotions return from the recesses of memory. Let me return to the last moments at the farm."

"You, Frank, said we had to leave at once, there was no time for goodbyes, or packing or taking anything bulky. You also said that our chances were not so good with Danica pregnant, Goldberg old and with a bad foot, and Geza old and frail. Nevertheless, all wanted to go."

"All agreed that they faced great difficulties, all agreed they did not want to go to prison, especially in the angry, vengeful attitude of the just reinstated Communists. All of them, she, they were profoundly saddened at having to leave the one safe place they knew. All felt that the American had brought this calamity into their lives."

"Yes, the bearer of bad news and bringer of calamities. Still a familiar theme, Maria, isn't it?" Alan asked.

She nodded, reluctantly continuing, "Then you, Frank, said that the American was in charge of the escape, that we had to follow his orders exactly, at once and without hesitation, and that he, she did not speak Hungarian, that she, he would speak in German and that you would have to translate. This was no problem; German was the lingua franca of central Europe since the imperial era, most educated people spoke it, and we all were used to it."

"Those staying on the farm should blame everything on the departing managers and claim innocence of any wrongdoing and act as obedient simple farm hands. We had hurried hugs, those who had them grabbed their few papers and photographs and we all piled into your taxi. Alan urged all to take their plastic raincoats. They were army surplus, olive drab, and could provide some camouflage in addition to keeping us dry in the rain."

"Frank was the driver, Laszlo sat in the middle because she, he knew the backroads of the area and could navigate, and Alan twisted in on the right, the two somehow managing to share the single front passenger seat. The other four of us squeezed in the back. The small car was tight and uncomfortable. He was overloaded, underpowered, and the springs bottomed out on every bump. We needed to stop several times to relieve painful leg cramps and had to push on uphill slopes."

3. Bratislava, Czechoslovakia

Frank continued with the narrative, "As I drove on, you, Alan, advised that we were headed to the Czech border. Several of us wanted to know why not Austria. We all feared the Czechs would send us back to the fraternal socialist Hungarian police. You said that Austria was too far, Czechoslovakia was only about 50 kilometres away, and at that point in time the Czechs were so overwhelmed by refugees from Hungary that they were helping to pass them through into Austria to get rid of some of the influx. That worked well for people with papers, not criminals wanted by the police."

"As wanted criminals, we could not leave Hungary through any of the official border crossings. Once in Czechoslovakia, you said we would get help if you could phone a number in Bratislava, the big Slovak city next to the Austrian border and close to Vienna."

"You warned that we needed to stay on the east and then north side of the Danube, although it was not the shortest way, because all the bridges and ferries were heavily guarded."

"We would have to crawl through a minefield and cut fences to cross the border. Alan said that if we crossed in a straight line we would be blown up by the mines, but there were several points where we could cross at an angle. You had to know the location of the starting point, and the exact angle. Alan and I had obtained the identical information from two separate sources; thus, it was considered reliable."

Frank drank some coffee, reflected for a moment, then continued, "Per Alan's instructions, I had procured a bolt cutter, small flashlights, two good military compasses, and a length of strong, thin rope, all hidden under the rear seat of the car. The bolt cutter was hard to get. I traded a radio of unknown provenance, a bottle of vodka, a West-German electric drill, and six packs of British cigarettes for it.

"Following Laszlo's directions, we zigged and zagged through muddy country roads. Once we got stuck in the mud, and we all had to get out and push. Once we saw a police patrol in the distance and had to go back and drive around them. It started to rain, lightly, heavy later."

"We stopped in a wooded area. Alan and Laszlo studied a map and argued in German. Laszlo took off his raincoat and several of us had to hold it as a makeshift tent to allow the unfolding of the map and study it in the rain. The paper map got soggy anyway and soon started to disintegrate. Alan and Laszlo got very angry in their argument, finally they agreed that we had to turn back several kilometres, where we ditched the car in a ravine, removed all papers and the license plates to be discarded elsewhere, and continued on foot."

"It was very cold. The rain increased and soon we were getting wet under our plastic raincoats that let water pass through the collars and sleeves. Our shoes were waterlogged. Dr Goldberg worried about hypothermia. His bad foot gave him great pain and he could barely walk. After about half an hour, we reached a gravel road along a chain link fence. As we were about to cross the road a military vehicle drove up and stopped in front of us. Alan whispered to keep our faces down and not move."

"The two soldiers sat in their vehicle, nice and dry, smoked and drank something. We all laid still in the muddy ground. We hoped our olive drab dirty raincoats would blend into the sorry winter landscape. I don't know if we were hoping or praying or just wishing. We hoped the approaching night would hurry up."

"After an eternity, the soldiers drove away. Alan said that their patrolling pattern probably would bring them back along the same road. He and Laszlo would look for the crossing point and cut an opening, then return for us, as it was easier for just the two of them to hide from the patrol."

"We sat in the rain for another eternity. It was freezing. Our hands and feet were numb. The solid farm woman seemed to be less affected by the cold. Perhaps she was better at hiding it. Alan and Laszlo returned at dusk. They had found the marked post and we all followed them along the road, ready to jump into the tall grass if we saw headlights."

Maria added, "Tell how cold and scared we were."

"I know. I was there, also cold and miserable," Alan agreed.

Frank nodded and continued, "I translated as Alan instructed: 'The minefield is clear in a diagonal line starting at this post, continuing on an exact geographical bearing, which we will follow by compass. The path is allegedly about three meters wide, but I do not trust the accuracy of that claimed width. We must stay in the middle, not stray to the sides.'"

"We will tie the continuous rope around our chest, left side over our shoulder, right side under the armpit, spaced at about three meters apart measured from shoulder to shoulder."

"I will lead by compass, and you will follow maintaining a slight tension on the rope, so that it maintains a straight line. I emphasise light tension, just enough to keep the rope straight. We cannot pull anyone along. We will have to advance on knees and elbows, moving at my pace. If I move too fast, pass the word along to me in whispers, and I will slow down a little. If there is a need to stop or discuss new instructions, we can lie down on our bellies to rest a bit."

"Do not stand or sit up at any time, keep your knees and elbows on the ground. The rain has softened the ground, which helps to avoid bruises. The rain will help us, the dogs lose scents, the guards are reluctant to stay out and get wet."

"If a spotlight suddenly turns on, close your eyes, lay flat and do not move, and do not look at it, because your eyes reflect the light and may be noticed. It is better you turn your pale faces towards the ground; they also reflect light. If the light is turned off, stay where you are and do not move, as they may turn the light on again after a brief interval to see if anything has moved or changed."

"I will lead, with one compass, followed by Laszlo, then Laszlo's wife Danica, then Maria, then Geza, then Goldberg, Ferenc last, with the other compass. If we must turn back for whatever reason, Ferenc will be the lead, on the reverse bearing. Any questions?"

"Dr Goldberg said, 'I believe Geza will not make it. He is limited by old age and does not have the strength. His body temperature is abnormally low, his pulse weak.'"

"Alan hesitated, then ordered a change in the line-up. 'Geza will go before last, just ahead of Ferenc. If Geza cannot continue, Ferenc will pass the word up the line, climb over Geza and untie him, maintaining the straight line, and we will continue crawling.'"

Maria inserted into the narrative, "We all looked at Geza, who listened quietly, then nodded his resigned consent. I felt so sad hearing those instructions. It seemed to me that an old man had been sentenced to death, just short of freedom. I thought that Alan was a cold-hearted cruel man."

Alan said, "Yes, I had to be. Our task was to save as many as possible. Okay, Frank, let us continue."

Frank narrated, "We crawled through the mud for a long time. The rain was heavy, the night was black. It was cold and miserable. We were soaked under the plastic. It was something unreal to crawl in the mud through a minefield in total darkness, hanging on to a rope, following someone guided by a small, magnetised needle."

"We stopped every couple of meters for Alan to check his bearing with a flashlight, under his raincoat. Goldberg reported that Geza did not want to continue, that he wanted to die on the Hungarian soil he had farmed all his life. Goldberg and I tried to change spaces so that we could place Geza at the end, to drag him along. Alan urged us to rush. Dr Goldberg then announced that he could no longer find a pulse, that Geza was dead. I untied him; we could not carry him. We searched him and took his identification papers, an old family photograph, a comb, a pen knife, and other pitiful possessions. We wanted to leave nothing that could connect him to anything. We said a prayer and left the old farmer laying in the mud."

"Alan urged us to keep moving. Once we saw a spotlight in the distance, on the Hungarian side. Vehicle mounted, it travelled along the road at the edge of the minefield, moving back and forth. It stopped before it reached us. Once we heard dogs, some distance away. Alan whispered that they were far and no threat, that around the Czech border the guards were short on dogs, that most of the dog units had been stationed along the Austrian border. At last, we ran into a chain link fence. Alan and Laszlo cut a hole, and we crawled through. Alan welcomed us to the Czechoslovak Socialist Republic."

"We were exhausted, but now able to stand up and walk. We remained tied to the rope, to avoid becoming separated in the dark. Alan continued in the lead, orienting himself by compass, now on a different bearing. It was slow going, occasionally by flashlight, on a few lucky moments by lightning illuminating the area."

"Once Alan fell into a small stream. We pulled him out by the rope. He was soaked down to his skin. The compass was still working in its waterproof case, his flashlight was dead. We tried to dry it and the batteries without success. It was a warning bell; we could not continue in the dark. We huddled under some trees and waited until dawn. Dr Goldberg, now the oldest in our group, had great difficulty walking, with great pain in his left foot. We were all shaking, coughing, and sneezing."

Frank stared at the coffee table, lost in some distant memory. Maria sat next to him and placed her arm on his shoulder. Alan was about to urge them to continue when he looked out the window and saw a Green Bay Packers flag moving rapidly above the shrubs in front of the garden. Then a small boy appeared, racing up the driveway on a Schwinn bike with fat tires, streamers on the handles, and his flag on a tall antenna. In no time, they heard doors slam and the boy entered the living room. He was about 6 or 7 years old, looked like a miniature Frank without a moustache. He was not at all interested in the visitor his parents introduced as an old friend and disappeared into the kitchen from where he yelled that Mom should buy more ice cream, the supply was low. Then they heard music from somewhere.

Alan wanted to proceed with the story. Frank obliged, "At the earliest light we were able to orient ourselves. Alan squished walking in his wet clothes, Dr Goldberg was in obvious pain, asked to be left on some roadside where someone would find him. Alan pleaded, argued, cajoled, ranted that we should continue for a short distance to a road, where we could stop and rest. Laszlo and I helped Goldberg to hobble along. It was a miserable journey. We reached a paved road in the early morning."

"We heard an approaching motor noise. It was an old tractor pulling a trailer loaded with beets. Danica was deputised to intercept. A dirty pregnant woman was less threatening than a group of dirty men. She spoke some Slovakian, had a Slovakian name inherited from a Slovakian mother, and managed to get a ride for the group until the next farm with a telephone. The steady rain had washed off some of the mud, but we still looked quite dirty. A police car passed us in the opposite direction, not interested in a bunch of filthy farmhands sitting on top of a load of beets. The second farm we passed had a telephone wire leading from the road to the house. The tractor driver was kind enough to drive us the short distance to the farmhouse and helped to introduce us and explain."

"The woman who greeted us spoke a little Hungarian and a little German. We explained that we got lost and separated from our guide, who had our papers to travel to Austria. If she would allow us to use her telephone, we could arrange to be picked up to continue with our journey. The phone call would be to Prague, and it probably would take a few hours for our ride to arrive. We would of course reimburse her generously for the telephone call and any other expenses she would incur on our behalf. She hesitated, looked at Danica and Maria, sighed, and agreed."

"A long-distance call had to be placed through an operator. Alan wrote down the number and she talked to the operator. When the slow connection was finally made, she handed the phone to Alan. It rang for a while, then Alan gave a long password in German, spoke to someone in English for some time, then handed the phone to the woman, who heard a fluent Slovakian speaker thanking her for her kind help, asking for her phone number, address, name of the nearest town, and requesting her help in letting her guests wash up and dry their clothes, offering generous compensation. She gave Alan back the phone, who had a further English conversation." Frank paused, looking tired, gestured to his wife.

Maria continued, "We were terribly embarrassed. Wet, filthy, soiled with incontinent mishaps, stinking. The woman called a girl and sent her to fetch her husband from the field. She then took Danica and me to a bathroom with a big wooden tub. We undressed and were able to clean up somewhat with wet washcloths and very cold water, while she heated two big pots of water on her stove. We filled the tub halfway with cold water. When she mixed in the hot water, we could have a sitting bath, with soap, in heavenly almost lukewarm water. The guys could clean up and wash in the same tub water. Alan offered Goldberg the first turn, which the doctor declined, explaining, 'My leg is badly infected. I don't want anyone to bathe in such contaminated water. Let me be last, then make sure the tub is emptied and rinsed out well.'"

Maria continued, "The farmer arrived at the house and had a short talk with his wife. He spoke some German and was able to converse with Alan, Frank and Laszlo. He was told that we had political asylum in Austria, that our ride and documents would arrive by evening, and that he would be reimbursed for food, clothing and whatever other expenses our visit caused. He was courteous, helpful, and did not ask many questions. He and his wife loaned us some ill-fitting but dry clothing. We washed our own clothing and hung it to dry around the kitchen wood stove, the warmest place in the house. They gave us a warm meal of boiled potatoes and beets sprinkled with some bacon bits and paprika.

"We all found a spot on the floor to lay down and sleep. Alan and Frank did not want to sleep at the same time. One of them was always up and awake, usually sitting on a straight-backed chair or walking around. Alan's gun and spare clips were discreetly passed back and forth."

Maria asked Frank if he wanted to continue. He shook his head in the negative. "Well, then," she said, "about seven in the evening a Volkswagen bus with diplomatic plates arrived with two young men, both fluent Czech and Slovakian speakers."

"We changed into our own clothing, still slightly damp and smelly. Our rescuers lavishly reimbursed the farm couple for their help. At first, they refused the money, but Danica took it and gave it to the wife, along with a hug, and guided the wife's hand to pat her pregnant belly, saying, 'You saved my child. Take the money,' pressing the wife's fingers around the folded bills. The woman looked at her husband, who nodded his acceptance. We shook hands, expressed our gratitude, and drove away."

Maria reminisced for a moment, then continued, "Along the way Alan and the two young men talked in English, which we did not understand. They were respectful and called him sir."

"Tense but uneventful hours passed. At times, the trip had an unreal feel, as if we were traveling in circles and never getting anywhere. I vaguely remembered some old Greek mythology about some guy trying to push a rock up a mountain and never succeeding. When we entered a village, it seemed that we had been there before in our circular itinerary. Alan talked about reaching Bratislava soon, that also sounded like a repetition of what he just had said before, over and over."

"We got hungry but were too dirty and smelly to stop at an inn. One of our rescuers bought black bread, cheese and soft drinks in a village. The food was heavenly. We were starting to regain hope. The following hours were relaxed, calming. Then, suddenly, adrenaline surged when we realised that we were in the outskirts of Bratislava."

"We were overcome with joy, relief, life and a future regained. City lights, streetcars, people, automobiles, bicycles, restaurants, civilisation, no troops or tanks in sight. We were astonished that we had reached the prize that you, Alan, had been promising throughout our ordeal. Bratislava had been the name of the unattainable, perhaps another false promise that we pursued in vain. Then we were there, and Bratislava became the name of salvation, it acquired an almost sacred connotation."

"We stayed in a big house for about ten days. Alan said it was a safe house. I did not know at the time what that meant. It seemed safe enough to me, and I did not know why Alan kept repeating that. We got real baths, toiletries, new clothing, regular meals, were able to sleep. We also were photographed and told to sign here and there. The documents were in English, and we did not have a clue what they were about."

"A few days later we crossed the border into Austria with the papers that had been prepared at the safe house. Dr Goldberg's leg was starting to smell. He was delivered immediately to a Jewish welfare organisation who had agreed to take him to a hospital and take care of him. Laszlo and Danica obtained political asylum in Austria. That's about it."

Alan said, "You are almost there. Let us finish."

Maria replied, "There is not much more to say. You provided housing, subsistence money, and told us we were to wait for approval of our political asylum in the United States."

"What else did I tell you?"

"You told us to get married at once, because Frank would be granted asylum for services him, he had provided, but that I had done nothing for the United States, and therefore I had to be her wife, I mean him, his, to be included. And I said that we wanted the priest who saved me to be him the one who married us, but since we could not go back, perhaps we could see he, him in the future to baptise our children."

"Go on."

Maria asked, "What else was there?"

"What was the rest of our conversation?"

"It was not nice. It was a mean-spirited conversation. You told me that the priest would not baptise any children, because he had been shot dead during the Soviet invasion for interfering with the arrest of a parishioner. I was, and still am, incredibly sad about it. I said that at least that was quick, and him, he did not have to suffer. And you said that no, that he had been shot in the stomach, the most painful bullet wound, that he had agonised for several hours before dying on the sidewalk next to the church door where I had been found."

"You did not have to tell me that. It was cruel. The whole situation was cruel, bad, inhuman. Our escape from Hungary was terrible, miserable, awful. I was lucky to get to a hospital, I had pneumonia, had nightmares for months."

"But you got out. What did you think? That it would be like in the movies, where the hero goes through the tale jumping from exploding airplanes into shark-infested water without wrinkling his tuxedo or messing up his hair? For Christ's sake, grow up, woman! You should know better by now!"

Frank interrupted, "Watch your manners and how you talk to Maria!"

Alan ignored him, and continued, "As far as these escapes go, ours was a successful one. Seven people started out, six made it across. Geza died of stress and old age. By the way, you probably do not know. Because of the physical and emotional stress of our escape journey, Danica's baby died in her womb, had to be surgically removed. And Dr Goldberg's leg had to be amputated. It could have been saved with proper treatment and medications. After his recovery, he was allowed to emigrate to Israel. They had more reason to complain than you do."

Maria's eyes filled with tears. The loss of Danica's and Laszlo's baby really touched her. She also felt sad for Dr Goldberg, who had been kind to her, but the loss of the baby affected her the most.

They talked about the days in the Bratislava safe house. Maria was getting quite ill and should have been in a hospital, but they decided it would be much safer to do so in Austria. Czechoslovakia's style of mild communism was like that of Hungary before the Soviet crackdown; however, there was an anxious feeling of foreboding in daily life. People were careful in what they said.

They reminisced about the feeling of euphoria when they received their papers and were able to cross the border into Austria. Maria and Ferenc had to get used to the fact that in Vienna police were viewed as protectors, not as feared oppressors. They were married in a Catholic church by a Hungarian-speaking priest. In lieu of a honeymoon trip, Maria was admitted to a hospital, where they kept her for a week.

Alan shepherded them through it all until Maria got a clean bill of health that allowed her admission to the United States. They enjoyed, like rich Western tourists, a wonderful train trip from Austria to Wiesbaden in West Germany, where at the big American base they said goodbye to Alan and boarded a U.S. Air Force plane to the United States and a new life.

The conversation returned to the present meeting in Appleton, Wisconsin. Alan looked at both, asking, "We just recounted the terrible experiences you had in Hungary and the help you received from kind people, at great risk to themselves, and the opportunity for a new life that was granted to you. Can you help me in finding a suitable bus company, at no risk to yourselves?"

Both looked subdued and slightly embarrassed. After a brief period of silence, Frank, holding his wife's hand, said, "Yes, we will help you in whatever way we can, without hesitation or arguments, as long as we do not put our family in harm's way. We have a moral obligation to help."

He looked at Maria, who nodded, then added, "Yes, I am in total agreement with Frank's statement. I am ashamed to be so difficult. I am scared. I am sorry."

Alan said, "Thank you both. Your help is a great relief. I deeply appreciate it."

Two young girls appeared, said hello to the stranger without interest, and disappeared into the house.

Alan resumed, "There is one more thing I need to add. Do you know what causes many troubles and human suffering? Someone reporting gossip or apparently suspicious activities without thinking about accuracy or consequences."

"Someone sitting at a hairdresser's confiding that she is worried about her husband's interest in foreign intrigue. Someone carelessly talking on a phone in a waiting room. Someone putting lives in danger for personal advancement or revenge for some petty grievance. Someone telling a friend that you are going to Europe on some secret errand."

"I have to trust you, Maria, not to screw things up by carelessly saying anything about undercover work anywhere, anytime, to anyone, not even to a priest in confession. I am not implying that I think you would be deliberately gossipy, but just reminding you of the danger of innocently letting something slip. It is a danger we all are exposed to, especially when we have been away from subversive activities for a long time. In Hungary, speaking carefully was a necessity and had become automatic. Here you lost the vigilance habit."

Frank was about to argue, but Maria responded, "Thank you for the trust. I will not endanger anyone by talking carelessly."

Alan reiterated his appreciation, and handed over a $9,000 cashier's check, advising that they were free to use it as they wished, as long as Frank appeared in Vienna and made the introductions.

He told Maria, "You can take the family to Europe, or if you change your mind, you can let Frank go alone and, I repeat, you can buy yourself a new Cadillac or a Packard or a Lincoln with the portion not used for Frank's travel."

He let them absorb this, then added, "Be patriotic and book tickets with PanAm or TWA, not British, Lufthansa or Air France. I will use one of those. I want to keep our activities totally separate. Let me know airline and flight info and what hotel."

"We need to exchange phone numbers. I need to see your passports, and before you travel, I want photocopies of your passports' information page. I will let you know a post office box where to mail them. I want to know this afternoon, no later than 6 p.m., how you will explain your sudden trip to Europe to your friends, neighbours, your kids, and their friends."

"I will meet you in Vienna and you will arrange the introduction to the bus people as soon as possible. I suppose you will be traveling under your real name. I never liked Yravszolok, it is dumb and not safe to use your own name spelled backwards."

Frank assured him, "It is easy to remember, and it has served me well for a long time, labelling me as the naïve innocent I was pretending to be, but don't worry, the alias was left behind. Now the whole family is Kolozsvary."

By late afternoon, the details had been worked out and Alan Mackenzie was enjoying a drink and a cigarette on the flight back to Chicago, where he would change planes and continue to Washington. He was scheduled to give a progress report on his mission the following day.

4. Vienna, Austria

Alan Mackenzie and Frank Kolozsvary took a cab to meet the bus people. Maria and the children went on a city sightseeing tour.

Alan was surprised that the meeting had been arranged at the owners' villa, not their offices, and he admonished Frank to avoid any surprises in the future; there was to be absolute clarity and up to date information in all things, no matter how trivial. Frank grunted understanding. He explained that the Hungarian partners of the bus company consisted of and old patriarch and his three sons, and that they would meet the Austrian partners later. As an afterthought, he added, "In the interest of sparing you surprises, you should know that their name is Rakosi, but they are not related to the former Communist premier Matyas Rakosi, whom they hate."

An elderly woman in a maid's uniform answered the doorbell. Frank announced them as "Kolozsvary, Ferenc, and Mackenzie, Alan, to see Herr Rakosi, Istvan."

"Please come in, he is expecting you."

They were led to a very old-fashioned parlour, with dark, polished antique furnishings and gloomy religious paintings. Alan hesitated to sit down on any of the museum pieces. They saw an old man walking towards them from a long corridor.

Alan commented, "He certainly is a much older patriarch than I imagined."

Frank explained, "He is not the father, he is the youngest son. They already looked old when I first met them, about twenty years ago. They were providing foreign transportation for a gymnastics team from the university and were helpful with some, ah, especially delicate imports."

He introduced himself as Rakosi, Sandor, and advised that the others were on their way. Soon the father, Rakosi, Istvan, and the two other sons, Bela and Josef, joined them. The conversation was in German. The elder Rakosi walked with two canes. He was nearly bald, with a few wisps of white hair over his ears, wrinkled, bent and frail, watery brown eyes, had a slight tremor in his chin, but his voice was clear and firm. Alan was fascinated by the slow, carefully articulated classical speech of the elder. He spoke with an Austrian pronunciation and with the elaborate florid courtesy of the bygone Imperial court. It reminded Alan of seventeenth century plays he had seen.

They talked generalities for a while. In his slow, measured style, Istvan asked, "Herr Mackenzie, I truly hope I am not infringing on your privacy by respectfully inquiring about the origin of your most elegant German. I used to have this undeserved pride of being able to recognise many accents; however, my limited skills do not suffice to place your accent in any particular region of origin. I would be most greatly pleased if you would kindly grant a favour to an old man and satisfy his curiosity."

Mackenzie felt a flash of anger. He had gone to Wisconsin hoping to get a name and an address. Then the simple inquiry turned into a complicated family vacation for five in Austria. Now he was being questioned by this old stranger about his private life. Alan was a skilled interrogator and recognised this skill in the old man. There were questions that could provide extensive information beyond that specifically being asked. Four pairs of eyes were watching him attentively. He needed their help and their trust, and he recognised he had to trust them, to a prudent extent, so he decided to take the plunge.

"Herr Rakosi, I am here at the suggestion of my friend Ferenc Kolozsvary. We go back many years and we have trusted each other with our lives, more than once. As Ferenc trusts you, I will be pleased to tell you about myself. My accent is hard to place. I learned German initially from my mother, who was born in Chile into a German family. My father was a Scottish mining engineer hired for several years by a Chilean mining company. He met my mother during a vacation in the south of Chile. They married and later moved to Colorado, where my father had a job with the Colorado School of Mines. I was born in Colorado. Later I studied German in college with professors from different countries for four years, planning to enter the foreign service. So, I picked up German accents and inflections from five different sources. I also speak limited Spanish and Russian. I will be pleased to answer additional questions, at least those that I can. I also would like to comment that this group interview is a most unusual booking of a bus tour."

"Yes, it may be more involved than customary, but you also have a requirement that is not a customary one," responded Sandor, the youngest son.

"What is so unusual about traveling to fixed timetable?" Alan asked.

"We almost always travel to fixed timetables. Most transportation systems do that. What you want is different. You want to choose the time, the date, the locality, and you cannot tell us when and where, only that it is in East Germany, a most difficult place to do anything off-schedule. In addition, you have a reputation of bad karma with bus trips into the DDR."

"I have been tarred with that unfortunate event many times," responded Alan.

Sandor said, "We have no problem; however, we pay attention to any gossip dealing with bus operations. It is our business. We also get blamed for what happens on our buses, no matter how remote the connection may be."

The discussion continued for a half-hour. Istvan, the patriarch, finally decreed that they would do business with Mackenzie and Kolozsvary, and the details could be worked out with his sons.

By some mysterious protocol, Josef, the middle son, took over. They talked in detail about what was expected to happen at the designated spot. Alan again had to explain the meaning of nothing, and that perhaps there would be a substitution of twins, perhaps not. There would be no change in passports. In either case, the tour would continue its scheduled run. There was also a concern about which region of East Germany, some being more difficult or completely off limits to tourists.

Josef wanted more details. "Are these twins male or female?"

"Male."

"Is the important one the one going in or the one coming out?"

"Let's assume the one coming out."

"Let's get rid of the assumptions. The one coming out is the prize. Right?"

"Right."

"Next question: Is this twin dead or alive? And if alive, is he barely alive or in good health and able to walk, talk or scream?"

"Alive and well."

"Does he want to get out or is he being forced?"

"He wants to get out and will collaborate with us."

"Young or old?"

"Age about forty-five."

"Is he well known?"

"In some circles. He has appeared in newspaper photographs as part of an entourage, but not as the newsworthy one. The public at large would not remember him."

"Do the other passengers know what is going on?"

"It's undecided at the moment. Probably three of them will know and be part of the rescue."

"Why three?"

"One will play the wife, the other two are a couple and will play close friends."

"If he is in good health and wants to get out, why do you need us? Why doesn't he just go away, take the train, or a bus, on his own?"

"I can't answer that, yet."

"Is he a prisoner?"

"No, but he may need help in leaving discreetly and getting to your bus."

"How far is that?"

"I don't know yet."

Alan said, "There is another factor that must be considered. If, and I emphasise the if, the defector indeed defects and joins the tour, there will be an extra person that has to be removed from the tour and rescued separately."

"At present, our assumption is that the exchange will occur early in the East German portion of the tour, and that the defector will leave the tour in Warsaw to join a different team, out of our control or knowledge. At that point, our original tour member will re-join the tour and take his original place."

"The added assignment is to safely transport the original tour member from the exchange point to his return to the tour in Warsaw. Nobody will be looking for the original legitimate tour member. He just must be kept safe and returned to us in Warsaw. I wonder if you would consider helping us out with this side show, separate from the bus tour. We would pay for this service whether or not the exchange takes place, and we would like to have this cost included in a single, all-inclusive, no-extras fee."

There was a brief whispered conversation in Hungarian between Josef and his father, who decided, speaking German again, "We will be most honoured if you would kindly consider us to offer assistance in the safe and comfortable transportation of your defecting distinguished client from a designated location in East Germany to our bus touring East Germany, and we would be equally honoured to separately care for and transport one original tour member from the point of exchange in East Germany to a return welcome in our bus in Warsaw."

Alan replied that he was pleased with the offer as this would be a much better arrangement than having to deal with another service provider.

Josef said, "You realise, Herr Mackenzie, that in order to provide connecting transportation between your client's point of origin and our bus we need to know more details, such as passwords and identification procedures, also a means of communicating with your client ahead of the transfer to plan the details. We subcontract these services to several East European experts, with whom we have worked for many years with most satisfactory results. Are you willing to trust our judgment? Please note that there are no guarantees in this, except the good track record we experienced."

Alan had to think for a moment. Anyone engaged to help in this operation would want some details and had to be trusted.

It seemed logical to go with the bus people. Kolozsvary wholeheartedly agreed.

"All right," said Alan, "we accept your recommendations. We would like, however, to make our payments for the entire tour to a single entity, namely your company. There should be no separate invoices for the side trip of our original tour member, fuel, consultants, sales tax, room service, toilet paper or whatever add-ons people may invent. Everything is included in your fee, absolutely everything. Can we agree on that condition?"

Josef replied, "Absolutely. We prefer it that way. We can go into details once you have a date and a location. No point discussing anything before then. We cannot even select the appropriate team until we know what is required. However, we do need an order of magnitude to quote you a fee for the entire service. Without going into names or details at this time, what is the rank of this person? Junior clerk or general manager?"

Alan hesitated, then replied, "He is the personal assistant and senior secretary of a member of the Politburo of the German Democratic Republic."

Josef was speechless, open-mouthed; Frank thought he looked like fish out of water.

Alan asked, "Is this out of your league? Did you assume we were trying to exfiltrate a janitor?"

Josef regained his composure, looked at his father, who nodded, seeming slightly amused by the son's discomfort.

"Yes, we can handle it," said Josef. "I just had not assumed anyone with that political weight. In a way, this simplifies things, as we now know what group we need to work with. There is only one group we can trust to deal with someone of that high rank."

Alan commented, "Is an administrative assistant such a high rank?"

Josef considered his response carefully, looked at his father and the brothers, then said. "Mr Mackenzie, let's not play word games. Nobody in this room is naïve. A secretary to a Politburo member is a keeper of information, of state secrets, a witness to secret discussions and long-range planning trends. He probably has more information, let us say more organised and catalogued information than the principal he works for."

"The disappearance of someone with access to such a vast array of secret information will stir up a massive reaction. We will have no problem hiding and transporting your original tour member, who remains unknown, does not exist, no one is looking for him. But the Politburo secretary is another matter. Everybody will be looking for him, and do not assume that it will be treated as missing person case entrusted to the local police. It will be a Stasi investigation, well-staffed, led by senior people and assigned top priority."

"Our firm, Neumann & Rakosi, provides transportation services. We look at passports when booking to insure we meet the visa requirements of the countries being visited. We do not check backgrounds. We collaborate fully with the authorities but do not do their work. We operate tour buses. Beyond that we know nothing, we don't want to participate in anything irregular, illegal or immoral that your tour passengers may be involved in. I am reciting all of this to remind you what we can and cannot do. You will need to train your twins to be prepared for a massive investigation, with personal interviews, fingerprinting, and intrusive questioning, by a ruthless police organisation that is very skilled in finding dissidents and other wanted types."

Alan responded, "I agree with your summation. I have dealt with the Stasi in the past and I have great respect for their nefarious abilities. You need not worry about my understanding of the limitations in the services you can provide."

Josef argued, "I am not worried about your experience and your abilities. I am worried about your passengers, your twins, whether they will be capable of surviving a hostile questioning. Will they manage the stress? I gather the twins are not experienced in this kind of activity."

Alan nodded and said, "Again, I agree with your concerns and the implied warnings. We, I mean my team, will be working on this aspect of the project. We will have to train and prepare the participants. Their success or failure is my team's responsibility. We absolutely must count on your team to provide transportation at the designated places and designated exact times, for the escaping twin and also for the original tour member who will detour into anonymity and later re-join the tour in Warsaw."

"That we can do," assured Josef.

Alan reminded him, "One price, Herr Rakosi. I need to repeat, one price, with everything included, no changes, no add-ons, nothing extra, no paper clips, rubber bands, parking fees, tips, one fixed price. Include whatever contingencies you deem appropriate. One fixed price, whether the exchange takes place or not, we will pay the fixed price."

"And please, Herr Rakosi, we do need your expertise and are willing to pay for it, but do not assume that because we lack your particular resources, that we are naïve and easily victimised, or that we lack the ability to protect our interests. I say this with respect and courtesy, and only to avoid misconceptions."

The elder Rakosi interjected, "Herr Mackenzie, I recognise that you are a skilled, experienced client, which pleases me greatly, as this is not a business for amateurs. We have a perfect understanding and I believe our venture will run smoothly and be profitable for all parties. Herr Kolozsvary was very accurate in recommending you to our tour services. Our conversations emphasise again the wisdom of networking with the participation of known good friends and trusted former clients."

Bela, the older brother, finally joined the conversation, "As you undoubtedly have noticed, Herr Mackenzie, Father approves any new business venture and any new players. Sandor manages operations, Josef does planning, and I am the financial guy. This is merely a meet and greet meeting that provides some background on what you can expect when you visit our offices for an actual booking. You will receive our printed rates for the various tours of Eastern Europe we offer, as well as hotel rates, meals, insurance, currency exchange requirements, additional costs that may apply, and payment conditions."

He continued, "For preliminary budgeting purposes, you may assume, in U.S. dollars, about $2,500 per person for a 16-day tour. If you have a full busload, say 30 persons, this is about $75,000. In view of the special requirements that you have, we will expect, in addition to the tour cost, a gratuity of 300% of the tour cost, which amounts to $225,000 to cover these special requirements. Adding the basic tour costs and the specials brings your budget requirements to $300,000."

"Your travel to Vienna, and your hotel prior to joining our tour, are by others, not included in our tour. The cost of our tour may be paid in Austrian, Swiss or West German currency, also US dollars, partially refundable per contract, if the tour fails through our fault."

"Please understand and agree that the gratuity will not be invoiced, taxed, acknowledged or recorded anywhere, is payable in advance in Swiss francs, all cash in used bills of assorted denominations, and is not refundable, whether the trip or any part thereof takes place or not."

"However, the gratuity will be refunded, and the tour cancelled, if the payment is submitted in new bills, or bills with consecutive numbers. You may arrange the next meeting with Sandor, who will introduce you as a new customer to our Austrian partners."

Alan asked, "What part of the business do your Austrian partners do?"

"They manage operations, bus purchases, maintenance, fuel, permits, taxes, drivers, mechanics, personnel, and insure a smooth, safe, comfortable, reliable transportation service."

Sandor rejoined the conversation. "For your planning purposes, I would like to point out that each country will require one of their own tour guides in the bus. By arrangement, they will be speakers of the tour's desired language, the most frequently requested being German, Russian, English and Japanese."

"In East Germany, the tour guide will wait for the bus at a location about one kilometre away from the point of entry; they are not allowed to get too close to the border. If there is a substitution of twins, it would be best for this to happen as close as possible to the beginning of the East German part of the tour, so that the German guide does not have much face time with the departing twin."

"Please," he added sternly, "be very aware that the DDR remains a closed, hyper-paranoid Communist totalitarian state. Their tour guides often are friendly, elderly, grandmotherly women; you feel relaxed and comfortable around them. Make no mistake, they are smart, alert, well-trained, fanatic agents of a police state. Trusting your guide with some personal political opinion or regime criticism can get you arrested, fined, and if lucky, deported. If they catch you in something more serious, you'll be in real big trouble."

Alan and Frank voiced their understanding. They agreed on a procedure for a future meeting in the office and decided that the current meeting had accomplished its purpose.

As they were shaking hands, the patriarch closed, "Herr Kolozsvary, thank you very much for introducing Herr Mackenzie to us. Our business depends heavily on referrals, and we are always grateful for the opportunity to be of service to a distinguished new client."

After a pause, he admonished, "Please, both of you, Herr Mackenzie and Herr Kolozsvary, I must respectfully remind you that we are old men, and old men have memories no longer as reliable as in youth. I beg your kind understanding that our frail memories may not remember that this meeting today took place, or that we ever met, or that we heard your names, or that you are interested in one of our tours."

"Also, the lady who greeted you on arrival has been our housekeeper for many years. She also is of advanced age, and she has the same memory problems. She probably will never remember that she saw you. However, if you decide to engage one of our tours, you will be introduced to the parties that can provide the high-quality services you require."

"Thank you very much for your visit. I trust you understand our memory handicap clearly. I wish you well in all your endeavours, and I am sorry that the passage of the years has so limited my ability to remember things and personally be of service."

5. Washington, D.C.

The first meeting had been with Charles Jenner in his old Georgetown house. Alan did not like visiting in the prestigious historic neighbourhood because it was difficult to find parking, but he was nevertheless charmed by the colonial aura.

Jenner had been Alan Mackenzie's boss for a time when both were stationed in Vienna. They had not seen each other for some fourteen years when Alan received a telephone call inviting him for lunch.

In their initial meeting, Alan had a brief tour of the house, and he and his host speculated about the many conversations and events that had taken place within these walls, built before there was a United States or a city of Washington. Much later Georgetown was incorporated into the newly created District of Columbia. During and after World War II the city outgrew the District and spilled over into the adjacent counties of Maryland and Virginia, and Washington became the generic name of the large metropolitan area.

In midst of the small talk, Jenner suddenly turned to business, speaking in the abrupt style that Alan remembered.

Alan commented, "I was wondering when you were going to tell me why, after such a long time, you …"

Jenner replied, "Shut up and listen. Abigail Williamson, the wife of our esteemed Secretary of State, during a conference about youth orchestra exchanges in Copenhagen, was approached by a high-ranking East German bureaucrat who wants to defect with our help. He is peddling the names of seven moles in our government, to be disclosed in instalments as our collaboration materialises. He has some peculiar conditions and there is a time limit. Secretary Williamson and the President discussed it, shared doubts, and scepticism, wondered whether this was a hoax or some kind of entrapment, then decided to pursue it. For obvious reasons, we cannot use the resources of our intelligence agencies to find moles within their own ranks. The President and the Secretary decided to find help among retired agents from way back. They found me and then I found you."

After a long discussion, Alan agreed to join the operation. The defector had requirements that precluded the typical escape or rescue mission. He insisted on disappearing without a clue, as if he had evaporated into thin air. He had to be taken out of the country without a trace.

They reviewed options well into the evening and decided that the best way would be to extricate the defector within a group, like a guided tour with tourists. It was further agreed to locate Alan's old assistant Ferenc Kolozsvary to help finding what else was needed. One of the President's wealthy financial supporters was happy to donate discreet funds, so money would not be an issue.

Mackenzie and Jenner had several meetings. Jenner had kept the Secretary of State informed. After the successful Vienna tour-bus engagement, Secretary Williamson decided to start attending meetings in person. There were privacy concerns about where to meet. The solution was for Williamson and his wife Abigail to have periodic dinners at Abigail's sister Madeleine, married to a retired Dr Charles Baker, and living on a ranch in northern Virginia. The press and the State Department developed no interest in these family visits. They had to wait two weeks for the Secretary's busy official schedule to allow him time to participate. Jenner's old age and failing eyesight made him afraid to drive after dark, so it was agreed that Mackenzie would give him a ride.

The Baker's country estate was a large Southern plantation-style manor, secluded in Virginia's horse country. The compound was hidden by a low hill from the two-lane highway, reached by a long curving driveway with white fencing. Alan at first approved of the privacy, then was alarmed by three long limousines: a government-issue black Cadillac with multiple antennas, a white Chrysler and a dark blue Lincoln, and several other very upscale luxury cars. A group of uniformed chauffeurs were talking and smoking in the parking area.

They met in a large parlour and introductions were made: Secretary of State Henry Williamson, Mrs Abigail Williamson, Dr Charles Baker and Mrs Madeleine Baker, the hosts, Mr John Stewart, Chairman of Stewart Investments and a fundraiser for the presidential campaign, and Charles Jenner and Alan Mackenzie, both formerly representing some of our country's clandestine interests overseas.

The men all had white hair, perhaps in their late sixties. The two sisters had beautifully styled grey hair with white streaks, age undetermined, probably also in their late sixties, both surprisingly attractive. All were suntanned and looked extremely healthy and fit, except for Charles Jenner, who was much older and looked frail and ill.

Madeleine Baker welcomed her guests, indicating that her sister Abigail wanted to have some conferences away from the press and society pages, and that the Bakers were pleased to make their house available. All were invited to a light dinner, and thereafter their meeting could take place in a very private salon. Snacks, desserts, drinks or whatever was desired would be provided, and they could stay as long as they wished.

The Bakers were elegant, gracious hosts and managed to keep the conversation interesting for all without ever hinting at the reasons for the meeting. Alan admired their relaxed social skills and speculated that these skills were the genetic legacy of generations of wealth and privilege.

After dinner, they moved to a spacious sitting room. Mrs Baker pointed out a sideboard well-stocked with food and drink, indicated a button to summon help if anything else was desired, and she and her husband excused themselves for the evening. The guests got coffee and drinks, lit cigars and cigarettes, and sat down.

Secretary Williamson started by narrating his conversations with the president and their decision to pursue the matter, and how to do it without involving the intelligence services. They were concerned about the possibility that the whole project could be an elaborate scheme to destroy some innocent American functionaries by fingering them as East German or Soviet spies. They decided that the only way to find out was to set some elaborate traps for the alleged moles; many details still being worked out.

The defector had offered seven names to be disclosed as the disappearance plans progressed. He informed that he had one high-ranking official in the White House, two each in the State Department and in the CIA, and one each in the FBI and the NSA. He left the choice to us, one name being available at the beginning of our collaboration to show his bona fide. We selected the White House mole, set a trap which confirmed his treachery, he remained unaware. Then we had him, and five others under consideration for promotions, investigated for any hidden embarrassments. We got two, including our mole, one for tax evasion and the other for child molestation. Both were fired quietly. The press heard about it, but it was kept low key, without details.

The State Department was trying to obtain the release of two stupid American students who had been arrested overseas, one in North Korea for stealing a political sign from a hotel, the other for graffiti and drug offenses in Singapore, both facing serious sentences. Secretary Williamson had used these cases as an excuse to see what his predecessors had done in the past to resolve these types of problems. He was able to request State Department files and discreetly search for names of agents, now retired, who had experiences useful in the matter at hand. The name of Charles Jenner appeared repeatedly, so he was found and invited to help. Williamson then suggested that Jenner should continue and lead the meeting.

Jenner had an unfriendly demeanour, speaking haltingly. "Thank you, sir. You found my name repeatedly in reports because I was station chief and wrote or signed the reports, but I was not the guy in the field who did the work. In our present circumstances, sir, I say that we omit the traditional chain of command and deal directly with Alan Mackenzie, who will be in charge in the field. If you concur, sir, I recommend that Alan lead these meetings and the planning of the operation. He is more security conscious than the rest of us. If we screw up, we may get reprimanded or fired. He was in a line of work where a mistake could have cost him his life."

He looked around the room, then added, "Here we have a bunch of uninitiated white-haired senior citizens playing middleman in cloak and dagger games that are usually handled by young, athletic men and women skilled in hand-to-hand combat and clandestine shenanigans you could not comprehend. I urge strongly that we should cut out middlemen as much as possible, starting with the communications within this group."

Secretary Williamson puffed on his cigar, then said, "This group of uninitiated white-haired senior citizens, as you so delicately put it, make the adventures of your young heroes possible, organise finances and rescues, and evaluate whether the offerings they submit have value. So, watch what you say if you want to remain on this team. You would not keep a job as a diplomat. However, despite your … your uninitiated way of expressing yourself, I concur that senior citizen Mackenzie should lead the proceedings of this group, subject of course, to appropriate supervision by the other senior citizens present."

Jenner said, "Yeah, okay," then added after a long pause, "sir," and looking at Alan, "Get with it!"

Alan said, "Thank you. You all know the broad outline of what we are trying to do. I will bring you up to date and answer what questions I can. I also will be asking many questions myself. One unending concern is security and the need to keep persons in the know to a minimum. When we arrived, I noticed a group of uniformed drivers by the cars, and I was uneasy about them knowing about our meeting. Could you tell me about them?"

Secretary Williamson replied first. "I have to use the State Department limo and their security. It would be highly suspicious if I were to drive myself anywhere. They are trusted fully, have high security clearances, and are privy to many meetings that rank much higher than this gathering."

John Stewart was next. He spoke with a faint Texas accent. "Mine is the white car, I don't like the dark funereal colours. I trust my driver more than I trust you, Mr Mackenzie. He has been my driver and bodyguard for many years."

Abigail Williamson concluded, "My sister and I spoke about that concern, more than once. The drivers and the household help are discreet, uninterested, and are trusted fully. The Bakers host many meetings and parties. They have a nice lounge for drivers and other staff to relax, watch TV, and enjoy fine meals. They are not a threat."

Alan thanked them, and addressing Secretary Williamson, added, "Sir, with respect, your comment about your driver's security clearance is appropriate, but we must remember that the traitors we are trying to flush out also have high security clearances. I must suspect and ask questions about everything. I apologise if my question appeared impolite."

Williamson grunted and asked, "On the question of trust, how trustworthy is that Hungarian sidekick of yours?"

Alan replied, "We have saved each other's lives a couple of times. I do not always agree with him, but I continue to trust him with my life, and vice versa."

Williamson thought about that for a moment, looked at Jenner, who looked bored and was yawning, then said, "Your former boss, Charles Jenner, reported to me that your friend acted like a real simpleton back in Budapest, pretending to be a spy and using his secret name, which was his real name spelt backwards, and everyone knew it. The Communists that rode in his cab knew all about his interest in rumours and intelligence and fed him a lot of false information, and I am told that he dutifully passed it on to us. What a waste of time!"

"Not at all, sir, we knew it was disinformation, and anything we heard through him told us what not to waste time on, saving us time and effort. He also provided us with particularly useful information about Hungarian and Soviet travels, activities and personnel changes, gossip, and scandals. He was everyone's friend, the cab driver to go to if you had a delicate transportation problem. He took party officials' mistresses to the abortionist, ferried illegal scotch for the police chief, delivered messages between opponents. Driving a taxi allowed him both unlimited transportation and freedom of movement, rare commodities in those places and in those times. He could procure anything, from cigarettes to permits to information. We worked with him for a long time and ended trusting him completely. We got out alive in the nick of time, thanks to his networking."

Williamson pondered the information, then changed subject to Cardinal Mindszenty's escape to the American embassy. "I read some reports that during his long imprisonment we, the United States, had analysed the possibility of helping him escape from prison. Your name appeared in some technical capacity. Nothing happened. Years later, when the ill-fated revolution started, he was released from prison. Were you there?"

Alan confirmed, "Yes, sir, I was in Budapest at the time, it was all over the news."

Williamson continued, "There were rumours and speculation about how Mindszenty managed to get to our embassy after the Soviet crackdown. You were there at that time. Any comment?"

Alan replied, "Yes, I was there and heard the rumours." Williamson asked, "Could you add anything?"

"No, sir."

"I heard that a commemorative plaque honouring Mindszenty was installed in a park in Santiago de Chile. That is pretty far from Budapest. Do you know anything about that?"

"Yes sir, I was in Chile at the time and heard about it. And in case you wonder, I was visiting cousins. My mother was from Chile. I might add, there were other Mindszenty memorials around the world, and in the United States, and I was not involved."

"You do not share much information. Some Hungarians seem to think that you were somehow involved in all the Mindszenty events."

"I don't know that I can comment on what they think."

Williamson gave no indication whether this exchange had been a test of some kind, and returned to the present project, asking, "Can you tell us more about our assignment?"

"Yes, sir. You know that Frank Kolozsvary found us a suitable bus line in Vienna. There remained three big unresolved items, one was timetable, two the location of the event, and the third was the passengers. Let me start with the passengers."

"The issue had been who the passengers in the bus would be, and how much could they be told. Frank Kolozsvary wanted to limit the search to the Hungarians in the U.S. He knows their culture and how to deal with them."

"How many do we have in the U.S.?" asked John Stewart. "About a few thousand perhaps? I never met one in the oil business."

"I had the same question," replied Alan. "It turns out the Hungarian speakers in the U.S. number over half a million, plus their many American spouses and children that don't speak Hungarian but have a friendly disposition toward the culture of the old country."

This surprised the audience, and they commented about the new knowledge. Abigail wanted to know if there was a Hungarian mafia, as we had Italian, Russian, Jamaican and Lord knows how many other mafias. Alan asserted that the Hungarians were not an organised crime group, that they just stuck together bound by language, history, religion, and culture, as did other ethnic groups in the United States.

After a pause, Alan continued, "Frank knew of a group of Hungarian emigres and refugees living in Long Beach, California. He sells insurance, had met them by chance years earlier and over time they became insurance clients. Most of them are retired, most on Social Security, all in modest economic circumstances, leading simple but content lives."

"They belong to a little theatre group, performing plays in high school and junior college auditoriums, having fun, and sometimes making some money with their plays, sometimes getting small jobs as extras in some movie. The theatre group includes several who retired from the movie industry, where they worked as camera operators, musicians, electricians, stagehands, costume seamstresses, and one woman was a make-up artist. About half of the little theatre group are Hungarian, the rest American by birth."

"Frank spent some time with them in Long Beach and heard their stories, made friends, and determined that they could make a happy bus tour in Eastern Europe if someone paid their expenses. I went to Long Beach with Frank, interviewed the group, and decided to extend the free tour invitation."

"They were of course curious about the free tour, and we had to hint that perhaps there would be an opportunity to help someone escape, perhaps to be aborted if someone talked, but the tour would be legitimate and continue in any event. They were thrilled to participate in the possibility of a real-life adventure. Some had to be excluded because they still might be on some Communist wanted list and were afraid to take a chance. A few were unable to travel due to health reasons."

"The group that will participate in the tour numbers twenty-two persons, most of them married couples. We have four singles. One is the makeup artist, who will play a crucial part. They all were instructed to get their passports in order, so that visas and other permits could be processed as a tour group by our own very carefully selected travel agency."

John Stewart inquired, "So far you have spent or committed money mostly for your and the Hungarian family's travel expenses, and for the bus tour and their so-called gratuities. Neither you nor your Hungarian co-conspirator have requested any payments for your own services. Please clarify that."

Alan replied, "Frank Kolozsvary and I are not doing it for money; we have retirement incomes. We do need to get reimbursed for expenses, mostly travel. We would expect comfortable travel, meals and lodgings. At our ages, we no longer can sleep in airports or railway stations or spend nights standing in the rain and survive on junk food or candy bars out of vending machines."

Stewart smiled and shook his head, saying, "I have no problem with any of the expenses, accommodations, what you eat or where you sleep. The amounts of money you are involved with are of no consequence. I have no money problems. I do have a problem with people providing free services; these have undefined costs. I like clear numbers; I do not like ambiguity or blank lines in some report. Please discuss my concern with your colleague and determine a regular compensation for your services and include it in your next report. You can give it to charity if you like, but only after I have paid it to you. Please do not argue with me about money, that is not your area of expertise. My money, my rules. Are we clear?"

Alan said, "Yes, sir. The 'do not argue' part is challenging, but we will comply. If I may ask, why are you financing this?"

John Stewart replied without hesitation, "Patriotism is a good part. I routinely contribute large sums to charitable and political causes that I consider beneficial to our country. This project has another great appeal for me. I had never been involved in secret cloak and dagger work. I find it exciting to be part of this, and I am having more fun than you can imagine. I haven't had so much fun since I won a hostile takeover of a competitor company and simultaneously beat an antitrust action."

Alan, impressed, said, "Thank you for the explanation. Your work is in a different world, I find it fascinating."

Stewart smiled again, and said, "Not so different from your world, Mr Mackenzie. We both try to defeat the bad guys, help our country, and at least in my case, make lots of money in the process. My tools are different. Mine are lawyers, accountants, banks, statisticians, and high-level private investigators. I suspect your methods are equally cunning, but your tools perhaps more weaponlike and your personal risks more physical and swifter. Your world is exotic to me. Each briefing about your progress on our project is thrilling. I look forward to every update."

Abigail remarked with a smile, "I find it charming to hear again and again, in the most diverse circumstances, some comment hinting about grass being greener or more interesting on the other side of the fence."

Stewart laughed, and said, "I don't think the other side of the fence is greener or better, I like my side just fine, but I do enjoy the opportunities of seeing exotic human endeavours, though as an observer, not a direct participant. Tell me, Mr Mackenzie, I heard about the betrayal of your busload of Hungarian agents in East Germany. I suppose the traitor got away with his deed, perhaps with a medal and a promotion. Do you know?"

Alan hesitated before answering. "Yes, he was promoted and well-rewarded for his courageous protection of peace and fraternal solidarity in the defence of justice and socialism. Unfortunately, a few weeks later he fell to his death from a tall church tower in Budapest. The police ruled it a suicide. The rumour mill said his hands had been tied behind his back."

None of the people present smiled or commented. At times, the thrill of participating in a cloak-and-dagger adventure was dampened when getting too close to that world.

Alan continued, "As you all know, the biggest item on our side was finding the bus line and a suitable group of passengers, which has been accomplished. We had to wait for the other two big items, location and timetable, which we now have. I heard from Charles Jenner yesterday, as you all have, that the date will be the 10th of April, and the venue will be the Politburo's retreat in the Wolkenstein Lodge, an isolated former vacation hiding place of the Saxon royalty, in the mountain range south of the city of Karl Marx Stadt."

"My colleague Frank Kolozsvary already has been in contact with the Rakosis, the tour operators, and they are in the process of obtaining all the tour approvals from the Czechs, the East Germans, and the Poles, and also making reservations in a suitable hotel not too far removed from the Wolkenstein Lodge. We have a little over a month until the … the … exchange date. It is tight, but doable."

"We must remember that the tour needs to start in Vienna and continue to Prague a week before arriving in East Germany. That leaves us three weeks, maximum. Kolozsvary and I are flying to Long Beach tomorrow to get all details organised. There is a lot to do. I will report to this group in about two weeks. We must communicate with our client directly to coordinate stuff. Can this be arranged?"

"We also need to know who the client is, so that we can study photographs and prepare makeup, haircuts, and so forth. We will need a sample of his clothing, business suit, shirts, ties, underwear, socks, shoes, everything, so that we can custom tailor a new set of clothing. We need a measurement of his head to get right hat sizes. We will need eyeglass prescriptions, better yet, a pair of eyeglasses. We need to know what he normally carries in what pockets, so there is no fumbling in front of a customs inspector."

"We need to know if he has any serious allergies or food restrictions. Does he need prescription medicines? Does he wear dentures? Is he right-handed or left-handed? Does he wear a hearing aid? Does he keep his pants up with belts or suspenders or both? What is his height and weight? Can we have a photocopy of his ID card?"

Alan looked around the room, then focused on the Secretary and Abigail. Henry Williamson answered, "We have set up a telephone link. We have a number at each end. Our end is in Austria, but the telephone is in an unoccupied place, electronically connected to a phone in another location. I believe most of what you want can be done by telephone. Getting a set of clothing and other things will have to be coordinated with him. So far, he only will speak with Abigail, she can discuss all of this with him."

Alan wanted to know, "Who set up the phone link?"

Williamson advised, "I had a State Department team do it, but they don't know who the users are. We often set up separate phone links for conferences or special situations. Routine stuff."

John Stewart commented, "It seems that now the real fun is starting. I can't wait to hear more details in the next briefing."

Alan responded, "I agree that a new phase has started, I don't know if I'd call it a fun part, but it definitely has to move fast, and it deals with real danger. The talking and planning phase is over. Once it gets underway a field operation acquires a momentum of its own, and the planning team's role becomes more that of an observer."

Abigail asked Alan to prepare a written list of the items he had requested before leaving the meeting, need not be typed, longhand okay.

Alan reiterated the need for the identity of the client. After some hesitation, Secretary Williamson said, "He is Bruno Hadler, Secretary to Politburo member Egon Lanz. I recommend that the name not be mentioned, and that the photographs needed for the makeup artist be nameless."

Alan agreed and summarised the situation, "We are now underway, and we still need some speedy decisions. We know the exchange location and the date; from there we can plan the before and after itineraries with the bus operators."

"I do clearly understand that our client must disappear without leaving a clue about who helped him or where he is going. The 'leave no clue' directive has been repeated several times in this meeting. Rest assured that all players will be made aware of this mandate, which, incidentally, is good practice in any event, and common in our business."

"Our current assignment is to get him out of East Germany, without a trace of course, and deliver him in Warsaw, all without involving government agencies. How does he get out of Poland, and where to?" He happened to be looking at Abigail at this moment and noticed a slight change in her pupils. She then exchanged glances with her husband and John Stewart. Alan kept the observation to himself.

Secretary Williamson answered, "Warsaw is the end of your assignment. Hadler has made his own private arrangements to disappear, after we spend a couple of days questioning him. Your job is to make him vanish from a heavily guarded Politburo conference in East Germany and deliver him in Poland without leaving a trace or a clue."

Alan pondered that answer. He had experienced abrupt assignment ends in his career before, decided not to argue, and asked formally if he had approval to proceed, reminding everyone that this would involve many people in many places and an intense amount of work.

Secretary Williamson said, "Yes, you are hereby authorised to proceed. You are in charge, and you have full authority. Please keep us informed. Please let us know if you need help with anything. Your contact for this group will be Abigail; she can get hold of any of us, as needed. You two can exchange telephone numbers and whatever other information is required."

Alan said, "There is one other thing. We had originally envisioned that the original twin was to disappear after the exchange, and be smuggled out of East Germany and into Poland by the same team who extracted our defector. There, claiming a lost passport, he could obtain a new one from an American Consulate. As our involvement ends in Warsaw, we should consider another option. The opportunity presents itself to reinstate our guy into the tour and return home with the group, if the defector no longer needs the twin's identity and passport."

Williamson reflected a while, then said, "I believe this will be a good solution, but I need to think it through. I will confirm it by tomorrow morning through Abigail."

Abigail asked Alan for his hotel and contact information in Long Beach and advised him that she and her sister would like to meet Frank Kolozsvary and, discreetly, some of the group. They had not decided yet whether to go on the next day or the day after.

Alan recommended that they book their tickets as soon as possible, as he and Frank had been unable to get last minute air tickets to Los Angeles, often having to wait several days.

Abigail responded, "Thank you, Mr Mackenzie, but do not worry, we never use public transit. I will let you know our arrival time and we can plan from there."

6. Long Beach, California

Alan flew from Washington and Frank from Appleton via Chicago. They arrived in California within an hour of each other and met at the airport, took a cab to their hotel, where they had dinner.

Alan reported on his Virginia meeting with the big players. The big item of course was the official go-ahead by the Secretary of State. Frank listened very attentively, as was his custom, asked many pertinent questions, and reflected for a time.

He was out of cigarettes, did not like the brand offered by Alan, waved at the cigarette girl, purchased a pack, and after she was out of earshot complained that buying cigarettes in a dining room was a rip-off, charging a dollar for a pack that cost twenty-five cents in the drug store or the supermarket. Alan reminded him of the convenience and suggested to plan ahead in the future.

Frank said, "On the subject of planning ahead, we need to talk about tomorrow and what instructions we will give our passengers. Before we go into that, I would like your real assessment of the Virginia meeting and the players. What you narrated was the sanitised children's version. Now I want the adult version and I'd like to know what is bugging you."

Alan laughed, "I am glad your antenna is still working and that you are paying attention."

Frank responded, "That is how I stay alive and sell enough insurance to support my family. So, what did your antenna pick up?"

"There are several items floating around in my head," Alan said. "First, as a general observation, the Bakers have some serious money. I know doctors earn well, but what I sensed was inherited old money, and old power, perhaps on the wife's side. None of my business, really, but something bothers me, and I don't know what."

"The answer will surface, it always does," commented Frank. "Are both sisters equally rich?"

"I don't know," said Alan. "I remember vaguely that during Williamson's Senate confirmation hearing the subject of money came up, and I believe he was found to be wealthy but not filthy rich. If the sisters had inherited a family fortune, it would have been noted in the confirmation hearings. So, we can assume that Madeleine is richer than Abigail. Let us put this on hold for now."

"All right, so what else is bugging you?"

"They had a large collection of luxury cars in their parking area. I inquired about the three stretch limos, which were explained, one of the State Department, one of finance man John Stewart, one of the Bakers. The other cars were not discussed. I considered asking, but I sensed this would not have been welcomed. All I feel sure about is that Rolls-Royces, Mercedes, Lincoln Continentals and Packards are not the vehicles of gardeners or kitchen help. It seemed to me that other powerful people were meeting elsewhere in the house, perhaps waiting to hear the outcome of our meeting. Pure speculation on my part, but as you pointed out, paying attention has kept us alive."

"Okay, next. What about Charles Jenner?"

"I think Jenner is out. He is too old and not healthy. His main function was to find the likes of us to do the tactical work. They may have kept him involved as a courtesy, but he pissed off Williamson with his comments about senior citizens playing games for which they were unqualified, and my guess is that he will no longer be invited. He really is no longer needed."

Alan continued, "What really is bugging me is a faint, very faint, perception that we don't know who we are dealing with, who the real power is. I entered the meeting sure that the real power behind our entire operation was Secretary Williamson, with the backing of the President, and that the contact with the defector was Abigail Williamson."

"You and I have speculated about what the defector would do after we extract him from behind the curtain. It is impossible to successfully disappear without some help. We were inclined to think that Henry Williamson had enough connections to make this happen without involving the State Department. When I left the meeting, I felt that the faint, very faint perfume of Madeleine Baker had displaced, very faintly, the faint, very faint, perfume of her sister Abigail, and that the clout of the Secretary of State depends on his service at the pleasure of the President, who in turn was on good terms with the people who financed his electoral campaign, one of the major donors being present at our meeting, and on friendly terms with the two sisters, with Madeleine perhaps a faint tad friendlier than Abigail."

Frank interrupted, "You are overusing the word 'faint', I think."

Alan replied, "I have the faint feeling that I am not. Anyway, moving on, when I asked about the security risks of having so many chauffeurs aware of our meeting, Abigail said she had discussed it many times with her sister. I wondered why they had many times previously discussed what I was questioning now."

"Then, when I asked Stewart why he was financing this operation, he had a ready, smooth, patriotic answer. I have a faint, very faint suspicion this was a memorised answer that he could give to any reporter or investigator without hesitation."

"I decided to bring up the subject you and I had been speculating about, namely, how does the defector proceed after we deliver him in Warsaw. Wilkinson abruptly told me that after Warsaw our services were not needed. And that at that point we can reintroduce our man into our tour group and retrieve his passport, in other words, the defector would have new documents. Our involvement with the defector ends in Warsaw, over and out."

"During this exchange I happened to notice a change in Abigail's eyes, then an exchange of glances with her husband and with John Stewart. Earlier during dinner, I also observed nonverbal exchanges between the sisters and Stewart. Vaguely I remember that Madeleine seemed to be the leader, which I attributed to her position as hostess, but at the time I did not pay attention. Now I wish I had."

Frank offered, "None of these … these premonitions, suspicions, whatever you wish to call them, none of these really affect our meeting with the passengers tomorrow, so we will continue as planned. However, I firmly believe you should not dismiss these thoughts. We both have picked up strange vibes with our instincts; sometimes they were nothing, sometimes they led to interesting information, but of no consequence, and then, rarely but oh so timely, we picked something that saved our skin in the nick of time. I guess we react to what we cannot pigeonhole or define or what leaves blanks on some list."

"It's curious that you chose those words," Alan said. "As I told you, Stewart wants us to bill for our services. He does not care about the money; he is bothered by a blank line on a ledger. I guess his survival instincts are well developed. Just so we can justify our pay, I suggest we base our billing rate on the highest income year from our tax returns of the last ten years, and that both of us bill at the same rate."

"I agree. Let us do the math later by phone."

They continued to rehash the project and their previous conversations but developed no new insights.

On the following morning, they met with the tour passengers in an empty small warehouse where the group rehearsed their plays. Alan had arranged for coffee, fruit, and donuts, and later a nice lunch, to be delivered to the warehouse, which delighted them all.

There had been no way to hide that the purpose of the trip was to offer someone the possibility to escape from East Germany. They had been told that the entire undertaking was a private venture financed by a very wealthy man, without any government help or involvement. It all being an amateur attempt, perhaps nothing would happen, or perhaps the client would be lucky and get out.

They were enthusiastic about acting on a real-life play. They all had known Frank for years, bought their insurance through him, trusted his advice on many subjects. After Frank introduced and recommended Alan, they paid rapt attention to what Alan had to say; they considered him the director of their play, and Frank the big boss who also was a technical advisor. They even brought two director's chairs, with titles but no names painted on the back.

The key roles were to be played by Richard Holley, who had agreed to lend his name and passport and become the disappearing twin, and Anne Miller, who would play Holley's wife. Her passport listed her under her real Miller name, not Holley. They concocted the explanation that she had married after she got her passport and would change to her married name when renewing.

The biggest contribution in the exchange of twins would be Anne Miller's professional skill as a make-up artist with many years' experience in the movie industry. She would convert the forty-five-year-old escaping twin into someone resembling the seventy-one-year-old Richard Holley.

Alan had been preoccupied about the time the transformation would take, and whether it could be done in a hotel room, without the facilities of a movie studio. She had performed a test run on a volunteer, with good results, but, in Alan's opinion, taking too much time. The time discussion escalated to the point that Anne quit in disgust. She was talked into returning and having a collaborative discussion with Alan, finally settling on a goal of forty-five minutes, which was achieved after two more rehearsals. Alan wanted to discuss the procedure and the time limit again in this meeting, the last before departing for Vienna, where they were going to do it again in a hotel room.

Anne said, "Stop worrying, the time limit will be met, and the results will be good. It is relatively easy to age someone. We do it in the movies all the time when the story shows the actor at different ages. It is much more difficult to make someone look younger, but that is not what we are trying to do. We are aging a guy to match someone else's passport picture. But be aware, this is not going to be 100% perfect, as you could achieve employing a wizard plastic surgeon, like in the Baker clinics."

Alan asked, suddenly very alert, "What did you say? What are Baker clinics?"

Anne replied, "Oh, this is trade talk. In the movie world, there is a lot of plastic surgery going on, mostly women trying to look younger, but increasingly also men. The favourite surgeons, if you are among the very few who can afford them, work in a small group of exclusive clinics founded by Dr Charles Baker. They have clinics in Virginia, California, Hawaii and Australia. They have their own airplanes and fly clients discreetly to their own five-star recovery spas." She wondered why Alan and Frank had big grins in their faces; she had said nothing funny.

Alan gave a speech about time limits again, reiterating that the changeover period was the most vulnerable, and that reducing this period of vulnerability was crucial. The happy rehearsal mood started to disappear with these time exhortations. Several threatened to quit if Alan continued with his time obsession. Alan retorted that he would rather risk losing a few people here in Long Beach than in East Germany and proceeded to repeat the reasons why time was so important.

No one left, but the hostility was growing. Frank whispered to Alan in German to cool it. Alan reminded him of the times they had managed to escape from something bad in the nick of time, including their escape from the farm.

The group looked expectantly at Alan, trying to guess if he was going to start the time limit exhortations again. One said, "You are extracting all the fun out of this with your time crap!" Alan started to get angry. "I am not extracting anything, I am introducing the reality that this is not a fun play, but a real-life act that involves real-life risks. It will be remembered as a fun adventure if all ends well. I am doing what I can to train you all to minimise risks. If you cannot handle the reality of what we are trying to do, now is the time to quit."

One couple asked if they could go to Vienna and Prague, then quit before East Germany. Alan replied, "Absolutely not. It creates complications and explanations. I am sorry, but I will not knowingly allow anything that calls attention or adds complexity, thus increasing risk. In view of your concerns, I would like you to withdraw from the tour, now. I think you would be nervous and attract attention. This is not a bad mark against you; on the contrary, I genuinely appreciate you letting me know your hesitation. That was the right thing to do. It is the mark of a good actor to know which parts to take and which to pass on. Perhaps you would be willing to help your colleagues with whatever needs doing at this end. And I ask the rest of the team to give a round of applause to these two who chose to forego a tour in order to avoid endangering the play."

They all clapped, and it appeared that goodwill remained all around. Alan reiterated that now was time to bow out for anyone who had concerns. There were no takers.

Frank commented in an aside, "That was a very unlikely twist from you. You are not well-known for kindness and forgiveness."

Alan replied, "I like 'not well-known,' for anything."

Frank noted, "Except for interesting bus tours." He got a vulgar swearing response from Alan, first in English, then repeated in German, for emphasis.

Timing issues aside, the preparations were complete. All passports, visas and other travel papers were in order. The Rakosis confirmed that all travel permits and hotel reservations had been secured.

Bruno Hadler had donated a full set of his clothing to an African charity in Berlin. The pickup was done by someone recommended by the tour bus operator, and the entire bundle found its way to Vienna, from where it was flown to Los Angeles. In Long Beach, a retired movie costume seamstress procured a matching size mannequin and produced several complete sets of good quality used clothing, including shoes, belts, and hats.

Two custom-made wigs were procured by Anne, as well as two sets of all the required makeup chemicals. There also were two sets of eyeglasses, toothbrushes, wristwatches, shaving gear, combs, and wallets. There was a pair of everything, to be carried in separate flights. Alan feared having to abort the mission if stuff got lost in transit.

The seething hostility against Alan that the group developed due to the time limit exhortations seemed somewhat under control. Everyone hoped that Alan would drop it. Frank kept a close watch.

A tour leader had to be selected, someone who could keep things functioning smoothly during the tour. Anne Miller was the ideal candidate, and Alan, Frank, and Anne herself wholeheartedly agreed.

In conversation, the fact emerged that in moviemaking the person in charge of makeup often controlled schedules and starting time for filming. No filming took place until the makeup was complete, even if directors had a temper tantrum. Alan saw an opening to reintroduce the time issue but had to drop it when it appeared that she would walk out.

Alan insisted that there should be a foursome playing two couples who were old friends, on the grounds that it would be easier to hide a newcomer in a cluster. Several couples wanted the part and were interviewed by Alan, Frank, and Anne. Anne nominated John and Barbara Crawford. They were reputed to be the most active members in their little theatre group, always learned their lines well, loved to act, and many times had improvised solutions to unexpected problems.

Frank had some reservations about John, who responded to questions about communism with, "I look forward to fucking the filthy Bolsheviks any way I can!" Frank insisted that he could not use this kind of language behind the Iron Curtain.

These countries were very touchy about insults and would not hesitate to impose hefty fines or jail sentences to teach the foreigners a lesson. They had a lengthy discussion about risking the entire operation by stupid talk. Frank agreed to control himself while on enemy territory but would not tolerate muzzling on home turf. Barbara promised to help her husband to curb his tongue. Alan, and after a while Frank, agreed to having the Crawfords in this key supporting role.

Alan observed to Frank that the John Crawford type was often courageous in dangerous situations. Frank said he preferred anonymity to heroics.

Next on the agenda was Richard Holley. Alan and Frank spent hours with Holley, training him to perform his role, albeit a very passive role, but to be played behind the Iron Curtain, not in a Long Beach little theatre play. After

Alan and Frank felt confident that Holley could handle the part, and the stress that would suddenly grip him in an unexpected complication, they invited Anne Miller to join the training session.

Anne seemed more at ease than Richard in handling the unexpected. She had many years of experience dealing with temperamental prima donnas, actors as well as directors, in all kinds of crises.

Alan and Frank were primarily interested in her troubled assignments rather than her normal successful routines where all went well, and everyone was happy. They discussed in some detail her dealings with temper tantrums, nosebleeds after the makeup had been applied, drunk actors slurring their lines and messing up their wigs and fake beards, and especially her dealing with inadequate time allowances.

In her experience, the worst time crunches and sloppiest jobs resulted from supporting actors quitting in disgust over some real or imagined affront, and the subsequent urgent, insane pressure to create with cosmetics and fake features a substitute to resemble the quitter and finish filming the last few scenes.

Anne was proud that she had been able to create a resemblance in a couple of hours. Alan intervened angrily, "Two hours is out of the question! Half an hour is generous, but you ganged up on me to agree to forty-five minutes. Let us not talk or dream or wish or reminisce about anything that takes more than forty-five minutes."

Anne yelled, "You really want me to quit! Why not just say so and spare us all this time pretence? I agreed to do a sloppy job in forty-five minutes. You cannot make chemicals dry any faster, no matter how you wish it."

Frank intervened, "This entire play will be dead before we even start. We have an agreement, let us move on."

Alan grumbled, "I only agreed to forty-five minutes because of the required drying time. I do not want to hear about anything that takes more than forty-five minutes."

"And while you are waiting for the face paint to dry, you will clean up and hide all your bottles, brushes and curling irons, hair dryers or whatever tools you use. You will have a well-organised and complete set of foreign plugs, adapters, transformers, extension cords and lights, so no time is wasted looking for the required gadget, nor for the orderly packing away of anything that looks more complicated than what a tourist may travel with. In forty-five minutes, there will not remain a single visible trace. Forty-five minutes!"

Frank moved carefully to stand between the two. Anne was red, pouting and breathing heavily through flared nostrils. Alan's face was hard, angry, and menacing.

Richard Holley had watched the exchange with some anxiety, and asked, "Are there many disagreements in the group? It seems to me that we are not ready, which is scary to me."

Frank reassured him, "No, we are okay. The issue of the time required to make-up someone to look like your passport photo has been the only area of contention. Both Anne and Alan have valid, real concerns about the metamorphosis time. They agreed on forty-five minutes. Alan considers it a maximum, Anne a minimum. Let us go through your role once again, which is by far more relaxed."

The plan was that Richard Holley would play the part of Anne's husband during the first segment of the tour, from Vienna through Prague. If the exchange at the beginning of the East German segment succeeded, the new Richard Holley would continue with the tour as Anne's husband.

As booked through the bus company, the real Richard would be rescued by a group of Hungarians who had established a service of itinerant labourers and farmworkers from Hungary, Czechoslovakia and Poland doing temporary contract work in East Germany. They were issued temporary identification cards and work permits, moved around as a group, and did not need passports or visas. Richard would stay at some farm in care of the Hungarians. Nobody would be looking for him, it was easy time. Further, the DDR did not restrict foreign travel by senior citizens, making exiting easy.

At the appointed time, they all would meet in Warsaw, where Richard would rejoin the tour and return home to the United States. The mysterious twin would be handed over to the mysterious businessman who would arrange for further travel. The tour group's assignment would end in Warsaw.

As had been agreed by telephone earlier, the two sisters arrived at the rehearsal warehouse in late afternoon. Alan and Frank noted approvingly that the platinum Rolexes had been replaced by modest watches, their customary small super brilliant diamond earrings and necklaces were gone, and their transportation was not a limousine but an Oldsmobile sedan, with a driver in a suit, not a uniform.

Alan introduced them to the group as Abigail and Madeleine, administrative assistants to the anonymous sponsor of their tour, who wanted to meet the group and wish them bon voyage. The sisters were friendly, low key, and got along well with the group.

One woman of the group asked, "Are you two sisters?"

Madeleine responded, "Yes, we are. We really were lucky to get jobs for the same employer. We work well together and watch out for each other."

The woman said, "You are lucky indeed. I could not work with my sister; we end up fighting all the time."

They chatted for a while, then Madeleine concluded the social meeting with a short speech. "Our boss is grateful that you are willing to participate in this adventure. If it succeeds as planned, you will have contributed to the rescue of a skilled professional who is a valued friend of the United States. As you all know, this rescue is being organised and financed anonymously by a patriotic businessman, as doing it through official channels could take a year of diplomatic and bureaucratic entanglements at great cost to the taxpayer. We wish you a happy, enriching trip through the mountain region along the Czech and East German border. It is a spectacular land of beautiful landscapes, fairy-tale castles, and historic cities. Enjoy, with our thanks and best wishes."

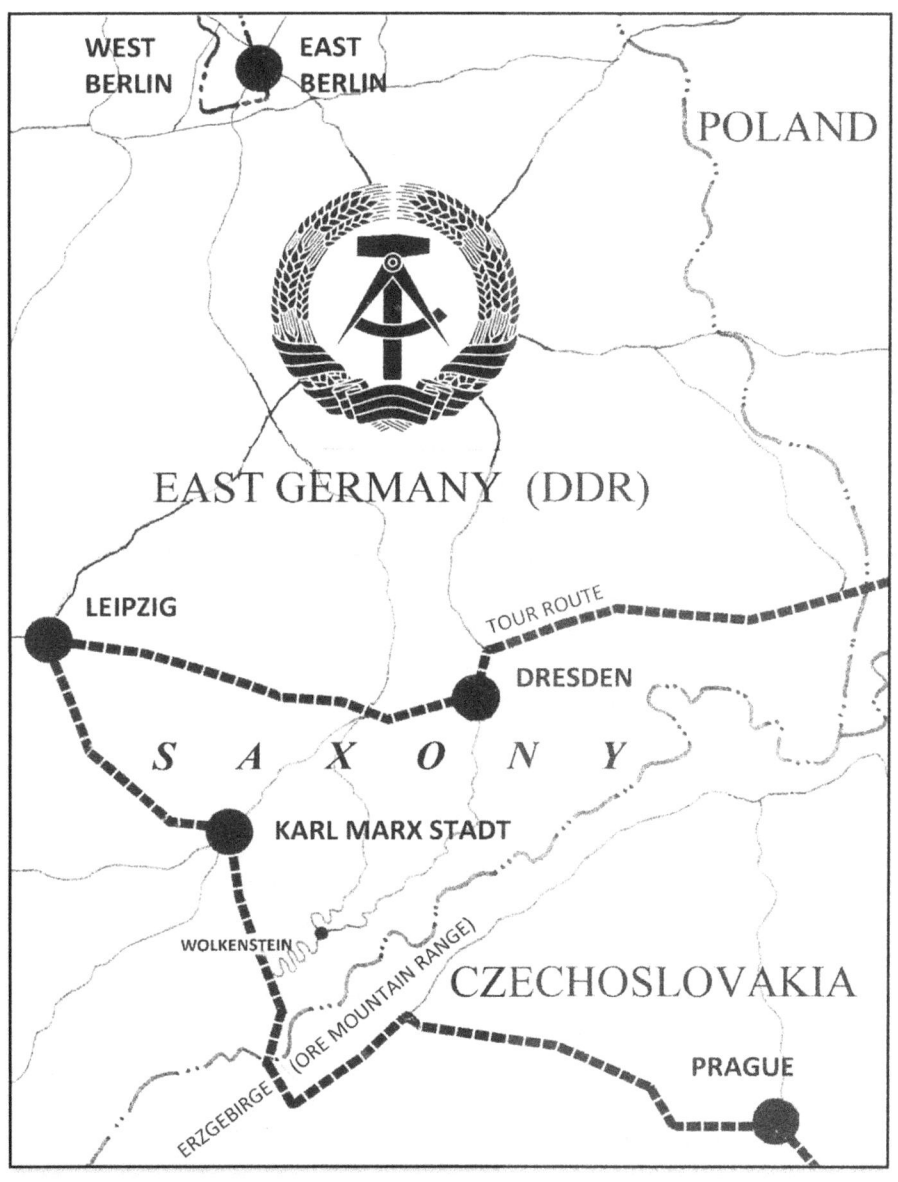

The map shows the region of the Erzgebirge (the Ore Mountain Range) at the borders of East Germany, Czechoslovakia, and Poland, highlighting cities important in our story. The territory north of the mountain range was the old kingdom of Saxony.

7. Prague, Czechoslovakia

Alan and Frank had first met the whole tour group in Long Beach. All were now reunited in Vienna, where two days of sightseeing were scheduled prior to start of the big tour proper.

The Austrian capital had much to offer in sightseeing, history, castles, palaces, churches, food, and entertainment, and most prominently, music. Vienna was not only the old imperial capital of the Hapsburg Empire and now of the modern Austrian Republic, but also the capital of European classical music. The stars who had thrived in Vienna included Haydn, Beethoven, Mozart, Schubert, the Strauss family, Mahler, Liszt, Brahms, Bruckner, many more.

The cultural offerings of the great city were so spectacular that they almost derailed the tour proper. Most of the group were inclined to skip the other countries and stay in Vienna the entire time. Alan had to remind them forcefully of their agreement to go on a tour from Austria to Czechoslovakia, East Germany and Poland, with all expenses paid, but the entire tour or nothing, no partial segments.

The next city to be visited was Prague, the ancient capital of Bohemia and now of the Czech Socialist Republic. Alan made it clear that they would leave as planned. He also made it clear that the tour had to continue exactly as scheduled or be cancelled. A further enticement was the assurance that the other countries also had much to offer, and that they all would be free to revisit any of these countries on their own at a later date if they felt that important sights had been missed.

This minor subversion was a good reminder for Alan, Frank and the two sisters that often matters considered settled were not; that players in a group, be it voters, consumers, or tourists, could change preferences and move in unexpected directions.

Neumann & Rakosi, the Austrian bus company that provided the international tour, also offered city sightseeing tours in Vienna. They did provide, within the allowable limited time, a well-organised guided tour of the main attractions of the city, featuring glimpses of the great Schönbrunn, Belvedere and Hofburg baroque palaces with their opulent interiors, the medieval iconic St. Stephen's Cathedral, the Vienna State Opera and the Johann Strauss and Wolfgang Amadeus Mozart monuments.

This was just a sampling of the many sights the ancient imperial capital had to offer, but it was so well done that the dissident tour members were mollified that they had seen the main sights of Vienna and looked forward to continuing with the big tour to Prague and beyond.

Anne Miller and Richard Holley, who had the two most important roles in the big tour, resigned themselves to miss some of the sightseeing in Vienna.

Anne Miller had to practice her cosmetic aging procedures under the constant obnoxious prodding by Alan, who was absolutely adamant that she be able to age a man twenty years in forty-five minutes or less.

She practiced on balloons and a few hired low-rate actors. They tried small variations in the procedures, like rearranging the tubes and small bottles, pre-opening some and not others, timing hair dryer use to dry lotions, how to shower and head shave a man in seven minutes, leaving clean-up to the end, using paper napkins instead of cloth, discarding items in the interest of speed, how to do it with inadequate lighting.

The adjustments saved a minute here and there, adding up. In one afternoon, Anne was able to repeat the procedure eight times in under forty-five minutes. Alan wanted two more tries. She quit in anger, saying she was going home, and stormed out, slamming doors.

Alan and Frank went looking for her, found her at the hotel travel desk where she just had purchased a ticket to fly back to California. She would not talk to them, went back to her room, and would not let them in.

After lengthy pleading to the closed door by Frank, who reminded her of his long relationship with her group and the many favours, problems, and other interactions with them that had been resolved thanks to his help, she opened the door, and regaled them with an angry summation of all the insults and abuse she had suffered from ignorant film directors and drug-crazed prima donnas. Now that she had retired, she was not willing to put up with insolent treatment.

Frank was soothing, understanding, patient, managed to get her calmed down. She agreed to continue with the tour but insisted on keeping her ticket in case Alan started harassing her again. Frank assured her that she would get reimbursed for the ticket, whether she used it or not.

"Don't you have anything to say?" she asked Alan.

Frank added, "Can we all call it quits and agree that her rehearsals are finished? You do realise, of course, that if she walks out, we would have to redo the whole thing with a new cosmetics expert, which would delay the whole thing for months or even get the project abandoned."

It was a not-so-subtle reminder to Anne that she could be replaced. The two men kept silent, let the message sink in.

Alan studied her for a moment, asked, "Do you feel better now? Are you able to have a coherent conversation?"

Frank started to object, but she interrupted, "Don't you know how to show some basic courtesy? Do you really think that this harassment will make chemicals dry faster or improve my skills?"

Alan responded, his expression serious, "I hope we don't have to replace you, not only because of the inconvenience of a postponement, but also because you are particularly good at what you do. However, I need to remind you that I also am particularly good at what I do. In this situation, Frank and I are trying to train a group of naïve amateurs to stay out of trouble in a hostile, dangerous foreign environment."

"We are not training you in hand-to-hand combat, the use of explosives or cryptography. We are training you to be able to continue doing what you do well, but under difficult, potentially dangerous circumstances. If we fail in our training, in my sole judgment, I will cancel the project. I will walk away if I feel that we are unnecessarily endangering ourselves or other people who depend on us."

"I am gladly agreeing that your training has been completed and that the quality of your magic is great. Our initial disagreement about time has been resolved; your time performance is acceptable."

"Nevertheless, I am not fully at ease with your irritation and stress tolerance. I have been harassing you about time and making you nervous by watching you work and standing too close while drumming my fingers, or by pacing back and forth."

"You were supposed to do ten procedures in under forty-five minutes. You did eight, then the stress got to you, and you stormed out. You confirmed my fear that you were borderline too vulnerable to stress and harassment."

Anne pouted but listened attentively and without comment.

Alan continued, "Generally I don't tell people being trained whether the testing in progress at any particular time is for stress tolerance or their knowledge of subject matter. I am telling you in the hope that a better understanding about my methods may help you manage your reactions."

"So far, all your rehearsals have been in safe indoor spaces, not as well equipped as a movie makeup studio, but nevertheless reasonably clean and safe. In a real-life escape behind the Iron Curtain, you may find yourself in a situation where the only chance to do your aging makeup magic is in a filthy public toilet or a baggage room in a bus terminal, with people surrounding you to hide what you are doing while others are banging on the door and yelling to open. Do you feel confident that you could handle that for forty-five minutes?"

"The luckiest outcome of that situation probably would be a sloppy job that may serve temporarily but would have to be redone later in another dirty uncomfortable place, but hopefully with more time and no banging on the door."

Frank commented, "That was a good explanation. I hope it will clear the air and allow Anne to get on her tour. I assume we are done with rehearsals."

Alan said, "No. We are not done with rehearsals."

Anne and Frank both were about to speak but kept quiet.

Anne crossed her arms and looked defiant.

Alan continued, "Look, Anne, you are angry, and your hands are shaking. You probably want a drink and perhaps need to use the bathroom. I propose you do one more makeup test, starting right now, no drink, no bathroom, and Frank and I will stand behind you and get in your way. Halfway through we may pretend the power failed and you must continue holding a flashlight in your mouth. No power means no hairdryer, and you must figure out where to hide to allow for drying time. Let us do this one, and I will not insist on the tenth one."

Anne demanded, "Your scenarios are absurd! Tell me one person who is ever required to do such work under such circumstances!"

Alan recited, "Emergency surgeons during storms and power failures, ambulance drivers extracting badly wounded traffic victims from a wreck, helicopter mechanics trying to fix an engine in the rain under enemy fire, hostage negotiators with diarrhoea unable to leave a desperate situation, firemen rescuing people from burning buildings, the airline pilot with an electrical fire in the cockpit while trying to land a passenger plane with a disabled engine. Shall I continue? How many more examples do you need? Who do you think has the better chance of success, the one who endured the training or the one who had a tantrum and walked away?"

She looked at her feet, did not answer. Frank tried to touch her shoulder, she recoiled. Alan remained quiet, serious, somehow projecting an image of indifference regarding the outcome of the intervention.

He repeated his questioning, "If you were a passenger in that disabled plane, who would you prefer to have as a pilot, the one who had trained for this emergency seventeen times, or the one who walked away from the training stress?"

There was no reply. He waited until the silence became clearly uncomfortable, and asked, "Okay, woman, are you capable of handling this or do you want to quit? And do not ask for time to think it over time. Time issues are not your strength; besides, we are out of time. By now, you know what you want. Let us have it."

She said, "You bastard …"

Alan interrupted, yelling at her in German, "It is forbidden to be disrespectful towards officials of the German Democratic Republic!"

Frank translated into English, yelling just as loudly. He could not suppress a smile, which she noted, and told him he was a bastard too.

Alan insisted, becoming angry and hostile, "Can you do the job, or will you quit?"

She looked at him, with moist eyes and a trembling chin, and nodded, then spoke, "Yes, I can do it and I will not quit. I would not give you the satisfaction!"

"Okay, I am glad you are staying with us. Let us go to my room. I have two Styrofoam heads with plaster faces that I got from the same theatre supply house as before."

"You must age one of them. Since you will not have to deal with showering, shaving and wig, you will need less time. Say we deduct ten minutes, so you have thirty-five minutes, starting now. Take your chemicals and utensils."

Anne started to say something, Alan shut her up with, "Do not waste time talking! Now you have only thirty-four minutes!"

She worked fast and diligently, gradually transforming the mannequin head from a young man to a senior. Alan and Frank kept talking in English, as the conversation became interesting or the joke approached the punchline, they switched to German. They also rattled things, moved chairs around and opened and closed doors, and switched off the light, forcing her to continue with a flashlight.

At some point, as she was carefully painting a faint vein, Alan approached her silently from behind and suddenly clapped his hands close to her ears, startling her and causing her to paint a jagged blue line across the mannequin face and kicking over a small cosmetic jar that rolled under the bed.

She started to complain, was told to shut up and not waste time. She tried to crawl under the bed to retrieve the small jar, but Alan stopped her, saying, "Let us pretend the jar rolled away into an inaccessible place. You will have to do without. Improvise, create colours by mixing, paint over the jagged line. You are the expert! Fix it, you don't have time to procrastinate!"

The shaking in her hands increased. She clutched her right hand with her left, used whatever objects of varying sizes that she could find in the room to prop her arms and continued with her artwork. As she was almost finished, Alan played the handclapping surprise again. She was furious, although the jagged line was smaller and easier to fix than the first time.

The work was finished, superbly done. Alan and Frank examined and praised.

Then Alan said, "You took forty-two minutes, you only had thirty-five! You really could benefit from another session."

Frank, standing behind Anne, held his hands closed in prayer and shook his head at Alan, no, no, no.

Alan continued, "However, since you are sort of delicate today, I will disregard that when I was willing to drop the tenth rehearsal, I was assuming that you would do number nine within the allotted time. Clean up your jars and tools. Leave no trace that a major makeup operation occurred."

"Enjoy your remaining time in Vienna and get ready to have a great time in Prague and points beyond. I am sure you will miss me, but I believe that under your weak veneer is a strong, skilled artist and actress, and that you will manage without my ongoing guidance."

She looked at her middle finger but elected to not make any gesture. Alan observed her with amusement.

Richard Holley's indoctrination was easier. His role was to be Anne's husband until the exchange took place, then go into hiding for the duration of the East German part of the tour, then rejoin the tour in Warsaw. The defecting German would play the role of Anne's husband during that period.

Richard would be cared for by members of the same team tasked with rescuing the defector, a group of East Europeans hired by the Rakosis. If there was no defection, Richard would continue with the tour and enjoy the vacation.

If there was a defection, Richard would disappear and spend a vacation playing chess or reading in a farmhouse, pretending to be a farmhand. He would be provided with fake seasonal migrant labourer identification and smuggled into Poland. He would not be wanted by the police, he was unimportant, no one would be looking for him, he did not exist. In Poland, as soon as the defector moved on to new handlers, Richard would return to his own identity and his tour group.

Both Richard and Anne looked forward to the tour and their big adventure. There remained that forty-five-minute time limit issue with Alan, but it was felt all around that it had been resolved, although the irritating friction between Alan and Anne would not go away.

The international tour started officially when they left Vienna for Prague. They enjoyed the beautiful Austrian scenery. During their days in Vienna, they discovered Viennese pastries and coffee and became addicted. They hoped that the food in Prague would be comparable. Their Austrian driver assured them that there was no cause for concern.

They could have crossed the border near Vienna at Bratislava, but the tour itinerary took them on a longer, picturesque two-lane mountain road. They crossed into the Czechoslovak Socialist Republic in midmorning.

They met their Czech tour guide, a short, heavy, potbellied man. He was knowledgeable and friendly, named Jan Bernasek. He wanted to be called Mr Jan or Mr Bernasek. The Americans opted unanimously for Mr Jan. Some tried to skip the 'mister' but were promptly corrected.

Mr Jan assured them that good food was a most important feature of their Czech tour. After they stopped in a small town for good coffee and a surprisingly large cake selection, the group felt confident that their Viennese addictions could be sustained in Czechoslovakia.

The bus reached Prague in the early afternoon. They had a late lunch in a historic basement pub, then went on a walking tour of the old town, largely intact as Prague had been spared the heavy bombing of World War II. The tour group was enchanted by the old buildings and the narrow winding streets.

They visited the Old Town Square and the Town Hall, then crossed the Vltava River, called Moldau in German, on the iconic Fourteenth Century Charles Bridge. The old bridge was of unusual interest to the engineering-minded members of the group, asking many questions that Mr Jan was truly pleased to hear and competently answer.

Dinner was in another basement pub, with traditional Czech cuisine, plenty of local Pilsner beer and a small band playing folk music alternating with jazz, a curious mixture that was presented well. The travellers were happy, now convinced they were going to enjoy Prague.

Next morning, they visited the Soviet War Memorial and were told the story of the heroic Soviet troops liberating Prague at the end of World War II and replacing the German flag with the Soviet one. Mr Jan narrated with passion the enormous sacrifice of the Soviet army, who lost thousands of their soldiers in the struggle for Czech freedom, yet in 1948 magnanimously relinquished Soviet control and supported the creation of the independent Czechoslovak Socialist Republic, bound in eternal friendship with their Soviet socialist brothers, and thriving under the protection of the Soviet Union.

John Crawford had some crude derogatory comments about the propaganda lecture in particular and the communists in general. Wife Barbara and friends Richard Holley and Anne Miller admonished him to shut up and reminded him of all the warnings they were given by Alan in Vienna, and before, in Long Beach, also by Frank Kolozsvary.

He grumbled that he knew his constitutional right to freedom of speech. The other three got quite aggravated and argued that his rights did not include jeopardising the entire group and the tour, reminding him that behind the Iron Curtain the U.S. Constitution was a foreign curiosity.

Since leaving Alan behind in Austria, Anne had become the de facto leader of the group. She was not as stern as Alan, and all liked her. She was very practical and not afraid of imposing order and preparing the way for the group, as well as for her upcoming role as the defector's wife and mentor. Before leaving for Prague, she distributed her makeup bottles and chemicals into four bags, each to be carried through customs in the baggage of a different woman, to avoid calling attention to an unusual quantity of cosmetics. After clearing customs, the bags were to be returned to Anne, a procedure to be repeated at each border crossing, to be ready for the new passenger, if any.

The tour continued with visits to the Ninth Century Prague Castle complex, museums, Wenceslas Square. They admired the 600-year-old astronomical clock, still with its original face, but the inner mechanism upgraded over centuries. Their tour guide was skilled in navigating the small old-city area, keeping variety, and finding new and different things only a short distance from the previous stop. They visited St. Vitus Cathedral, and places where Wolfgang Amadeus Mozart and Bedrich Smetana had lived and worked. After the Smetana Museum, they went to a small concert of Mozart and Smetana music.

Their Austrian driver called his company every day and reported the progress of the tour and the news of the moment. On their third and last day in Prague, the tourists were taken to several arts and crafts shops, including one where skilled wood carvers made beautiful sculptures for churches and museums, using techniques developed over centuries and passed on from generation to generation. During their sightseeing, the tour had encountered several shops that sold puppets, an ancient, disappearing artform that seemed current and popular in Prague.

Mr Jan told his tour members the history of the puppets of Prague and Bohemia, explaining why puppetry remained important in modern Prague. In a charming, interesting way, Mr Jan narrated that in the Seventeenth Century the Kingdom of Bohemia came under the rule of the Austrian Hapsburgs, who abolished the Czech language and instituted the mandatory use of German in schools, commerce, and government.

The only venues that allowed the use of Czech were puppet shows performing ancient fairy tales. The Bohemians consequently fiercely promoted puppetry, and through this medium managed to keep the Czech language alive until it was allowed again. The beloved puppets continued their chatter and pirouettes to the present times, in Czech and in other languages, embracing serious drama and current events.

That evening in the hotel bar, two young men approached the table of the four friends, asking for Richard and Anne Holley. Having confirmed they had the Holleys, the strangers introduced themselves as Istvan and Janos, explaining that they, or one of them, would be taking Rick Holley into hiding if and when the twin behind the curtain appeared on the scene to take Rick Holley's place.

They were invited to pull some adjacent empty chairs and sit down at the table. They declined the offer of a drink.

Istvan was the better English speaker of the two, and he did most of the talking, but Janos also took part in the conversation; they said it was important to get used to people's voices.

Istvan explained, "If and when the escaped East German appears to take your place, the transfer of identities must be immediate. You must leave at once. One of us, perhaps both, will take you in our car to a nearby farm, where you will stay for a while. We will provide you with farmhand travel papers and later deliver you back to your comrades in Poland, probably in your Warsaw hotel. We will be in communication with people in the bus company. They will inform us of any itinerary or time changes."

"Take a good look at our faces. You must recognise us. We will say something that includes Alan's name, like 'Alan says hello' or 'greetings from Alan', but there will be no further explanations or introductions or secret handshakes."

"You must always keep your suitcase ready and closed, in your hotel room, or with other luggage when it is being moved. You will not need your suitcase while sightseeing, but it should be closed and ready in your room, or in the bus luggage compartment with the other suitcases. We will leave you with a green name tag for your suitcase, so we can find and recognise it quickly if we must search through a luggage pile. Please attach it today. There will be a matching suitcase for the defector, with his clothing. He is of a slightly different size."

"Now repeat what I just have told you, so we can hear and recognise your voice, and so we can be sure that you understood what we told you. Here and now you can ask questions; when the moment comes, you will have to leave immediately, without time for goodbyes, introductions, or questions. You may be able to nod or wave to your wife if she happens to be in the room. You may have to leave without seeing anyone. We will contact your wife and let her know."

Rick Holley repeated what he had been told to the satisfaction of his interlocutors.

Anne asked, "Will you appear during business hours, or do we need to expect a middle of the night visit?"

Istvan replied, "We don't know. It all depends on when the defecting twin shows up. It could be lunch time or midnight. I suggest Rick lay out his clothes at bedtime so that he can dress quickly, and I mean fireman-on-fire-call quickly. If you forget something, too bad. Perhaps we can buy a replacement, perhaps not."

"We will check the contents of your suitcase. If the stuff you have is incriminating in any way, we may have to replace it with local Czech or Polish manufactures."

"Now I want you, Mr and Mrs Holley, to listen very carefully. There will be a quiz at the end. What you need to understand very clearly: Rick should not take his wallet or his passport. The arriving twin will use the same passport and travel documents. They will be returned to you in Warsaw. I suggest you keep passports and wallets in Mrs Holley's purse for the duration. Do not, I repeat, do not take your passport; give it to her for safekeeping. Now please repeat this, both of you. And I hope Mr and Mrs Crawford paid attention, as they will be part of the charade."

John Crawford answered for both, "I have never seen so much crap just to take a lousy bus ride. You Commie bureaucrats should …"

Istvan brusquely interrupted, "Mr Crawford, listen carefully, and Mr and Mrs Holley, listen even more carefully. Safe travel in the socialist countries of Eastern Europe depends on being quiet, anonymous, courteous, and non-political. If you can adhere to those simple guidelines, your trip will be tranquil, at times slow and bureaucratic, but generally enjoyable."

"However, if you want to make juvenile political speeches, you may find out to your deep regret that it is the wrong thing to do. We want no part of that. We want our clients to arrive safely at their destination."

"Let me be clear about our concerns. As a matter of fact, if Mr Crawford had been our client in this assignment instead of Rakosi's, we would have cancelled our participation right now, within seconds of his negative comments. We would return his money in cash within a day and refuse to do business with him ever again. I hope that Mr and Mrs Holley understand that we will walk away, refund your money, and never remember knowing you, if you do not want to follow our instructions. It is not worth the risk. Are we in agreement?"

John Crawford was visibly angry but did not say a word. Barbara Crawford and the Holleys said they understood and agreed.

Istvan waited a few seconds, then repeated, "Are we in agreement? The question was primarily directed at you, Mr John Crawford. You must decide, now, or we will decide, now. Will you behave and keep your mouth shut? Let's hear it."

John grumbled, "You wanted me to be quiet, so I am being quiet and saying nothing."

Istvan got up and said, "Goodbye, ladies and gentlemen. We don't play parlour games. Find yourself another service provider."

Janos got up as well, advising, "The bus company will refund your money tomorrow." Both men left.

The four travellers remained seated, without knowing what to say. Barbara was red with anger, veins bulging on her forehead. John was pale and chagrined. The Holleys looked serious and determined.

Anne broke the silence, "We will continue without you, John. We have invested too much to quit. I have a prepaid open ticket from Vienna to Los Angeles, which I will transfer to you. You can go back to Vienna by train in the morning and catch the plane from there. I suppose we can say that you got sick and wanted to return home. And you, Barbara, please let us know by morning if you want to continue on the tour or return home with your husband. I also will talk to our bus driver and call Alan for further instructions. Good night."

She got up, also Rick Holley, and they left together. As they were waiting for the elevator their driver appeared. They seized the opportunity to discuss the problem caused by John Crawford. The driver said that in East Germany any changes in a guided tour would cause further problems and invite scrutiny.

The driver said he had a safe way of communicating with his bosses in Vienna to request instructions and advised Anne and Rick to keep quiet about the development, as their room may be bugged, and not use the phone, under any circumstances. He also urged that the Crawfords be reminded not to discuss any of this in their room.

Anne went back to the bar as the Crawfords were leaving and brought them up to date and asked to wait until they got guidance in the morning.

Barbara Crawford informed Anne, stuttering, "I will also return to California, but I will go on a separate flight. Right now, I am so angry I can hardly breathe, and totally stressed out that I cannot even yell at John until we get back to Vienna. Rest assured; we will do nothing until we hear from you tomorrow."

John was still pale, broke his silence with, "We should never have come to these fucking communist enclaves. I will be glad to get out of here and never again look at their fucking puppets, cuckoo clocks, crumbling slums and greasy grub."

He went on using increasingly vulgar language and attracting attention. Barbara started to cry, which attracted more attention. After they left, Anne assured the bystanders that her friends had a marital dispute and that they were going to be loving and friendly again by morning. A few spoke English and translated for the others. The bystanders nodded knowingly, dispersed, some smiling.

In the elevator, Barbara yelled at her husband that he had hurt and humiliated her, in the process endangering the whole tour. She had much more to say but choked on her tears. As the elevator arrived at their floor the opportunity of a private lecture was gone.

They did not talk in their room. He said goodnight, she did not respond. Both slept poorly, with much tossing and turning. He tried to talk several times as they both lay awake, she refused to acknowledge him. Both eventually slept, having nightmares.

In the early hours of the morning, their nightmares became astoundingly real, both feeling a strong hand covering their mouths and someone whispering in their ears that if they kept quiet, they would not be hurt, but if they did not keep quiet, they would be savagely beaten up.

As instructed, they nodded affirmatively and the hands were slowly lifted, but remained within an inch of their faces. A night table lamp was turned on, and the Crawfords recognised their recent acquaintances Istvan and Janos, dressed as hotel maintenance men.

Indicating silence with a finger over their lips, the intruders pointed the terrified couple towards the bathroom. After the four were inside, Janos closed the door and turned on the bathtub water wide open and flushed the toilet.

Istvan whispered, "They do not have recording equipment in the bathrooms. They do record in the bedroom. Now listen very carefully."

"We did not want to continue with you. Mr Crawford's stupid talk calls attention and is extremely dangerous. Unfortunately for us, you are not our direct clients. We are attempting to protect you on behalf of one of our oldest and largest clients. They are our client, not you. They requested, as a special favour, that we try to keep the tour group intact, as initially booked, as we go into East Germany."

"Abrupt changes in a listed, approved visitor group attract attention. Considering the special circumstances involved with this tour, attracting attention is something we need to avoid at all costs."

"We agreed to honour our client's request and try again to obtain your assurance of good, silent behaviour, so that the tour can continue as originally booked. We agreed to do this one time only."

"We were also allowed to warn you about what you risk if you agree to behave and then renege on your promise and start your insulting talk again. If you endanger us, you will fall down some stairs or have a traffic accident. Any of these events will break a leg. If you cause us severe harm, it may be both legs and both arms. As you can imagine, these injuries can be extremely painful and inconvenient. And as you cannot imagine, the medical services and the long convalescence in an East German prison hospital are harsh."

"If you cause us harm, I can assure you that we will find you, no matter where you try to hide, or how good you think your locks are."

"We will visit you at breakfast, a few hours from now. At that time, we need your decision. You can promise to behave and continue with the tour, or you can leave the tour. Personally, I hope you leave the tour. You cause too many complications and too much drama. In either case, we will do our best to ensure the safety, comfort and transportation needs of Mr Holley."

Next morning as the four travellers were having breakfast in the hotel dining room, the two young men reappeared and sat down at their table.

Istvan started, "Mr Crawford, we have been requested by the sponsor of this tour to offer you another chance. Please respond clearly, do you wish to continue on the tour on our terms or go home?"

As his three companions watched anxiously, a grim-faced John Crawford said, "I will continue with the tour and follow your instructions, albeit under protest. I will not loudly criticise the communist swine during this tour. But do not expect me to applaud their Marxist lectures or pretend to admire their bullshit."

"I can only offer my silence. Do not expect love or subservience. Now it is your turn to respond clearly. Is my silence sufficient? If it is not, I will leave."

Istvan pondered his alternatives, then acquiesced, "Your colourful vocabulary reflects your intellect in a convincing way. You convinced me that yes, your silence will do, that is all we can ask for. However, please be reminded of the consequences that were explained to you. Now I guess we can continue our conversation of yesterday. Thank you."

John nodded; the others looked relieved. Janos took over the narrative, now addressed primarily to Rick Holley.

"Mr Holley, while you are in our care, and if you keep your mouth under control, you will have one of the easiest assignments in the entire tour. Everyone will be looking for the defector, nobody will be looking for you. You do not exist, there is no record of your entry to any country, you will become a humble migratory farm worker, you are not important, you will be safe, provided you behave and follow our directions, quietly."

Istvan took over again, and asked Rick Holley to repeat some of the instructions, asked a few questions of the others, declared them fit to travel on to East Germany, provided they did not engage in political commentary.

The two wished them a safe tour and left as quietly and unobtrusively as they had arrived.

On their last day in Prague, they all had concluded that although smaller than Vienna, the Czech city offered a similarly rich cultural experience, thanks to their excellent tour guide. When he was not reciting the obligatory socialist dogma, Mr Jan could be a charming and interesting companion. He knew a lot about food, guided them to good restaurants of various types, and thoroughly enjoyed partaking in the offerings.

That evening the travellers felt content and relaxed. There were some guilty introspections about overeating, and perhaps some stomach aches. They had participated in a feast of tasty, heavy, hearty winter dishes of roast pork with dumplings and cabbage, bread-like dumplings to soak up rich sauces, potato pancakes, boiled fruit desserts, Czech pilsner, coffee and after dinner drinks with fruits, cheeses and assorted snacks.

Mr Jan commented, patting his pot belly, "I am glad we had the opportunity to offer you a traditional Czech formal dinner. I have heard some of you wondering if you had overindulged. I can assure you that you have not. Czech food is light and fluffy. Tomorrow you will experience German cuisine, not even closely as gourmet as our simplest Czech potato soup. I highly recommend the chocolate cake with whipped cream and glazed cherries with your nightcap. Tomorrow morning after a proper breakfast we will tour some of the interesting Prague suburbs and then travel towards the mountains. It is a beautiful ride. I will remain as your tour guide until the frontier with the German Democratic Republic, where a German colleague will become your guide."

"By the way, have you tried the caraway crackers with Brie cheese? They make a wonderful bedtime snack, with some ice cream and a shot of plum brandy."

8. Wolkenstein, East Germany

The small town of Wolkenstein, among several neighbouring similar towns, has been a picturesque resort since the thirteenth century. Located at the foot of the Erzgebirge, the Ore Mountains, in a region of rocky mountains, granite cliffs, hot springs, waterfalls, and spectacular views of river valleys, it has attracted visitors from Saxony and other parts of Europe for over seven hundred years. Over the centuries the nobility built hunting lodges and the Wolkenstein castle.

The town proper has a population of about 4,000, with a similar number scattered in nearby villages and rural resorts. Among these is Wolkenstein Lodge, a former nineteenth-century spa and hotel requisitioned by the East German government as a retreat for senior officials and a perfect site for unobtrusive conferences. The Politburo held their yearly spring retreat there, to determine party policy before the Mayday celebrations. The lodge is about four kilometres away from the castle and the tourist areas, affording great privacy.

Bruno Hadler went twice for walks around the grounds of the lodge, especially to reconnoitre the terraced gardens facing the river. The spring thaw had released enormous quantities of water from the mountains. The runoff past the lodge was violent, foaming, noisy, beautiful. The only relatively calm spot was along the terrace wall at the foot of a waterfall.

The surface of the water was about four meters below the lowest terrace floor, a good jump. It would be a standing jump, feet first, in case the water depth was not as assumed. There were no guards along the river, which, along with the high cliffs, provided a formidable defence against any intruders. His scheduled rendezvous time would be in total darkness. He feared jumping without being able to see, although he knew he would be on a tether.

After an early dinner, the Politburo members and some of their staff returned to Berlin in their special train. All cars had returned from the railway station, and with the Politburo gone, the atmosphere in the lodge had become more relaxed. Ministerial secretaries and other staff would stay for the evening to organise paperwork, type minutes, and take care of loose ends, returning by car in the morning. Bruno spent some time discussing the day's closing conference with colleagues, had a drink and announced he was tired and had decided to retire early and finish his paperwork in the morning.

He instructed his driver to be ready for departure at ten next morning. He was scheduled to travel alone, with just the driver, which suited him fine. This and the late departure hour would allow more time before his absence caused alarm.

He paced the floor in his suite, worried and restless. He reflected about other defectors and traitors and wondered how they had felt on the eve of their betrayals. His next thought was the realisation that his betrayal's eve had been some time ago, and the planned escape of this day was just another step in a journey long underway.

He had to abort his exit twice because of people milling about. He became increasingly anxious about the time as he waited. On his third try, the corridors and intervening rooms were empty, and he managed to leave the building unseen. The trip through the gardens was more difficult. The only light was from a quarter moon, intermittently interrupted by clouds. He descended the steps down to the river, got lost once, then found his way to the lowest terrace. They were going to wait for him for one hour, between nine fifteen and ten fifteen at night. They had insisted on not scheduling full hours; for some reason nine to ten had not been acceptable.

He arrived at the designated space about nine forty. He could not see the other side of the stream; in the daytime he had estimated it to be about fifteen meters wide at this point. His rescuers would be equipped with night vision goggles and see him.

As instructed, he stood by the railing in the centre of the terrace and held out his arms to form a tee. In a few seconds, he saw a weak green light blinking three times. He raised and lowered his arms three times to acknowledge the signal, then moved to his left, out of the way at the end of the small terrace.

Shortly thereafter he heard a faint pop and a thin rope with a padded three-pronged hook came flying and hooked on the railing. He grabbed it and pulled in a heavier rope attached to a harness, trailing two ropes from across the river. He slipped the simple harness, just a large loop, under his armpits and rolled up the initial slim rope and tied it around his waist. He had some difficulty with the hook, but got it tied to his back. Leave no traces was the agreement.

For a fleeting moment, he weighed that he still could abort his escape and continue with his position in the party and lead a comfortable life. And his thoughts also turned to the many before him who had faced their last chance and made their decision. And as he had realised repeatedly, his decision had been made long time ago.

He climbed over the railing, stood on the narrow ledge facing the river, raised his arms three times, and took a deep breath. Within seconds, a powerful pull yanked him into the icy water. The shock was so intense that Bruno knew he was going to die. The pain was unbearable, he was paralysed, all the cold shower training proved useless. He felt he was being pulled in a regular, strong rhythm, but he could not time his breathing and started to swallow water. He was barely conscious when they pulled him out.

He was dragged into an overheated van and given first aid. He resumed breathing on his own, his wet clothes were cut away, they dried him with large towels, rubbed some lotion on his naked skin, then dressed him in warm clothing. He drank strong coffee laced with sugary brandy from a thermos, and they kept exercising his tingling arms and legs. Soon he started to return to normalcy.

They were traveling on a bumpy road without lights, the driver looking weird with his night vision goggles when the others could see him during the few moonlit breaks in the clouds.

When they reached a paved highway, two of them got out and listened intently and scanned in both directions looking for vehicle lights. They let a truck pass. After a quiet wait, they decided to enter the highway, turned on the lights and travelled normally.

They were three young, very fit looking men. They spoke little, in German with a foreign accent that Bruno assumed to be from a Slavic language but could not be sure which. His rescuers did not answer questions, except to advise that they were taking him to his tour bus rendezvous.

About this time, there was banging on Bruno's hotel room door. One of his colleagues, secretary to a minister, had decided to skip a planned sightseeing side trip with his group, and return directly to Berlin. He knew Bruno had no passengers and called him to get a ride. There was no answer. The hotel switchboard operator kept trying at intervals, without success. Then they knocked on his door, but there was no answer. After a long interval, they decided to call security, which was handled by the national political police, the Staatssicherheitsdienst, the Stasi, for the duration of the Politburo conference.

The Stasi captain in charge was annoyed about the disturbance. He assumed comrade Bruno Hadler was screwing a clerk or a maid in another room, and that he would be quite angry when found. And the Stasi guards would of course get blamed for something. High-ranking bureaucrats could be a difficult, vindictive bunch.

After a while, he had no choice but to get the hotel night manager to unlock the room. The room was empty. Papers and binders were arranged in good order on the desk, obviously work in progress. Briefcases and luggage were half packed, another piece of work in progress. Outdoor clothing was still in the closet. Nothing was touched, and the room was locked again.

The next step, publicity, was now unavoidable. Comrade Hadler was paged on the hotel's public address system. After a while without a response, the loudspeakers asked staff and visitors to report if they had seen Hadler, and to start a room by room search of the lodge. By eleven in the evening, the search had been completed. Comrade Hadler was not found. The captain had worried that they would find Hadler in some embarrassing situation; now he was worried that they would not. He called his superior in Karl Marx Stadt, a bad-tempered major. The major was distracted with something else when he received the call and had not paid attention. He asked, "Are you calling me to report a goddam missing person? Isn't this a matter for the local police? They deal with domestic issues, errant husbands, teenagers that did not get home when they were supposed to. And they will not be interested until someone has been missing for two days. How long has your man been missing?"

The captain stuttered, "A … about two hours, comrade major."

The major screamed at his subordinate, "You stupid idiot! Is this a joke? Are you drunk? You better start explaining again, from the beginning! What kind of an officer are you?"

The captain explained again, slowly and carefully from the beginning, and the major now understood that they were not dealing with an errant husband but with the disappearance of a high-ranking Politburo secretary. He questioned the captain about the details. There were only two access driveways to the lodge, both scheduled to remain heavily guarded until the last conference participants left next morning. There was no other access.

The site was surrounded by steep granite cliffs and a raging river. Hadler's two administrative assistants had been taken to Hadler's suite to examine the paperwork; they determined nothing was missing. Everyone had been questioned. They could not find a clue or an explanation.

They speculated about possibilities, concluded that if Hadler had gone for an evening walk and fallen off a cliff or into the river, a body would be found by morning. If he had been kidnapped by a mountain-climbing enemy sabotage team, he could not have gone far. They assumed that it would take about an hour to kidnap him and carry him down a cliff and to the highway to a waiting vehicle, which would have a head start of about one hour.

The major then ordered roadblocks on all roads leaving Wolkenstein at locations one and a half hour of travel time away. He also ordered searching all hotels, campgrounds, and trailer parks within that distance. He did not think anyone would be found but concluded that his actions would be scrutinised by his superiors, and that it was safer to be overzealous rather than underperforming. He further instructed that the roadblocks would be staffed with help of the local police, but that hotel and similar searches would by Stasi personnel only.

The major decided to go to Wolkenstein. He gave orders to get his car and to assemble a detachment of twenty men to be trucked to the lodge to assist in the search.

By nine o'clock in the morning, the colonel commanding the Karl Marx Stadt station was informed. By noon, the Stasi general in charge of the region had been informed, and soon thereafter the Politburo in Berlin.

The consensus at all levels was that the disappearance would be resolved by the end of the day, but that it was prudent and necessary to mount a full police action until then.

9. Karl Marx Stadt, East Germany

In about an hour, Bruno Hadler and his rescuers reached the outskirts of Karl Marx Stadt, as the old Saxon city of Chemnitz had been renamed under the Communist regime. This was the first city in the German Democratic Republic scheduled on their tour, and the designated site of the high-risk exchange of twins. As they were about to make a left turn across the highway, they saw the flashing blue lights of a police car coming in the opposite direction, followed by a truck carrying troops. They let the police vehicles pass, then entered the hotel parking area.

They waited in the van until about ten minutes before eleven. Two of the unnamed rescuers went into the hotel to register, one stayed in the van with Bruno. They had reservations for a late arrival, not customary in East Germany, but tolerated for tourists. The clerk said that the reservations were for three and wanted to know where the third guest was. He was told that the third had to straighten something in the car and would be coming in soon with the luggage. The clerk hesitated, said his shift ended at 2300 hours, and his colleague would have to finish processing the registration when the third guest came in, as all three had to be processed together to match the reservation. The night clerk was apprised, handed the two passports and the partially completed form, and all was declared to be progressing in order.

The two rescuers went into the bar where a tour group had gathered for a nightcap. They mingled with some of the tour members until the barkeeper announced that it was past eleven and that the bar had to close soon, with lights out by 11:30. The guests started to leave. The two men went back outside, one stopping at the reception desk to tell the night clerk they were going to get the missing third member of their party to help bring in their luggage and finish checking in. The clerk nodded and repeated that all three had to be accounted for because the reservation was for the three. Soon they appeared with the third companion. Two stayed to make sure that the papers and the third passport were in order, the other went to their room with the luggage. The bar closed on time. The night clerk was becoming impatient with the constant going in and out of the three men, but now he was tranquil that all names and matching passports were accounted for. The outdoor guards checked license plates of cars and tour buses, all was well, it promised to be a peaceful night.

Not all was peaceful. In Room 72, a disoriented, fatigued Bruno Hadler became Richard Holley, and was introduced to Anne Holley, his new wife, and told that he could not sleep yet, that he had to be aged some twenty years, now, immediately. They shaved his head, he had to shower, was towelled dry by the woman and a strong, older guy.

Sitting in his new American underwear he was fitted with a glued-on wig of shaggy grey hair turning white, and under a bright light, his new wife, the retired Hollywood makeup artist, proceeded to apply wrinkles and age spots. His eyebrows were dyed, he acquired bags under his eyes and some visible veins on his neck and hands. A face cream turned into wrinkles as soon as it dried but remained flexible. He was assured that the wig and the makeup were shower resistant for about ten days if careful.

He tried on new eyeglasses in a heavy dark frame, the vision was perfect. He also tried on clean but used clothing and shoes, which fit perfectly. Then they took him to the bathroom mirror. The image he saw left him speechless, he was shocked by the change. He was shown his American passport, with a closely matching photograph that could not pass detailed scrutiny but was quite adequate for a routine viewing by police or customs. All conversation was in English. When he spoke German, they totally ignored him. A new reality crept in.

Hadler was really exhausted and wanted to sleep. He knew he had about twelve hours before they would start looking for him, but Mackenzie's instructions to his team had been brutally clear on this, and the team was complying.

Alan had told them repeatedly, "He will not have twelve or three or seven hours; he will have an unknown period of time, he may have no time. If he is becoming someone else, it must be as close to instantaneous as possible. He has a good chance of survival when the metamorphosis is complete. He, and you all, have no chance if they catch him with his pants down while changing uniforms."

Alan had rehearsed the procedure with them in Long Beach and again in Vienna until they all were fatigued and disgusted, but they had learned their assignments.

Anne, and John and Barbara Crawford, the couple in the role of old friends, now had their turn. They spent over two hours with Hadler rehearsing names, answering hypothetical questions and getting their stories straight, especially rehashing their interaction with the East German tour guide who had joined them in the afternoon and during dinner had shared conversations circulating from table to table.

An exhausted Bruno Hadler was allowed to crawl into bed, where he collapsed into deep sleep. After an hour, he was awakened brusquely by the others, who yelled at him to recite his address in Long Beach, about his last job before retirement, his favourite sports teams. Half asleep he stuttered but managed to give the right answers in his accented English. He was asked why he spoke with an accent if he was American born, he yawned convincingly and said he had been raised in Austria and didn't really use English until the family returned to the United States. It seemed that he could survive routine questioning.

Anne put her makeup bottles and brushes away and went to bed. There were two beds in the room, which made things easier.

At four in the morning, the Stasi's favourite hour, there was a loud knocking on the door and a voice announcing a Stasi inspection, ordering to open. Anne got out of bed and opened the door. Two Stasi officers came in, holding their passports and a list on a clipboard, accompanied by a scared-looking night clerk who functioned as an interpreter. They announced that they had to search the premises, which they proceeded to do with speed and efficiency.

They opened and closed drawers and suitcases, looked in the bathroom and in the closet. They opened the passports and compared their faces with the photographs, asked why hers was not in the name of Holley. They looked at the photographs again, carefully comparing with their faces, first hers, then his. Anne was standing to the right of Rick, about a step back. The Stasi man was distracted by Anne's nightgown, which had become unbuttoned and showed too much of her right breast, not quite covering her nipple. After a good look, he closed the passports, saluted, and left. Then they heard the banging on the next door. Anne buttoned her gown, saying, "Don't get any ideas!"

Bruno smiled and nodded, "Danke, thank you."

They did not sleep well, with much tossing and turning. At daybreak, Bruno started to sleep more soundly, but was awakened by Anne with, "Okay, Rick, time to get up. We need to show up on time for breakfast and tour the city."

He mumbled, "My name is ... Richard."

Anne scolded, "Not for your wife, you dummy. I and our friends call you Rick, only strangers use Richard, some try Dick, but you don't like it, and you tell people, with a smile, that you prefer Rick, or Richard. And I am your wife Anne Miller, in case you forgot. What were you dreaming? Come on, say my name, and call me sweetheart, dear, sweety pie, honey, and Annie. Let's hear it."

Bruno had difficulty transforming himself into Richard, or Rick when talking to his wife and using terms of endearment. She kept insisting that he use these terms or her name in every sentence until he got used to it.

At one point, he stuttered, "Yes, d-d-dear," and Anne burst out laughing. It embarrassed him, but he ended joining in the laughter. This little moment somehow broke the ice and the two started to feel friendly towards each other.

She guided his dressing, selecting shirts and socks, and a long dark red windbreaker with a blue lining. He thought it was a little too colourful, she advised that he had been wearing it since Vienna and everyone remembered it. He was impressed that everything fit so well.

As they headed towards the hotel dining room, they encountered a heavy-set stern-looking woman coming in the opposite direction.

"That's our tour guide," she whispered. "Wave at her and say 'good morning' in English."

Rick did as he was told, Anne waved as well, the tour guide nodded and wished them a good morning as she walked by.

"Now," she said, "we must continue our friendship with the Crawfords, John and Barbara. We have been a foursome since Long Beach and we will continue to sit together. We call them John and Barb. Okay, Rick?"

"Yes, dear sweety honey pie."

"One such term at the time, please. 'Dear' is the best all-around expression. Don't get too sugary, at least until you learn more of the nuances."

"Yes, dear."

The Crawfords joined them and talked about the dawn inspection of their room. They decided to sit at the same table they had occupied on the previous evening for dinner, with Rick's back towards the spot where the tour guide had sat.

Alan had warned them that the tour guide could be one of the most dangerous officials they encountered, as he or she might be familiar with the faces of high-ranking members of government and recognise a similarity in Rick, especially if he or she was informed about the disappearance of Bruno Hadler.

They had the same waitress as before, and they all said hello and acted familiar. They had ordered their breakfast when their guide appeared in the dining room and asked for their attention. She wore a dark grey pant suit with a white blouse. She might have been in her fifties, with short brown hair, a serious expression, and shiny steel rimmed glasses. She spoke German-accented but fluent British English.

"Good morning, dear guests, and again, welcome to the German Democratic Republic. As you know, I am tour guide Seifert, and I will be guiding you throughout your visit in our country. Some of you have asked me about last night's inspection of the hotel by our security officers. We apologise for the brief interruption to your sleep, but they had to investigate a potential disruption to our democratic peace, which requires eternal vigilance against revanchist anti-proletarian foreign infiltration. You need not be preoccupied; your tour is properly documented and welcomed, and we all can enjoy this opportunity for strengthening our international friendship. And you can rest assured that our law and order institutions will protect you throughout your tour and guarantee your comfort, enjoyment, and safety. We will depart in one hour and we will be having fun touring our beautiful city of Karl Marx Stadt."

In a low voice, John Crawford imitated, "Vee vill depart and vee vill haf fun vis Karl Ma …"

Barbara admonished, "Don't do that. Remember Alan's stern warnings and instructions to not argue, make fun, criticise or in any way antagonise them. We had a very traumatic night-time visit from the mafia goons in Prague. Have you forgotten their retaliation warnings?"

"Again, remember Alan's many cautionary lectures. Last night's visit by the cops should have taught you, again, the importance of following his instructions. Again, again, again. When will you get it?"

"You are right. I'll watch it."

Rick warned, "Actually, Barbara's reminder is more dangerous than what John said, because it tells of conspiracy, while John's comment was just impolite and stupid. Do not that kind of exchange repeat. You also must assume that some of your hotel rooms might be equipped with recording apparatus, which will record everything for in depth later analysis. We use, they use exceptionally good equipment, from Japan. It would be good if you could take turns privately warning the other travellers to follow their security instructions exactly, mit … with precision. This has to be done today, before to rooms returning."

The rest of the breakfast conversation was describing life in Long Beach and making Hadler repeat it. His English was stilted and needed much practice. As they had been trained, no one asked a single question about Hadler's real name, position, or reason for his defection.

The tour guide was walking around the tables and chatting briefly with her charges. One asked, "Do you have a first name?"

"Yes, of course," she replied. "What do we call you?"

"Guide Seifert is appropriate," she said and moved to the next table. She asked their names at each table and checked them off on a clipboard.

When she reached their table, the four were apprehensive, but it all went smoothly. She asked about their hometowns and whether this was their first visit to the German Democratic Republic. The Crawfords inquired about her hometown, and she replied it was a village. She asked whether they were members of the intelligentsia, a question they pretended to not understand. She then asked about their jobs prior to retirement and seemed pleased that the Crawfords had been electrician and seamstress, and the Holleys office clerk and beauty shop attendant. After some further small talk, Seifert left, commenting that it was nice to see real people having fun on an overseas vacation.

After she was gone, John Crawford wanted to know, "What or who are real people, and what or who are the unreal ones? And what the fuck is intelligentsia?"

Barbara scolded, "You were going to watch your tongue. I do not want to call attention and invite trouble because you are acting stupid. It really worries me. Why can't you understand?"

John nodded, "I am sorry. I am not used to monitoring every word. That's not how we speak at home."

Rick Holley explained that intelligentsia meant the educated professionals, scientists, managers, and officers. He had observed the exchange with interest, while Anne had watched him with interest, commenting, "You are entering a different world."

John Crawford grumbled that all the guide's questions had already been asked and answered in writing on their visa applications.

They assembled in the parking area and boarded their bus. Their tour guide started to narrate about the sights they were about to see. She was deeply knowledgeable and answered questions easily unless the question had something to do with politics or DDR economics. Everyone soon got used to it and all went well.

The hotel was on the outskirts of the city. As their bus proceeded the mood was relaxed and happy. The passengers were chatting and enjoying the foreign views, observing with interest the mixture of old buildings and new socialist concrete apartment complexes. They had travelled about fifteen minutes when they were stopped at a police checkpoint.

The bus was directed to an adjacent yard, and driver and tour guide were ordered off. They had a lengthy conversation with the police, then two policemen boarded the bus and asked for names and passports.

They went from seat to seat, asked the passengers to get up and move to the aisle, then looked under the seat and in the small carry-on luggage compartment above. They wrote something on a clipboard and moved to the next seat, where they repeated the procedure. The young cop who checked the Holleys and Crawfords seemed bored and slightly embarrassed.

Outside they opened all luggage compartments, then inspected the underside of the bus with mirrors mounted on a wheeled dolly guided by a long handle. Upon arrival of another bus, the police were ordered to finish the inspection of the Americans without delay and take care of the new arrival.

As they resumed their tour the mood had changed. There was less small talk. They were glued to the windows and watched the scenery go by. There were no questions and no smiles.

During the predawn Stasi inspection of their hotel room, Rick Holley had wondered what had triggered the inspection, but did not associate it with his own disappearance, which he expected not to be noticed until some six hours later. With the bus inspection, he started to fear that it did relate to him.

He could not figure out what might have caused an early discovery, but the heavy police activity and the two inspections only a few hours apart made him suspect that someone or something important was involved. He did not consider himself that important, but if a problem involved the Politburo, everyone up and down the chain of command would do his utmost to avoid getting blamed for duty dereliction or lack of socialist zeal if things turned out bad.

His travel companions did not know of his high rank; therefore, they must be assuming that the DDR was the police state depicted in the American propaganda. They had no idea that Rick faced execution if caught betraying state secrets, which was best not known, as they would be too nervous and attract attention.

Karl Marx Stadt was often referred to as the Manchester of Germany, sharing a dusty, grey industrial physiognomy with the English city. They day was overcast. The city seemed particularly drab to the Southern California tourists.

The first stop on their tour of the city was the huge Karl Marx monument, a seven-meter-high stylised head sitting on a six-meter stone base, roughly the height of a four-story apartment building. Behind the statue, on the façade of the large district council office building, the slogan 'Workers of the World Unite' could be read in several languages.

Tour guide Seifert proceeded to give her guests a biography of Karl Marx. She was animated and talked with surprising passion about the worldwide influence of his teachings and his books, especially *Das Kapital* and *The Communist Manifesto*. They learned about the collaboration with Friedrich Engels and the glories of Socialism, Communism and Dialectical Materialism.

Someone asked if Karl Marx was born in the city, and if that was the reason for the name change from Chemnitz. Tour guide Seifert explained that the East German Politburo renamed the city in 1953 to honour Marx on the 70th anniversary of his death, in recognition of the city's industrial heritage, which includes Europe's oldest machine tool factory, established in 1852, and the connection with Karl Marx's crusades to improve the lives of industrial workers enslaved by the Industrial Revolution, and his efforts to unite and save the workers of the world.

In response to follow-up questions, Seifert explained that Marx did not have anything to do with the city named after him. He was born in Trier in the Rhineland, studied in Bonn and in Jena, worked in Cologne, Paris, and then London, where he remained until his death.

John Crawford jokingly asked his wife if he could ask the guide if there was going to be a quiz. She responded with a truly angry look, and Anne Holley told him that his sense of humour was tiresome and dangerous. Rick added that something unusual was going on with all the police activity, recommending that accordingly unusual discretion be exercised. The other three sensed Rick's fear and became afraid in turn.

The tour continued for another day with visits to two castles and their museums. In the afternoon, they stopped at a place that sold souvenirs and postcards, and they were asked to purchase a minimum of one post card per person and write how much fun they were having. The guests should address the cards. The tour guide would collect and mail them. The postage was included in the tour, no charge. Rick said they would photocopy the cards and record the addresses. He was concerned that his handwriting may be recognised by someone, so John Crawford wrote Rick's card, and Barbara wrote the two cards for the Crawfords.

That evening they had dinner at the hotel. The mood was jovial, perhaps the passengers had already noticed that the exchange had been made, but gave no indication, and just enjoyed the great adventure, probably the most exciting thing they had done since retirement.

The following morning, they were scheduled to continue to Leipzig for two days and then continue to Dresden. There was some police activity in the parking area, but they seemed more interested in the busloads of younger passengers, perhaps those under fifty.

10. East Berlin, East Germany

That evening, Politburo member Egon Lanz was sitting down for dinner in Berlin. He was annoyed that his senior administrative secretary had not reported in yet. He should have arrived by now, and Lanz needed to coordinate paperwork and prepare for the upcoming Politburo meeting. The duty clerk reported that comrade Hadler still did not answer his telephone. Lanz ordered, "I want him found, not later or after dinner, but now! And you better pass this along, not as a request but as an order. Is this clear?"

Halfway through dinner a nervous duty clerk announced that they could not find comrade Hadler and that a Stasi officer wanted to see comrade Lanz.

The officer, a major, was led into the dining room. He saluted and apologised for interrupting the comrade's dinner, but he had been ordered to deliver a message in person.

Lanz asked, "Since when do we use senior officers to deliver messages? What next, you will also deliver my mail?"

"No, comrade. The matter at hand requires confidentiality and that is why I was sent."

"Well, then, speak up."

The major was fidgety for a moment, then reported in a crisp military style, "Comrade Hadler is missing since last night. We have Stasi personnel searching the area around Wolkenstein, in a circle that reaches Karl Marx Stadt. Because of your rank and his position on your staff, his disappearance has been taken very seriously and kept confidential. My superiors will contact you in the morning and bring you up to date. The Stasi will also be requesting your assistance in investigating what could have happened."

The conversation continued, with a detailed report about the chain of events, and many questions. After dismissing the officer, Lanz telephoned a few of his Politburo colleagues.

Lanz stayed up late pondering about the significance and the fallout of his senior secretary's disappearance, and how it might colour the politics within the party hierarchy. The longer he thought about the problem, the more his anxiety grew, as it started to sink in that Bruno Hadler had access to a huge amount of state secrets. He felt his heart rate go way up. He was undecided about calling an ambulance, postponed it as his heart started to slow down, but remained quite worried about his health, ultimately about survival.

The Central Committee of the Party was the ultimate power and authority over state and government. The most important day-to-day work was undertaken by the Politburo, the small circle of senior party members comprising between 15 and 20 members plus a few non-voting participants. All the members were experienced political operatives, jealously defending their turf with intrigues, backstabbing and sycophancy, waiting for an opportunity to take advantage of a rival's misstep.

Lanz hoped that Hadler's body would soon be found, and the matter determined to be an accident, but he could not be sure, and he knew he had to prepare for the possibility of a kidnapping or a defection and the subsequent very thorough investigation into Lanz and his staff. He was particularly concerned about Walter Ulbricht, the General Secretary of the Central Committee, who had served his apprenticeship under Stalin and Khrushchev, and Erich Honecker, his ambitious understudy.

Membership in the Politburo provided high perquisites and entitlements, but it did not guarantee immunity from the Stasi apparatus. The Stasi bosses would take their cue from Ulbricht and his inner circle to calibrate the intensity of the investigation of comrade Egon Lanz and staff.

A regular Politburo meeting had been scheduled in Berlin for a week after the Wolkenstein retreat. The important political issues already had been discussed and adjudicated in Wolkenstein, thus the Berlin meeting had a short agenda, ending early.

There were several questions about the disappearance of Bruno Hadler, directed to comrade Egon Lanz but answered by Chairman Walter Ulbricht before Lanz could formulate his reply. Ulbricht requested that Lanz, Stasi chief Erich Mielke, and foreign intelligence chief Markus Wolf stay behind for a little while to discuss the case.

The rest of the group was sent away, in Ulbricht's words, to conduct affairs of state and not waste time on a police matter. They all would have liked to stay and find out more about the disappearance and the investigation. All were concerned about what Hadler knew and how a disclosure of these secrets would affect their own fiefdoms.

Erich Mielke was wearing his four-star general uniform, as was his custom for official functions. He was heavy-set, with a round face that smiled often, and enjoyed the limelight. Three-star general Markus Wolf almost always wore civilian clothes and remained inconspicuous in the background, obsessed with secrecy. He was tall, thin, pale, and reputed to never smile. Both were well known, feared, and professionally respected in the Western intelligence services.

Walter Ulbricht, supreme leader of the German Democratic Republic, looked serious, professorial, balding, with his sideburns, moustache and goatee turning grey. He wore rimless glasses over malevolent steel blue eyes. His voice was soft and slightly higher in pitch than one would assume in someone so powerful. People who were misled by his grandfatherly, academic appearance and did not take him seriously regretted it.

Ulbricht fixed his look on Mielke and asked, "Do you plan to tell me again that no progress has been made, comrade general?" Mielke nodded and replied, "Yes, comrade chairman, unfortunately, that's the case."

"Is this above the Stasi capabilities? And why do two senior generals have to be involved in this investigation?"

"No, comrade chairman, it is not beyond our capabilities, but we have not resolved it. Not yet. And general Wolf and I are both involved to ensure that the investigation of the disappearance of a Politburo member's most senior assistant is handled efficiently and discreetly. Once we resolve the case, I will offer recommendations to you on how to announce or not announce it to the public."

"Who is leading the actual investigation?"

Mielke replied, "A colonel Schmidt is in charge, Alfred Schmidt. He has about twenty men at his disposal, the majority officers. They all are bright and experienced."

Ulbricht looked at Wolf, appeared to want to ask something, then turned to Egon Lanz. "And what do you have to say about your missing man? Did you hire and promote a deserter?"

"No, comrade chairman. He has been my secretary for over five years, working diligently and energetically for the party, for the Politburo and for me in all the tasks assigned to him. He has never said or done anything that would make me question his loyalty or his competence or his faith in socialism."

"I do not know why he disappeared. I can assure you that this is of the greatest interest and concern to me." Looking at Mielke, he added, "I have complete faith in our state security service so ably led by you, comrade general. I will do everything in my power to assist your team in the investigation."

Ulbricht stroked his goatee and allowed himself a slight smile. Perhaps he enjoyed the diplomatic reiteration that now it was the Stasi's responsibility to resolve the problem.

After an awkward pause, Ulbricht asked the question everyone feared, "How much does our missing secretary know? I remember seeing him in some of our Politburo meetings and events. I suppose, Comrade Lanz, that you granted him a top security clearance. What was he working on? How much damage can we expect? As you know, I am scheduled to meet with Brezhnev in the Kremlin. Does the situation require immediate coordination with the Soviets? I don't want to get ambushed by fallout from this crap in the midst of high-level talks."

Lanz replied, "His main focus was research into long range energy planning, and prognosticating future coal, oil and natural gas needs in our country and foreign regions, as well as investigating energy sources of interest to us. He also assisted me in other activities."

Ulbricht pondered the implications, asking, "May I assume that he had access to many of your activities and also Politburo proceedings? Now he has disappeared, with substantial classified knowledge that could be very damaging to our country if disclosed to our enemies. Making it short, how bad is it?"

A pale Egon Lanz answered, "Very. It is very bad."

Ulbricht stared at his fingernails for a moment, then commented, "That is not what I hoped to hear, but at least it puts a dimension on the potential damage."

Lanz said, with a light stammer, "Unfortunately, comrade chairman, that is not all. It is much worse. He did not work on all my projects, but he had unlimited access to my files, my office safe, my agendas, my travel schedule, and all my interactions with the Politburo."

Ulbricht stared at Lanz for a moment, then got up and paced the floor, for what seemed a long while to the other three. Markus Wolf speculated that Ulbricht was more worried about fallout with the Kremlin clique than damage to the fatherland, and that Lanz and Mielke were afraid of what Ulbricht may do next. Wolf was not particularly preoccupied about himself and enjoyed watching the others squirm.

Ulbricht finally stopped his pacing and asked, "I have heard the story in bits and pieces. I want to hear a clear, chronological summary of what happened and where the investigation stands. Comrade Lanz, Comrade Mielke, Comrade Wolf?"

General Mielke said, "I guess that's my territory. After the Politburo members left the Wolkenstein lodge, a group of the most senior secretaries and their clerical support stayed to organise and type meeting minutes and deal with administrative chores for the Politburo before returning to Berlin."

He consulted his notes and continued, narrating the chain of events and the change in travel arrangements that led to the early discovery of Bruno Hadler's disappearance.

After Ulbricht left, the two Stasi generals stayed to rehash the case, without staff. They had collaborated privately many times. When alone, they could ignore protocol. Mielke was the very able administrator and master politician navigating the party bureaucracy, Wolf the obsessively secretive fanatical technical wizard of foreign intelligence. They liked their jobs and did not covet each other's position. Without rivalry they could analyse all the known facts about Hadler's disappearance and speculate and fantasise about what might have happened.

Many alternatives and far out speculations were discussed and abandoned. The conclusion remaining was always the same: Bruno Hadler's disappearance was a voluntary defection with foreign help, not a kidnapping or accident.

Both generals would have liked to relegate the incident to a missing persons pending case file, to be handled routinely by junior staff. Hadler's linkage to the Politburo made it political, and chairman Ulbricht's interest and his preoccupation with the Kremlin's reaction elevated the political stakes.

At a lull in the conversation, Wolf asked, "Who do you think will replace Ulbricht?"

Mielke stared at him for a moment before answering, "You do realise that this kind of speculation could get you arrested if heard by the wrong people."

"Who is going to report it? Are you going to report my own question to me? Come on, general, this is a valid national security concern. We both need to be prepared to face a new leader and remain part of the inner team, while maintaining alertness and continuity during the transition period."

Mielke nodded in agreement, but asked, "Why are you bringing up this political stuff while we are talking about a missing bureaucrat?"

"Because, comrade general, if the disappearance of a senior bureaucrat with access to all secret Politburo proceedings coincides with a change in our highest leadership, my suspicion of foreign involvement will change from suspicion to conviction. We, not just you and I, but the whole security apparatus would be dealing with a massive problem for our republic."

The conversation changed to generalities while staff brought in coffee and snacks.

After they were alone again, Wolf continued, "We all have speculated about this, with every participant concluding that the disappearance was an act of foreign intervention, but hoping that a body would be found. It is still early in the investigation, but the discovery of a missing body is being recognised as wishful thinking. We have searched very, very thoroughly, with dogs, instruments, equipment and a large, experienced staff."

Mielke asked, "Do you suspect the Americans?"

Wolf thought for a while before replying, with hesitation rather than his customary assertiveness, "It is possible, but unlikely. I don't sense CIA vibrations. There is something devious, different about this case. It has a complicated twist; here I am following my instinct, not any known fact. The twists I am suspecting could be British, Chinese or Israeli," adding after a long pause, "or Russian, perhaps just inherited from Stalin, the grand master of unexplained disappearances."

Mielke was surprised, asking his spymaster, "You have an overactive imagination, General Wolf. Have you perhaps been rereading too many of your own case histories?"

The introduction of a Russian angle affected the speech of the two generals, becoming slightly more formal. Even among the highest ranks, discussions about the top political leaders were inducement to speak carefully, especially if it involved both Ulbricht and Brezhnev.

Wolf explained the reasoning for his suspicions. "Comrade General Mielke, you are the head of our state security, and I have no doubt that you have noticed the changes in behaviour in Chairman Walter Ulbricht. He is worried about Kremlin reactions and unsure whether to involve them. In the past, Ulbricht would threaten troublemakers with reporting them to Stalin, or later Khrushchev. These two seemed always willing to step in. Stalin is gone, so is Khrushchev, and now we are linked with Leonid Brezhnev. This linkage seems to have weakened over the last year. Today we witnessed Chairman Ulbricht being worried about Brezhnev's reaction to the disappearance of a secretary—granted, a high ranking one with access to many of our secrets."

"It is rumoured that Secretary General Brezhnev is seriously ill. Our information is a couple of heart attacks, diabetes, and assorted pancreatic and pulmonary ailments. Not a good prognosis."

"Perhaps Ulbricht's experienced political antenna is picking up some unspoken message from the Kremlin. Perhaps Brezhnev wants to push Ulbricht into an early retirement by means of little tortures and demotions. There is no doubt in my mind that Comrade Chairman Ulbricht is on his way out. I do not know what forces are at play, perhaps we'll find out, perhaps we won't. However, I wish to reiterate that we, the guardians of our country's state security, should be prepared to guide a smooth transition with clear allegiance to a new leader while remaining in our posts."

Mielke nodded. Wolf wondered if that meant agreement or just that he had heard. There followed a long period of silence. Both generals could handle silence to an extent that most people could not. Both had learned early in their police careers that this skill was a useful interrogation tool and enjoyed watching people squirm waiting for a question or a word.

Mielke finally said, "Let us keep the succession theories for another day and finish our discussion of disappearing Politburo secretaries. What happens next?"

Wolf summarised, "We have exhausted all the conventional procedures and searched for all normal and logical potential leads. You are familiar with that old saying that when all normal leads are exhausted, only the remaining abnormal could hold the key and must be investigated. That is what I intend to do."

"By a stroke of luck, the disappearance of Hadler was discovered shortly after he left the meeting with his colleagues, which set a time limit and consequently limited the distance he could have reached by motor vehicle, assuming of course that he managed to climb down from the lodge and rendezvous with accomplices on the highway."

"We rounded up all the vehicles within that distance and time limit. They all were stopped, questioned, inspected, and checked with vehicle registrations. They were confined to their hotel for another day and will be allowed to continue on their travel tomorrow, except a few cars and a couple of trucks."

"What was the problem with these?" asked Mielke.

"One of the truck drivers was arrested for trying to smuggle into the DDR a stash of Italian pornographic publications, the other had problems with his paperwork, I believe his cargo manifest. He is being held until they unload the truck and check it out. The cars had a few that were more interesting. One guy was wanted by the police for domestic violence, one woman had an expired driver license, we also had a drunk driver."

"And we had another one, this was a real prize. He was arrested for making an illegal U-turn at a police road block and fleeing. After a chase, he was caught and arrested for fleeing, speeding, resisting arrest, drunk driving without a license and in a stolen car, draft evasion, repeatedly spitting at policemen, urinating in the police car, then spitting on the neck of the cops in the front seat on the ride to the station, where, although handcuffed, he fondled and insulted female staff, bit the fingerprinting clerk, spit on the photographer's camera lens, then started a fight in the drunk tank, and bit the two guards who subdued him and dragged him to solitary, where he remains."

"I don't remember the exact sequence of the spitting and biting, and we don't know how this guy had so much liquid in him to enable all the spitting and urinating. The two young cops who initially caught him were thrilled for all the intercepted crimes they could list in their service experience record."

The two generals had a laugh about the incident. Mielke wanted a copy of the police report as a conversation piece. Wolf promised to have it sent, then continued, "In addition to some seventy cars and trucks, we tracked and inspected five buses. One from Poland returning home with a high school tour, one of our own regular municipal suburban buses, another from an Austrian bus company with a bunch of American retirees on a budget tour, one bus from our own state tourist agency with a team of Angolan soccer players scheduled to play in several of our cities, and one French tour bus with tourists."

"They all were checked out thoroughly twice and discreetly followed after they left Karl Marx Stadt. All the passengers had been individually inspected, their documents thoroughly checked, both in bright sunlight when they entered our country and again at four in the morning when they were unprepared and groggily half-asleep. The foreign buses of course were chaperoned by our own tour guides around the clock as soon as they entered the country."

"Our municipal bus carried only a dozen locals. We checked them out and let them go. The foreign buses, and our own tour bus carrying the Angolans, will not be allowed to leave the country nor this area for several days, until we check them out again. They were notified today. The Angolans made a big fuss and threatened to file a complaint through their embassy."

Mielke advised, "They did already. I just heard from the foreign ministry. They want us to be friendly with our African socialist allies and support friendly international sports events. It seems that the players are quite angry at having to miss training time and possibly some scheduled games."

Wolf replied, "Being angry is usually the first reaction when we start questioning someone, especially if it is a group. They find strength in numbers and want to show off in front of their team members. When we are through with them, they will be peeing in their pants, terrified at the prospect of a twenty-year prison term for collaborating with enemies of our country. If they know anything, they will tell us. If they know nothing, they will invent something. At that point, they will admit to everything and sign papers as we direct, in exchange for a reduced prison term, perhaps one that would allow them to play soccer in the prison yard after five years of good behaviour."

"Do you think our disappearing man painted his face and sat in the bus among a bunch of African blacks? Assuming he could have reached the highway. Are you serious?" Mielke asked.

"Yes, I am serious, but not in the sense that Bruno Hadler could be transformed into a Portuguese-speaking negro inserted into the visiting soccer team. I told you earlier that we had exhausted all realistic clues and options; therefore, what remains is the pursuit of the least realistic, the absurd. Accordingly, we start with the most absurd option, which seems to be a connection with the busload of blacks. Perhaps they saw something, perhaps they gave a hitchhiker a short ride, perhaps someone was bribed to mislead us in some way. Perhaps, if all investigations fail, someone like Chairman Ulbricht may accuse us that we didn't check out the black soccer team, and we'll have the pleasure of informing him that we did."

"Which bus is the next least likely, or most likely, or however you can label your reverse selection process," Mielke asked. Looking at his watch, he added, "Keep it short, I have to go soon. Please continue."

"Next in the absurd category would be the Polish high-school group. They are mostly teenagers but accompanied by several teachers and one political adviser. Our disappearing man could conceivably be incorporated into this group of white males of similar age, mid-forties. This would require the cooperation of our tour guide as well as students, teachers, political officers and driver. Not likely that all could be turned into accomplices, unless … unless our colleagues in the KGB were somehow inserted into the game by comrade Brezhnev. Far out and perhaps absurd, but we are looking at the absurd."

"Not to mention documents, wigs, photographs, motive, how to fool us, and other details," interjected Mielke.

Wolf responded, "Yes, there are many details, but if we pursue the basic premise, I believe we can also work out the details. Remember that some of our greatest successes started out with a hunch, unlikely and unreal, until we figured out all the absurd details and the hunch became a clear resolution."

"That leaves two buses, continue," Mielke urged.

"The Austrian bus with the American seniors would be next, in the decreasing absurdity scale."

Mielke asked, "Does that then mean that the decreasing absurdity scale matches an increasing counterpart likelihood that something will be found?"

"Yes, I think buses three and four are more likely to produce something of interest than the first two. Let's start with the Austrian bus, which belongs to a company owned by Austrian and ethnic Hungarian partners. They organise low budget tours into our DDR and other fraternal Eastern European socialist republics. We have seen them on many tours, always friendly and efficient, following all the rules, liked by all our staff, and not likely to become involved in anything that may jeopardise their excellent business relationship with the host countries."

"What are the passengers like?"

"A group of retired Americans, former manual workers, clerks, electricians, seamstresses, carpenters, beauticians. No intellectuals, military, or political types. We got copies of their visa applications. Most of them worked for the movie industry in the Los Angeles area. They all seem to know each other from work. Some go on tours together, and some participate in amateur little theatre plays, mostly in local schools and retirement homes. Quite a few have Hungarian names, have resided in the United States for many years. We sent their names to our colleagues in Budapest, but they found nothing of interest. It would be difficult to hide a younger man among the seniors, even if he were given a white wig and some myopic eyeglasses. The one characteristic that makes them interesting is that they would be the easiest to enrol in some plot as a group. They are familiar with each other and seem to collaborate in many ways."

"How about papers, background checks, home stories?"

"All their passports and papers are legitimate and current. We confirmed their home addresses and travel story by phone with children, relatives, and house sitters. Where we did not get a phone answer, we sent our local agent to check and talk to neighbours. They are clean. The only thing that keeps me interested is that they are the most likely to function as a cohesive group, perhaps willing to participate in some shenanigans just for the fun of an adventure. As you know, comrade, our business thrives on suspicions, intuitions, coincidences, the recognition of something interrupting a pattern."

Mielke looked at his watch again and asked, "Tell me about the fourth bus."

"A group of French socialist and communist tourists from Le Havre. About the same age as Hadler, who could have disappeared into this group easily, if they had let him. They argue a lot among themselves, seem to be enemies on soccer issues and friends on social issues. Our tour guide is worried about the non-stop arguing, he wonders if it should be ignored or if he should call the police. Our Stasi officer told him to calm down and call police only if their arguments turn into fist fights. The bus company is a French outfit. They make DDR tours two or three times a year."

Wolf had been called out to deal with an emergency phone call and missed part of the meeting where Hadler's case was being discussed. Mielke summarised the highlights. Wolf wanted to know whether they had discussed photographs, and could the Stasi announce the disappearance to the public and circulate Hadler's picture in newspapers, police stations, post offices, and television. Mielke replied in the negative, advising that the Presidium had unanimously vetoed publicity, and warned Wolf that they had been very stern about making sure that some idiot subordinate did not ignore their directive. It might change later; for now, great care was required.

The two generals felt oppressed by the feeling of impending doom that could befall their country if all the secrets stolen by Hadler ended in the hands of foreign enemies, and even worse, if all became public knowledge.

General Mielke got up and started to put on his greatcoat. He thanked Wolf for the report, and they agreed to meet again in a few days, sooner if something urgent developed. Before parting, they decided that Wolf would go to Saxony and shadow the tour buses and really turn up the heat on the investigation. It was clear that they had to resolve the mystery or let the buses out of the DDR. Keeping them longer would risk a big diplomatic mess. The Angolans already had started this process.

11. Leipzig, East Germany

After having seen the gigantic sculpture of the head of Karl Marx in their previous city, the tour members did not expect to be impressed again by monumental art or architecture, but they were surprised.

The first landmark to be visited in Leipzig, the German Democratic Republic's second most populous city, was the Battle of Nations Memorial, commemorating the defeat of Napoleon Bonaparte by the alliance of Prussia, Austria, Sweden, Russia, and the German states of the Confederation of the Rhine. The 100-meter-tall monument, about the height of a 25-story building, was the largest war memorial in Europe.

After his disastrous Russian campaign, Napoleon had tried again to impose his domination over Eastern Europe. His depleted army was unable to prevail over the allies in the 1823 battle of Leipzig, in which over 600,000 soldiers clashed. Napoleon was forced back into France and exiled to the island of Elba the following year.

Tour guide Seifert gave a lively narrative of the famous battle, managing to incorporate some comments about the wonderful outcome when the German speaking peoples allied with the Russian people, as now could be seen by the friendship of the German Democratic Republic and the Union of Soviet Socialist Republics. Her passengers were getting used to the periodic Communist commercials, treated it as a TV commercial back home, and enjoyed the rest of her excellent historical presentation.

That time long ago, an international array of armies had started a day in Leipzig in high spirits. At the end of a brutal three-day battle, the survivors, both winners and losers, were wounded, bleeding, filthy with mud, sweat, blood and excrement, numb from terror and exhaustion.

For the four busloads of foreign tourists, the monument tour in Leipzig had also started on a high note. They were rested, interested, pleased that everything was proceeding well, and looking forward to the day. At the end of the day, they were very upset, scared and fatigued. Their predicament was nothing compared to the historical slaughter, but to the present-day tourists, the day had turned sombre.

As the Long Beach travellers were leaving the war memorial their bus was stopped by police and directed to a parking area. Two other buses were already there, and another appeared shorty. A Stasi officer boarded and ordered everyone to get out and wait for an announcement. Tour guide Seifert and the Austrian driver had to follow the Stasi man to a small building across the parking area.

They returned after a while. A grim looking Seifert informed the group that the ongoing anti-terrorist investigation was continuing and that in order to protect the security of the German Democratic Republic and the safety of our dear visitors, the tour would continue as planned only until Dresden, but not be allowed to continue into Poland until further notice. The tour would remain in Dresden, pleasing accommodations would be provided, and there would be plenty of sightseeing. As soon as the investigations had progressed adequately, the tour would be allowed to continue. She would take questions later when more information and guidelines became available.

Richard Holley, wife Anne and friends John and Barbara Crawford were left speechless and in a cold sweat.

John spouted, "Goddam Krauts, what the fuck …" and was angrily interrupted by Barbara: "Watch your mouth, especially right now! Don't start that careless complaining again. You had agreed to watch your tongue. Hold it until we get back, that is if we get back."

The three Americans stared at Richard, hoping for guidance. Anne asked him to become Bruno Hadler again for a moment and think what would happen next and what they should do, attempt to flee, keep pretending, or do something else.

After a tense period of reflection, Richard said, sounding very tentative, "I think they haven't found anything. I think they don't have a clue about what they're looking for. I think they are getting pressure from above to resolve the matter. I think that having nothing new, they are going to recheck what they had checked before, hoping to find something they may have missed. I think the whole circus has to do with my disappearance. I don't know why it started so soon and why it became so active."

"Those are the thoughts I think, the assumptions I have thinking in my head. Now then let me tell you what I not just think but for sure do know. I know that cornered Stasi operatives are a very dangerous group. I know they are going to escalate their investigation into a very obnoxious, obsessed procedure. I know they are going to record all our conversations in buses, hotels, bathrooms. bedrooms, restaurants, and any outdoor spaces that they select. I know they will arrest you for any infraction, no matter how trivial, just to keep us a little while longer to see what they seeing can. They probably will install recording equipment in this bus while we sightseeing are. If we need to discuss anything in private, it will have to be whispered in a very low voice into your ear. Ja, very low voice. Now there is nothing we can do, except being ve ... very careful. Und don't write nothing in writing. Written papers can be reappearing at the wrong moment. Besser, be ... better let all others at once to know that everything are being recorded, emphasise that is so in every single thing in every place, at all times. every time, und not just listened to, but for later analysis recorded. And that probably will be effective zu ... be before we return to bus."

All four, including Richard, noticed that Richard's English deteriorated when under pressure. He stuttered slightly, his accent became more pronounced, parts of German words crept in, and some of his sentence structures drifted away from English usage.

John Crawford glowered at Richard, demanding, "What are you going to do about your speech, before you get us all in trouble?"

Barbara jumped in, starting to give her husband another warning about watching his language, which he interrupted angrily, "You want me to watch my speech? I am not the one unable to communicate in English! You better point your bitching where it belongs and remember to ..."

Richard, suddenly projecting a more assertive image than at any time before, admonished them, "Both of you! Be quiet and listen! We are facing a serious risk. Please clearly note that I said 'serious', not 'fatal' or 'impossible.' Pay attention. It is not a crime in the DDR to speak faulty English. Sedition, treason, kidnapping, and a very long list of other crimes against the state are serious matters. Protecting us against these is where we need to concentrate our efforts. Let's do it, step by step. Not all at once, but one step at the time. I know the system better than you do, so pay attention to what I advise. There are other parts of our tour where you know best, and in these I will follow your advice.

We have suddenly a changed situation and additional scrutiny that we had not expected. Right now, it is imperative that everyone in our group be fully aware of the changed circumstances, and very especially, that everything we say or do will be recorded. We must be prepared as of now!"

The Crawfords and Anne managed to relay the warning to the other travel companions, while they all were loitering in the parking area. When they re-boarded the bus, everyone was glum but informed.

The Crawfords and Anne also had to contend with a new worry. Up to know they had assumed that Richard was a defecting minor bureaucrat. Then, when Richard became assertive, they sensed that they were dealing with someone of a higher calibre. Richard had not raised his voice and remained polite throughout his short harangue, but somehow conveyed very clearly that he was someone in a position of great authority, whether through his own rank, or whether he projected power in a position representing someone of a very high rank. They compared notes later, found that all three had the same conviction. The newly estimated high rank of their travel companion also explained the increased police activity and the new inspections and the delay in being allowed to leave the country. If they were abetting a high-ranking defection, the level of risk was obviously much higher than previously assumed.

After lunch, the tour continued with the worldwide heritage of Johann Sebastian Bach. They visited the Lutheran St. Nicholas Church and the St. Thomas Church, where Martin Luther had preached, and where Bach directed the musical activities and composed his most important works during the 27 years he lived in Leipzig. After they visited Bach's grave, they were treated to a concert of Bach's music. The calm, regular, comfortable, glorious rhythm of the great man's music and the sacred historical surroundings helped to dispel the sombre mood of the travellers. Richard was particularly touched, and his mood change helped to dispel the fear that had overwhelmed him, Anne, and the Crawford's earlier in the day. The four were touched that they were listening to music and in surroundings from long ago, spanning centuries that had seen many events that deeply affected humankind. Later, at dinner, others on the tour commented that the concert had a similar calming effect on them, putting in perspective a tour delay of a few days compared to the much bigger fears and problems that had been dealt with in the old churches since long before Bach composed his music.

The change from pleasant day to one less pleasant was not limited to old battles and modern bus tours. Colonel Alfred Schmidt had started his day in a positive frame of mind. He had been informed that General Wolf would be joining the investigation in person. Schmidt was uneasy about Wolf's visit but attributed it to the prominence of the missing secretary. They decided to remain in Leipzig for the day and set up set up their field office in Dresden on the following day, which was the scheduled arrival date there for the bus tours. Wolf had requested two private offices, for himself and an assistant. Schmidt had arranged these and was ready for the high-ranking boss, with whom he had spoken only once but whose reputation was well known. He also had issued the orders to stop the four busses from leaving the country and not be allowed beyond Dresden, about one hour's travel time from the Polish border.

Everyone involved had worked to capacity for several days without finding anything. Schmidt hoped that Wolf would finally realise that there was no choice but to distribute photographs and involve the public and the press.

Schmidt had assumed that General Wolf would appear in Leipzig in civilian clothes and remain seated in some dark corner in the background, observing and analysing, as was his custom. Wolf shocked everyone by appearing in full dress uniform, pulling rank with every gesture and being obnoxious to the extreme in asserting his power. Schmidt realised that he was going to have a rough time.

Wolf wasted no time in criticising the collective work of the group of Stasi officers assembled in front of him, concentrating his vitriol on colonel Schmidt, their commanding officer.

After a long, stunned silence, Wolf demanded, "Does no one have anything to say? Not only is your collective performance deplorable, but you seem to have become deaf mutes!"

Colonel Schmidt stuttered, "Co … comrade general. I would like to respond to your comments. We all agree that we have not found a single clue, and not for lack of trying. As you know, we have been pursuing two parts to the mystery, one being how our man got out of the lodge and down to the highway, and the other, how he got away from there, assuming that that is what happened and not something totally bizarre that no one has imagined yet."

"The first part, getting away from the lodge, is the most mysterious. He either managed to sneak past our own Stasi guards, or somehow get across the river. Sneaking past the guards seems the more likely possibility, crawling through the bushes and down the granite cliffs, except no traces, no footprints were found. There still is snow on the ground, and where the snow melted it is muddy. We speculated about fantasies like helium balloons or cables and pulleys to get across the river, but no traces of any kind were found. We had commando divers from the navy check it out. They could deal with the freezing temperature but because of the violent current and the rocks declared it not swimmable, even if hanging on to a rope. We found no clues, not even microscopic ones."

"The other part, the highway, assumes that somehow, he made it to where he got a ride on a car, a motorcycle, a bicycle, a bus, or a truck. By luck, his disappearance was discovered early, and we were able to limit the search area. We intercepted all traffic. We found some interesting petty lawbreakers, but no missing politburo secretaries. We found nobody suspicious, dead or alive. We questioned everyone, hoping someone might have seen or heard some little clue. We found nothing. Having run out of options, we again request you reconsider the release of photographs and involve the public. Someone may recognise …"

Wolf screamed, "Shut up! Are you stupid? Don't you understand your orders? The highest authorities have decided to keep this disappearance quiet for now, and the instructions were clear, to all of you, that we would not announce this to the public, nor would we issue photographs to local police or others, like tour guides or hotel staff. Are you trying to contradict your superiors? Do you think you know better?"

Schmidt had not been yelled at like this since basic training, nor had he ever heard a general having such a fit.

He stammered, "No general, I was just inquiring …"

Wolf resumed his yelling "Don't be an idiot! Don't you think we all know about the use of photographs in the search for missing persons or escaped criminals? Every local cop knows this! It was decided at the onset of this investigation to keep it quiet, not public!"

Wolf looked at the officers, one by one. His expression was particularly menacing, intimidating. They all hoped not to be selected for questioning, and jumped when Wolf roared, "You pretend to be elite counterespionage officers! Dammit, goddammit! Start thinking and acting like one! You especially should be fully aware that because of the privacy concerns the investigation was assigned to the counterespionage unit of the German Democratic Republic's state security service, not the local cops!"

"What is the fucking matter with you all! How in the hell did you pass your entrance exams? You are wearing the uniforms of officers in our most elite service! Do you think these uniforms are just props for your social life? Perhaps you should be wearing the uniforms of maintenance men in a sewage treatment plant! If you still are under the effects of whatever you recently smoked, you probably would screw up our sewage system because the maintenance manual is printed in high-German and doesn't have enough pictures!"

One young officer cleared his throat. Wolf noticed it and asked him he wanted to say something. The young man shook his head in the negative, and a furious Wolf screamed, "Is that how you respond to a superior officer, by shaking your head? Goddammit, not only is this outfit's performance deplorable, but you men don't even know the basics of military discipline! What's your name and what are your duties? No, forget it. Report to Colonel Schmidt later and I will see you both after this meeting, as well as anyone else who needs guidance."

"Listen men, we have an assignment that has both political and time pressures. Let's move our asses much faster! Do you think we got the assignment to assist the local cops? So, once again, we got the assignment due to the political sensitivity and the privacy concerns. This is a high-ranking state matter, not a fucking goddam neighbourhood missing person's case."

"Have you forgotten what in the hell we do, why we exist? It is a disgrace that I even have to ask the goddam question! Don't you remember that we are trained to catch spies and saboteurs without photographs, names, addresses, locations, dates or even countries?"

"Most of our cases start with a suspicion that some state secret found its way to where it was not supposed to be! We know nothing, except that there is a suspicion, which may be nothing! That is what our unit deals with! Vague suspicions without any goddam clues! We have to catch spies and saboteurs that may or may not exist! Most of our energies are burned away trying to figure out if what we are trying to solve even exists!"

"If you don't like it, I can arrange your transfer to an infantry unit to train draftees in mud logistics. Or, if it is your idea of police work, you can join the rural cops and staple photographs of wanted criminals on lampposts or post office bulletin boards. So, stop contradicting my orders! Is that understood, Colonel Schmidt?"

"I am not contradicting you, general, I just …"

"Goddammit, you are doing it right now!"

Schmidt was very pale and obviously uncomfortable. He took a deep breath and said, "I am sorry, general, for my bad choice of words. I am a career officer and fully understand and believe in the chain of command and the obedience to my superiors and my duties to our country. But I also believe in doing my best in the performance of my duties, which means that I must use all means at my disposal to resolve the task assigned to me. This includes soliciting guidance from my superiors. I believe my superiors will provide this guidance if it is within their purview to do so."

Wolf commented, now in a normal voice, "I suggest you choose your words with care, colonel."

Schmidt nodded, saying, "Yes, general, thank you for the warning. I have a couple of questions. The first is whether we should contact Bruno Hadler's ex-wife. They divorced several years ago. She is remarried to one of our diplomats, currently stationed in Cuba. Hadler has no other relatives, and no children. Since we are questioning everyone even remotely connected to …"

"No, do not contact the ex-wife. What's the other question?"

Schmidt hesitated, then asked, "Comrade general, since we cannot publish photographs, would it be possible to just show them to our officers and to the tour guides on the busses? I think all our officers, knowing who our mystery man is, have looked him up in news photographs or government rosters and have a good idea of the man's appearance. The tour guides know someone important is missing, but not who. Perhaps seeing a picture would trigger a memory."

Wolf admired the colonel's guts in pushing the photographs but was not inclined to encourage a subordinate's independence. He let him dangle for a while, then responded, "Yes, colonel, you may show photographs to the tour guides, but not leave them. Concurrently, have someone compare Hadler's photograph with all the passport photographs, including women and the negros from Angola."

This seemed to startle Schmidt, who asked, "Do you think they could have substituted someone on a bus?"

Wolf grinned, "We are discussing far out possibilities. Perhaps Hadler has been painted black and is now in the soccer team."

Schmidt questioned, "Would that not require a passport substitution? We know beyond a doubt that all the passports are legitimate and were used to enter the country."

Wolf answered, "Perhaps there was no passport substitution. Perhaps there was only a person substitution, using the same passport. Then we have an extra person running loose. Perhaps a body by now, but we found no unexplained bodies. However, if there is a substituted person in the area, he could have a fake passport that would suffice for a perfunctory check by low-ranking transportation clerks or the local cops, not scrutinised by us."

Schmidt nodded, fascinated. Wolf grinned, "There are all kinds of possibilities, even without photographs in every post office or lamppost, don't you agree?"

Schmidt agreed, smiling carefully. The general reminded him of a sleeping bear, who may only appear to be sleeping.

The rest of the officers cautiously started to relax. For a moment, they feared that their colonel would be fired or transferred, but now it seemed that Wolf had calmed down.

The remainder of the day and the following day passed in frantic activity but without arguments. Wolf spent most of his time on the telephone with his Berlin headquarters but was immediately available between calls to participate in the missing secretary project. They reviewed all their previous investigations, and then one more time, with Wolf and Schmidt breathing down their necks.

Wolf gathered the group for what he called 'a final Leipzig meeting' to set strategy for Dresden and to inform them of Berlin developments.

He looked at his officers and started, "We are running out of time. In Dresden, we'll have a few days, at most, to find and arrest any wrongdoers, or let them go. If something is discovered after they cross the border, we still could grab them with the help of our Polish counterparts, but that gets messy. So, we better concentrate our efforts to resolve the mystery in Dresden."

"We have investigated and speculated about how our man got out of the lodge. We determined that he could not have gotten past four sets of our guards on the two paved access roads, and that he could not have crawled through the shrubbery and down the cliffs without leaving a single footprint, trace, broken twig. We also dismissed helium balloons, overhead cables or some other contraptions being set up without being noticed by guards, staff and guests. Therefore, let's not waste any more time on landside escapes and concentrate on the river. The river route was also investigated without finding clues or believable theories. However, here we may find our break due to one very special fact, which is that the river was not guarded, because it was considered safe from invasion due to all the physical barriers."

"The politburo security planners always looked at the river side as a possible intruder route, never as an escape route. The physical obstacles are the same in any direction, but the big, very big factor in our investigation is that the river side was unguarded. It was the one location where something could have been constructed, assembled, or launched without being observed."

"Accordingly, by tomorrow morning I want everyone's theory on how to escape across the river and get to the highway. Forget all the impediments discussed before. Your assignment consists of figuring out a way of crossing the torrent of fast-moving freezing water whipping and splashing between rocks. Assume you are a prisoner of war planning your escape. Consider everything, including the fact that you can have resources and help not available to a POW. Give it your best. Remember, a POW may have a long time to plan something. You all have until tomorrow morning. Colonel Schmidt and I will question each of you and we'll discuss your plan as a group."

"I also would like to share some good news, well, perhaps they are good, perhaps not, but news, nevertheless. We had a team in Berlin examining comrade Hadler's apartment. Two officers and several civilian Stasi technicians examined everything and found nothing that could have any connection with the disappearance. Their departmental commander and I gave them a motivational speech to encourage a repeat, more thorough examination of the premises."

Colonel Schmidt smiled to himself visualising the 'motivational speech' the Berlin team had enjoyed. One of his officers across the room noticed the smile, understood and smiled back. Soon a few other officers joined in. Wolf also noticed and decided to join the gesture.

"Well, gentlemen, I am glad to note that you find some humour in hearing that your colleagues in Berlin also needed a lecture. You all got the mild, bland version reserved for delicate, innocent young virgins who still can be taught. However, don't forget, always keep it somewhere in the back of your minds, that our country rewards success, but also that reprimands for sloppy work and dereliction of duty can be escalated to demotions, prison terms and executions for treason."

No one knew whether Wolf was threatening or joking, but there were no more smiles.

Wolf continued, "One of the technicians found a large-scale map of Hong Kong, its printing date coinciding with the date of a trip by a couple of politburo members and Hadler to attend a conference on energy. The trip, several years ago, was no secret and is of no use to our investigation. We had a Chinese speaker study the map for anything interesting. He found that it was a run-of-the-mill tourist map available everywhere, but there was a small legend in Chinese listing a catalogue number and the fact that it was a second printing, done one year ago, long after Hadler's official visit to the British colony."

Schmidt commented, "That's very interesting. It fits your theory that this whole show does not have a CIA pedigree. It could be American, but another agency."

Wolf nodded. "Yes. Or this could be a Chinese or British connection. It also could be a very clever piece of disinformation. There is more. Hadler has several books about China, and a large Chinese-German dictionary. These were all printed before his trip, therefore explainable. He also has a large world atlas. Laboratory examination determined that it was most frequently opened to a map of Southern China. Some spots on the edge were determined to be coffee stains. It seems that our man spent some time looking at this map. Anyway, these are clues, but we don't know yet what of. I have a team in Berlin pursuing the China angle. I'll keep you all informed if we find something. For now, I want everyone to figure out a good way to escape across the river, and from there to the highway, where he must have gotten transportation."

"If his transportation was in one of the busses, he must be taking the place of someone who was on the bus before the event. That means someone is moving around in our country illegally. We need to find him as well."

The tourists spent their second day in Leipzig sightseeing in historical places and museums. In the afternoon, they wrote the mandatory postcards for mailing by the tour guide. They started to enjoy the procedure and started to write funny things, pretending not to suspect that all would be read by some bureaucrat. They enjoyed figuring out typical American jargon, slang, jokes, and sports references that would make the censors waste time trying to figure out what it meant. They found much material in stories and plays dealing with

American rural life in the South or the West by the likes of William Faulkner and John Steinbeck, thoroughly enjoying retelling and mixing up parts and characters of some of the classics.

On the following morning, they continued their tour, traveling to Dresden on a scenic route, and regaining their confidence.

They stopped for a bathroom and coffee break along the way. Richard and his three companions sat in a booth away from other ears to whisper about their predicament. Richard had regained his composure and was firm in his reassurances that all would be okay. He pointed out that there were other buses involved, which he considered evidence that the Stasi were fishing, not pursuing a clue. He also pointed out that the Stasi had not posted photographs or involved the local police, considered evidence that they wanted to keep it quiet. He reasoned that any passport checks would done by junior staff, probably bored by now. He was convinced that his makeup would hold and that any coincidental resemblance of his elder persona to the much younger missing politician would be dismissed as coincidental.

They discussed again what had been discussed before about what to do if Richard could not answer or remember some detail about life in Long Beach. They had settled on blaming memory on beginnings of Alzheimer's, not unusual in their senior age group. The tour interruption in Dresden continued to be the main preoccupation. They kept reassuring each other that Richard's skilled, Hollywood level professional makeup would hold.

"The one thing that worries me," Richard concluded, "is that one of us could get nervous during a passport check, trembling or stuttering, which, if noted, would lead to more thorough questioning that we could not survive. Do any of you have tranquilisers that we could take?"

The Crawfords had some sleeping pills, which could be used in advance of an inspection, even if it caused them to fall asleep later in the tour. They hoped that these pills would work as well as tranquilisers to calm jitters.

The one thing that could not be faked was fingerprints; however, they had been fingerprinted when they began the tour, when the real Richard was among the travellers. This item had been taken care of.

Next morning the Stasi officers assembled in a large briefing room at their Dresden regional headquarters about eight in the morning. Everyone was dressed in pressed uniforms, shaved, combed, looking sharp and polished, in contrast to the previous days when fatigue had allowed loose ties, rolled up shirtsleeves and wrinkled uniforms. The officers had arranged to have their clothes washed, dry cleaned and pressed overnight. Wolf and Schmidt noticed and complimented the men for returning to proper military decorum. There was a new energy in the team. They felt that the days of banging their heads against a brick wall had come to an end and that some breakthrough was imminent. Their fear of General Wolf was tempered by the expectation that they would learn something from the legendary head of their service.

Colonel Schmidt started, "The general and I decided we would interview each of you privately, one by one, to avoid being influenced by the words of your colleagues. We want to hear your unedited, personal theory on how the escape across the river can be accomplished, no matter how crazy your idea may seem. Afterward we all will discuss it as a group. Initially, we need the uninhibited input of your collective brains."

Wolf added, managing to sound threatening without raising his voice, "Remember, gentlemen, we had above average education and training, and consequently, are supposed to have, and use, brainpower to resolve mysteries without clues. In this case, we are almost there. We have a defined event, name, place, date, time, and distance parameters, we are operating openly and officially in our own country, not trembling in fear of discovery in some foreign miserable hiding place. Colonel Schmidt, shall we start?"

Schmidt pointed to a lieutenant sitting in the front row. The three of them stood up and headed to an adjacent interview room. Wolf gestured to wait and asked the selected officer, "How much sleep did you get last night?"

"Not enough, general."

Wolf and Schmidt exchanged looks. Wolf nodded and Schmidt asked all to pay attention. After a pause, he addressed the group in a conversational tone.

"Yesterday General Wolf admonished one of you, and for the benefit of all of us, that in order to function efficiently, this team has to maintain military discipline and clear communications. One last time, if you cannot answer a simple, direct question clearly and responding precisely to what has been asked, I will remove you from this team and reassign you to a different unit. Let it be clear that we will not allow you to answer questions from a superior officer with head shaking, mumbling or with answers to questions that were not asked. If you don't know the answer, clearly state so. Is that clear? Does anyone wish to be transferred? This is your chance to be transferred at your own request without reduction in rank or endangering your pension. However, if we must fire you for insubordination, disobedience, disrespecting superiors or for plain stupidity, your career is over."

There were no takers. All ranks, lieutenants, captains, two majors, remained silent.

Getting back to his target, Wolf asked again, "How much sleep did you get last night, lieutenant? Do you understand the question? I did not ask you if you thought you had enough sleep."

"Yes, general. I understand the question. I slept four hours."

"Thank you."

Wolf then requested to start the interviews with someone else, to give the ashen-faced lieutenant a chance to regain his composure.

The interviews proceeded swiftly. Each officer was asked for name, rank, assignment, or role in the subject investigation, and how much they had slept. Wolf seemed to want to assess their level of fatigue or sleep deprivation. Two of the men were sent to rest for six hours after they had submitted their river crossing theories, with assurances that this was no reflection on their good service, and that they would be of more value to the investigation if they were not so fatigued. Both Wolf and Schmidt took brief notes.

After their interviews, the officers were led to a large conference room, where they had coffee and snacks, and enjoyed smoking and comparing notes, separated from any contact with those still waiting their turn.

Meanwhile, at the hotel they had just finished breakfast. Tour guide Seifert was addressing her tour group and arranging for international telephone calls and updating the group about all the travel arrangements that had to be changed. She could deal with the schedule changes in East Germany and would remain as their tour guide until they departed for Poland, where the Polish tour guide would take over. She admitted that her biggest problem was that the DDR authorities were unable to give her a firm departure date. They estimated between two and four days, which was no problem on the German side, but no arrangements could be made in Poland without dates.

She further reassured them that no additional costs would be incurred on the German side for the extended lodging, meals, and sightseeing, and that the Austrian bus company would collaborate without additional charges. The question put to the travellers was to choose between extending the tour time to visit all the cities originally scheduled and change their plane reservations or skip the Wroclaw tour and go directly to Warsaw and keep their airplane reservation as scheduled.

They all voiced their concern about additional costs. A few had no problems with extending the return date, but the majority did not want to postpone their return home due to previous appointments and commitments, plus house-sitting and pet-sitting arrangements. It was soon decided that they would keep their Warsaw departure date and skip the Wroclaw visit. Tour guide Seifert and the bus company would make all the arrangements as soon as the elusive dates could be pinned down. Several of her charges thanked her for being so helpful, told her how much they appreciated her and how they wished she could continue as their tour guide in Poland. She beamed with pleasure and even blushed.

Having finished with the discussions relating to the delay in their departure to Poland, Seifert outlined the tour program for the day, which was dedicated to the World War 2 bombing, to be followed in subsequent days with visits to a porcelain factory and several museums that had been reconstructed. They boarded their bus and started towards the old city centre area.

Back in Vienna, having finished all business in Austria, Alan Mackenzie was packing to fly to Warsaw to meet the tour group upon their arrival. He had no idea about the delay in East Germany. The phone rang, it was the hotel reception desk, informing Herr Mackenzie that he had received a letter by messenger. Alan asked that it be delivered to his room. It was from the bus company, in German, with an attached unsigned English translation.

To Our Esteemed Clients:

In all our tours, we fully cooperate with the authorities of the host country and render them all assistance in the performance of their duties, to ensure compliance with the local regulations and the safety of our passengers, and to maintain the cordial relationships that allow us to provide you the high level of quality, courtesy, comfort and safety that has always been the hallmark of our international tours.

We just have been informed by the honourable authorities of the German Democratic Republic that our tour will be detained in Dresden for a few days, pending an internal investigation of suspected law violations in the area. We will be allowed to proceed to Poland as soon as the local investigation is complete. Our bus is in a group of four international tour buses, all facing the same situation. We do not foresee any problems with our bus except the time delay.

Perhaps some of you may have in the past experienced a delay with another transportation company that resulted in additional costs for lodging, meals and cancellations. Please be assured that it is our policy to not charge for any additional costs related to an unforeseen delay or time extension. Neumann & Rakosi will pay for all additional expenses caused by the delay, including meals and lodging, added airfare fees, and incidentals. We will do our best to make your additional days on our tour as comfortable and pleasant as possible, with our most sincere apologies for any inconveniences.

Thank you very much for your truly appreciated patronage.
Faithfully yours,
Dr Werner Neumann
Managing Director
Neumann & Rakosi International Tours Ltd.

Alan felt as if he had been punched in the stomach after reading the letter. All the emotions of years ago, when he was notified that an entire busload of his trained agents had been send to their deaths, returned, and hit him hard. He sat on the bed, trying to figure out what to do. His first decision was to order a pot of coffee from room service, his second was to open a small bottle of gin from the mini-bar and drink a gulp. He chain-smoked until the coffee arrived, then he called Frank Kolozsvary, who already had returned home with his family.

It was four in the morning in Wisconsin. A sleepy Frank answered the phone, became quickly alert when he heard Alan's voice. They joked briefly about operating on Stasi hours, then Alan read him the letter. Frank asked to call back in about ten minutes and not from the bedroom, where Maria was waking up and asking who had called.

Frank called back through the intermediate secure phone line that had been set up by the State Department, which showed up on the hotel switchboard as if originating in Austria.

Alan reread the letter aloud several times, both the German and English versions, Frank listening carefully for word nuances. They concluded that the letter had been written or drafted by Istvan Rakosi, the elder of the family, in his florid courtier's German syntax, and that it was specifically directed to Alan, to reassure him that they did not expect a repetition of events of long ago. They further concluded that the marketing goodwill about no additional costs was a clever reassurance that the Stasi didn't have a firm clue and were still fishing, therefore that no additional consequences were likely except the loss of a few days, that the Warsaw departure date was still applicable, and to keep cool and proceed as planned.

They also decided that Alan would notify Abigail Wilkinson, then fly to Warsaw as planned, and that Frank would fly to Los Angeles as fast as possible to man some of the Long Beach phones that may receive difficult inquiries.

After fretting about the time difference with Washington, he decided to call anyway and leave a message for Abigail to call Frank for an update, as he, Alan, probably would be on the plane to Warsaw by the time she got up. Surprisingly, Abigail's phone was answered immediately by a male voice, who politely inquired about the purpose of the call. Alan said he just wanted to leave a message regarding a European bus tour, was told to hold. In a brief moment, Abigail was on the line, sounding totally awake and self-assured. She listened to Alan's detailed report and the letter, thanked him for the update, and advised that she would give Frank a ride to Los Angeles to get him there as soon as possible, and that she would of course inform her husband, who would consider State Department involvement if a tour group of American citizens was accused of something and arrested in East Germany.

Alan called Frank to report, but his phone was busy. He later found out that Frank had been talking to Abigail, who had called immediately and instructed Frank to be ready at the Appleton airport at eight in the morning Central time to fly to Los Angeles.

Maria was agitated at the escalation of a project that she had assumed finished after their Vienna trip. Frank reassured her that he was going to Long Beach, not Eastern Europe, because his assistance was crucial due to an emergency in Europe. She wanted to know if again a busload of Hungarians was going to be executed. He told her that this time it was Hungarian-Americans, she resented him joking about it. Both then decided it would be smarter to drop the discussion, and they hugged and kissed as he left for the airport.

At the Stasi headquarters in Dresden, all the individual interviews had been concluded. Wolf and Schmidt had a brief private meeting in an office, then joined the large group in the conference room.

Colonel Schmidt started, "Thank you all for your thorough analyses. It was remarkably interesting that you all reached essentially the same conclusions, the differences being primarily in details and in elements that you couldn't resolve. Curiously, what seemed insoluble to one was easily solved by another, who had an unresolved element of his own, but clarified by someone a few interviews down the line."

"Now we need to confirm our consensus, first the getting across the river, then the escape from the Wolkenstein Lodge area. General, do you wish to comment?"

"Not yet. Please proceed with your summary, colonel."

Schmidt continued, "What emerged is a consensus that the river crossing could not be assisted by overhead cables, as this would require a pole or another structure on each side of the river. It was clear that the cables could only be discreetly anchored on one side, and that our man would have to be in the wild ice water and dragged across."

"This scenario requires two sets of cables, better said ropes, one to pull our man across, and the other to prevent him from being dragged downriver by the current. The upriver rope would basically function as a pendulum, able to move a weight sideways but remaining at a fixed distance from a point above the crossing. The lower rope would pull the man sideways, across the river."

"Another issue is that the ropes can be anchored only at the opposite side of the river, as no structure could be erected on the lodge side without being noticed, which in turn requires that the ropes would have to be thrown across the river, about fifteen meters, too far to throw across by hand."

"There are harpoon shooting guns and rockets that are used for rope throwing in maritime rescues or comparable operations, but guns are loud and rockets highly visible in the dark. There are quiet compressed air guns, but they can only propel a light load. The solution is to shoot a light thin line with a compressed air device across the river, to hook on the railing at the lodge side with a padded hook that leaves no mark. This thin line would be attached to the two heavier ropes, which could be tied together, as at the bottom of a vee. Our man could then pull the ropes across and tie them on himself. He could also coil the thin rope and the hook and take them with him, leaving no traces."

General Wolf interjected, "Here we had several discussions about how many people were needed for the river rescue. The majority felt that two men were needed, one for each rope. The basis for the determination was the need to economise manpower to the minimum. This is the desirable way in most cases; however, this operation is so elaborate and well organised that it seems to not be on a low budget. I think that we should assume sufficient manpower to secure a successful operation. My feeling is that they should have at least three, perhaps four men, dealing with ropes, equipment and vehicle. Adding our defector, they would have to hide and transport four or five men, plus equipment. So, we can forget bicycles, motorcycles or small cars. We are looking at vans. I also assume that anyone being dragged across an icy torrent banging at rocks without a padded thermal suit will need some assistance when they pull him out. Colonel Schmidt, please summarise the second part, the getaway scenario."

The officers in the room were awake, interested, pleased. There was a palpable feeling of achievement, of relief, of something hard to define, but clearly a reaction to progress, to seeing a path leading to resolution of the problem they had been obsessing about.

Schmidt shared the feeling of accomplishment, continuing with, "Thus we get our deserter across the river, out of the water, at the foot of a ten-meter rocky cliff. He is helped in climbing up, or carried if he is unable. At the top is a small observation area with a few picnic tables, with a good view of the Wolkenstein Lodge. This place is closed in winter, screened from the road by shrubbery. Here we find a level gravelled parking area, where a vehicle, we assume a van, could be waiting, a place to change into dry clothing, hide equipment and provide escape transportation."

Wolf joined the narrative with, "At this point, we reached another wye in the road, where we had to choose between the obvious and the counterintuitive alternative. Typically, escapes near a frontier trend towards crossing the border as soon as possible, getting the hell out of the country, as far and as fast as possible. Wolkenstein is near the Czech border, the obvious direction. As you all know, our border was tight. At night, all road crossings are closed, and crawling through the shrubbery in rocky cliffs, mud and snow, cutting holes through fences, abandoning and hiding a vehicle, all in the dark, soon forced us into accepting the illogical other direction, getting deeper into East Germany, and hiding until more favourable escape circumstances become available."

"In our debriefing, the majority of you favoured an escape by a private car or van. By a stroke of luck, comrade Hadler's disappearance was discovered early enough to block roads immediately and contain the search in a manageable area. The problem with the car theory is that we intercepted only two vans, a number of small cars and a number of trucks. We checked them all, very thoroughly, both the vehicles and the people. We held them for days and then checked them again. We found a few anti-socialist petty criminals, but not comrade Hadler. We had to let them go."

"The only other vehicles left were four international tour buses and a local transit bus. The local bus and the local commuters were cleared easily, leaving only the tour buses. One of the buses belongs to our own tourist agency, but for this investigation we will treat it the same as the foreign buses."

"It seemed, it still seems, totally absurd that Hadler escaped hiding in one of the tour buses. However, we had exhausted all the logical, reasonable, rational options we could think of, without finding a solution, leaving only the illogical, unreasonable, irrational options to explore."

"The question always was how to insert someone into a bus tour. The passengers are required to have extensive documentation, they are supervised by our tour guides, they eat and sleep in designated hotels. Adding a passenger would require the collaboration of the entire tour group and hotels along the way. It is impossible to suddenly add a passenger to a tour without it being noticed. So, this issue became part of the brainstorming assignment you all got yesterday evening. This morning we had the consensus that the only possible way to incorporate Hadler into a tour was to substitute him for someone else on the tour, who would have to disappear. We decided to leave the … the double, for lack of a better word, to another, separate investigation. Right now, the pressure is on finding Hadler, not his double. It was also agreed that Hadler would have to use the same passport used by the double to enter the country, to get past our usual checks. Colonel Schmidt?"

Schmidt informed, "This morning we received the results of the comparison of Hadler's picture with the passport photos of the tour passengers. There was no match. We also had asked the tour guides to select a likely match, someone who could be disguised as Hadler. They picked two in the French group, about the same age as Hadler, and one in the American group, much older."

Wolf said, smiling at the colonel, "It seems that the photographs, at least in the limited way we have used them to date, are not as definitive as we may like. We will check out the three selected possible matches later, just to make sure. Right now, we need to cast a wider net. The only fool proof identification method we have nowadays are fingerprints. Please arrange to have them all fingerprinted, at once. Include all tour passengers and drivers in the four busses. We may skip our own tour guides."

Schmidt asked, "That involves over a hundred people. Do you want to involve the local cops or use our own? We have only limited fingerprint processing capability in the Dresden station. No problem doing it, but it may take all day."

Wolf replied, "Let's keep it in house. Stasi only, Dresden station only. We already have Hadler's print on file here. I don't care how long it takes; they are not going anywhere."

A sergeant came into the conference room, apologised and handed Colonel Schmidt a message, who read it and told the others, "We have a second complaint from the foreign office regarding our detention of the Angolan soccer team. Their diplomats are getting hysterical. A man from our foreign office is outside waiting to complain to comrade general Wolf in person, insisting on seeing him right now, immediately."

Wolf ordered, "Arrest him for interfering with a state security investigation!"

Schmidt smiled and commented, "He'll be out in a day."

Wolf agreed, "Yes, but that foreign office flunky will have learned something of the world outside of the fluff he is used to. On second thought, I also want to know what idiot sent him, especially with that insolent demand for my immediate attention. Perhaps we should teach him a lesson as well."

Schmidt assigned a lieutenant to take care of it all.

After some thought, Wolf ordered, "I want to start the fingerprinting with the Angolans. Get our own Portuguese interpreter and listen attentively to what I am saying right now, I want to advise them slowly, in very plain, very clear, undiluted, unequivocal, undiplomatic language that we will arrest anyone who complains." After a pause, he cracked one of his brief, rare smiles and added, "It is not likely, but it certainly would be interesting to find Bruno Hadler's fingerprints on the hand of a fake black African soccer player."

12. Dresden, East Germany

In Appleton, Frank Kolozsvary arrived at the small Outagamie County airport about a quarter to eight. His instruction had been to wait in the airport's single waiting room. He expected a small private plane, perhaps for ten or twelve passengers. He saw no small plane; they probably had not arrived yet. The only plane on the tarmac was the regional turboprop to Chicago, where you changed to a bigger plane, sometimes a jet, to go anywhere.

He watched a jet land, uncommon in Appleton. He did not recognise the airline. He went to the coffee shop and ordered a coffee and a donut for breakfast. As he was taking his first bite a loudspeaker announced that Mr Kolozsvary's plane was waiting and to proceed towards the boarding area. He took another bite of his donut and a gulp of coffee.

The boarding area was deserted except for a young man waiting for him. He had a sedan at the gate and drove them to the private aircraft terminal, where the big jet he had seen landing awaited. Frank was surprised at the size of the plane, not his concept of a private plane.

A uniformed young lady greeted him and invited him to board. She followed, raised the power operated stair, closed the outside door, then led him to an elegant cabin with large, widely spaced seats. He chose a window seat. As he sat down the engines started, and soon they were airborne. The leather seats were superbly comfortable. Frank played with all the adjustments, up, down, tilt, footrest, headrest, swivel right or left, tray up or down, all power operated from clearly labelled buttons. Then he settled down to look at the landscape below, a view he always enjoyed when he could get a window seat. After a while, another young lady offered him breakfast. He asked if he could have coffee and a donut.

"Of course, sir." She gave him an appraising look, then offered, "If you prefer, sir, we can also offer you ham and eggs, fruit, toast, choice of juices, or an omelette, or an assortment of cereals, bagels, cold cuts, jams and marmalades, yoghurts and pastries, and your choice of coffees, teas and hot chocolate."

Frank decided to indulge and selected the ham and eggs full course with all the extras, enjoying the treat.

He asked whether he was the only passenger. The attendant informed him that Mrs Williamson, Mrs Baker and their staffs were aboard, that they were in conference, and they would be joining him soon.

His food arrived on china plates and cups, real silverware, crystal glasses, plus small crystal jars of condiments with little silver spoons, and cloth napkins. It all was served promptly with great courtesy. The young woman vanished out of sight, later reappeared magically to refill his coffee cup. Again, Frank had to adjust his concept of how the very wealthy travelled in their private aircraft.

As they were flying over the Rockies, Abigail Williamson appeared, regal and attractive, as always, and greeted Frank.

"Good morning, Mr Kolozsvary. It was fortuitous that we could combine our travel. It gives us an opportunity to strategise. I hope you have been looked after."

"Good morning, Mrs Williamson. Thank you, and yes, everyone has been very attentive. To be frank, I am hugely impressed by your airplane. My usual travel arrangements are spartan in comparison. What is the plane's range without refuelling?"

"We can fly cross country, reach Europe from the East coast, Hawaii from the West. My sister is expecting us in the conference room, please join us."

The conference room had an opulent décor and furnishings, featuring an oval conference table with twelve chairs. A young man and a young woman in business attire were gathering documents and folders from the table, then disappeared through a side door. Frank could briefly hear a typewriter and some conversation.

Madeleine Baker, looking as stunning as her sister, greeted Frank, and they sat down at the table. She ordered coffee and offered pastries. Frank shook his head, but she smiled at him and ordered some light Danish pastries.

Frank observed the sisters with a certain awe. Here were two women, probably in their late sixties, with grey hair turning white, beautifully groomed, slight wrinkles, different persons but obviously related, with similar old-fashioned names, similar superb social graces, and elegant demeanour. As Alan had observed in his Virginia meeting, the sisters radiated an aura of upper class inherited from generations of wealth and privilege.

Abigail started, "We seem to have a serious situation in Dresden. Up to now, everything was happening as Alan Mackenzie had planned and we expected a happy ending in a few days. Then, as I understand from my last conversation with Mr Mackenzie, the disappearance was discovered way ahead of the expected time, we do not know why, which reduced the head start of the escape to only a few hours. The East Germans started investigating immediately. Subsequently the scope of the investigation and the resources assigned to it increased beyond what was expected for a missing person's case. We do not know why."

"It seems that all inspections had been passed without any problem. Now suddenly in Dresden, the tour is detained and not allowed to leave East Germany, implying a new expanded investigation. Then we get that letter from the tour company, implying that not all is lost, yet. Is that the situation as you understand it?"

Frank responded in the affirmative and submitted a detailed analysis of what he and Alan had discussed and concluded, the essence being that the Germans had not found anything, that they were still fishing, that they suspected passengers in four buses. The main danger was a possible repeat passport check in bright daylight, this time more careful than the routine earlier checks.

The two sisters were intelligent quick learners, fascinated with the glimpse into the dark world of espionage and defections that Frank, in a limited way, could explain. The three had an interesting, analytical conversation. Frank felt that the only thing the people on the tour could do was to distract the policeman checking passports at the right time, perhaps assisted by the fact that the group included a number of amateur actors, a profession skilled in make-believe.

During a pause in the conversation, they drank coffee and ate Danish pastries. Frank had two, acknowledging Madeleine's complicit smile. He was tempted to ask a question, then decided against it. She noticed the indecision, asked him to spill it out.

Hesitating, Frank asked, "I was wondering how you and Mrs Williamson managed to get dressed, get to the airport and fly to Appleton from Washington DC or Virginia in three hours. We talked on the phone at dawn."

She pondered the question for a moment, answered coldly, "Why should you want to know? What made you assume I was in bed, or in Virginia, or away from an airport? How does this relate to your assignment?"

"The phone number you and Mr Mackenzie have is not a Virginia or Tokyo or South Pole number, but our number, just a number that you may use to communicate with me or Abigail, not to find out what we are doing or where. That phone number will reach us anywhere in the world if we wish to be reached. The operator answering the call also may accept messages if we wish to get messages."

Frank apologised, embarrassed. "I am deeply sorry for my question. I just have a general interest in logistics, not specifically in your travel. I should have considered that I may be giving that impression. Please accept my apology, and my thanks for your clarification."

She studied him for a moment, asked, "There is something else you can't decide whether or not to share. What is it?"

Frank admitted, "My previous question to the contrary, I have stayed alive by having an analytical mind, thinking before asking, and following a well-developed instinct. Alan Mackenzie and I have shared our gut feelings over many years, and usually found them accurate predictors, or close enough."

"Based on nothing but intuition, totally unscientific, Alan and I believe that our present predicament is due to a change of some kind in high levels of the DDR. We don't know if our defector is more important than we assumed, we don't know if he is a lesser rank that happens to have knowledge of something of very high value, or if his disappearance somehow got mixed into some power struggle or internal rivalry or a fear among their leadership, something unknown to us. However, Alan and I feel certain that on the last day in Leipzig or the first day in Dresden the style of their investigation changed."

"They seem to be moving more swiftly, more things are happening. I had a careful conversation this morning, in Hungarian and on the secure line in Vienna, with one of the Rakosi clan, the Austrian outfit we booked the tour with. Their driver reports to his office on the status of the tour every day by telephone. He also noticed the change, noted that decisions are fast, that immediate compliance is expected, and that the German tour guide is extremely stressed."

"Alan and I discussed it a length. We believe that the investigation has been removed from the regular Stasi security team and transferred into their counterespionage agency, which is a different kind of outfit, with high calibre leadership."

Abigail was excited about the supposition and commented that this would be of interest to her husband and the State Department, who often had to formulate policies based on rumours, hunches and fragmentary information.

They continued their conversation. Both sisters were fully updated on every detail Frank could contribute.

Abigail said, "We have an awfully bad situation on our laps. Madeleine and I and our husbands will help in every way we can. We rely on you and Mr Mackenzie to deal with … with your specialised skills, as you may decide. We have no expertise in that. However, we have considerable resources. We can provide money, transportation, accommodations, connections, experts in many areas. Let us know what is needed. We will be instantly available day and night for the duration of this crisis. Please keep us informed twice a day, even if nothing is needed."

"I have arranged for a car and driver for your use. He will provide transportation, communications or whatever you may need. He is totally reliable, vetted, available twenty-four hours every day. If he needs to sleep, he will provide an equally qualified substitute."

They landed and taxied directly to the private plane terminal. Frank saw several large private planes on the tarmac, most of them anonymous, showing only the registration number. The wealth that these planes represented was impressive. Frank was particularly awed that this was private wealth, not government-owned perks for high-ranking officials.

Two limousines, one Oldsmobile sedan and two vans were waiting at the foot of the stairs. The sisters, each with some staff, left in separate limos in opposite directions, Frank got the Olds with a young driver, well dressed in a business suit. A large staff group with briefcases and some suitcases disembarked behind him and headed towards the vans.

In Dresden, on the way to the ruins of the old city centre, tour guide Seifert started her passionate narration of what she considered the greatest war crime of the Western imperialists, the firebombing of Dresden in the last weeks of World War II.

She told the driver to park on the open square across from the ruins of the Frauenkirche, the historic Our Lady Church, and addressed her American tour audience. "The war in Europe was coming to an end. Most of the remaining fighting was in the north of Germany, and east of Berlin. Dresden was not in the fighting, as it was not a military target and could not contribute to the German war effort. It was a city of great Lutheran and Catholic churches, museums, libraries and palaces, great examples of European Renaissance and Baroque art and architecture. It was an historic city, the old capital of Saxony."

"At war's end, its non-military status attracted some 300,000 refugees seeking shelter from the bombing elsewhere. Dresden had no air defences, no anti-aircraft guns, no searchlights, nothing. It was an open city. It was expected that the rapidly advancing Soviet army would liberate Dresden in a matter of weeks. Then, between February 13 and 15, 1945, in four separate air raids, 722 British and American bombers dropped some 4,000 tons of high explosive bombs, followed by fire-bombs. The intensity of the bombing devastated the city's historic centre."

"The ensuing fire that raged in the central parts of Dresden made superheated air rise with such force that it created a vacuum on the ground, ripping trees and bushes out of the ground, sucking people into the fire, suffocating those spared the flames."

"The city remained ablaze for weeks. Thousands of fires could be seen from 100 kilometres away. People were still dying from smoke inhalation and burns. Thousands of firemen, those from Dresden who had survived in the suburbs, and many from nearby cities, carried on an exhausted battle against the fires. Then the bombers returned, twice, on March 2 and April 17, allegedly to bomb remaining railway yards and military targets, actually to destroy the remainder of the city before it could be liberated by the Soviet forces."

"This wanton destruction of a great city and the murdering of over 25,000 innocent civilian men, women and children, plus an unknown number of victims who just disappeared in the rubble, is a tragic, colossal example of the Western imperialist criminal behaviour that is at the root of the necessity of our freedom-loving socialist countries to maintain a strong defence capability."

"The British and American war criminals who were guilty of this insane destruction and the mass murders of thousands never were arrested or tried. They walk around free, show no shame, and spit on the socialist ideals that keeps our democratic republic free and safe."

Seifert paused to catch her breath, observing her American audience with defiance. She was surprised by one of her tour members asking whether she had read Kurt Vonnegut's *Slaughterhouse-Five*, depicting the bombing as experienced by the author, who was a prisoner of war in Dresden at the time. She said she had heard about the novel, but not read it. There was a lively exchange involving Seifert and several other tour members who had read the book.

The tour guide had not expected such a knowledgeable and articulate tour audience. On other tours she had guided there had been no such reaction to the narrative of the Dresden bombing. This group was different, she should watch them more carefully. Perhaps it was the high number of Hungarian names, perhaps some of their families had been closer to the Dresden bombing than the typical American.

She added what in her mind was a conciliatory closing statement. "The destruction of Dresden is one of the great tragedies of the Second World War and it must be told. However, we are careful to teach our children that the people of the United States and of the United Kingdom are not to be blamed for the warmongering excesses of their imperialist, capitalist governments. We hope that someday all the peace-loving people of the world will be united and in harmony."

John Crawford started growling about 'this crock of shit', and was interrupted by Barbara and Anne at once. Rick Holley observed him clinically, assessing how long he could survive in a closed, fanatic, politically correct society without getting arrested for a careless something. Probably not long. John Crawford had become a real loose cannon, adding to the worries of the other three.

They had managed to reduce their agitation about the delay in getting out of the DDR and the extra scrutiny that the delay undoubtedly would enable. The only defence they could think of was to distract the guard assigned to check the individuals against passport photos. They rehearsed their lines and acting every chance they had. The unbuttoned nightgown during the dawn inspection had been a great help. They had to find something equally effective. They discussed an unbuttoned blouse and planned how to stage it. It was still undecided whether to keep the defence strategy within the four or include others, a decision that could not wait.

Arriving back at the hotel, the bus of the touring Americans parked next to the tour bus of the Angolan soccer team, where they had some commotion. Tour guide Seifert went to investigate, returned promptly to explain that the authorities, attempting to minimise the inconvenience to the esteemed visitors to the DDR, had decided to expedite the departure of the tour buses by fingerprinting all passengers, thus being able to confirm expeditiously that all were law abiding legitimate visitors and need not be delayed further due to other investigations in the area. Perhaps they still could leave in time to include Wroclaw in the tour.

The Austrian bus driver needed to telephone his company about the new expected date of continuation into Poland. In his phone call, just in passing, he mentioned the fingerprinting and that everyone in his bus was pleased that soon their legitimacy as tourists would be confirmed and they would be allowed to proceed. This statement would undoubtedly please the Stasi telephone conversation monitors.

John and Barbara Crawford, and Anne and Rick were so upset that they feared attracting attention like a blinking neon sign. Barbara needed to vomit but managed to hold it back until she got to her bathroom in the hotel. Later they found out that the Angolans had refused to be fingerprinted because someone connected to their group had been arrested, then two more were arrested for arguing with the police. It was late in the day, so the police decided to postpone the fingerprinting to the next day.

John Crawford went into an angry tirade against Alan Mackenzie for having lured them into a dangerous situation. The other three let him have his temper tantrum without interruption, as they were outside of their hotel room. They could only hope that they were not being recorded.

John went on and on, that Alan Mackenzie and that guy Frank with the Hungarian surname had presented the substitution as the simple adventure they had experienced in the first few days in the DDR, then it abruptly escalated into some big investigation with the entire Communist police force getting in the act. The other three did not say a word.

After a pause, John demanded, "Why fingerprinting now? We were fingerprinted already before we started on this stupid odyssey!"

Rick abruptly reverted to his assertive Bruno Hadler persona and admonished John, "Wir … We are in a bad predicament. You are part of the problem, and this part of the problem can be fixed by you up shutting your mouth. Do not comment about the situation unless I ask you to. And you, Barbara, do not get defensive about your husband, not in this context. Our group was fingerprinted before my disappearance. Now they are looking for Bruno Hadler's fingerprints."

"They have not found a trace of my disappearance in any logical place; therefore, they are searching in illogical places, which may include me hiding among the passengers in one of the tour buses. The previous set of fingerprints was made before my disappearance."

John asked, "Why are they fingerprinting the Africans? Do they expect your paleface can be hidden among them?"

"I don't know. Perhaps they do not want to leave any stone unturned, perhaps there is something else going on with the blacks. Our driver heard from another driver that two or three were arrested by the Stasi."

Anne wanted to know, "What is next? What do we do now?"

Rick prognosticated, "I assume they will complete the fingerprinting tomorrow, that is fairly fast. Then the prints go for study, perhaps here in Dresden, more likely to Berlin, where clerks compare them manually, one at the time, which is a slow process. That may take a second day unless they work through the night. Anyway, I assume nothing will happen for a day, perhaps two. That gives us a few hours to think. Perhaps I need to disappear. This also would have consequences and complications for you. I really need to think." Looking at John, he added, "Without being distracted by dangerous antisocialist commentaries."

John nodded but gave him the middle finger.

Anne asked, "Do people back home know about the new fingerprinting requirement? They know of course about the delay announced earlier."

Rick assured them, "Yes, the bus company certainly knows, and I am sure they would have notified any interested parties. I noticed that our driver phones his bosses every time we park near a public telephone. He has plenty of DDR experience and he really seems to know the hurdles of international calling using our system."

Frank Kolozsvary settled in his Long Beach hotel room and called Maria to let her know where he was staying. She told him he had two messages, one from Alan in mid-morning, who was about to board for London, where he would transfer to Warsaw, and he left his hotel number in Poland.

Next, she told Frank, "The other was from a Mr Rakosi in Vienna, who wants you to call him back as soon as possible. He asked and we spoke in Hungarian. He speaks in a convoluted, funny old-fashioned way, but very charming, very polite. He would not leave a message, except that he was most eager for you to call him back. He left two numbers."

Frank and Maria chatted briefly about household and children, then he called Vienna, with dark premonitions.

The patriarch Istvan Rakosi answered in German, then they switched to Hungarian.

"Mr Kolozsvary, thank you kindly for calling back. I am sorry to disturb you in your busy schedule. If this is an inconvenient hour, I will be pleased to call you back at a more propitious time."

"No, Mr Rakosi, this is a good time. What did you call me about?"

"I had called you about a trivial matter that may contribute to the enjoyment of the tour by one of your friends. As you know, we strive to provide the most enjoyable travel experience, which often is enhanced by little gestures and courtesies."

"When you were booking the tour, one of your friends, I made a note, here it is, a Mrs Anne Holley, with her husband Mr Richard Holley, was concerned about returning to California in time to attend a play that she had expensive, hard-to-get tickets for. She had a conversation with another lady who had tickets for a later performance of the same play about trading tickets, but they did not think it necessary."

"We just were notified by our tour driver that there was a further delay by the DDR authorities, but that they would fingerprint all passengers to expedite travel. We all were pleased with the fingerprinting decision, which would confirm our identities as tourists and allow us to proceed."

"However, since we still do not know the new departure date, I most respectfully suggest that Mrs Holley exchange the tickets with her friend, so she would not have to worry about the dates and enjoy her tour."

"If you can reach her in Dresden, please be kind enough to remind her of the ticket option. We could of course also remind her, but I feel this reminder is more appropriately suggested by a family member or a friend."

"Anyway, Mr Kolozsvary, this is why I called. I know it is a trivial detail, but as I never tire of emphasising, these little gestures contribute immensely to our passengers' enjoyment of their travel experience, and consequently, to our success as one of Austria's best international transportation companies. Thank you very much for returning my call and listening to my suggestion with such patience and courtesy."

Frank thanked Rakosi for the suggestion. He sensed that the older man was most eager to get off the phone, now that the message had been given. Frank was stunned by the new fingerprint threat. Fingerprints could not be hidden under makeup, wigs, and fake glasses. It was utterly discouraging to fail this late in the game. He could not reach Alan and realised that he had to deal with this by himself.

He telephoned Abigail, got Madeleine in two minutes. He explained the latest bad news, advised that he would call her back later after he had some time to formulate a plan of action.

He drank a coke and smoked, wondering why Rakosi had gone through this elaborate presentation. The patriarch was very bright and very experienced in navigating the murky border between East and West. Perhaps his courtier's speech was just a guise to appear innocent, senile or stupid, just as Frank had once used his surname spelt backwards as his password to play the innocent Hungarian peasant wanting to be a secret agent.

He wrote down the words the old man had used in the telephone conversation, as well as he could remember them. One part of the message obviously was to warn him about the new fingerprinting development, but this information also would have reached Frank from other sources.

As he and Alan had done many times before, he tried to distil the essence of the message into three or four, no, better just two words. He reminisced about some highlights in this reduction to a minimum process; two distillations ranked high in his memory. One was 'Save Mindzsenty' and the other 'Escape Hungary'. Every action or inaction thereafter was measured against these two words. The two-word simplicity of what really mattered was a powerful compass.

He started to feel sick with the chain smoking and the endless sugar and caffeine that he craved. He kept it up until he felt confident that for the problem at hand the two magic words were 'Ticket Substitution'. He then went out for a walk to clear his head and start thinking about means and methods.

As he walked around within a few blocks of his hotel he became aware of the Long Beach street landscape. It felt foreign, without a doubt still American, but not northern Wisconsin, nor Chicago or midwestern. It brought back some memories of out-of-town assignments he had participated in during his previous life in Hungary, also his irritation with the American, Alan Mackenzie, who could not speak Hungarian, but, speaking German or English through interpreters, could force a whole group to intensely focus on one specific goal, and then really piss people off by insisting on speed, on adhering to absurd timetables that later proved to be lifesavers.

Crossing at a street corner without paying attention he was rudely awakened by squealing tires and a car horn, followed by an angry driver yelling at him to watch where he was going. The traffic incident woke him up from his reminiscences, also reminding him of Alan's often abrupt interventions when he caught someone daydreaming. The culprit was, often in front of his colleagues, reprimanded, reenergised, and refocused on the task at hand.

Back at the hotel he called Abigail, again getting Madeleine. He told her he needed help and that they had to move as fast as possible. She advised that his driver would pick him up in a few minutes and bring him to meet with her.

Remembering being awed by his host's elegance, wealth, and grooming, he shaved again, brushed his teeth and changed into a clean shirt, newest tie, and polished his shoes with a hotel towel. As he reached the front door of the hotel the Oldsmobile arrived, the driver jumped out and opened the rear door. Frank would have preferred to sit in front but decided to not call attention to his proletarian upbringing.

Trying to orient himself, he asked the driver, "Where are we going?"

"To the 'Cottage', sir, a pied-à-terre the family owns in Beverly Hills."

In Dresden, Rick and his three companions were in low spirits. They would have liked to stay up late to discuss their problem and try to figure out what to do. They also knew that the hotel rooms had to be off limits, due to the danger of eavesdropping by the Germans. They managed to have some private space by getting approval to go for a walk along the Elbe river.

Guide Seifert asked others, several joined the walk, where they broke apart into small groups, some just finding a quiet spot and looking at the great river and the lights on the opposite shore. Others walked with the guide and listened to her talk about historical landmarks. There were requests to take a river cruise if the schedule changes allowed. Seifert said it could be arranged.

The four conspirators concluded that nothing could be done for the moment. Rick felt certain that the leaders of the escape operation would have been informed about the latest events by the bus company and that better brains would be working out a solution during the night, which they probably would transmit to them in Dresden early in the morning.

They had a restless night. Fear kept them wide awake, tossing and turning, extremely frustrated about not being able to talk. Barbara seemed the most affected physically, continuing with stomach problems and vomiting. Fear also muzzled John Crawford, who controlled his urge to express his derogatory opinions about the East German communist regime. For the four, hoping the new day would bring some instructions, fearing it would not, the gradual, slow appearance of dawn seemed to take forever.

In Beverly Hills, the evening approach appeared too fast to Frank, who knew he had to resolve things before the morning in East Germany, nine hours ahead of California time.

As they reached their destination, Frank thought that he would not have called the mansion the 'Cottage'. Again, he had to control his proletarian upbringing and keep it very private.

Madeleine Baker met him in a large sitting room, with several groupings of easy chairs, sofas, small tables with four chairs, a large fireplace, a grand piano, and at one end of the room, a theatre-size curtain that probably covered a movie screen. Frank would have loved a guided tour of the place.

She had changed clothes since that morning on the plane. As always, she was impeccably dressed and combed, looking rested, radiant, alert. She was friendly greeting him and offered coffee or whatever he would like. He declined the coffee and requested ice water.

She looked at him intently, then smiled and commented, "You probably had too much caffeine, sugar, nicotine and stress for one afternoon. Perhaps some herbal tea may help you calm down."

"Thank you, madam. I didn't think it was so obvious."

"The ice water gave you away. Believe me, I have been in such situations. Now, you indicated that we had some urgent business to attend. Do we have additional bad news?"

"No, madam, no additional bad news, just what I reported to you earlier today, which is pretty bad. Please allow me to bring you up to date on the details and the proposed course of action."

His ice water arrived in a tall cut crystal glass, as well as a pot of hot water, a little lacquered box of assorted herbal teas, a sugar bowl, a small cream pitcher, and a porcelain teacup with a silver spoon. She had what appeared to be an espresso.

He related the events of the day since his phone call home, including all the details he remembered, including his anxiety in deciphering the real message that Rakosi had conveyed, then how to implement the solution hinted at.

He explained, "Rakosi will not say or write anything that will incriminate him. He is obsessed that everything he says or writes will be intercepted by someone. Hence, his real message is always hidden in some reasonable, real, verifiable information."

"Why do you think he is helping us?"

"Primarily because trouble with any of his tours is bad for business, and secondarily, we have a relationship that goes back over twenty years, during which we always were careful to protect his company from trouble, always punctiliously did our part, always paid very well without arguing or negotiating, and lastly, but not least, we both wholeheartedly belong to the monarchist Catholic Hungarian diaspora. He has three sons in the business, and two Austrian partners."

He paused, then continued, "May I ask a question about … about your and Mrs Willliamson's roles in this … assignment? When we started, it was our understanding that Mrs Abigail was to be our client. Alan and I are honoured to work with either one of you or both. Our concern is that now, as you are becoming more actively involved in our operation, it has become more important that we have a clear understanding of our roles, to avoid confusion or misunderstandings at some critical moment."

Madeleine replied, "As you know, the original contact with the defector was through Abigail at that Copenhagen conference. After our high-ranking government leaders decided to pursue this operation without involving government operatives, they found Mr Mackenzie and pulled him out of retirement. He then found and enlisted you. Secretary Williamson is much too busy at the State Department to be of much help. About that time, it all was getting too complicated for Abigail to coordinate by herself, so she invited me to partner with her."

"We have worked together on many projects, get along superbly well, and soon we became interchangeable. Now we have the possibility that they find the defector on our bus, arrest all the passengers, and turn our little game into an international scandal, in which case it is best that the press does not find the wife of our Secretary of State loitering in the wings. Abigail must be in hiding for the duration, and you have my undivided attention and many resources at your disposal."

"Thank you, madam. Now you will participate in some real subversive secret chess game with the East German Stasi, their state security service. I have a suspicion that they have involved their very competent counterintelligence division, further bad news for us. Our best chance is winning a few chess moves, perhaps not a checkmate, but keeping the game interesting and gaining time. Do you play chess, Mrs Baker?"

"Not well, but I understand the complexities and possibilities the game offers."

"As I related to you, the telephone call from Mr Rakosi included a suggested theatre ticket exchange that would remove any anxiety two of the tour guests may have about missing a performance and losing the cost of their tickets due to a delayed return to Pasadena."

"I told you about the process of distilling the crucial meaning of a message or a crusade down to a few, preferably two words. Here the two words are 'Ticket Substitution'. But why are the theatre tickets so important? Perhaps Rakosi was hinting at substituting a different piece of paper, say a fingerprint card."

Madeleine commented, "This is fascinating, now I'm hooked." She opened a box on the table and offered Frank a cigarette. Having had a pause of several hours, Frank was craving his nicotine again. He accepted, was soon surprised at the highly aromatic smoke. She explained it was Turkish tobacco and offered other varieties if he so desired.

Frank continued, "We need to convey to our four targeted tour members a message, a telegram, that instructs them to switch names on their fingerprint cards. What I have in mind is that our defector does not get fingerprinted, but that someone else gets fingerprinted twice, once under his own name and once under the defector's name."

"I am assuming that they will not be checking fingerprints against passports or visa applications; they have those matches already. My guess is that they just will be looking for Bruno Hadler's fingerprints. They will not notice that two of the over a hundred sets of prints from the four buses are duplicates."

"Sounds complicated. Why not a phone call?"

"Because phone calls are listened to by the Stasi, and it is too easy to miss some important detail. If they get it in writing, they can study the words and figure out what needs to happen."

"But won't the Germans intercept the telegram?"

"Yes, madam, they will. That is why we need to word it carefully, as Rakosi did in his phone call to me. The Stasi need to think it has to do with some silly worry about a theatre ticket exchange, our four people need to figure out that one of them must get fingerprinted twice and another not at all. You and I will have to develop the right text."

"I look forward to the task. All this is new to me and quite different from my usual assignments, which usually involve fundraising for charitable institutions, museums and performing arts. I suggest we both write a draft, then discuss and combine."

Frank added that there was more. "While we work on the text, could you assign someone to find a play or concert that would fit certain dates, and after we make a selection, purchase four tickets or make prepaid reservations for the four names I provide as well as the dates needed. We need to do that overnight because of the nine-hour time difference with Dresden."

"What if the tickets are sold out?"

Frank replied, "I am sure you could find a way, through friends, recipients of your financial assistance, performers, ticket sellers, bribes, whatever. It is now about seven in the evening here, and the deed must be done tonight."

She was not used to be given orders but realised that Frank now was the one who had to be in charge and who knew what needed to happen. She rang a bell; a uniformed maid appeared and was instructed to find two people and send them in at once.

She asked, "Why do you need actual tickets? Do you really think the Germans are going to hire an investigator or send an agent to check that four tickets to some show were actually sold to or reserved by certain people?"

Frank advised, "Probably not, but not impossible. The telegram will catch their attention, not because of anything we are saying, but because it is unusual. Mild and innocent, but not common. I am sure they have not seen this particular message before."

"They are against a wall. They obviously have not found their fugitive, they are out of time, they have pressure from above, they want to keep it quiet, it is an embarrassment, therefore we see no photographs on wanted posters or on front pages of newspapers. They are scared that they will miss their man, and will do anything, no matter how remote or unlikely, to find him. I am scared that they will succeed because we missed some trivial small detail. So, yes, I think we need actual tickets."

They started to write drafts of the telegram. She was a better writer; Frank still was intertwined with Hungarian grammar. He could write business letters in English without a hitch. What they were drafting was more delicate and had exceedingly high stakes.

Within fifteen minutes, an older woman in a business suit appeared. She was introduced as Madeleine's senior secretary and given the assignment to find plays or concerts meeting certain criteria and playing between given specific dates in the Los Angeles/Long Beach area, preferably popular, sold-out events. They discussed some parameters and she left, returning in about twenty minutes with three options. One was a charity fundraiser at $500 a person. Frank said that was not an expenditure that his clients could afford. The other two options were less expensive. They settled on the Arthur Miller play 'Death of a Salesman', played by some well-known movie stars teaching in always sold-out performances by a college theatre class, and at $75 per person, affordable.

A young man in a business suit appeared and was assigned the task of getting four tickets, no matter how or at what cost, for two dates. Frank explained that the first date was crucial and fixed, perhaps it could be extended by one day only, preferably not, and had to be in the names of Anne and Rick Holley, it being very important that there was a written record of their names, in a reservation log, or a payment ledger, or on a list of tickets to be picked up. The second pair of tickets needed to be in another couple's name, which Frank provided, and the date should be about two weeks later. The second date was approximate.

Madeleine added, "This must be completed before noon tomorrow. I am available at any time day or night if you need me or if I need to speak to someone."

"Yes, madam, I will take care of it and confirm as soon as it is done. In view of the time pressure, I will have to ask some of the colleagues to assist me."

Madeleine instructed, "Do whatever you need. Get all the help you need but be done before noon tomorrow."

"Yes madam, thank you."

Frank and Madeleine returned to drafting an innocent telegram with a hidden message. They decided the telegram would be from a female friend to Anne Holley. Madeleine was much better than Frank in this role. They worked on several versions, settling on the following:

Hi Anne,

I heard your tour was extended a few days. You had worried about missing the Arthur Miller play if your plane was late. Now you will miss the play for sure, so I will switch tickets with you. We talked about it but did not follow up. I will go on the date you reserved, you can go on mine, which is two weeks later. They got their money, so I do not think they care whose names are on the tickets. I found your tickets. Relax and enjoy the extra days. All is well at your house. Alan says hello.

Love, Mary.

Madeleine summoned yet another young man in a business suit and asked him to have the telegram typed, brought back for a final reading, then take it to the telegraph office and have it sent for immediate delivery in Dresden, East Germany. He brought the typed version in a few minutes, was approved by Frank, who added the instruction that the telegram be sent in duplicate to Anne Holley, one in care of the tour guide, and one in care of the hotel, to ensure that Anne would get it in the morning. Frank furnished addresses and other details.

Madeleine invited Frank to stay for dinner, which he accepted. He was surprised when asked what he would like to have, as if it were a restaurant. He figured it would be safe to ask for meat, potatoes, and a vegetable. Madeleine asked for something with a French name, and added appetisers, soup, and salad for both. Frank was worried about so much food but was surprised at the superb quality and what he considered very small portions. They had a glass of wine, a small dessert and coffee.

Frank fleetingly remembered the many times when dinner had been a piece of soggy black bread, standing in freezing rain in some filthy alley, fearing for his life, praying for escape or rescue. His hostess was very observant and asked him if he cared to share his memories. Frank said he had remembered some dinners in his past that had not been as pleasant as the present one. She understood that he could not get into details.

They talked for a couple of hours about their current project. He narrated, highly edited and limited, some clandestine events and projects that echoed some of their current anxieties. She was fascinated by this glimpse into a world far removed from hers. He in turn managed to get glimpses, also highly edited and limited, into her world, so far removed from his. Both enjoyed the evening.

One of the young men who had been sent on assignment, Frank could not tell them apart, returned and reported that the telegrams had been sent, the second set of tickets had been purchased, and that the first one, the one with the crucial date, would be available in the morning. And that she would receive phone calls and complaints from one person he had to push a little hard. Madeleine told him not to worry, thanked him, and reminded him to get the promised tickets in the morning, not letting up the pressure.

Frank wanted to know, just out of curiosity, what reason she had given for the urgent ticket demands. She said they were helping a friend who had solemnly promised to get tickets to that specific show to celebrate a wedding anniversary. He had forgotten to do it on time. Now they were unavailable, and he would be facing a big fight with his wife if could not get the promised tickets.

She added, "In aristocratic circles, they love this kind of stuff and will eagerly participate. It is fun and games, at times expensive. Recently someone in our charity group helped to rescue a friend who had been entrapped having a torrid affair with an underage girl on a tropical island where he allegedly was on business. The underage statutory rape entrapment had a high price."

"Subsequently he donated substantial sums to one of our charities. The wealthy cocktail party circuit thrives on such gossip. I suppose this stuff happens in your circles as well."

Franks said, "Of course." He did not say that the payoffs in his world were on the order of getting a good deal on the financing of a used car.

Madeleine and Frank agreed to meet for breakfast at the Cottage about six in the morning, in consideration of the time difference with Europe. His driver took him back to the hotel in Long Beach.

From the hotel he was able to reach Alan, who was at his hotel in Warsaw. Frank brought Alan up to date. Alan agreed with what had been done and prepared to wait on pins and needles for the outcome, like the rest of them. Alan would remain in Warsaw, hoping for the safe arrival of the tour and preparing for the second exchange, Bruno Hadler masquerading as Richard Holley for the real Richard Holley, scheduled to arrive from his hiding place to reunite with his passport and his friends.

At the hotel in Dresden, Anne Holley got her telegram at the reception counter. The four read it, then went for a walk in the hotel garden and pretended to look at and discuss some replica baroque sculptures, while analysing the telegram, with an intensity fuelled by fear and hope.

Rick read the key sentence aloud: "They got their money, so I don't think they care whose names are on the tickets."

Pausing, he repeated it aloud as: "They got their fingerprints, so I don't think they care whose names are on the tickets."

It was an epiphany. They had been fantasising about avoiding the fingerprinting, now salvation depended on including fingerprinting, except for Rick. The immediate question was who would be fingerprinted twice, the obvious choice being John Crawford.

It was assumed that the clerks would not know their faces and not require passports, just go by names on a list. Rick was convinced that their whole exercise was to find Bruno Hadler's prints, therefore they only would be comparing the new prints with Hadler's, and finding no match, moving on to the next one.

The dilemma was of course not with the fingerprint clerks, but their travel companions and the tour guide. They probably could enrol the entire group to look the other way, but not tour guide Seifert.

They went to the dining room to have breakfast. Tour guide Seifert appeared promptly at their side and cheerfully handed Anne a telegram. Anne opened it, told the others that her friend Mary was trading performances of a play, so they need not worry about returning on time. Anne added, "That's nice of her. I'll thank her on my next postcard." She laid the telegram on the table, and they returned to their conversation. Seifert seemed disappointed that the telegram had not generated greater interest.

The tour travellers had finished breakfast and were having coffee and cigarettes, discussing the upcoming sightseeing schedule. Seifert returned to the dining room and announced that they would have their fingerprinting completed before the sightseeing, so they would have the day free and clear. Someone asked what the procedure would be. Seifert responded that two functionaries would be sitting at a table and calling the travellers by name. Everyone's name was already typed on the cards and the process would be quick. After the printing, they could wipe their fingers and sign the card. Then they could leave.

The signature requirement was unexpected. Rick wrote his name on a paper and told John Crawford to copy it several times.

"Don't try to match my handwriting. Write as you normally would write. You are not copying a signature; you are just writing a name. The clerks are only interested in having a completed form, with name, file number, ten fingerprints, signature box filled in blue ink, place where done, date. The one key thing you must, absolutely must remember is that for this crucial moment you must be Richard Holley. You must respond to the Holley name when called. After you do the Holley appearance, you revert to being John Crawford and go through the fingerprinting process again, hopefully much later."

At that time, the African soccer players were herded into one end of the dining room where the fingerprinting table had been set up. There were two civilian fingerprinting clerks and three men in uniform. The uniforms intensely worried the Crawfords and the Holleys.

John moaned, fortunately in a low whisper, "Now we are really fucked! I wish we could offer them Alan Mackenzie as a sacrificial lamb! He led us into his dangerous adventure under false promises. This was supposed to be …"

His wife hissed, "Shut up, John!"

He retorted, "Then what? Do you look forward to getting arrested by the fucking Gestapo? I will not go quietly. Alan did mislead us. I definitely will …"

"You definitely will shut up!" interrupted Rick Holley. "Let me be the guide when dealing with a system I know well, and you don't! Incidentally, these are Stasi, the DDR State Security, not Gestapo, KGB, CIA, FBI, MI6 or Mossad. They do not like to be mislabelled. Just shut up, listen, stay alive and free to go home. Do not screw up things at the last minute! Do you want to cause troubles for them or for yourself? It seems to us that it is a simple choice."

He looked at the other three questioningly. They nodded, John last and sulking.

Rick continued, "They use uniforms for discipline and intimidation, not fingerprinting. I think they brought in the muscle because they apparently had some problems with the blacks. The Stasi like order and obedience. I do not think they will be checking us, unless one of us is overheard bitching about the system. Do you understand that, John?"

John nodded. The two wives reacted angrily at the nodding.

Barbara demanded, "Speak up! I want to hear you saying that you understand that today, now, may be our last chance and that you will not screw it up. If you want to spend time in an East German prison, I probably cannot stop you. But do not drag me down with you. Let me go home and divorce you! And do not nod, you bastard, say it clearly so we all can hear it and judge whether you understand!"

John sulked, reluctantly assured the others that he understood and would do his part. He even apologised for his carelessness.

Rick commented, "If you do your part well, we really will screw the Stasi, and I think you will experience great satisfaction in doing it. Just think about their frustration and internal blaming and repercussions."

John nodded, then remembered that nodding was presently not acceptable, promptly spoke the words, "Yes, yes, I like that image. Let us screw them!"

He would have enjoyed knowing that Stasi officers also had been reprimanded hard for nodding.

They observed the fingerprinting of the soccer team. It proceeded smoothly, with names being called, then fingerprinted, hands wiped, card signed, then the next name called. Once a white guy who was with the Angolans started to argue about something. One of the uniforms raised a cautionary hand and all was quiet again. The clerks worked in a relaxed rhythmic way, looking at hands rather than faces.

Tour guide Seifert kept hanging around the fingerprinting table. It was obvious that they could not play a substitution in front of her. Rick suggested that the others could stage a distraction.

Anne Holley moved swiftly and talked to all of them, asking with the greatest urgency that they must distract the tour guide while John Crawford or Rick Holley were called for printing, that the success of the entire tour depended on that. No time for discussion, all must act now.

She suggested they could stage a family argument using the dialog of a recent play they had performed at a high school auditorium. One couple who had participated in the play was not on the tour. They concluded it did not matter; they could skip their parts. As an added benefit, the truncated dialog could contribute to confuse any eavesdroppers.

Anne also cautioned that if the tour guide noticed her going around and talking to the entire group, they should, reluctantly of course, admit that Anne was asking all to participate in buying the tour guide a gift.

The Angolans were finished and were leaving. Two of the uniformed men left with them, one stayed with the clerks. Anne suggested that John Crawford wear Rick's dark red windbreaker when impersonating Rick. It did not quite fit John, who was bigger, but it could be worn open.

Two names were called while the tour group assembled to one side, where they started talking, gradually louder, attracting the tour guide's attention. The next names called spelled disaster, with John Crawford and Rick Holley being called at the same time. They were stunned, this development had not occurred to any of them.

Anne was standing a few feet behind tour guide Seifert, who appeared to lose interest in the group's discussion. Anne raised her arms like an orchestra conductor and waved them up to increase volume. Seifert turn around at that moment and caught Anne's raised arms, which Anne managed to convert to a slow stretch, commenting that she missed her yoga class. She asked the guide whether she practice yoga, Seifert said no, but that she attended a gym on a regular basis, adding praise for the excellent health and fitness programs and facilities that the socialist state offered to its citizens, all for free.

At that moment, the discussion in the group became agitated and louder. Seifert went to investigate. She was surprised at the loud exchange; this tour had been so polite and quiet.

Back at the fingerprint table a scared John Crawford, pretending to be Rick Holley, submitted to the fingerprinting. The clerk had seen trembling hands before, frequent with people being fingerprinted by the Stasi. He grabbed and rolled John's fingers with an experienced firm hand and got good prints. John wiped his hands and wrote Rick's name on the signature line of the card.

The other clerk was told in broken German that Mr Crawford had to go to the bathroom and that he would be right back. Meanwhile Mrs Crawford could be printed. The clerk nodded in agreement, found her card, and proceeded.

Guide Seifert was still trying to figure out what the group argument was about. She convinced them to lower their voices and resolve their issues more harmoniously. Behind her Anne Holley signalled a thumbs-up with a big smile, resulting in the immediate lowering of the volume of the discussion. Seifert was proud of herself for being able to calm everyone down.

She was told that the argument had been about the politics of raising funds to start a social club for seniors in Long Beach. Seifert commented that in the

DDR the socialist state lovingly cared for their senior citizens and provided social and cultural facilities for their enjoyment, all for free.

In the men's toilet, Rick got his dark red coat back. John thoroughly washed and scrubbed his own hands to remove all trace of fingerprinting, then, waiting for the clerk who had not printed him before, presented himself at the fingerprinting table as John Crawford. Just at that moment the uniformed Stasi man came over and asked the fingerprint clerk something, soon the two were in a longer conversation, and John got an intense stomach ache suddenly facing the danger of again getting the clerk who had previously fingerprinted him as Rick Holley.

John was overcome with fear of being recognised and had to plop down on the nearest chair, feeling sick. The Stasi man and the clerk noticed his abrupt collapse and came over to see to him. They called the tour guide to translate, John explained that occasionally he had these episodes of weakness if his sugar level went down, that it went away after he had something to eat, and not to worry. He just wanted to have his fingerprints done and then go and get some sugary snack. This seemed to pacify everyone. The finger printing clerk was equally skilled with trembling hands as his colleague had been and guided the process with firm hands and got good prints. John was given the card to sign; for one spinning, terrifying moment he could not remember whose name he must use. They noted his discomfort and suggested he lay down for a rest.

The French busload was next on the fingerprinting agenda, and the American tour was free to leave. It was about eleven in the morning. Seifert announced the sightseeing program for the afternoon. The group decided to stay at the hotel with some time off and not leave until after lunch.

They all needed time to calm down, especially the Crawfords and the Holleys. Barbara Crawford was nauseous from the stress and again ended up vomiting in the bathroom. John Crawford's hands would not stop shaking. Anne and Rick were jittery but calmer than the other two. They all had drinks from their room minibars, including Barbara. They smoked and tried to regain their composure. They were reassured by Rick that the Stasi were not going to compare fingerprints with those of their travel companions but only look for Bruno Hadler's prints.

They did not know how long the Stasi would need to check all the prints from all the buses. The hope was that they would be allowed to leave in time to do some sightseeing in Warsaw and then depart on their scheduled flight.

Seifert had said that if they were required to stay an extra day in Dresden, they could go on an Elbe River tour.

The first stop in the afternoon was a spectacular ceramics museum exhibiting historic porcelain figures from Meissen and Dresden, as well as modern ceramics that faithfully reproduced the old styles. In a whispered conference in a corner, a group of the travellers decided to buy the tour guide a gift. They found a porcelain figurine scene of a grey-haired woman pointing at something and speaking to a small, attentive, smiling adult audience. They all thought it beautifully represented tour guide Seifert. They were shocked at the price, hesitated, one said that they needed the guide totally on their side and that settled it. They pooled money and had it gift wrapped.

Seifert noted that they had bought something and seemed pleased that her tourists had liked something enough to buy it and pay the price. Porcelain figures were some of the most valuable art objects produced in Saxony over the centuries.

They spent the afternoon visiting museums and buildings that had been reconstructed since the war. Seifert also pointed out the many ruins that still awaited funding. The rubble had been cleared, which somehow made the ruins look sadder, like naked skeletons without name or history.

That evening after dinner they gathered in a circle and asked the tour guide to join them. Seifert looked very apprehensive and hesitant. The woman that was the best actress and speaker in their little theatre group gave a beautifully worded short speech thanking tour guide Seifert for her knowledgeable lectures and for taking such good care of the travellers, who were pleased to present her this little gift hoping she would remember her American senior citizen group.

They urged her to open the package, warning it was very fragile. Seifert was astonished at the large porcelain display with many figures clearly depicting a scene of a teacher, or a tour guide, all dressed in the elegant style of the Renaissance royal court. She started to cry and stuttered her thanks. She tried hard to compose herself, tears over a gift from a capitalist group probably was not encouraged by her bosses. Her audience consoled her and asked not to worry, that surprises sometimes brought out some tears. They told her that they had had several conferences to agree on an appropriate surprise gift.

After she calmed down, she confessed the whispered conferences of the group had worried her, thinking that she had done something wrong and that the group was preparing a group complaint.

Anne Holley hoped Seifert would not get in trouble for getting a present and being emotional on the job. John Crawford hoped they would jail her for antisocialist behaviour, fraternising with the enemy, and dereliction of duty, to get another Communist propagandist out of circulation. Barbara Crawford asked him if he would like to get back to Long Beach or rather enjoy his ongoing stupid talk in an East German jail.

They all had drinks and the evening ended well, although there was no news about permission to continue their tour into Poland.

13. Warsaw, Poland

Colonel Schmidt and two other officers were reviewing stacks of reports, notes, and forms, separating them into various categories, searching for anything remaining to be done. An orderly came in to announce that several tour guides and bus drivers were waiting for the day's instructions and wanting to talk to the commandant about whether they would be allowed to continue to Warsaw.

Schmidt agreed to see them, starting with the Polish school group. After a brief conversation, they were given approval to return home to Poland. The German tour guide would remain in Dresden to wait for reassignment.

The Angolan soccer team was next. They were told to wait in the hotel until the disposition of the arrested members was determined. No one was to leave the hotel grounds for sightseeing, shopping, or any other reason. Their bus was not allowed to leave the parking lot to refuel or for any other reason until further notice. Complaints or disobedience would be cause for further arrests. Inquiries from Angolan diplomats or emissaries from the East German foreign ministry were to be referred to Colonel Schmidt, who reiterated the consequences of complaints or disobedience. The German tour guide would remain with them for the time being to assist with translations.

The French had brought their entire team to the Stasi station. They were an energic, belligerent, young crowd, the kind that worried small town police forces on a Saturday night or in a soccer game. A few of the more vocal ones engaged Schmidt in a passionate discussion about socialism and the need for more collaboration between the freedom-loving East bloc and the oppressive capitalist regime of the French Republic, with plenty of arguments among themselves. A few spoke rudimentary German; the rest exhausted the two interpreters who tried hard to keep up.

Soon Schmidt tired of the theatre, yelled at them to shut up, and asked if they wanted to proceed into Poland or not. The interpreter repeated it in French, yelling in imitation of Schmidt. It quieted the group. They listened to the message that they would be allowed to leave if they kept quiet and the local police had no pending issues with them about violent arguments in the bus and breaking the peace outside of their bus. About an hour later they got their exit permit. As soon as their bus moved, they all started to yell and sing the Marseillaise, with waving and many unwise hand and finger gestures at the uniformed East Germans.

Tour guide Seifert and her Austrian driver were starting to worry about being the last ones received by the commanding officer. When called in, she was awed by having to deal with a Stasi colonel. Her usual interactions about travel permits and such were typically with a sergeant of the local traffic police.

Colonel Schmidt asked them about their trip and whether they had seen or suspected anything out of the ordinary and questioned them extensively about their American passengers. He had a list in front of him, read the names aloud and asked for commentaries about each. Seifert was complimentary about her charges, who were of retirement age, did not cause troubles or engage in arguments. She pointed out that several in the group had read about the bombing of Dresden, and that the discussions and questions were civil. They were interested in the historical background of the places they had visited, and generally easy-going and friendly.

She said two of her charges were complaining more than the rest put together; one was a woman who complained about everything, the food, the weather, the hotel, the bus, everything, fortunately in a soft voice addressed to her henpecked husband, and the other was a guy who periodically had something critical or unfriendly to say about socialism, communism, and our fatherland. His wife periodically shuts him up. He is stupid, irritating and ill-mannered, but nothing that interferes seriously with anything. As I said before, they were an easy-going group, enjoying their vacation, which they viewed as a grand adventure. Seifert mentioned, "They even bought me a present, which surprised me, and said some nice words about my work."

Schmidt asked, "What did they give you?"

The tour guide answered, "They got me a porcelain table piece, here in Dresden, shows a woman lecturing a group."

"Very nice. You will note it in your tour report, yes?" Seifert said.

"Yes, of course." She hesitated, then asked, "Comrade Colonel, could you let us know when to expect resumption of our tour into Poland? They would like to take a riverboat tour on the Elbe if we are staying in Dresden another day, but if we are leaving today, they want to have quick tour of Wroclaw, where they originally were scheduled to spend two days."

Schmidt asked the driver, "Have these arrangements been coordinated with your office and the Polish authorities?"

"Yes, colonel. My bosses in Vienna were informed of the delay and they got in touch with our representatives in Warsaw to rearrange hotel and tour guide assignments. They all understand that you had to investigate a local legal problem and instructed me to collaborate with the DDR authorities in every way. I have driven tours in the DDR many times, always a pleasant, orderly, interesting event. Sometimes our clients are a young, unruly bunch, as seems to be the case with our French colleagues, and sometimes we have a quiet, intellectual, polite group, as is the case in this tour."

Schmidt thanked the driver for his words, and asked, "This question is for both of you. If you had to point out one item that was peculiar to your present tour, not typically found in your usual tour, what would it be?"

The driver answered first, "From my point of view, I found it unusual that there was not a single complaint about the bus, my driving, the length of time until the next bathroom stop, or anything related to the tour services provided by my company. There was this one lady that tour guide Seifert mentioned, but she complained about everything, to the tour guide, never to me, so for me, there were no complaints on this tour. Typically, we have had some grumbling about something, so far never serious and always easily explained or fixed."

Seifert's comment was, "I agree that it was a noticeably quiet and orderly group, with the two exceptions noted. For me, the uncommon item in this group was that about half of them were Hungarian speakers, and a few spoke German, with an old-fashioned Austrian lilt. Some of the couples spoke Hungarian with each other. None wanted to speak German with me, they were embarrassed about having forgotten so much, especially grammar. They all have lived in the United States for a long time, so we spoke English."

Schmidt asked, menacing, slowly and carefully, "Can either of you think of a reason, or harbour a vague suspicion or a vague concern, that could perhaps result in a recommendation to delay your departure from the DDR?"

Both driver and guide recognised this as a dangerous type of question that politicians and Stasi officials asked when questioning someone, especially when the goal of the inquiry was undisclosed. Both thought about the implications and future liability that might result from a yes or a no answer.

Both hesitated before answering, and both avoided a simple yes or no, noted by Schmidt with interest.

The Austrian driver spoke first, "My biggest anxiety on this trip, and it was a very mild anxiety, was to run too low on fuel when detouring from the main roads for sightseeing. We are not allowed to go below a quarter tank. The castles and waterfalls are fascinating, but the twisting rural mountain roads do not have facilities that provide diesel fuel. I cannot think of any other anxiety. The only reason for being unable to depart would be lack of fuel. I never experienced this in the DDR."

Seifert explained, "I harboured various vague suspicions and anxieties during the tour. One was that I feared inadvertently getting in the way of whatever investigation was taking place in the area. I had no concern about our group. They all are fully documented tourists on a supervised tour booked well in advance."

"Then I noticed that our passengers had various small group meetings with whispered conversations that stopped when I approached. I suspected vaguely that they perhaps were organising a complaint against me, but I had not a clue why they would have a complaint. Later I found out that they were whispering about buying me a surprise present, the porcelain I told you about."

"I also worried that they would become very terribly upset and troublesome when the tour was interrupted, but they accepted the situation with good grace. The only issue was deciding whether to extend the tour to include all the scheduled cities in Poland and change their plane tickets or keep the scheduled flight home and skip the Polish cities. Extending the tour was offered as a no cost option; however, they decided to keep their plane tickets and return home as scheduled. There was no argument, all very amicable."

"I don't know whether any of the concerns I just described fit your criterion for a reason to delay their departure from our country."

Colonel Schmidt looked through his binder, finally told the driver in formal bureaucratic style, "You are free to leave the German Democratic Republic and continue your tour into the People's Republic of Poland. Please hand over your documents so we can stamp and sign them."

Turning to Seifert, the colonel asked, "We are about 100 km from the Polish border. How far are you scheduled to remain as their tour guide?"

She replied, "I get off in Görlitz, right at the Polish border. From there, I will call for my next assignment or go home if they don't have anything scheduled for me. The Polish tour guide is scheduled to join the tour at the customs house on their side of the border."

After the driver got the travel papers to take his bus out of the DDR, Colonel Schmidt shook hands with them and wished them a safe journey.

Soon they were under way. In about two hours, they arrived in the small city of Görlitz, where they had lunch and then said their goodbyes to tour guide Seifert, who looked sad standing on the sidewalk next to a small suitcase and clutching her gift box of Dresden porcelain figures. They all waved; she waved back as the bus drove away.

They went through the fastidious German border controls without difficulties and then crossed into Poland. They were joined by their new tour guide, a thin and tall young man, who was talkative and friendly. He held up a sign on white cardboard with his name: Andrzej Leszczynski, pronounced it in Polish, then added that foreigners often had difficulties with Polish names, and therefore suggested they call him 'Andy', for which he got applause. He said he was sorry that their Polish tour had been cut short. They were going to spend the night in Wroclaw, where he would try to show city highlights in a brief mini tour early in the morning and then proceed to Warsaw, about seven hours away.

As they travelled from the border towards Wroclaw they started to relax and savour the awareness that they had gotten out of East Germany safely. Now the trip would be easy and worry-free.

A feeling of euphoria took hold of the four lead collaborators, John and Barb Crawford, and Rick and Anne Holley. As they became too demonstrative Rick had to ask them to tone it down.

"I think we are going to make it, but we are not there yet. In Warsaw, my twin, the real one, will rejoin you, and I will disappear. Only then can you start relaxing, but with great care. Remember the Stasi is one of the most competent secret services on earth. They have not closed the file, and they will not close it until they get their man, or the world ends, or the DDR collapses, whichever comes first. Be careful, for your own sake. You had a great adventure, do not let it become a great nightmare."

The other three smiled, then turned serious and voiced their agreement without argument. John's hands had stopped shaking. Their collective blood pressures had returned to approaching normal. Barbara's stress-induced nausea ceased. Stomach aches eased, then disappeared.

Alan Mackenzie had arrived in Warsaw in the morning, as did Abigail Williamson. They were staying at the same hotel and met for lunch in Abigail's suite. They speculated about the delay of the tour in Dresden, and the intensity of the police activity.

Abigail asked, "This operation became more complicated and scarier than what you had presented to us. Did you miscalculate, did the years of retirement atrophy your dexterity, or did something happen that you did not consider?"

Alan disliked the implied criticism but controlled his temptation to say something offensive. It probably would be educational for the rich bitch to be told more about the rough, untidy, unpredictable life-threatening aspects of undercover work, but, as he had to do many times in the past, sitting across from politicians, station chiefs, employers, inquisitors, or expense account clerks, he explained politely and tried to educate patiently.

"Let me respond to each of your questions first, then I would ask that you allow me to share some general information that may help you understand some aspects of secret endeavours."

"Regarding your first question, no, I did not miscalculate. We allowed sufficient time and had sufficient training to accomplish the rescue of a high-ranking defector from a police state despite unexpected events and changed circumstances. As a matter of fact, we calculated odds and contingencies well, we even had a little extra time. I did not miscalculate the readiness of a bunch of elderly retirees and amateur actors to improvise under stress. They performed well, despite a level of stress not encountered in high-school plays."

"Your second question was whether my years of retirement had atrophied my dexterity. Here my answer also is no, at least as it relates to our project. Yes, age has taken its toll on my skills. I can no longer parachute behind enemy lines or infiltrate a terrorist organisation or crawl through a jungle for several days to photograph some secret activity. This kind of stuff was not required in our agreement. My head has not atrophied. I believe my intellectual output has actually improved, as I could concentrate on our project rather than having to split my time among several."

"Your third question was whether something happened that I did not take into account. Here the answer is yes, something did happen, but I don't know what. My best guess is that someone's travel plans were changed, leading to the early discovery of the disappearance, hence limiting the time for escape, this in turn limiting the search area. The intensity of the search, and the early insertion of the Stasi, their superb state security system, makes me think that there was some situation in high levels of government that added energy to their search. As originally planned, we expected to have about twelve hours to get far away. As it turned out, we got about two hours until the disappearance was discovered, not enough time to get far."

Abigail asked, "How do you know all this?"

Alan explained, "Some of the intelligence came from the Austrian bus driver, who turned out to be exceptionally observant and very skilled in dealing with unusual situations. He communicated by telephone with the Rakosis in Vienna, and they forwarded information to me and my partner Frank Kolozsvary. From that, we connected the dots. As I told you before, retirement has not dulled my brain."

Abigail commented, "I bet you are relieved that the job is finished. It was a most interesting experience, quite stressful at times."

Alan disagreed. "Mrs Williamson, please let me explain some things, as I requested before answering your questions. The first thing we need to be truly clear about is that the job is not finished until …"

She interrupted assertively, "Mr Mackenzie, the deal was that you rescue the defector, smuggle him out of East Germany and hand him over to me here in Warsaw."

Alan responded, "Exactly, but we are not there yet. Your man is not here yet. The disappearing twin, the real Richard Holley, must be reunited with his passport and his tour group, as soon as the defector shows up. The real Richard is here in the hotel already, in my room. We can make the exchange there, or any other place you select, and I approve. The exchange must take place after the Polish tour guide departs and the group leaves the bus, but before they register in the hotel and make arrangements to go to the airport tomorrow."

Abigail said, "I prefer to make the exchange in the morning, after the people who will take care of the defector arrive. The urgency is gone, you are out of East Germany now."

"I am sorry, madam, we are still in a Communist country with close political and police ties to the East Germans. It is crucial that the exchange occurs in the right place at a time when it would not be noticed. That window of opportunity is small, and we cannot afford to miss it."

"You are arguing with me, Mr Mackenzie. I have been involved from the beginning. I was the first contact with the defector. I participated in the search and then your selection as the leader of the clandestine extraction. Please don't treat me as a naïve observer."

Alan held her gaze for a moment, "Please do not take it as argument, Mrs Williamson. Please accept my advice, advice based on many years of doing this kind of work for our country. My position is not much different from that of your lawyer, your doctor, your accountant, your mechanic. You can accept expert advice, you can disagree, you can fire us, but you cannot overrule or change our professional judgement. In my case, you have the added complication that it would be exceedingly difficult, for you or your husband, to get a safe second opinion on time. You do not have the time. We are talking a matter of a few hours, not days."

"I respectfully must insist that we continue on full alert until the exchange has taken place. I will assist in the safe return of our tour collaborators to Long Beach, and you or your team will manage the deserter's further journey. I would have liked to continue assisting you with that segment, but I am okay with ending my assignment here in Warsaw. I am used to a type of business that is highly compartmentalised, with few knowing the whole story. For me, it was a great adventure, and it was wonderful to brighten my retirement with participation in one more escape from behind the Iron Curtain."

Abigail responded firmly, "I have made arrangements for tomorrow morning. It would be inconvenient to change them. I do not intend to do so."

A frustrated Alan tried again, "Please let me share some comparable situations I experienced in the past. On several occasions, we exchanged captured spies, often on a bridge between West and East Berlin on a rainy night. After an exchange of signals, there always was a tense wait, counting minutes, footsteps, distant noises. In most cases, a man walked slowly across the bridge from each side, with a heavily armed group waiting at each end, and the exchange was completed without incident."

"On two occasions, the exchange failed. In one, our man was shot in the back after crossing, and their man managed to escape running across. On another occasion, there was no shooting. The exchange was made carrying sedated men on stretchers, exchanging stretchers at midpoint. We found out too late that the body on the stretcher was not our man, but a sacrificial nobody that looked like our man."

Abigail commented, "Those are interesting cloak-and-dagger stories. I suppose there is a reason you are telling them now."

Alan replied, "Yes, madam, there is. We lost two American intelligence officers because the prisoner exchanges were changed from the originally agreed-upon plan. The shooting on the bridge happened because we delayed the exchange for one hour so that a congressman from an intelligence committee could watch the exchange. On the other side, the Stasi officer with whom the exchange had been negotiated ended his shift, and his replacement knew nothing about the deal and ordered the killing."

Abigail was getting abrupt, "And what about the substituted man on the stretcher? Who delayed that?"

Alan explained, "The stretcher event was not a delay but an early start, too soon. A clerk saw that the anesthetised man on the stretcher was ready to go. He phoned the other side about doing it early, they had no problem, so they proceeded with the exchange. The right man arrived exactly on time, but the exchange had already been done. Later our man was caught, kangaroo court tried, then executed."

Abigail commiserated, "I am sorry for the men who got killed. However, they were caught trying to escape the country. Our man is already out. They no longer can prevent his escape."

Alan argued, "True, they cannot prevent his escape. They can find him and kill him before he can be interrogated. If they kill him, whatever knowledge we expected him to share will be gone, out, final. Death is final. There are many types of information that can only be elicited verbally, especially if we are trying to discern enemy trends or fears or distant goals. These are abstract, they cannot be explained in a few sentences or some numbers, like reporting that the enemy has 150 tanks behind that mountain range."

For the first time in their conversation, Abigail seemed to be receptive to Alan's reasoning. Observing small details and word inflections during their discussion, Alan sensed at some intuitive level that the information they expected from the defector had more to do with the Politburo's long-range planning than any current issue.

She pondered his arguments for a while, then said, "We will make the exchange tomorrow morning. I am committed to that."

Alan insisted, "But why? Why not make the exchange as soon as the bus arrives? Both twins will be in the building, available for further travel. Why can't we close this chapter today?"

Abigail looked upset, retorted, "Please do not continue arguing with me. We cannot make the deserter disappear today and connect him with his next team until tomorrow because for some twelve hours he would be unaccounted for. We cannot break the chain of custody. He must remain part of the tour until he gets transferred to his new group. My new team will fingerprint him, give him a physical and scrutinise the passport he used on his escape. They want to make sure that we are handing over the real prize and not a substitute exchanged in the middle of the night."

It was Alan's turn to become slightly more receptive to her reasoning. He proposed, "Why not figure out something that would solve both our concerns? I suggest that when the bus arrives our defector hides in my room and lends the communal passport to the real Rick Holley to rejoin the tour and register in the hotel. After registration, the passport is returned to the defector for processing tomorrow morning by his new team, as you have planned. After your new team takes custody, you return the passport to its original owner to travel back home. This would not require a change in your plans. It assumes that the hotel will not be required to keep the passports overnight; if they keep them, we will have to improvise."

Abigail reflected a while, then agreed to the back-and-forth passport switching if the other team approved.

Alan thanked her, adding, "If something unusual happens that requires swift action, can I count on your unhesitant cooperation in dealing with the emergency? My understanding, since our first meeting in Virginia, is that I am in charge and responsible until we safely deliver your man to the designated party. I need your clear agreement now. Trying to decide or approve or negotiate anything when seconds count can be fatal. And I assure you, I will protect you and our man no matter what it takes, with or without your cooperation. If you do not cooperate with me, you will cause unnecessary, worthless pain and complications for yourself and others."

"I say all of this with respect and courtesy and hope you will understand the necessity for procedures that can be quite different from what you encounter in the business world. Think of our current phase as landing a large airplane low on fuel after a long flight. You selected the airport; let me handle the landing."

She sighed, pouted, then sarcastically grumbled, "Yes, captain, sir, you may land the plane, and yes, captain, sir, I will fasten my seatbelt, stow my tray, move my seatback to the upright position and follow the crew's instructions."

They agreed to meet in the main lounge before the expected arrival time of the bus. Abigail had to be there, as she was the one person the defector knew personally since his initial approach, and the only one he communicated with until his escape from Wolkenstein Lodge. Alan knew all the others from Long Beach and Vienna.

Back in Dresden, the Stasi task force was disbanding, and the officers were returning to their other pending cases. Colonel Schmidt and General Wolf had a telephone conversation summarising the situation. They agreed to close the Dresden operation but continue in Berlin, microscopically examining Bruno Hadler's apartment and all correspondence, paperwork, and phone records, and maintaining an open case file until they caught their man. Berlin headquarters also set up a task force to analyse what state secrets Hadler could have accessed, and what countermeasures were required to offset or at least reduce the damage.

It weighed heavily on everyone that they had not caught their man. Damage control now replaced the manhunt as the primary preoccupation of the Politburo and the Stasi.

Schmidt's group had prepared a four-hundred-page summary of the disappearance investigation, each clue or hypothesis on a separate page, giving a brief narrative, investigations conducted, witnesses if any, and disposition of the task. The entire file was being sent to Berlin.

Wolf approved of the thoroughness and thanked Schmidt, adding that it was great to have 100% coverage of all the angles investigated and discarded, to avoid unnecessary repetitions, and for use as a training manual.

Schmidt commented, "Actually it is about 98 or 99%. We excluded the traffic violations, as these have their own police reports, being sent to Berlin in a separate file. However, there are three items that we did not close. We had assigned an officer to compare the tour member passport photographs with photographs of comrade Bruno Hadler, with the idea that we would thoroughly check out anyone showing a resemblance. Three names emerged, two on the French bus, and one American. We did not pursue that because the fingerprints from all four buses definitively did not include Bruno Hadler's. There was no point in further examining the three named passengers."

"The only bother is that we cannot claim it as a 100% summary. Some future inquisitors may accuse us of incomplete work without bothering to find out why. If I had to do it again, I would check them out, just to be able to claim 100% completion."

Wolf agreed. "The 99% figure is usually an irritant. It clamours for an explanation or a disclaimer that nobody wants to hear. There have been some famous cases where the result of a battle or a race was claimed as 99% successful. Let's get rid of the 99 and make it a 100%. Now we need to involve the Polish Ministry of Public Security, or whatever they are called this week, but I do not want to do it at the ministerial level, to avoid curiosity and publicity. Additionally, let us make sure, if we do this, to truly make it a 100%. Do you know anyone at the SB who could do us a quiet favour?"

Schmidt replied, "As a matter of fact I do. I have worked with a colonel Surowiecki a few times and exchanged favours. He speaks fluent German. Let me call him and see what we can do. I'll keep you informed."

Schmidt called the Sluzba Bezpieczenstwa, or SB, as it was usually referred to, the Polish counterpart of the East German Staatssicherheitsdienst, or Stasi. He spoke to his colleague and explained that they were trying to locate a petty criminal who kept getting away by impersonating foreign tourists. The Stasi suspected he may be impersonating one of three tourists who just left the DDR towards Warsaw. One candidate was an older American, traveling in an Austrian tour bus, the other two French, both traveling on the same French tour bus.

Would it be possible for the SB to go to their hotels and verify that they were the persons listed on their passports? The passports were good, they had been checked and certified, so no need to spend time on that. The Stasi would greatly appreciate a thorough body search, checking for cosmetics that change appearance, fake beards, wigs, fake prescription glasses, wrinkles, tattoos, body scars from surgery, and a very careful face comparison with the passport photographs, done in bright light. If wigs or aging were used, they probably would be of high, professional quality, so they need to be pulled or scraped hard. It did not matter if the suspects were insulted or inconvenienced. It also was especially important that the search be conducted on the evening of their arrival. Do not wait until night or next morning.

If one of them was a fake, he should be arrested. The Stasi would promptly extradite him through channels. Any expenses incurred by the SB would immediately be reimbursed by the Stasi.

If all three were legitimate, they should be free to go, with apologies or a kick in the arse, the Stasi did not care which. Surowiecki hated the Americans and the French and was happy to oblige. He also was glad to help the Germans and collect some credits; usually it was the SB that needed assistance from the Stasi.

Schmidt sent him the personal details of Richard Holley and the two Frenchmen, as well as bus and hotel information.

Alan and Abigail sat at a small table from where they could watch the entrance and the reception desk. They had coffee and cake and talked about Warsaw. She had been in the city several times, which surprised Alan, who had been assigned there frequently. Rick Holley remained in Alan's room. They wanted to minimise the public visibility of the two Rick Holleys until the exchange was completed. The grand hotel bars and restaurants were popular meeting places for the high-ranking politicians and party officials who could afford it. The former Politburo secretary had been socialising in these places many times during Warsaw visits. Alan worried that someone, colleague, or waiter, might recognise the fugitive from his profile or some other characteristic that the artificial aging had not camouflaged.

Alan's anxieties raised Abigail's stress level; however, he did nothing to calm her down. She seemed inclined to think that their current situation was like a real estate transaction in escrow, where all terms had been agreed upon, with only routine paperwork remaining. He worried that project-end complacency lowered people's guard, at times with dire consequences. She reiterated several times that she had not heard yet from her other team about Alan's proposed modification, therefore the tomorrow morning schedule remained valid.

Alan had updated Rick Holley about the tour adjustments, warned him about Abigail's refusal to change the exchange time, and instructed him to remain close to the phone, even while using the bathroom, in case Alan had to give him emergency directions.

The tour bus was approaching the outskirts of Warsaw, headed to the hotel on the most direct route. Guide Andy kept pointing out features, making a valiant effort to say something interesting about parts of town that were never included in the sightseeing itineraries. His audience, especially the aspiring actors in the group, admired him for improvising ways of telling the drab story of a drab factory building, citing the products made there and the happiness those goods spread across Poland. He pointed out pioneer streetcar lines that changed the demographics of the city, told interesting vignettes about the many churches, and pointed out sites that were important during World War II. He also repeated how sad he was that their tour had been delayed at the cost of missing the important sights of Wroclaw and Warsaw.

As they arrived at the hotel there was already another tour bus unloading passengers and luggage at the main entrance, and they parked to wait. Andy took the opportunity to say goodbye to his American tourists, wishing them a safe journey home and hoping that they would return to Poland to visit great places with plenty of time. They thanked him and gave him a round of applause. He bowed and left towards the hotel side entrance.

The group decided to use the traffic pause to thank their driver for his superb service, presenting him with a gift from Dresden. He opened it carefully and found a porcelain stagecoach with four white horses, all in the royal livery of the kings of Saxony. He was very touched and thanked them profusely in English and in German. They asked him where he was headed next, it was the port of Gdansk, where he was to pick up a group from a cruise ship and drive them on a tour through Poland, Czechoslovakia and Austria.

The bus ahead moved on and they drove to the front entrance. As the passengers were exiting the bus, the driver took Anne Holley aside and told her that an unmarked police car had been following them at a distance since Wroclaw. On the outskirts of Warsaw, the unmarked car was joined by a regular police car. He thanked Anne again for the beautiful gift, wished her a safe trip, and, with their eyes meeting and holding her hand, urged great care and wished her good luck. The hotel crew took in the luggage and the passengers shook hands with their driver, all mutually wishing each other a safe trip.

Anne urgently conferred with her three co-conspirators. Rick was convinced that the Polish SB had been co-opted by the Stasi for another inspection or investigation. He was sure that the cops would do nothing in the public areas, but wait until everyone was in their room, to avoid publicity.

The panicked four decided that Rick would immediately head to the nearest men's toilet and hide in one of the stalls. The other three would wait until the last moment to join the line at the hotel registration. They were hoping for something, not sure what it could be. Perhaps a bright idea, perhaps the cavalry would arrive at the las minute, as in the old Westerns, and save them.

Looking towards the glass front of the hotel entrance, Alan recognised the Austrian bus driving up. He and Abigail got up and went to have a closer look. There was the usual crowded scene of luggage and people coming and going, people departing paying their bills, people arriving registering and handing over their papers, all presenting a somewhat disorderly appearance. Abigail commented that the Poles could learn some hotel management from the Americans, Alan suggested that at present slow and confused was better.

Alan recognised Anne Holley standing in line and went over to say hello. She was panic stricken and stuttered what their driver had reported. Alan asked where their defector was, she said he was hiding in the nearest men's toilet. Abigail joined the conversation, she had become pale, without a word to say.

Alan became aggressive and said, "Listen, women, the cops following the bus is not a coincidence, it is called surveillance. Once you are in your rooms you will be questioned, and Rick Holley will have an interrogation like he never had before, probably including a rough physical. For all of us, the only way out is for the real Richard Holley to be in place, endure the abuse, and stick to his American birth, citizenship, history, and that he just had an interesting tour through four countries. I will produce the real Rick Holley in a matter of minutes; the fake one must disappear, not tomorrow but now."

"You, Mrs Williamson, will go to the men's room, talk to our defector, and tell him to remain hidden, and no longer respond to the name Holley, even if called out repeatedly. He will have a new identity in the morning, according to you, and he will spend the night in your suite. We will move him out of the toilet as soon as the real Richard Holley is reintroduced into the tour."

Abigail said, "I have no intention of going into a men's toilet in Poland or deviating from the schedule my people worked out. We will make the change in the morning as we had discussed."

Alan looked at her with disbelief, then said, "Listen very carefully. There is no time for games. We are in an extremely dangerous situation. You will do exactly as I tell you. First, you …" She interrupted, "No, I will not. You are not my boss; I am your boss and I fully …"

Alan tried not to raise his voice, but managed to project the anger he felt saying, "Shut up, Abigail Williamson. You may find yourself in a Polish jail, with accommodations far below the standards you are accustomed to, just for being stubborn and naïve, a bad combination."

Abigail insisted, "My husband will promptly take care of any situa ..."

Alan lost his patience, "Shut the fuck up! I am trying to keep several people alive and out of harm's way. Do not be a stupid idiot! Do not risk finding out too late what it feels like to have a gun stuck in your mouth and a police nightstick between your legs! By the time your husband's position, assuming he still would have a position, gets you out, you will have been damaged forever! There is no time for arguments."

"You can have a fight with me after this is over, with your life, position, and privilege intact. Right now, we need you! Get the fuck into that toilet, send any witnesses away, and talk to Hadler, alone. He will recognise you, perhaps you will initially not recognise him. It is imperative that he sees you. You are his initial contact, the only contact he has been willing to deal with until his escape."

Abigail was red-faced, speechless, furious. After a pause, she mumbled that she did not speak Polish and therefore could not tell men to leave the men's toilet. Alan said there was no time to coach her, so he would go with her to solve the problem. Then he called Rick Holley from the nearest house phone, told him to meet them at once in the men's toilet near the main lobby.

Alan went into the toilet first, saw a man about to enter one of the stalls, grabbed him by the collar of his jacket and pulled him back, pointing towards the door with his thumb, telling him in English, German and Russian to go elsewhere. The man, who was big, young and muscular seemed undecided, then left. Another man at the lavatory was about to wash his hands but decided to leave as well. Only one pair of feet remained visible under the stalls.

Alan then called in the two women and instructed Abigail to explain the situation to comrade Bruno Hadler. The two went through some greeting ritual that could have been passwords, then the stall door opened a crack and Abigail was asked to show herself, walk and talk. Hadler then opened the door, shook hands with her and looked at Alan and Anne. Abigail was surprised at the changed appearance, but there was no doubt that she was looking at the real Bruno Hadler.

Alan introduced himself and explained, "I am the technician who Mrs Williamson hired to engineer your escape. And you know Anne, your tour wife."

There were some smiles. Abigail wanted Alan to explain, but he referred it back to her, as moments earlier she had seemed eager to handle the situation on her own way without Alan's advice, and she had to coordinate the next phase of the escape with a new team. She took a deep breath, then explained in a clear, firm voice that Bruno would spend the night in her suite pretending to be her lover, and that it would be best to keep his makeup intact for now. He would receive new instructions tomorrow.

At that point, the door opened and the big young man who had been told to go away moments earlier reappeared. He was angry, started yelling at Alan in Polish and punched him on the chest, hard, feeling at ease overpowering the white-haired older man. Alan almost lost his equilibrium, wobbled but remained standing, then hit the young man in the side of the neck with the edge of his hand with lightning speed, and the big guy fell to the ground wheezing, having difficulty breathing. Alan kicked him in the stomach, which caused him to urinate in his pants, then grabbed him under the arms and stood him up leaning against the wall, slapped him on the face a couple of times to get his attention and held him against the wall until he could stand and breathe on his own. The man was terrified, all bravado gone.

Alan gestured silence holding a finger over his lips, and the man nodded. Then he pointed at the door and with his fingers gestured walking away, and the man nodded again. Alan looked at him for a moment, then gestured a warning index finger, and implying other consequences by dragging the edge of his hand across his own larynx. The man nodded again, this time more vigorously. Alan released him to leave with an unsteady walk, wet pants, quite shaken and obviously in pain.

The two women were astonished by Alan's speed and shocked by his violence, became scared of him and of being mixed up in such a situation. Bruno Hadler found the interaction interesting and reappraised Alan differently from his initial impression.

After Abigail recovered her composure, she asked Alan hesitatingly, "When you tried to send me to clear the men's room, did you expect me to deal with that kind of situation?"

"No, madam, I expected you to use charm, money bribes, courtesy, whatever your imagination could conjure. If you did not succeed, or if things appeared threatening, I expected you to leave and come to see me."

"You are a dangerous man."

"Yes, madam, that is correct."

The door opened again, and all prepared themselves for another rough scene, but it was Richard Holley, the real one. The two Richards looked at each other with surprise and amusement. The German shook hands with Richard and Alan, bowed slightly and said thank you, then bowed and kissed the hand of his tour wife, with a more emotional thank you.

Alan interrupted the ceremonies and urged Abigail to take Bruno into her suite at once and keep him there, out of sight. He also instructed her to resolve how to deal with the chain of custody issues that she had argued earlier, and to get it done today.

Alan added, "Tomorrow morning I expect you to call me and advise that the new transfer has been successfully completed. Only at that time will you be off the hook. Until then I expect that we can count on your continuing cooperation and active collaboration, and until then I expect everyone here to follow my instructions. Are we all clear and in agreement? Please say so, in words."

He looked at Abigail, who nodded and said, "Yes, I will collaborate and obey your instructions, but only in connection with this undertaking."

"Thank you, Mrs Williamson."

The others followed suit. Alan then addressed Anne and Richard, "This panic attack could be a false alarm. Very unlikely, but theoretically possible. In my judgement, based on experience with many cases over many years, there is a 99% chance that the SB, the Polish internal security organisation, will knock on your door and test that Richard is indeed Richard, and not an escaping criminal impersonating Richard."

"These security organisations favour the hours of three or four in the morning for their surprise visits, but they have been known to vary their routines."

"It is important that you assume less time rather than more. It is imperative that you, Anne, spend the next few hours bringing Richard up to date on what took place while he was away from the tour. I assume you may have a few hours, but just in case they come after you within minutes, you should have covered all major events at least once, even if just briefly."

Anne was worried about suitcases not matched to the right Richard, as the two men were of slightly different sizes. Alan conceded that this may cause a problem if someone had to change clothing but considered it a minor risk compared to getting caught trying the exchange suitcases. The decision was to leave the suitcases alone.

Anne and the real Richard went to register at the hotel front desk. Alan, Abigail and Bruno Hadler went up to Abigail's penthouse suite in the freight elevator, sharing part of the trip with laundry bins, food carts, vacuum cleaners, and argumentative Polish-speaking maids trying to explain that they should not be in the freight elevator.

Alan insisted on a quick tour of Abigail's suite, looking into every room and closet, and admonished Hadler in English and in German that he had no papers and should stay hidden until morning, then follow Mrs Abigail Williamson's instructions. He also reminded Abigail that it still was Alan's show until the morning changeover. She did not argue.

Anne and Richard joined their group in the front lobby. Alan had insisted that they all be aware that Anne's husband had changed back to their friend and little theatre colleague as it had been at the beginning of the tour. They looked at Richard with interest, no one said anything dumb. They resisted the temptation of shaking hands or asking about Richard's tour. They all realised that there had been a second successful exchange of twins, and without any fugitive in their midst, they all felt that they were no longer in danger.

The quartet of John and Barbara Crawford and Rick and Anne Holley waited for the elevator together. They had rooms on the same floor. As the doors started to close a uniformed policeman held it open, and five men entered the elevator, two in uniform and three civilians. All passengers were headed to the same floor. There was silence during the short ride; four of them feared that their thumping heartbeat would be heard. They realised that the few hours assumed available for coaching Rick had evaporated.

The group walked down the long corridor together, looking at room numbers. The Crawfords reached theirs first. The four agreed to meet for dinner in the hotel dining room in an hour, secretly hoping dinner would not be grub in a Polish prison.

When they reached Holley's room, the five from the police looked at a card, one said in English this is the number they also are looking for and asked whether he was Richard Holley. As soon as he confirmed it, badges were flashed, and the English speaker said that they were from National Public Security, the SB, and ordered all into the room.

One of the civilians seemed to be the leader. He spoke a little English but communicated through the interpreter for anything requiring more than a simple sentence. He was anxious because the previous investigation of the two Frenchmen confirmed beyond a doubt that the Frenchmen were legitimate, impersonating no one. He concluded that the criminal, if there was one, would be impersonating someone in this third and last group, accordingly, he instructed his team to be extra thorough and check everything.

The leader explained that they were looking for an escaped criminal who impersonated foreign tourists to get away. He pointed out one of his companions as a medic who would conduct a body search. He ordered Anne, the medic and one of the uniformed men into the bathroom to examine Anne. The other uniform remained by the front door.

Rick Holley tried to complain about Anne being forced into a body search, was told to shut up or risk having his teeth broken with the butt of a gun. She came out in fifteen minutes, buttoning her clothes with shaking hands and purple with anger. Rick's turn was next. He was told to undress completely. The medic examined every inch of his body, photographed his surgery scars, examined his rectum and his genitals, and his ears. There was a slow, careful examination of his wrinkled skin, they swabbed parts with an alcohol impregnated cotton, pulled his hair in all places, checked his eyes, inside of his nose and his mouth, examined teeth and photographed them, scraped his skin in various parts.

They examined his clothes and the contents of his pockets. They compared his face with his passport photograph under a very bright light, measured his height and checked his weight. They let him get dressed and proceeded to check all luggage and all clothing, and the contents of purses, wallets, pockets, and shopping bags. They looked at clothing in the suitcases again, dumping it all on the bed. They held up Anne's underwear and joked in Polish. Then they held up a pair of men's pants and commented about them. For a scary moment, Rick feared they would ask him to change clothes and find out that what was in the suitcase did not fit him.

They seemed to be getting angry, behaving in a brusque, insolent way. Rick and Anne grew proportionally more worried, not knowing what to expect.

The five policemen had a quiet conversation in Polish, then announced that the inspection was over. As they were leaving Rick impulsively told them that they should apologise to Anne. The leader responded that Rick and Anne should apologise for wasting the police's time.

After the police left, Rick and Anne were exhausted. They did not feel like straightening their things and packing again. They pushed everything on the floor and laid down on the bed for a while.

Anne was crying. She felt violated, humiliated, scared, helpless. Rick tried to console her, although he himself could have used some calming. They rationalised that they should be dancing euphorically for having passed the inspection, but emotionally they were drained and not in a celebratory mood. They called the Crawfords and rescheduled their dinner date for an hour later, commenting only, in a very sanitised way, that they had a police inspection, but everything was okay.

Anne sobbed, "I keep thinking at every crisis that it is the last one, then we have another, and another, and another. Since we are leaving tomorrow, I suppose that today's insulting, ugly, vulgar episode was truly the last one."

Rick advised, "No, you cannot count on anything. We still have the airport exiting procedure. In our times, getting out from a Communist country is frequently one of the most exciting events of a trip behind the Curtain."

Back in Dresden, Stasi Colonel Schmidt received a telex from SB Colonel Surowiecki certifying that the suspects, two French and one American, had been inspected very thoroughly by the Polish security service and proven beyond a doubt that they were the persons described in their passports. There were no wigs, makeup, fake wrinkles, hair dyes, evidence of plastic surgery, absolutely nothing unclear or suspicious. A thorough naked body examination confirmed age, weight, height, eye colour.

Schmidt telephoned Surowiecki to discuss the inspections. They agreed that nothing else could have been checked. The only additional information was that the two Frenchmen had vowed to file a complaint with the Polish government. Surowiecki wanted to know how to explain it; Schmidt advised him to tell the truth, that they were trying to catch a petty criminal who kept getting away by impersonating foreign tourists.

Surowiecki asked, "Shall we let them leave Poland? They all are scheduled to depart tomorrow."

Schmidt advised, "Let the French depart. Hold the Americans at the airport until I advise you whether we want to hold them or extradite them back to the DDR. I suppose we will let them go, but not yet. I will telephone you in the morning with our request. Meanwhile, the Stasi and I thank you very much for your help on this matter. We owe you, and I will let my superiors know about your splendid cooperation. I hope you will call me whenever we can be of assistance to you. It is so great when we can strengthen the fraternal bond between our socialist nations through mutual assistance."

Later Schmidt called General Wolf and brought him up to date. Schmidt ended his summary with, "The problem I have is that I don't really know if I have a definable, specific problem that can be tackled, or if I am just feeling the frustration of not having found our vanished man. My instinct keeps tugging at my gut and my mind that we overlooked some simple detail, perhaps something obvious that is staring us in the face, but we keep looking beyond."

Wolf commiserated, "I know, comrade colonel, I understand your frustration well, as I experience it often. But I am glad you are again thinking and sensing like an intelligence officer and not as a playground cop. Anyway, it seems that our Polish colleagues did a good job examining and clearing our suspects. What are you going to do?"

Schmidt explained, "I told them to let the French go, and I have no second thoughts about them. The Americans, however, are where my gut acts up. I told the Poles to let them go to the airport but not allow them to board until I authorise it. I am holding them overnight just in case I have a flash of enlightenment in the middle of the night."

Wolf asked, "Are you going to hold up the plane if you need more time?"

"No, I'll let the plane go, to minimise the diplomatic whining that undoubtedly will ensue if we keep them from leaving. If we ask the Poles to arrest a few and hand them over to us, the diplomatic reaction will grow louder and involve higher levels of government. Your level, I suppose."

In the Warsaw hotel, Alan confirmed at the front desk that their bus to the airport had been reserved and scheduled for the right time in the morning. Then he called the airline to confirm tickets, passengers, boarding time. He was advised that they had the passenger list and the tickets reserved, but that there was a boarding hold ordered by the national security police. The agent said that typically these boarding bans were lifted after the security people detained the person of interest they were looking for, and the American passengers would then be allowed to board and have their luggage loaded.

Alan called Abigail and asked to meet with her to report. She refused, he reminded her brusquely that until the morning she was supposed to cooperate without arguing and told her he was on his way and would be at her suite door in a matter of minutes.

He knocked on her door, had no response, then banged hard and repeatedly until she opened.

She was angry and hostile, told him, "I don't want to see you. You were insulting and rude to me, and horribly violent to a man who just wanted to use a restroom. I choose not to mingle with people indulging in your kind of behaviour and I will not tolerate it from you or anyone else! I ask you to leave or I will call security!"

Alan was highly amused. "Mrs Williamson, you just made the funniest statement I heard today. It is nice to have something to laugh about in midst of danger and complications. Let me ask you, what do you imagine a bellboy or a young man from hotel security can do to me?"

"Let me add, I will keep you and your refugee alive and well until tomorrow morning, with or without your cooperation, when the transfer to a new team has been successfully completed, that is, when I hear it from you and I am convinced that you are not being coerced."

"Let me remind you of something else that you saw but choose not to remember. The roughness in the rest room was not because the man wanted to use the facilities, but because he physically attacked a senior citizen. He was young, big, strong, and angry, and he hit me really hard. So I pushed back. I believe he learned something, and his future manners will be much improved."

"Also, let me enlighten you a bit more. He was lucky that he hit me. I let him wobble away. If he had attacked you, he would have been carried to a hospital emergency facility unconscious on a stretcher."

She pondered what she heard, reluctantly said, "I understand your reasoning for resorting to violence, and I understand we all behave according to our own reasons and beliefs, but your beliefs are not my beliefs."

Alan retorted, "You may not like my style, or that of some of our specialised military units, but we are the people who protect your freedoms, who will rescue you from sinking ships, who allow you to criticise our bad manners in accordance with your own beliefs and without breaking a fingernail or messing up your hairdo."

She asked, with hostility, "Are you starting to become insulting again? You explained your rationale for violence, but you have not acknowledged, explained, or apologised for treating me like an uneducated idiot and insulting me with vulgar, filthy language. What gives you the right, in your own mind?"

He thought for a moment, then said, "I will try to enlighten you again about the dark world you chose to touch lightly at its edges. Cloak-and-dagger stories are the subject of interesting conversations in parties and the subject of good action movies."

"In real life, cloak-and-dagger actions rarely use cloaks or daggers anymore. Nowadays it is firearms, elaborate disguises, electronics, encrypted communications, technical and scientific knowhow, photography, wireless, powerful puppet masters, and skilled, highly trained field agents. For this brief explanation, you may include me in the field agent category."

"In the traditional puppet theatres, the puppeteer behind the scenes pulls strings, with great skill, and through the strings, controls all movements of the marionettes, puppets, some scenery, making them jump, dance, hug, fight, sway in the wind, and through their movements, tell a story."

Abigail interrupted, "And your point is what? Are you going to illustrate things for me with a children's story? Do you think I do not understand adult language? Why should I listen to this?"

Alan answered, his voice becoming irritated, "You should listen to this because it may help to keep you and your protege alive for another twelve hours. It will also serve to illustrate to you how quickly I can irritate you enough for you to forget your exquisite manners. How would you react if someone slapped you, fondled you or spit in your face?"

"Back to puppets. Unlike the puppets on stage, those in the intelligence business, cloak-and-dagger if you wish, often have no physical linkage with the puppeteer. Yes, there is training, instructions, preparations, goals, patriotism, loyalty, fear, hatred, revenge, whatever long list of words you may add, but the bottom line is that the puppet in the field is alone, there are no safe strings to guide his movements. He must survive by his wits, he must evaluate and improvise with limited resources and often, and more critical, limited time. The story may be planned in detail by the puppet master many months ahead, then, in real life, the circumstances change abruptly, and the puppet, now alone, has two hours or a few minutes to figure out an alternative. I must repeat, there are no strings to pull him up or guide his steps."

"Often, he has to inform other players under his care, motivate them, at times convince them, make them aware of impending danger when they don't want to listen, or don't believe the seriousness of a situation. In normal situations, the issues can be discussed in comfortable chairs, with coffee and cigarettes, or over a fine meal, and a consensus is gradually arrived at. In the field, you must learn to choose between 'fight or flee' and decide at once, in a matter of minutes, at times in a matter of seconds."

"In our project, as in many of these transactions, timing was crucial. There had to be an exchange of Bruno Hadler and Richard Holley on the first stop in East Germany. A new Richard had to be created on arrival, while changing tour guides concurrently. The switch was successful, there remained the task of changing the appearance of Bruno Hadler. I had to push really hard in Long Beach and in Vienna to rehearse making the changeover in a minimum time. Several times in Long Beach and in Vienna, Anne Miller, alias Mrs Anne Holley, threatened to quit, as did a few other members, because I was pushing too hard on the time issue, and being angry, abrasive and rude."

"We assumed we had about twelve hours until the disappearance of Hadler was noted. Something happened, causing the discovery in about two hours. Two hours, not the twelve we were counting on. A massive manhunt was instituted almost immediately. We had a surprise inspection by the Stasi at about four in the morning. Fortunately, the appearance changeover had been completed, and by a lucky miracle, the Stasi man did not notice the face difference between Hadler and the passport photo of Richard Holley. He was tired or distracted; perhaps fate was on our side."

"Anne Miller realised that Bruno Hadler had escaped the firing squad and she had escaped a long prison term by having completed the makeover before the surprise four a.m. inspection by the Stasi. Alan Mackenzie suddenly became a hero and icon of salvation, and his short-fused bad temper was gratefully understood."

Alan continued, "With a head start of only two hours, the search radius was relatively small. The vanished secretary could not have travelled too far in two hours, therefore a massive manhunt in a reduced area was indicated. With the originally assumed head start of twelve hours, a massive manhunt could not have accomplished anything, as the area to be covered became too large."

"The tour passengers, although not professionals, had enough coaching to improvise, and to figure out how to get help discreetly. Later in the tour, an unexpected fingerprinting session that would have identified Bruno Hadler was announced for the following morning. Our driver telephoned his bosses in

Vienna, who understood the danger and the urgency, then developed a suggestion on how to escape the trap and telephoned my partner Frank Kolozsvary in Wisconsin, who understood the coded message and devised a plan, coordinated and drafted a message with Mrs Madeleine in California, cabled it in concealed language to the team waiting for salvation in East Germany, who understood the message and implemented it with about half hour to spare."

"I was on my way to Warsaw and did not hear about this until I reached my hotel. We hoped that once all were in Warsaw the surprises would be over. However, after the bus arrived, we found out that the Polish state security was after us, no doubt at Stasi request. We had an unknown amount of time to make Bruno Hadler vanish and reinstate the real Richard Holley into the tour group. We were able to make the exchange in the rest room. We took Hadler to your suite, Anne and Holley went to the front desk to register. They were the last of the group, the line was gone. They were processed swiftly and went up to their room."

"In my line of business, it is useful to note things, memorise numbers like telephones, addresses and license plates, and pay attention to the clock, the time."

"Watching the time, I noted that from the Hadler/Holley exchange to the arrival of Polish security in Holley's room, twenty-three minutes had elapsed."

"Please note this number, Mrs Williamson; twenty-three minutes separated Bruno Hadler from the firing squad and several in the tour group from a long prison term! You wanted to wait until next day! Are you listening?"

"Yes, Mr Mackenzie, I am listening."

Alan continued, "We were under extreme pressure. You argued with me, insisting on keeping your arrangements for next day. You complicated an already complicated situation even more. I explained the concerns to you, but you were stubborn and unwilling to adapt to the circumstances. Nice conversation had no effect, so I had to resort to rougher language. Now you are upset and sulking about being insulted. You should be grateful that you have Hadler in your suite, and that the tour members are all accounted for and relatively safe in their own identities."

Abigail complained, "You did not need to use such vulgar language. I am not …"

Alan raised his voice, "Mrs Williamson, yes, you needed some strong language. You ignore polite explanations if they do not fit your preconceived agenda. We seem to be headed into another argument. I suggest that it would be much easier to trust my experience and follow my instructions until you are out of Polish airspace."

Abigail asked, "What would you have done if I ignored your yelling? Hit me?"

"No, madam, nowadays I only hit people in self-defence, and I don't hit women, although there have been cases where a lady attacked me with a machete or a firearm and I had no choice."

"Your main question is what I would have done if you did not collaborate. What I would have done, probably, is leave you standing there by yourself, and kidnap Bruno Hadler and go into hiding, until the tour people were home safe, and you were out of harm's way. Then I would contact you and deliver Hadler to you, in a place and manner of my choosing."

She pouted for a while, then concluded, "I believe it is best that we exchange apologies and then start fresh again."

Alan said, "I agree with starting fresh, but not exchanging apologies. There is nothing to apologise for, on either side. I am only interested in keeping all of us, including you and Mr Hadler, safe and in good health. Nobody needs to know that you got involved in a situation that was unfamiliar and that this unfamiliarity led to arguments. As far as the world is concerned, you performed brilliantly in some extremely dangerous circumstances."

"But please, let me be the guide in this business, it is my area of expertise. And do not forget how close we were to disaster! Twenty-three minutes!"

"Please note also how the time issue keeps getting worse. At the beginning, we had planned twelve hours head start, which abruptly became two, and we had a surprise visit from the Stasi that same night. Later we had to figure out, overnight, how to escape the fingerprinting entrapment, and next morning, how to implement it, which we did with half hour to spare. Today we were surprised by the unexpected involvement of the Polish security and had to remove Hadler and re-insert Holley in a truly short period of time, which turned out to be twenty-three minutes!"

There was a long silence. Alan was more able to manage long silences, Abigail was not. Eventually she took a deep breath and asked, "What did you want to see me about?"

"To report on the latest impediment to happiness. I inquired about airport transportation and flight reservations, found out that the airport bus is scheduled, and all air tickets are confirmed, but there is a police hold placed on our group that prevents us from boarding or loading baggage."

She was astonished. "Oh God, what now? Why do we have a problem with the Poles?"

Alan explained, "Because they were asked by the East German Stasi. I guess the Germans had second thoughts about letting us leave, or they found something new to connect us to the missing bureaucrat. The Poles can hold us, whether we like it or not, and they are more inclined to please the East Germans than the Americans."

Abigail stated firmly, "This is not acceptable. Delays do not fit my schedule. I will tell my husband if I must. We will leave on time. Tell the Poles not to mess with my rights!"

Alan asked, "Are you joking? I hope you are trying to be funny. If you are serious, you will …"

She cracked a smile, said, "You should have seen your face. It clouded over real fast. Do not worry, I was joking. I heard and understood all your explanations, and I will follow your directions concerning this project until we all are out of Polish airspace. I mistakenly and naively assumed that we were safe and done once we were in Warsaw. What do we do now?"

Alan responded, "Please don't joke about all this. I do not scare easily, but I am scared because too many things did not go as planned. We do not know why, perhaps we will never know. Right now, we still are not out of the Stasi clutches."

"My plan is to follow the only option available, which is we will firmly stick to our story that we are American retirees on a tour. We have no escaped East German politicians in our midst. They have checked us out many times. We are who we are. There is no reason to prevent us from going home. It is obvious that they have found nothing, but keep fishing, hoping to net something. We are of an age group that the East Germans allow to emigrate, as seniors are no longer productive and burden the state with their welfare costs. Why are they delaying us?"

"I will stay in Warsaw until the tour group people are out safely. If they keep holding them until they miss their plane, I will have grounds to go to our embassy and ask for help. I believe at this stage your husband will use the resources of our State Department to get them out. The Communists have at times held individual Americans and other Westerners imprisoned on trumped-up charges, triggering a slow, political, and difficult diplomatic effort to secure their release. I do not believe they can hold an entire busload of senior citizens for no reason. In my opinion, the worst scenario is a delay of a few days in a fine hotel. We do not have any escaped East Germans in our midst, we have not met any, we don't know what they are talking about."

"The only danger I see is that they may have an individual in their sights and question him, or her, until panic sets in and the story spills out. If they discover that the group was involved in a conspiracy, they can hold the entire busload for trial. That could be an interesting international scandal. I do not believe this is likely to happen. I mention it only because too many unlikely things have happened, and I am getting spooked, and I want to make you aware of the situation."

Despite his reassuring words to Abigail, Alan worried that assuming that innocent tourists were safe was not a reliable assumption. In the following morning, the tour checked out of the hotel and boarded their airport shuttle, although Alan had been unable to get confirmation of their departure permit. He went to the airport in a taxi ahead of the group, in hopes of being able to get more done in person than by telephone.

The airline and the airport informed him that if they did not receive clearance for the tour group at least twenty minutes before departure time, they would be left behind, with their luggage, as they could not load the luggage in less than twenty minutes, and the airport authorities would not allow a departure delay due to a police hold on some of the passengers.

Alan reported the situation to the group gathered in front of the check-in counter, next to their pile of suitcases. He reassured them that they had nothing to hide, there were no escaped criminals hiding in their midst, therefore the worst that could happen is that they would remain in Warsaw for a couple of days. The costs of the delays, including airfare, would be reimbursed.

After a pause, Alan added, looking at John Crawford, that any stupid criticisms of the Polish government or political system could delay the departure even further, urging all tour members to curb their anger about the delays.

Crawford argued, "Why in the hell do we have to pussyfoot around now? As you said, there are no escaped criminals in our midst. Why do not we start acting like Americans and exercise our rights to free speech and our right to complain about lousy services rather than kowtowing to a bunch of Communist bureaucrats. If these assholes keep interfering with our travel plans, we should inform our embassy and get it fixed at once! What are we paying taxes for? I am getting really sick of all the bullshit!"

Alan admonished angrily, "If you raise your voice to spout your suicidal complaints again, I will call the police and request they arrest you for disturbing the peace and insulting Poland! They will not read you your rights; here you do not have any! And our embassy can request and negotiate and submit protest notes, and perhaps obtain your release after several months. The Poles have three Americans imprisoned for over half a year on various vague charges, with no release in sight. Do not count on fantasies of a quickie rescue by our diplomats. My job is to protect you all and return you safely to Long Beach. If I must sacrifice one of you to save the rest, so be it. Your wife already promised you a divorce if they arrested you through your own stubborn juvenile stupidity. Perhaps that matters to you."

John Crawford was furious and started to rant loudly, "I know my rights and I will not tolerate your telling me what I can or cannot do. Keep your fucking lectures to yourself! And I certainly will file a complaint with …"

Alan interrupted the tirade by calling on the machine gun toting soldiers guarding the luggage pile and asking in English that they arrest Crawford for troublemaking. They only spoke Polish and none of the languages Alan spoke, so they had to summon an interpreter. One of the soldiers moved next to Crawford, who angrily pushed him away, for which he got promptly and roughly handcuffed.

An airline employee appeared to translate, shortly thereafter a lieutenant. Alan explained that everyone in the group was terribly upset with the delays in East Germany that made them miss the sightseeing in Poland, and now with the delay in boarding their flight home without explanation. Mr Crawford had lost his temper and was disrupting the entire waiting room. Alan agreed that Mr Crawford was motivated, but that did not excuse his behaviour; others on the tour were suffering the same frustrations without losing their civilised manners.

A group of onlookers had gathered around to observe what was going on. An airline supervisor arrived and tried to defuse the situation. He alternated speaking English and Polish, suggesting that since the plane was about to depart, it might be easier all around to let Mr Crawford leave with the rest of the tour, provided his tour companions had no objection and subject to good behaviour.

Alan said, "No."

The supervisor asked, "Who are you? What is your relationship to these people?"

Alan explained, "I am the tour organiser and responsible for the passenger's lawful behaviour while guests in your country, and for their safe return to California. Besides, we still do not have clearance to depart, so that scenario is a moot point for now."

The lieutenant said he would check on the status of the hold. He went into an office and called State Security, had to explain everything several times and was eventually connected to a Colonel Surowiecki, who listened attentively and asked him to stay on the line while he made some inquiries.

Surowiecki phoned Colonel Schmidt in East Germany and requested a decision about holding or releasing the tour. They discussed the developments briefly. If they held the tour group in Poland, the case would have to move to a higher level, and the police action would become an international political business. Schmidt did not have a specific clue to investigate that would justify holding the tour group in Poland further. He reluctantly advised Surowiecki to release the hold and let the travellers leave Poland, to be confirmed by Schmidt in writing by telex immediately. He thanked his Polish colleague heartily for his assistance and collaboration. They parted on good terms, pledging ongoing mutual cooperation.

At the Warsaw airport, the lieutenant received his answer and reported the welcome news to the group and the airline. Baggage handlers started to load the luggage on a cart to take to the plane. They were stopped by the airline staff, who announced that the luggage loading had ended, with the plane's cargo doors closed and the conveyor belt on his way back to the terminal.

The euphoria of the passengers evaporated as fast as it had risen a few minutes earlier. Alan went to talk to airline supervisors. He could not reverse the luggage situation, but it was agreed that the passengers would be allowed to board with hand luggage but leave the checked baggage behind in Alan's care, for later shipment.

Alan returned to the waiting area, instructed all to board at once, that he would arrange to have their luggage shipped separately at no cost to them.

Richard and Anne Holley remained behind with Barbara Crawford, who asked, "What about my husband?"

Alan replied, "Your husband is being arrested. I will let you know where you can write to him. You are free to fly back to Poland to attend his trial at your own expense, if you can get a visa."

The airline representative asked Alan if he could not drop the charges and let Crawford leave with the group, that it would be so much easier all around and that lessons had undoubtedly been learned.

Alan said, "No. He was admonished many times, and given a final warning of arrest if he continued endangering the group by his insolent behaviour."

Barbara started to sob. John was about to say something. Alan warned, "Do not open your mouth for any reason. Do not speak, do not yawn, do not sneeze. If you are asked anything, answer by nodding. I can assure you that if you are unable or unwilling to learn your lesson of silence, that I will change your present mild discomfort and apprehension into real pain and fear. Do you understand, are you paying attention this time? Think carefully before you reply."

John Crawford nodded in the affirmative. His chin was trembling, and a pitiful subservience had replaced his previous belligerence.

The lieutenant, the airline supervisor and the airport functionary were having a discussion in Polish. They returned to Alan's group. The airline supervisor proposed to Alan, "Would you be willing to drop the charges if Mr Crawford promises to behave and is released to his wife and his friends Mr and Ms. Holley? Right now, the police have not filed an incident report and the matter could be closed with a warning."

Alan asked, "Why do we keep giving all the insolent petty troublemakers a pass? They repeat their behaviour with contempt for the people who want to travel in peace with courtesy and good manners. How many times is enough? Two, three, eight? How many repeats do you think a judge would allow? Well, now we have the opportunity to find out."

The lieutenant said, "Please be aware that we could let him go whether you drop the charges or not."

Alan replied, "Please be aware that if you do that, I will file a complaint about your support of troublemakers rather than law-abiding visitors."

The loudspeakers announced the last boarding call for their flight. They all looked at Alan. Barbara Crawford sobbed that John was not a bad man, he just was naïve and not used to a strict environment. Anne Holley reminded Alan that John had been a splendid help in dealing with the inconvenience of an unscheduled fingerprinting session that lasted all morning, and that he had been a reliable, good companion throughout the trip, even if he had a careless tongue.

The airline supervisor asked, "Are these four staying, or just one? I must notify the gate. Once they close nobody will be allowed to board, and you will miss your flight."

Alan finally agreed, "Okay, he can go. I will withdraw my complaint, you can uncuff him, but I will appreciate a police escort until he boards. If he tries to run away or does something stupid, I hope you catch and then keep him, even if you have to shoot him."

The airline supervisor phoned the gate and advised that four more were coming and gave their names to check off.

Anne Holley approached Alan and told him, "You are a dangerous man."

Alan replied, "Yes madam. I also am your salvation. Incidentally, this is the second time I have been labelled as dangerous by a woman since yesterday."

"Were you also the other woman's salvation?"

"Yes indeed. It seems that many people need salvation in the last days of our tour."

They shook hands, and wished each other well, looking forward to meeting again in Long Beach.

She boarded her flight, he remained in Warsaw to arrange for the luggage forwarding, staying at the airport to watch the plane with the tour members take off.

He called the Rakosis in Vienna, they agreed to take care of the luggage for an additional fee, first transferring all to their Vienna office, and from there to Long Beach.

14. Long Beach, California

On the second week after returning home, the tour group started to attend their regular Thursday little theatre evenings again. These simple events could be social, or play rehearsals, or just friends sharing homemade cakes, soft drinks, beer, gossip, caffeine and nicotine, or advice on lawnmower repair. Occasionally they had special events or celebrations. Everyone understood the simple rules, which basically consisted of not having any.

A few times a year the group's large Hungarian contingent organised old homeland remembrance parties, where they cried about their lost ancestral country, perhaps lost youth, and had fun sharing Hungarian music, dancing, and party food with their American-born children, who in turn introduced their immigrant parents to the strange American popular music and the even stranger American sports. The non-Hungarians in the group enjoyed the exposure to a culture that seemed exotic in Long Beach, California, participating with great enthusiasm.

Among the many ethnic-themed groups and clubs scattered across the United States, the Long Beach group was particularly successful. They did not even have an official name, although, if required to announce their participation in a play, they called themselves the Pacific and Danube Actors Guild.

Their lack of an official legal structure often created problems when required to meet insurance requirements to perform in school plays or similar places. The local insurance agents could not find a formula to ensure a group that did not exist as an entity. Individual policies for all participants proved cumbersome and, in many places, unacceptable, especially in public schools.

One of their group had participated on a radio talk program dealing with financial and insurance matters, and related the problems encountered by an unorganised group trying to obtain liability insurance for the group.

Two weeks later the radio talk participant received a letter from an insurance broker in northern Wisconsin who had heard the radio program, and who offered to resolve the problem. Both had Hungarian names. They talked by telephone, first in English, then, O joy, in Hungarian. The broker had to get a license to sell insurance in California, which was done promptly. Thereafter a liability policy for the group was obtained. The broker paid for legal advice by a California lawyer out of his own pocket and rented space for a small California branch office in the warehouse where the group rehearsed.

One of the experienced retired women in the group got a part time job staffing the Long Beach branch insurance office. She relayed questions and problems to Wisconsin, where immediate action was taken, a clear response was returned promptly, including all relevant information. In some complicated issues, telephone consultations were available, in English or Hungarian, friendly, helpful, truthful, free of charge.

Soon the Wisconsin insurance broker Frank Kolozsvary became a valued resource and friend to the Long Beach group. Within two years, he carried all the house, life, automobile, boat, group health, liability, and business insurance policies for the entire group. He paid their premiums when they could not, gave good free advice, honestly said when he did not know the answer or could not advise or help. He meticulously collected personal data and his customers got birthday and Christmas cards in Hungarian, also in other languages when appropriate. Three dual nationality couples couple got theirs in Hungarian as well as Italian, Spanish and German.

Frank visited his Long Beach office only three times a year, but he was always so instantly available that no one thought of him as an absentee broker. From time to time, he brought his wife Maria and children, combining his business trip with a family vacation. They always participated in one of the Thursday evening reunions, with hot dogs, pizza, ice cream, and enjoying the eclectic company for all age groups.

The American-born members of the Pacific and Danube Actors Guild participated as eagerly as their immigrant colleagues, and all were enthralled to perform amateur Shakespeare plays with some strong Brooklyn, German, Spanish and Hungarian accents. Their audiences loved it, and many a serious piece was interrupted by laughter when somebody could not pronounce a word or forgot his lines. Their most successful productions were those featuring famous characters speaking in totally unfitting accents.

Now the entire Guild was reunited again for their Thursday gathering, the twenty-two who had gone on the tour and the thirty or so who had stayed in

Long Beach. The discussion about having a party turned towards having a celebration in honour of Frank Kolozsvary, for his out-of-the-ordinary shepherding of their insurance needs, for helping his clients in need, for giving free advice on many issues for many years, and now for providing a great thrilling acting adventure and an overseas tour for a group of amateur actors living in an uneventful retirement.

The tour's Mrs Anne Holley had returned to her maiden name of Anne Miller but remained as a sort of tour leader. She was tasked to contact Kolozsvary to invite him and his family to the party and coordinate dates. He refused, courteously and friendly, insisting firmly that such party should include Alan Mackenzie, and perhaps someone from the tour's sponsor. The group agreed and appointed Anne to organise it with Frank and Alan. The cost would be shared equally by all members.

Frank called Abigail's number. As always, a polite male voice answered and inquired about the purpose of the call. Frank said he wanted to invite Mrs Abigail and Mrs Madeleine to a party of the European bus tour group. About an hour later the call was returned by the same male voice, who said the ladies would attend if their schedules permitted, depending on date, location and time. Location was the warehouse in Long Beach, any Thursday or Saturday in the following month, at seven in the evening. Pizza and picnic type food and drinks would be provided.

A Thursday three weeks hence was agreed upon. Abigail called next day and offered to cater the event. Frank thanked her but felt that any fancy catering would make people uncomfortable. He reminded Abigail that many of the group were living on Social Security, and although most owned their modest houses, their lifestyle was thrifty. She insisted and offered to provide whatever level of food they felt at ease with. She also argued that the group may appreciate a 'Thank You' from the wealthy patron of their tour, and that this could be a tad more festive than what the typical Thursday meetings offered.

Abigail asked, "How many people? And do they have chairs and tables for everyone?"

Frank replied, "About one hundred, perhaps hundred twenty if they bring more family members. And no, they cannot provide seating or tables for that many. They have about three dozen folding chairs and some folding tables. They stand or sit on the floor when they have a crowd, which is rare."

Abigail talked him into accepting her offer of rented tables and seating for everyone, plus a large serve-yourself buffet of foods considered appropriate by Frank, who additionally requested that no vans with a Beverly Hills catering company signage would deliver the goods, and that the food should not include anything with French names. She laughed and assured him that all deliveries and removals would be in unmarked vehicles, in true cloak-and-dagger fashion.

They proceeded to go through an item-by-item list of acceptable foods, favouring pizzas, salads, fruit, ice cream, small sandwiches, chips and dips, pickles, varieties of beverages. Frank summarised it by saying that 'picnic food' covers it. She laughed again, told him that she had been on picnics where they built a ballroom dance floor on the beach in case someone wanted to dance.

Frank commented that that was gross, the kind of stuff that triggered revolutions. She replied that after the people got their revolutionary governments, they went through extraordinary efforts to escape their revolutionary paradise and get into a country where it was possible to make money and spend it on anything they wanted, be it a beach dancing floor, endow cancer research in a university, or earn a decent living selling insurance and buy a house and two cars.

Frank said nothing, she insisted, "Are we in agreement on what is or is not gross and unfair? Would you rather be back in a communist paradise?"

Frank capitulated, "No, I would not like to be back under the system we escaped. I apologise for my unthinking comment."

Abigail's next question was, "What music will you have?"

Frank expected another put down when he answered, "We have a record player with a loudspeaker, and some of our people play violin, guitar, accordion, piano and clarinet, but we don't have a piano. And we have quite a few good singers."

Abigail pondered this, then commented, "I believe in some ways your group is wealthier than my group. You have things of great value that cannot be bought or rented for the occasion."

She asked about dress preferences, there were none, and whether Alan Mackenzie would be there, yes, he would, and would she meet Frank's family, yes, they will be there.

The celebration was well-attended, ages ranging from babies to very senior elders. The guests were surprised at the tables with tablecloths, china dishes and silver, chairs for all, and the large assortment of offerings on a twenty-five-foot-long buffet counter with four waiters assisting. Frank had checked up on the food upon arrival, was pleased to confirm that everything was in the categories he had approved, nothing weird or with French labels in sight.

Frank was also pleased to see that the delivery trucks were anonymous, that the two sisters were dropped off in the Oldsmobile rather than a limousine, and that the two also had dressed down to suit the occasion.

The guests appreciated the high quality of the catering and commented that hot food and drinks were kept hot, and the cold stuff and drinks were kept cold, without temperature change. The heating and cooling equipment attracted some restaurant old timers, who examined it with interest.

Anne Miller gave a welcoming speech, announcing the group's appreciation of Frank Kolozsvary and their gratitude for his many years of support and friendship. She gave a brief narrative of how Frank had become such an important part of their group, all the way from Wisconsin.

There was applause and cheering. One voice yelled that Frank had made a lot of money from selling insurance to the group, several yelled back that others also had made money off the group but giving nothing in return. There were vignettes by several elderly people who shared how Frank had helped them in times of stress and financial hardship, to more applause.

Frank's turn was next. He thanked them for their kind words, for maintaining Hungarian culture alive and well while loving and respecting their new country, and for being loyal customers so he could make more money, which caused laughter and requests for a congressional hearing.

Anne Miller returned to the podium. "There is another side to Frank that we did not know. He arranged for our participation in an exciting, real-life play, like our group never had performed before. The fine food and the party set up you see here today is a thank you to our group by the anonymous sponsor of our great acting adventure. It is better to let Frank tell the story."

Frank responded, "I will pass the buck and the microphone to my old colleague from Budapest, an American with the classic Magyar name of Alan Mackenzie."

This was greeted with joking about unfitting unpronounceable names, evolving into a funny impromptu sketch about a simple-minded Scot trying to retrieve his luggage and explaining in English the spelling of his name to a simple-minded Hungarian clerk in a luggage storage room, with people behind in the waiting line urging them to hurry. The amateur actors were quite good and created an interesting play with the confusion created by the different pronunciation of letter names in English and Hungarian. There was much laughter and good applause.

Alan took the microphone, and said, "Hello. I have met many of you while preparing for your tour. For new acquaintances, I will give you a brief background. I used to work for our government as a commercial attaché negotiating trade deals in Hungary, East Germany and Czechoslovakia. In Budapest, I got to know Frank Kolozsvary, then a graduate engineer driving a taxi, who soon became indispensable as a supplier of scarce goods, information, and introductions to government officials. He knew everybody's birthday, what they needed, what problems they had, and he volunteered to help wherever he could, and when he could not, he would find help elsewhere. He could find anybody and anything."

There was recognition, knowing nodding and smiling from the audience. Some wanted to know how he got paid.

Alan continued, "You will have to ask him about his pay. We worked together on many projects. Gradually, cautiously, he let me know his real feelings about the Communist regime, his disappointment, and his anger about what they were doing to his country. Over time his views got him into trouble with the party. He lost his job, and feared arrest. We both managed to get out of Hungary in the nick of time during the Soviet invasion. We lost contact with one another thereafter."

"Years later, when I already had retired, I was invited by a former colleague to consult about helping a minor bureaucrat escape from behind the Iron Curtain. The escape was planned and financed by a wealthy American as a private enterprise, without government involvement, for purely patriotic reasons. I remembered Frank Kolozsvary, the guy who could find anything, and invited him to join the conversation."

"We discussed many ways of helping with the escape. Not having government resources, we had to figure out a different way, eventually narrowing the options into the simple solution of hiding our escapee in a group of tourists and sneaking him out as part of a tour group. The guy being rescued was unimportant and we did not expect anyone to come looking for him until weeks later. The solution required a collaborative group of people who had the right disposition against communism and who could act the part. As we all do when we do not know what to do, we do call Frank."

The audience started to smile, then erupted into laughter as Alan said, "Yes, I asked Frank, who just happened to know a group of little theatre actors who had the right political disposition and might be interested in some adventurous acting assignment. The rest you know."

"Now I would like to present Mrs Abigail Williamson and Mrs Madeleine Baker, whom some of you have met, to relay a few words from our tour sponsor."

"Hello, I am Abigail. My sister and I are honoured to be invited to your celebration, and equally honoured by your acceptance of our employer's contribution of refreshments. We did not know what to do to insure we provided what you enjoy. Therefore, we decided to do what you all seem to do, we do ask Mr Kolozsvary."

This was greeted by laughter and acknowledgements.

Abigail continued, smiling, "All the food selections were approved by Mr Kolozsvary, therefore all praise and/or complaints should be submitted to him."

"He also was most helpful in coaching us for this adventure behind the Iron Curtain. The businesses we are familiar with in our daily lives are far removed from foreign adventures."

"Working for a wealthy, generous entrepreneur, we periodically become involved in some detour that attracts his interest. When this occurs, we must learn fast and find an expert to help us out, more easily said than done."

"Our initial involvement in this particular detour was with Mr Mackenzie, who introduced us to Mr Kolozsvary. Then we joined the many who could ask Frank for help in solving problems, find anything, from deals on insurance to bus rentals behind the Iron Curtain. We learned that if you do not know what to do, you do call on Frank, and then you do."

"Mr Mackenzie and Mr Kolozsvary worked as a team, and we cannot imagine what would have happened if one or the other had not been involved. We are grateful to both, but today's celebration is organised by the Pacific and Danube Actors Guild in honour of Mr Kolozsvary, so we must primarily applaud him. All I can say, Mr Frank Kolozsvary, is a heartfelt thank you for your help and guidance, and also to your family, who must tolerate the many absences and long hours of a husband and father who works all the time."

People applauded; Frank took a bow. Then the sister took the microphone.

"Good evening, I am Madeleine Baker. I work with my sister Abigail for the same employer. We often share projects, as in this case. I wholeheartedly agree with what has been said about Frank Kolozsvary. He is a rare find."

"I would like to talk briefly about another angle. The rescue, or escape mission, that brought us all together was a private enterprise by a compassionate man, who met someone who wanted to escape, and decided to help him. Our simple scheme to sneak him out of his country could have worked, and perhaps he would have been here celebrating with us."

"The escaping man joined our group for a short time, and we expected to have him here today to celebrate the event, but apparently he got cold feet and did not return with us. The tour was nevertheless great fun, and we are glad we tried."

"However, we would be extremely grateful that this story is not spread as a tale of some rich guy screwing up a rescue and causing great harm. This was not a failure; it was an undertaking that was abandoned before completion. No one was hurt. We want to keep it that way. If a rumour about a fantasised daring escape reaches the wrong ears, an innocent man behind the Iron Curtain may get arrested and horribly mistreated. Let us not do that. We want to remember the tour as tourists and actors in what could have been a real-life drama. There were no troubles, you played your parts well. We want to keep the story simple and quiet. Thank you all, thank you very much."

There was applause and nodding agreement. Anne Miller took the microphone and reminded all that Mrs Abigail had acknowledged Frank's family putting up with his working hours and suggested that the family also deserved applause.

Frank and Maria and the children were called to the stage. They got a nice round of applause, parents and the two girls smiling and waving, the young boy, the miniature Frank, looking angry, with arms akimbo, ready to pick a fight. They made a lovely picture. The scene reminded Alan of a political family just having won an election.

All participants were obviously enjoying the food. It was what they were accustomed to and what they liked, except that the quality and variety offered was outstanding. The younger set was thrilled to eat whatever they wanted in whatever order, like dessert first, followed by pizza, then another dessert, plus cake, not a word from parents observing but lenient for the occasion.

Anne Miller announced that speeches were over, and that next the program would consist of music and dancing, the choices alternating between the selections of the elders and those of the young crowd. Anne then re-joined Alan, Maria, Frank, Abigail and Madeleine, Rick Holley and the Crawfords at their table. Frank's children had joined the youth group at the other end of the building. The principal players now had a private moment to themselves.

The conversation drifted to a recollection of the tensest moments of the tour. The nine persons at the table had experienced different parts, or shared parts from different angles. It was interesting to learn the rest of the story.

In any conversation about the close calls, their luck, and their ability to deal with the unexpected, the narrative invariably drifted back to Alan Mackenzie and his stubborn, single-minded, strict leadership and training.

Anne Miller related how angry she was with him about the time limits he imposed on difficult makeup sessions. Maria Kolozsvary reminisced about Alan's management of their escape from Hungary, without going into the details. Abigail complained that he could exhibit unnecessary violence and insolent vulgar language, attributes she did not want to be exposed to again, without saying what had happened when or where. Frank and Alan said they shared a long history of joint adventures and close calls, noting only a few carefully edited generalities. Others around the table had less intense experiences with Alan, but felt similar cautious respect for the man.

Surprisingly, it was Abigail who acknowledged that Alan's guidance and demanding discipline had saved their mission and some lives. She spoke elegantly and eloquently, ending with, "My gratitude and respect cannot be repaid by presents. However, I have a gift for Mr Mackenzie that may prove useful in some future interaction."

With a big, happy smile she handed Alan a gift-wrapped package. He opened it, finding a large, hardcover book titled *Good Manners and Polite Language in the Diplomatic Service*. Alan laughed with the others.

A woman approached the table to remind Anne's group that all had promised to sign a poster for someone who had been transferred out of state. Anne got up and asked the visitors to stay there, they would be right back.

As soon as Alan, the Kolozsvarys and the sisters were briefly alone, Abigail returned to the subject of unwarranted violence and vulgarity.

"Did you really have to be that brutal in word and deed? I feel I should complain to someone, but I don't even know how to explain what happened."

Alan suggested, "Your honour, I wish to report an act of violence. I was in the men's toilet of a hotel in Poland peacefully having a meeting about smuggling out a criminal wanted in two countries. I was talking to this senior citizen when a big and muscular young man came into the restroom yelling in Polish and with his fist hit the senior in the chest, almost knocking him over."

"The senior managed to remain standing and defended himself by hitting the assailant in the neck. The assailant fell down, nearly passed out. The senior kicked him in the stomach, causing him to wet his pants, then he picked him up by the collar and leaned him against the wall, slapped him in the face a few times to return circulation to his head, and using a clearly understood sign language, taught the man that he should remain silent, get out of the bathroom, and warned him of terrible damage if he did not follow his instructions."

"Or, if you prefer a simpler alternative, you could say a degenerate pervert went into a men's room and tried to beat up a senior citizen, but the senior defended himself successfully and the pervert fled."

Abigail scolded, "I resent your making fun of a disagreeable incident. I am offended by your attitude. There is nothing funny about any of this."

Alan said, "I agree with you that this is not funny. I was trying to show how ridiculous the incident becomes when you try to explain it in a few words. I might also add that there is nothing funny about being charged with espionage, sabotage, and treason in a Communist police state. You have no rights. You are guilty when charged. There is no bail, no appeals, no lawyering, no nothing."

Abigail objected, "Yes, I am not arguing about their behaviour but yours, which is no …"

Madeleine interrupted, "Look, it is done, it is over. Let us drop it."

Alan was becoming impatient, assured them that he no intention of dropping anything and reminded Abigail sternly about the circumstances, "We are having this celebration because we managed to interchange two lawbreakers in the nick of time. Remember that I was truly scared that we could run out of time, and I watched the clock."

"Perhaps you forgot; I have not. That time interval is still engraved in my memory. Polish security arrived twenty-three minutes after we made the exchange. Please remember this number, you probably will never again in your life be exposed to such a situation. Twenty-three minutes separated Bruno Hadler from the firing squad and several in the tour group from a long prison term. You planned to wait until the following day! I did not have the book about nice manners with me at the time, nor could I have read it in twenty-three minutes."

"I will match your gift with one of my own. I will choose for you one of the several available good books about the legal, ethical, moral and practical duties of ship captains, aircraft pilots, ambulance drivers, firefighters, policemen, doctors, nurses, emergency medical personnel, and others engaged in saving lives in emergency conditions."

"They will attempt to save your life with or without your cooperation. In those desperate, violent situations, you may be yelled at and insulted if necessary to get your attention, and physically restrained, undressed or anesthetised if need be. Those events are not covered in the Miss Manners books. However, I am sure both of us will learn something about appropriate behaviour in different environments from reading our gift books."

Abigail was blushing and angry. There was silence around the table, until Madeleine broke the ice. "I think these emergency interactions are necessary but not courteous. I hope we do not base our relationships on what is said or done in panic situations. Let it go, both of you, please, let us enjoy the success of our mission."

Frank commented with pleasure, "We can be confident that that pervert will no longer be prowling toilets to beat up seniors. I bet he will be overly cautious when opening doors or if a stranger looks at him."

Alan concurred, "I am sure he learned something. Judging by his size, he must have been the school bully, not used to push-backs. I would like to meet him alone in an elevator, get close and say hello, to see how he reacts."

Madeleine could not suppress a smile. Maria frowned, but with a hint of amusement. Abigail shook her head in disbelief. The discussion ended as their table companions returned.

On the little stage, four women were singing melancholic songs very beautifully, accompanied by a violin. They sang Greensleeves and Shenandoah in English, and La Paloma in Hungarian. There were some tears in the audience.

After long applause, loud rock and roll started at the other end of the building, and some of the people moved in that direction. The change of entertainment seemed to work without a hitch, with people moving back and forth and participating or not.

Among the large audience there was conversation about sports, local politics, business, and much gossip about the movie industry that was or had been the employer of most of the people in attendance. The decor in the warehouse was primarily movie posters, children's drawings, and a large American flag. They had a bookcase with assorted paperbacks, everyone free to borrow, take or add. A large sheet of plywood served as a bulletin board, where one could find an eclectic assortment of notices offering astonishing variety.

Abigail and Madeleine had observed the place and the proceedings with interest. They were used to have their lawyer read the small print in the contract before organising any activity. In this warehouse, there was a thriving social life functioning without rules, contracts, lawyers, or fights.

Abigail wanted to know, "How do you manage to function without rules or legal guidance?"

Anne answered for the group, "But we do have rules. Everyone follows them; therefore, we have no problems."

Abigail wanted to know, "But what are your rules? Could you share some of them?"

Anne again, "Yes, I can give you all of them. Last person out turns off the lights. We take turns selecting activities and cleaning. We share stuff and watch out for each other. Sometimes we post a sign-up sheet to select dates for something. We keep us informed about movie jobs as extras, always a big treat. Small groups talk about shared interests. That is about it."

"Don't you write anything down? How do you pay rent and utilities? How do you handle disputes?"

Anne thought the questions were curious, but answered, "Yes, we do write things down and put it on our bulletin board. We pay rent and other expenses by check. We opened an account in the name of three of our members. We give them the money and they write the checks. We do not have serious disputes. Small arguments get discussed and settled, or we flip coins. People come and go, some move away, some return. It is easy, it is nice, it is practical."

Abigail commented, "Sounds like a socialist utopia."

Anne suddenly became intense, "We don't like anything that is labelled socialist, Marxist, communist. Please do not label us with those. Our friends have had enough contact with communists during the Korean war or escaping from behind the Iron Curtain. We are just a private voluntary group sharing a warehouse as a clubhouse for fun and friendship."

Abigail nodded, "I agree with you. I used a wrong label because I am not familiar with your style of uncomplicated, friendly, and successful circle. You may be surprised, but I am admiring your group and learning."

The locals did not mention the husbands of the two sisters. They knew that one was the Secretary of State and the other a wealthy retired surgeon owning several clinics. Nothing further was said.

Unavoidably the discussion returned to highlights of the tour, among them the last-minute arrest of John Crawford instigated by Alan at the airport. The sisters had been subsequently informed by Alan.

John admitted, "I know I get into trouble by speaking my mind and that in doing so I caused some anxiety."

He paused, then continued, addressing Alan, "However, nothing happened with the Communist cops because of my comments. At the end of the tour when we were boarding, you pulled that needless stunt of having me arrested. We worried during the entire tour about getting into trouble with the Stasi. I certainly never imagined that I would get stabbed in the back by you in the closing minutes of our tour."

The ensuing uncomfortable silence was broken by Madeleine, "Mr Mackenzie, could you comment about this event? I am sure Mr Crawford and the rest of us would be pleased to learn your reasoning."

Alan looked around the table, trying to read the mood of the participants. He guessed John Crawford defiant, Barbara Crawford embarrassed, Abigail and Madeleine politely attentive, Frank amused, Maria worried, Anne Miller tired and resigned, Rick Holley curious. There was another long silence.

Finally, Alan explained his hesitation. "I was trying to decide how to respond. One option, for me quite tempting and difficult to resist, was to get up and leave without saying goodbye."

"I concluded that John Crawford's comment was not malicious but innocent, and that walking out would unfairly offend everyone around this table and all the nice people participating in this pleasant celebration. Therefore, respecting innocence, I will attempt to explain a few things."

"We all are innocent, naïve, about some things, and we all are knowledgeable about other things. As we have discussed several times before, in emergency situations you must rely on the experts on the type of emergency at hand. It may be a medical emergency, or a mechanical failure, or a situation endangering an escape."

"In emergency situations, there is no time for nice seminars. In the comfort of hindsight and safety, it is easy to criticise the brusqueness, the skill, or the apparent lack of judgment of those who saved us."

Alan paused, looking at Abigail and John Crawford. Abigail held his gaze, Crawford looked down. The others had varied reactions, some nodded.

Alan continued, "John was incredibly lucky that he did not get in trouble with the Stasi over his freedom of speech. At the airport, his luck was about to run out."

"Airports are the absolutely dumbest place to make threatening remarks. Perhaps Mr Crawford, and perhaps most of us, are not aware that public airports are among the most jittery of government institutions. They worry about smugglers, hijackers, illegal immigrants, drugs, sabotage, aircraft safety, flight operations, fire prevention around aviation fuel, public health issues, passenger safety and comfort, crowd control, luggage handling, extraordinarily complex maintenance of aircraft, ground services, equipment. They worry about communications, air navigation and traffic control. Let's not forget cleaning and maintenance of large buildings, food service, garbage removal, urban transportation, and everything else."

"The official paranoia of the place will get you arrested for making threatening remarks, for joking about bombs, or for disorderly conduct. This applies in Warsaw and Los Angeles and everywhere else. If you do not believe me, go to your local airport, and make some jokes about bomb threats. You will regret it."

"The only difference between here and Warsaw is that here they read you your rights and follow a legal process, there they do not, and your quick trial will be in Polish, consisting of reading the charges and imposing sentence. Penalties are probably comparable, accommodations and food probably not."

"While I was trying to get you boarded on a flight that already had closed its luggage handling and was about to depart, still desperately dealing with lifting a police departure hold and the local bureaucracy, you went on and on with your incredibly stupid ranting, getting louder and louder. I warned you that I would have you arrested, which you ignored."

"I had been watching the armed guards loitering around. As you got louder, they took an interest and started to move closer. Luckily, they did not understand English, but your tone of voice was an invitation to intervene. One of them moved close to you, you stupidly shoved him, and got yourself handcuffed."

"If you think that that was a brutal Communist tactic, go out to the Los Angeles airport, make a scene, then hit or shove an American cop, and see what happens. In Warsaw, you were about to be arrested, and the only way out that occurred to me was to lodge a complaint and request your arrest, to separate you from the group, and pre-empt the police action."

"If they had arrested you, you would have spent some time in a Polish prison. Since I initiated the action, their natural response was to not cooperate with the foreigner and not get involved with the problem within his group. With me lodging the complaint, the charge changed from threatening airport security to a squabble within a group of tourists on their way out, and good riddance."

"Luckily, the scheme succeeded. Often, the desperate last-minute solution attempts fail. In our case, the guards and the airport and airline managers were eager to get rid of the trouble and avoid the paperwork."

"That is all I want to say. I am really tired of having to explain in polite conversation why I had to take certain actions in dangerous emergencies. I hope it clarified things. However, I will not answer questions or explain this further. I want to talk about something else. If the subject comes up again, I will leave."

A blushing John Crawford looked at his hands and mumbled, "I am sorry." His wife, looking unhappy, added, "Thank you for your explanation." Abigail and Madeleine both looked him in the eyes and very clearly and slowly nodded their approval. Similar gestures and words of appreciation were repeated around the table.

The conversation continued until late in the evening. Abigail and Madeleine were fascinated by the Long Beach group. They talked at length about little theatre acting and how to make do with minimalist props. They heard the story about their plywood tree that hinged in the middle so it could fit into Harry's station wagon. In one show, the tree collapsed in mid-sentence, to great applause.

"And who is Harry?"

"Harry is the guy who owns the station wagon in which we carry the folding tree."

The stories were silly, funny, quite removed from the formal, serious environment the sisters lived in. They asked many questions about working in the movies behind the scenes, as electricians, makeup artists, caterers, stagehands, extras. They had stories about the stars and the directors and drinking problems and temper tantrums. A few old timers had worked in the movies since the silent era in the late twenties.

The magic world of make-believe that surrounds the movie industry never ceases to fascinate. Alan, Frank, Maria, Abigail and Madeleine enjoyed the stories, especially the unusual viewpoint of the support workers, so different from the public view presented in the press. The moviemaking stories were as interesting to outsiders as cloak-and-dagger stories, except that the movie stories could be told, and the secret world had to remain so.

Madeleine asked, "Do you use this place only one evening a week, or do you have other activities?"

Anne Miller responded, "Oh, we have a lot going on. At various times, especially on rainy winter days, we have children's activities like tricycle races for the small ones, roller skating, ping-pong, folk dancing, play rehearsals, birthday celebrations. We rent the place twice a month to a square-dancing group. Once someone used space to modernise his motorboat, others to build bookcases."

Abigail asked, "Don't you worry about personal safety or thefts in this area, especially after nightfall? The neighbourhood does not inspire confidence."

Anne assured, "It is not an unsafe area. It is an economically depressed area, but we do not think it is unsafe. We leave nothing valuable, there is nothing to steal. The adjacent warehouses have nothing of interest to steal."

"The warehouse next to us stores temporary fencing for events or construction sites. The next two are vacant, the next one stores vinyl siding. Our warehouse had been vacant for some time, that is why we can rent it cheaply. We hope it continues to be available. The owner wanted a two-year lease, but we could not afford to make the commitment. He said he would try to find a new tenant. Meanwhile, we keep enjoying it. At night, we usually leave in a group and feel confident that we will not have any muggings."

With a slight shift of direction, Abigail asked Alan if he ever had been mugged. Before Alan could respond Frank burst into laughter, so contagiously that the others ended laughing with him.

Alan gave the question some thought, answered, "Yes, but I don't do muggings well, so they were not successful."

Frank started laughing again, leaving to the imagination why attempting to mug Alan was so funny. Abigail, remembering her own witnessing of the Warsaw men's room incident clearly, and the discussion just a few minutes earlier, decided to not pursue the subject of violent self-defence any further.

There was curiosity about Alan's and Frank's adventures, but the two were notoriously tight-lipped about their pasts. They narrated carefully edited short stories about the secret world, little or nothing about their own involvement.

The conversations moved on to other subjects. Many kept returning to the buffet, worrying about their diet but indulging just for the day, and enjoying meeting and interacting with people from other parts of society and quite different occupations.

When they said their goodbyes, there was a sense of loss. The great adventure was over. There was a feeling of camaraderie with the players, accompanied by a yearning for doing another chapter, but the play was finished. It was a feeling the actors knew well.

The caterers removed all their furniture and equipment promptly and cleaned up, leaving several stacks of beverages and canned goods, with compliments of the two sisters.

At the door, Madeleine asked Alan and Frank whether her little explanatory narrative about the fugitive aborting his escape would be believed by anyone.

Alan replied, "Absolutely not. The participants and those who stayed behind are fully aware that we extracted a high-ranking communist defector, triggering a massive police action. However, they are discreet. They learned discretion dealing with powerful, vindictive stars. If they talk about it to strangers, they will use the sanitised version you narrated. You did the absolute right thing with your story. They will be grateful for having and sharing an official fake version for public consumption. They are used to heavily edited official versions. I am sure you noticed how careful they are when telling movie star stories. No identities or statements that could bring retaliation. They enjoyed the tour and the real-life play. It probably was one of the best acting jobs they ever had."

All guests went home. The last one out turned off the lights.

15. Appleton, Wisconsin

Alan remembered his restlessness during his first flight from Chicago to Appleton, Wisconsin. Now he felt totally at ease, and ready to take on another assignment, should one be offered, not a likely event. This time he had decided to drive, as he had just purchased a new car and was enjoying every moment behind the wheel. He went to the same motel he had used before. After settling in, he telephoned the now familiar number.

A woman answered, and he asked to speak with Mr Yravszolok. There was a long silence, then she said he had a wrong number. "Please, madam, in that case, may I then speak with Mr Ferenc Kolozsvary? I am an old acquaintance of his. I'm just passing through Appleton and I thought I'd call to say hello."

There was another long silence, then she said, "She, he is retired."

"So am I. I just want to say hello. Could you please ask him to the phone, or would it be more convenient if I stop by your house? My name is Alan Mackenzie. He will …"

She interrupted, "I know who you are. Wait." She started laughing, then he heard a muffled brief conversation in Hungarian.

Kolozsvary came to the phone, also laughing. "Better you come to my house for dinner, we are expecting you. It was hard to remain serious while re-enacting our first conversation."

Several months had passed since their last meeting in Long Beach. It was late October, autumn had set in. The trees were turning, it was getting cold, the days shorter, and the good people of Appleton were preparing for the Northern Wisconsin winter. The talk of the town was an upcoming game in nearby Green Bay, with high hopes for a Packers victory.

Alan enjoyed the season and the American small city pulse on this crisp autumn Saturday. He drove past the house on Lee Street to look some more at the neighbourhood. Someone was installing a canvas cover on a trailer-mounted boat. In another house, they were taking in their garden furniture. Next door a man was on a ladder cleaning gutters. A neighbour was stacking firewood. Kids on bicycles were wearing padded jackets. Two women were planting something in a garden, and in several gardens, trees were being pruned. Nice cars were being washed, and ball games were in progress. At one house, there was a scent of freshly mowed lawns, on the next block the scent of wood smoke was in the air. It was a prosperous, peaceful scene, and Alan had a fleeting thought that the preservation of such scenes had been the purpose of his life's clandestine overseas work.

The welcome at the Kolozsvary house was warm and friendly, quite a long way from the hostility of his earlier visit. Alan had brought presents. For Frank, a genuine Hungarian plum brandy, with an alcohol content far exceeding what was legal in Wisconsin. Maria received a large leather-bound book of Budapest photographs from the time before the Soviet intervention, the girls each got a doll in Hungarian traditional costume, the boy a wooden statue of an old Hungarian hussar officer with a big moustache, and the children each got a package of assorted Hungarian candy and chocolates.

The dolls were a big hit with the girls. The hussar was studied for a while by the boy who commented that it looked like Dad, but boys don't play with dolls. Alan agreed but suggested that the hussar should not be contemplated as a doll, but as a guard to be placed on a shelf to guard the boy's territory and possessions. He thought about this for a moment and then smiled and nodded his agreement.

The sweets were not inspiring, far less wonderful than remembered, but the Hungarian wrappers were admired and discussed. Maria had missed those candies for many years, remembering them from her childhood, imagining them to be of much higher quality. The wrappers brought out tears, nostalgia, and childhood memories. She asked the children to open the wrappers carefully to avoid tearing, she wanted to save them.

The kids wanted to know why Mom was crying over photographs and low-class candy and commented that Dad would not be crying over his bottle of nostalgia. Frank told them that Hungarian plum brandy was so powerful it made grown men cry. They listened politely to explanations of nostalgia and memories of youth but did not seem convinced. They commented that they also would have escaped a country where the candy was so bad.

The young boy asked Alan, belligerently, why he made Mommy cry every time he visited. Alan said he was sorry that his visits revived memories of sad events of the past. The boy started to argue. Maria quieted him, assuring him that it was necessary to remember important events that happened many years ago, lest we forget our history and all we have learned. She explained softly and patiently until everything was okay.

Maria asked, "Where did you get this Hungarian stuff? I am amazed that the candy wrappers are still the same, except for that small notice of manufacture by a 'people's enterprise', meaning the state."

Alan admitted, "I had to bypass Frank to keep it a surprise and use one of his competitors in the 'finding' business, in this case an outfit in Vienna specialising in Czech, Hungarian and Polish melancholy. I got their name from the Rakosis."

They asked Alan about his flight, and he disclosed that he had driven in his new car.

Frank asked, "What did you get?"

Alan grinned, "An overpowered muscle car, a new Mercury Cougar XR-7 GT, with the biggest engine."

They all went out to look at Alan's new toy, glowing bright red with a white top, unanimously declared beautiful. The kids suggested to their parents to remember Alan's colour choice when buying another car. Maria surprised everyone by asking to drive it. She and Alan sat in front, Frank and kids in the rear.

After seat adjustments, Maria commented that the hood seemed too long compared to her car. Alan instructed her how to start it, they all listened to the throaty, deep purring engine sound. Alan checked for traffic front and back, there was none. He then advised Maria that the big engine was heavy to drive and that she needed to step really forcefully on the gas to get it moving.

She did as told, was shocked by the engine roar, the intense acceleration and the squealing of the rear tires burning the pavement. Instinctively, she stepped on the brake hard, stopping as if hitting a brick wall, with tires squealing again. She had never driven a car with power brakes.

She sat still for a moment, then got out and told them in a huff that if anyone laughed or joked about her, they would not get dinner, and walked towards the house. She returned after a few steps and added that the car was unsafe and that it squealed like the pigs in a farm where she once had lived.

Frank commented, "Well, there you have the text for a new commercial extolling the virtues of the Cougar."

Alan agreed, "Yes, I screwed up with that 'step on the gas' encouragement. Should I apologise to her?"

Frank replied, "I am impressed. You do not apologise often. Take her some flowers, a few, don't overdo it. If you let me drive, I will take you to the nearest florist."

He moved to the driver's seat. Small voices from the back seat urged him to step on the gas, like Mom, that was cool.

Frank asked. "What did you pay for this basic transportation, over three grand?"

Alan said, "I got a customised brand-new car with all the manufacturer's bells and whistles, something I had never done in my life. I figured this was my last chance. I traded in my trusted Hudson sedan plus paid four thousand cash. And I have absolutely no buyer's remorse, I am thrilled."

"How long did it take you to drive here?"

"From Maryland, near Washington DC, to Appleton was about sixteen hours driving time, plus stops. Two days of driving fun."

"No speeding tickets?"

"It came close. On one occasion, I tried out a thrilling maximum acceleration at a turnpike entrance, zero to the seventy-mile speed limit in a few seconds. I passed a cop in an unmarked car at the entrance ramp. He followed me close for several miles. I got tired of him, pulled over and waved him down to ask why he was following me.

He said he was hoping to give me a ticket for reckless driving. I said I had not broken any laws. He said that anyone burning rubber with smoking screeching tires in a red Cougar was going to get a ticket for something, sooner rather than later. He said his dream was to arrest me after a chase. He had the horsepower advantage driving a Dodge with a big Hemi, and probably was the better driver, doing it for a living while I was fooling around behind the Iron Curtain. I guess we both indulged in some daydreaming. We talked cars for a bit and parted company".

Back at the house Maria accepted a small bouquet and Alan's apology for his boyish prank. She was pleased by the peace offering but admonished both men to behave like responsible adults and stop the teenage hot rodding.

The conversation shifted from Alan's new toy to Frank and Maria's new toy, a newly acquired television set, which had turned the whole family into addicts.

Frank reported, "We decided to splurge and got a TV with a giant screen, 24 inches. Can you imagine that? It is like going to the movies. It also can show pictures in colour. With a new antenna on the roof, we get six stations, and two of these transmit programs in colour several times a week. Our old set had an 11-inch flickering green screen. The new technology is astounding, the pictures are clear and steady."

Frank demonstrated the features and all the adjustments for sound and colour. With the new roof antenna, they no longer needed to adjust the antenna arms on the set every time they changed stations. The set was huge, they had placed it in a corner. The TV tube was about thirty inches deep and generated a lot of heat.

The cabinet was mounted on casters so that it could be easily turned around to reach the rear access panel to replace tubes. Everyone was familiar with the Sunday evening drama of having to rush to the nearest open drug store to test radio tubes and buy replacements, hoping to get it done in time to watch the rest of the show. Some people bought extras of the tubes that burned out most frequently.

After dinner, the children were allowed to watch a program on the giant TV in another room, then goodbyes and bedtime. The three adults stayed in conversation with coffee and cigarettes, and tried out the brandy, which required much ice water to douse the flames in the throat.

Their conversation returned to the bus tour. The great adventure was finished, all bills had been paid, and Frank and Alan had each received an unexpected $5,000 bonus with a slightly scented thank you card from Madeleine.

Madeleine had also arranged, through Frank, to have an attorney organise the Long Beach group into a simple legal entity of a social club under the name of the Pacific and Danube Actors Guild. After that was qualified, Madeleine, again through Frank, paid for a two-year lease on the warehouse and donated one hundred folding chairs and several long folding tables.

The Guild, as they now insisted on calling themselves when not required to use their full legal name, were convinced that all the gifts and legal status had been entirely Frank's doing, despite his disclaimers. Frank grumbled that the Guild was ready to nominate him for sainthood and he wished they would stop the fawning.

Frank and Alan had kept each other informed about these developments by telephone, but not discussed them in depth. They usually limited discussions about suspicions, dangers, feelings, and fears to occasions where they could face each other, in person and privately, rarely including others, except, in this case, Maria.

Frank asked Alan, "Do you remember that, when you reported on your Washington meeting and getting mission approval, you were, in my opinion, overusing the words 'faint and faintly' in your narrative, primarily in connection with Madeleine's faint, very faint perfume? I clearly understood that 'perfume' was not limited to a scent, but also included power and influence."

Alan concurred, "Yes, of course I remember the words, and clearly, the extended meaning of the word 'perfume'. As a matter of fact, some faint doubts and questions about this entire affair keep fluttering in my brain, disappearing for a while, then suddenly reappearing."

They talked for a while about the frustrating process of catching and saving fleeting, slippery, intuitive thoughts, concluding, as they had many times before, that the only way to shake out the key parts was to keep talking, and if need be, starting at the beginning and telling it all again, and again, somewhat as they did in intelligence debriefings.

Alan continued, "My analysis of the matter is that Abigail was the initial contact and the designated team leader but moved into the background whenever there was a concern about implicating her husband or the State Department, reappearing when the danger was assumed to have disappeared. But that is a detail, a logical, simple explanation of two sisters collaborating with each other."

Frank smiled, "We have had variations of this type of conversation before. Let me have a turn at forwarding the narrative to the next level. I agree with your assessment that the collaboration of the sisters is a procedural detail."

"There is a part in this entire affair that does not fit. It reminds me of those geometry puzzles in math classes where they give you a set of numbers or equations or shapes and you are supposed to pick the one that does not belong. The puzzles are easy to solve starting the first course, gradually increasing in difficulty, at the end of the final course practically impossible to understand, much less solve."

"I suspect that a similar problem was faced by the Stasi, leading to the unusual intensity of their investigation. Something did not fit, they could not find it, therefore they threw people and resources at the problem, could not resolve it, and remain severely humiliated and angry. That vision fills my heart with joy!"

Alan concurred, "Mine too! Remember what we were taught in Budapest by our most experienced mentors? That, as you do in mathematics, half the solution of a problem is first stating the problem. They encouraged us to state the problem in two or three words, preferably two. The difficulty, and the beauty, of the two-word definition is that the two-word limitation usually fits only a narrow set of conditions."

Frank's smile was turning into a grin. "My two words are 'Wrong Premise', but I cannot prove them yet."

Alan countered, "My two words are 'Moles Subservient'."

Maria and Frank asked simultaneously, "What is the meaning?"

Alan explained, "Subservient means it is part of the issue but in a secondary, subordinate rank."

Frank was jubilant. "'Wrong Premise' fits! The moles are not the premise, the moles are the excuse!"

Alan concurred, "Yes, we have a double set of two-word solutions. We are saying that the moles are subservient, therefore we are operating on a wrong primary premise. If the unmasking of the moles was the excuse but not the ultimate prize, then we must answer the next question, the big one, what was the ultimate prize?"

Frank was euphoric. He advised, "As part of my insurance business I read many trade publications with news about the insurance industry, proposed legislation, and future business trends. Usually it is boring stuff, periodically I learn something of interest. Read this!"

He handed Alan a magazine article highlighted with a pink marker. It was a well-researched article about the need of the insurance industry to reinvent itself to catch up with the changes in international commerce, especially in the energy sector.

The narrative recounted that the energy sectors' traditional insurance models were initially based on the coal industry, later had to adapt to petroleum, a mineral that had different extraction, transportation and storage requirements. The risk analysis models had slowly been adapted to the transition from coal to petroleum. The emergence of new power sources, like natural gas, geothermal, solar, hydro and new-generation nuclear had not been sufficiently taken into account. The key word was 'sufficiently'.

The author noted that the industry was ignoring tremendous profit potential by not offering insurance programs suited to specific branches of the emerging technologies. Other areas where the industry was lagging was in the geographic and geopolitical changes in energy production. Traditionally coal and oil came from specific regions. These had changed. Who would have thought that Norway would become an oil exporter, or that the Soviet Union was becoming a natural gas exporter?

There were ongoing new explorations, new developments in nuclear power, modernisation of existing electrical generation facilities.

The article further noted that the insurance industry's lobbying efforts were geared towards regulatory issues and modifying existing systems to be more favourable to underwriters, but not particularly creative and forward thinking. The industry always seemed to favour insuring for risks that could be analysed, measured, and have an actuarial statistical basis.

Frank and Maria moved to the other side of the room and conversed in a low voice, to let Alan read the long article. Frank was in a celebratory mood and poured everyone another brandy.

Alan read on. The author advocated that the insurance industry should become involved in a project long before regulatory approvals or building permits were in process, long before anything could be built or measured. He acknowledged that in most fields the insurance protocols and regulations were well-established.

Obviously, no one could be part of the early beginnings of something that had been built years ago; however, he pointed out that there were a few opportunities to get in before the beginning, primarily in the emerging markets of Eastern Europe. It was rumoured that East Germany and Poland were depleting their coal reserves, thus ensuring a big market for Soviet natural gas exports, which meant pipeline systems that could spread to other socialist countries and even extend to western parts of Europe.

Any insurer who could make the right call and join in early, could reap immense profits creating customised insurance programs and underwriting them, and consulting, guiding, risk analysing and planning the liability exposures in distributing energy. The insurers' traditional reluctance to insure what cannot be measured militates against their early involvement.

The author advocated that the industry should attempt to investigate this potential market and obtain what information they could.

It was acknowledged that countries behind the Iron Curtain were particularly hard to read, but the potential for huge, long-term underwriting and project management profits should encourage the effort.

Alan finished reading and commented, "I am impressed. I did not understand some of the insurance jargon in the latter part of the story describing the applicability of various insurance policy types and the issues affecting the development of new actuarial algorithms, but the essence of the message is crystal clear, that those who can get inside information and act on it will reap huge profits."

Maria disclosed that she felt her English was totally inadequate when trying to understand insurance contracts and was pleased to hear that Alan had the same problem. She laughed and said, "I guess that means we have to keep Frank."

Frank said, "I am so relieved you want to keep me! It would be so hard to drag a new Hungarian lass through a muddy minefield that I don't want to go through that again. Now that my job is safe, I would like to suggest alternative explanations of our recent adventure."

"As we all know, comrade Bruno Hadler's area of expertise is energy analysis and management. We all were fixated on his identification of moles within our government, which he meticulously delivered as agreed. We were not interested in the East Germans' understanding of American energy issues. We knew our own energy issues and did not need their assessment."

"Having become more educated on international energy considerations, I have reached the conclusion that the inside information on East bloc energy issues is as big a prize as uncovering moles. This, of course, makes the oilman who financed the rescue a person of interest."

Alan interjected, "Actually, he is not an oil man, but a finance man who specialises in the long-term financing of energy-related enterprises. He is the oil people's banker. It appears he touches money only, not dirty oil extraction or sales. I am sure he has mastered many of the get-in-early procedures advocated in your insurance article."

Frank continued, "That is even better. It all is starting to fit together well. Looking at insurance opportunities I was exposed to the importance of energy futures. I am sure your devious mind also has some variations on the subject."

Alan conceded, "Yes indeed. I have several ideas rattling through my overactive brain. In order to solidify my thoughts, I would like to have some additional bits of information."

Maria asked, "Like what?"

Alan replied, "Like who is the leader of our rescue mission, and like is this a government-sponsored event or a private enterprise at its most devious?"

Maria was happy to introduce her opinion. "I am convinced that the orchestra conductor is Madeleine Baker, and that the whole deal is private, with the government as a subcontractor providing specialised manpower, like you two, Alan and Frank."

Frank asked, surprised, "Why? What makes you so sure?"

Maria explained, "Because he makes …" Frank interrupted, "Don't you mean 'she'?"

"What you asking?"

"She is a 'she', not a 'he'."

"Oh, for God's sake, don't be such a picky bore. You, he, she, them, it, whatever, understood me, my, her, she, me, mine, his, its, hers perfectly!"

Alan intervened, "Let us stop the marital grammar squabble! You can slug it out later!"

Maria, giving her husband a defiant look, returned to her narrative, "I was saying that he, him, I mean she, Madeleine Baker is the orchestra conductor because she makes the decisions, she ends arguments, the big meeting was at her house, she handles money and payments, she replaces her sister when there is a suspicion of danger, she is the older sister, therefore the bossy one. When Alan and Abigail were arguing about Alan's vulgar manners and violent behaviour, Madeleine looked at the bigger picture and stopped him and her from more arguing."

"How do you know she is the older sister?"

"Woman's intuition. Plus, I observe while you guys scheme and talk."

Alan and Frank recollected their analysis of Alan's meeting at the Baker's estate in Virginia and his faints impression of Madeleine's faint perfume being faintly stronger than Abigail's, and the visual fondling between Madeleine and moneyman John Stewart.

Maria objected to 'visual fondling' and Alan changed it to 'visual contact'. She shook her head and muttered something about men. Frank and Alan retaliated by shaking their heads and muttering something about women, all three ending with big smiles.

Both Frank and Alan agreed with Maria's nomination of Madeleine as project leader. It fit with every scenario and every contact they had had with the sisters.

Frank looked at Alan, commented, "I know your expression of unsaid, undigested ideas. Why don't you spit it out and let us help to unravel it?"

Alan agreed, "Yes, let us dissect the strange thoughts. I need to get back to our two-word summaries, especially to your 'Wrong Premise'."

"I was always bothered by the lack of detail regarding the Copenhagen meeting between Abigail and Bruno Hadler. The initial contact in defections always has been subject to intense scrutiny. In this case, it was implied that the vetting and the acceptance was done by the Secretary of State, with presidential approval, and with help of old retired station chief Charles Jenner, who found me, and who later got himself fired for antagonising his employers by pointing out that they were inexperienced and unqualified to deal with clandestine matters."

"The feeling lingering in the back of my head today became explainable in words because of our conversations. It seems that I thought, but could not rationalise it, that Hadler did not contact Abigail offering the moles in exchange for help in disappearing. I now am convinced that Hadler was selected by us for his knowledge of energy matters behind the Iron Curtain. I think he was probably approached not by our government, but privately on behalf of John Stewart, probably in some foreign conference. Stewart has enough money to hire top talent to ensure that Hadler would not double-cross him or turn into a double agent."

"My guess is that Hadler is, or was, a loyal East German, unwilling to betray his country, and that he was manipulated carefully and cleverly to stay in touch without betraying anything to anyone."

"Perhaps it took a long time to turn him. Perhaps they had something to blackmail him on, perhaps he was totally clean and unwilling to accept the customary bribe of, say, a hundred thousand dollars, but was given the option of having a crippling accident or, say, five million dollars, top quality cosmetic surgery, relocation to a safe place, in exchange for participating in monthly planning conferences about Eastern Europe energy issues. Perhaps in Copenhagen he met with Abigail to accept the deal rather than having the accident."

Frank wanted to know, "What about the unmasking of moles embedded in our government?"

Alan theorised, "I think that it was a real deal. I think they wanted something they could offer our government to accept the defector. In his position as secretary to a Politburo member, Hadler had access to all kinds of information not necessarily related to his assigned tasks."

Maria said, "It seems that we are approaching the end of the story. A lot has happened since your initial visit. I was so worried about being dragged back into the terrible situation we had escaped long ago. I was worried about endangering the children by becoming a revenge target for some fanatic, I was worried of losing Frank to some crazy, dangerous rescue mission."

"When you came, you assured us that all you wanted was some names and addresses. As it turned out, we got more involved than that. We enjoyed the family trip to Europe, and, I hate to admit it, we enjoyed the sense of participating in an exciting adventure. As a bonus, I was pleased to help inflict some pain onto a Communist group. We do not often get the chance."

"I thank you both for allowing me to participate in events, analyses and troubleshooting sessions. And Alan, I apologise for being so worried and difficult at the beginning of this endeavour, and I thank you from all my heart for your keeping your word and not dragging my family into harm's way. I will always welcome you as a friend in our house."

She was teary-eyed and could say no more.

Alan consoled her, "Please don't let your little son see you cry again. He will try to kick me out of your house or call the police. And, dear Maria, thank you for your kind words."

"I often remember our scary, miraculous escape through the minefield and wonder what happened to those of us that survived. I knew you lived in Wisconsin and that Frank had built-up a successful insurance brokerage."

"I also knew when you became American citizens. I was contacted by the government to confirm details of your circumstances entering the country, and they also wanted to know whether I could think of any reason why your application should not be accepted. I was genuinely happy to endorse your application."

"Years later, well into retirement, I received a phone call inviting me back into action. Thereafter I managed to find your home number, and the rest you know. I thank you both for helping to bring this case to a successful conclusion."

Frank commented. "I am so glad we figured out the mysteries surrounding this adventure. Perhaps we are not guessing every detail, but I am no longer kept awake trying to figure out what pieces I am missing. I guess officially the explanation will be the tale Madeleine told us in Long Beach."

Alan narrated, as if giving a lecture, "A compassionate wealthy American wanted to help a humble man escape from behind the Iron Curtain. They had planned to hide him in a tour group to sneak him out of the country, but at the last moment our man changed his mind, and nothing happened. The tour continued and everyone had a good time."

"I could make it shorter, of course, but I think this is about the right size explanation, if it ever comes up."

Frank commented, "Speaking among ourselves, I would love to know how the escape proceeded after we handed him over, where they relocated him to, what the bribe was, all the details, not to harm anyone, just out of professional curiosity."

Alan and Maria shared the wish and the curiosity but knew they would never be told. Alan and Frank had worked on many cases, often separated into segments with their involvement limited to one isolated segment. Few got to know the whole story, usually station heads or higher ranks.

One case where they knew the whole story was their escape from Hungary after the Soviet takeover. They stayed until late into the night reminiscing about Budapest and their lives.

After the traumatic recounting of events during Alan's first visit, the subject matter was no longer a taboo, especially for Maria. There was a certain liberating feeling about being able to reminisce. It also was an opportunity of finding out details about some part of the story. All three had long wanted to know some trivial part that only one of the others knew.

They agreed to keep in touch and visit from time to time. Alan invited them to stay in his large house in Maryland and use it as a base to visit Washington, DC and its vast offerings of museums, famous buildings, art galleries and activities for the whole family.

Alan and Frank talked by telephone occasionally. Maria joined in briefly, remaining friendly.

One day Frank received a newspaper clipping from Alan in the mail. It was a short article from a financial newspaper reporting that a consortium of financiers led by John Stewart had agreed to invest nine hundred million dollars in an East European natural gas pipeline network, and an additional five hundred million in a joint venture with Scandinavian and Soviet enterprises to distribute natural gas in the Baltic region.

The article noted that the financial inner workings of the East bloc politicians are so inaccessible to Western investors that any venture with countries behind the Iron Curtain is a huge gamble based on guesswork. The East's long-range energy policies are as inscrutable as their financial plans. Most analysts concluded that the returns on the subject investments would be below expectations and take a long time to materialise, unless some major political changes occurred in the East bloc, an unlikely development.

Ingram Content Group UK Ltd.
Milton Keynes UK
UKHW020620170523
421882UK00005B/118